12/2011

SUPERVOLCANO
ERUPTION

SUPERVOLCANO
ERUPTION

HARRY TURTLEDOVE

A ROC BOOK

ROC
Published by New American Library,
a division of Penguin Group (USA) Inc.,
375 Hudson Street, New York, New York 10014, USA
Penguin Group (Canada), 90 Eglinton Avenue East, Suite 700, Toronto,
Ontario M4P 2Y3, Canada (a division of Pearson Penguin Canada Inc.)
Penguin Books Ltd., 80 Strand, London WC2R 0RL, England
Penguin Ireland, 25 St. Stephen's Green, Dublin 2,
Ireland (a division of Penguin Books Ltd.)
Penguin Group (Australia), 250 Camberwell Road, Camberwell,
Victoria 3124, Australia (a division of Pearson Australia Group Pty. Ltd.)
Penguin Books India Pvt. Ltd., 11 Community Centre,
Panchsheel Park, New Delhi - 110 017, India
Penguin Group (NZ), 67 Apollo Drive, Rosedale, Auckland 0632,
New Zealand (a division of Pearson New Zealand Ltd.)
Penguin Books (South Africa) (Pty.) Ltd., 24 Sturdee Avenue,
Rosebank, Johannesburg 2196, South Africa

Penguin Books Ltd., Registered Offices:
80 Strand, London WC2R 0RL, England

First published by Roc, an imprint of New American Library,
a division of Penguin Group (USA) Inc.

First Printing, December 2011
1   3   5   7   9   10   8   6   4   2

Copyright © Harry Turtledove, 2011
All rights reserved

 REGISTERED TRADEMARK—MARCA REGISTRADA

LIBRARY OF CONGRESS CATALOGING-IN-PUBLICATION DATA:

Turtledove, Harry.
Supervolcano: eruption/Harry Turtledove.
p. cm.
ISBN 978-0-451-46420-0
1. Volcanoes—Fiction. 2. Natural disasters—United States—Fiction.
3. Yellowstone National Park—Fiction. I. Title.
PS3570.U76S87 2011
813'.54—dc23   2011031876

Set in Sabon LT
Designed by Elke Sigal

Printed in the United States of America

SUPERVOLCANO
ERUPTION

I

Colin Ferguson woke up with a hangover, alone in an unfamiliar double bed. *Not* the best way to start the morning. "Fuck," he muttered, and sat up. Moving made his headache worse. Even the quiet four-letter word seemed too damn loud, always a bad sign. The inside of his mouth tasted as if something had died in there a week ago.

Thick maroon curtains kept out most of the daylight. Most, but not enough. He felt like an owl squinting at the sun. Yeah, he'd done a number on himself, all right. Bigtime.

"Fuck," he said again, not quite so softly this time. Here he was, in a rented room in.... For a second or two, he no-shit couldn't remember where the hell he was. The hangover just hurt. Not remembering honest to God scared him.

If it hadn't come back to him, he could have got the answer from the telephone book. The nightstand by the bed was a two-shelf unit attached to the wall. No drawer—using one would have cost an extra seventy-one cents a room, or whatever. Multiply that by a raft of rooms and you knew why Motel 6 never lost money. The top shelf held a phone and his watch, which was *that* close to falling on the uncarpeted floor. On the bottom shelf lay the phone book and a Gideon Bible bound in bilious blue.

Motel 6. Jackson, Wyoming. The day after Memorial Day. He *did* remember. "Fuck," he said one more time. Back when he'd set up this vacation, Jackson, Wyoming, had seemed about as far from the L.A. suburb of San Atanasio as he could get. As far from the fiasco he'd made of his life.

What was supposed to be a laugh came out more like a raven's croak. That was one of those jokes that would have been funny if only it were funny.

You couldn't get away that easily. Most of the time, you couldn't get away at all. Being a cop taught you all kinds of lessons. That one stood pretty high on the list.

He'd slept alone in that not very comfortable double bed because Louise, his wife of close to thirty years, was currently living in sin, as the saying went once upon a time, with her aerobics instructor back in San Atanasio. And he'd slept alone because . . .

"Fuck!" he said yet again, this time in genuine horror. Bits and pieces of the night before came back to him. You always remembered the shit you most wished you could forget. He'd slept alone because he'd tried to pick up a waitress half his age and struck out as gruesomely as some poor, hopeless high-school kid flailing away against Randy Johnson in his prime.

Christ! No wonder I tied one on, he thought. Shame—and a bladder full to bursting—propelled him to the head. It was as severely functional as the rest of the unit. Its walls were just as thin, too. A guy in the next room was taking a leak at the same time as Colin. The other guy finished and flushed—a space-age *whoosh!*—long before Colin did.

After his own *whoosh!*, Colin fished three aspirins out of his travel kit. They sat on his tongue while he filled the plastic glass with water. Once he'd swallowed them, he brushed his teeth. That got rid of the dead animal.

He pulled off sweatpants and a ratty T-shirt—elegant nightwear—and stepped into the corner shower stall. The head was set into the outer part of the ceiling, and pointed in at the control and the soap ledge. That struck him as weird, but it worked okay.

He made the water as hot as he could take it without boiling like a lobster and stood under it for a long time. A Hollywood shower, he would have called it in his Navy days. He was surprised the shower head didn't have an automatic cutoff. If he could think of it, some Motel 6 bean counter could, too, and probably would.

By the time he came out, the aspirins were starting to work. He figured he'd live. He wasn't so sure he wanted to, but he figured he would.

Up till now, he'd done everything in near darkness. If he planned to shave without cutting his throat, though, he needed to turn on the light over the sink. If he did . . . Another interesting question, but, he decided, not one for right now. A cop who aimed to end things could always find a quicker, neater way than a disposable Bic.

He flicked on the switch. The vicious photons made him flinch. So did the ancient alky who peered out of the mirror at him. Sallow, sagging skin. Gray stubble. Not to put too fine a point on it, he looked like hell.

Scraping off the stubble helped . . . a little. So did Visine . . . a little. He still had all his own hair, and the stuff on his scalp, unlike his whiskers, was only beginning to frost. Once he combed it, he didn't look too much older than he really was.

"Coffee," he said—the first word besides *fuck* that had come out of his mouth this morning. He could get some down at the front desk, but the coffee here was as chintzy as the rest of the operation. He quickly dressed (jeans, sweatshirt, denim jacket over it, Angels cap—the calendar might say June was starting, but Jackson was cool and Yellowstone, seventy-odd miles north and over a thousand feet higher, was downright cold). Then he went down to his rental car and headed toward the national parks.

Bubba's was a lot closer. They brewed good coffee there, and cooked enormous, delicious, artery-clogging breakfasts. And they opened at half past six, so you could feed your face and head out for wherever you were going.

"What can I get you today, dear?" the waitress asked when Colin sat down. She wasn't young or cute, but she said *dear* as if she meant it. *Maybe I should have hit on somebody like her last night*, Colin thought—too late, as usual.

Aloud, he said, "Coffee—and a big bowl of vanilla ice cream."

It was the best hangover fighter he knew. It made people give him funny looks, though. Not this gal. It didn't faze her a bit. She just nodded. "Hurt yourself last night, you say?"

"Oh, maybe a little," Colin answered dryly.

"I'll get it for you right away, then. And I'll keep the coffee coming." The waitress bustled off.

Caffeinated, his stomach greased against the slings and arrows of outrageous single malts, Colin drove out of Jackson: past the park with the elk-antler arches at each corner, past the visitors' center, and north out into open country. Yellowstone was still more than fifty miles away, but he didn't care. He wasn't fighting traffic, the way he would be on the Harbor Freeway or the 405. A lot of the time, his little Ford seemed to be the only car on the road. Things here would get more crowded later in the season, but they hadn't yet. No one even checked his receipt when he came to Grand Teton National Park—the ranger station at the southern entrance was closed and empty.

Off to his left towered the Grand Tetons themselves. One of his guidebooks said that was French for Big Tits. The sharp, jagged, snow-topped mountains didn't make him think of boobs.

They reminded him of a cat's back teeth, made for shearing meat into swallowable chunks. Whose cat's back teeth? Maybe God's.

Even the guidebook allowed that only a very lonely French trapper could have imagined those mountains were breastlike. Colin wasn't so sure the book had it straight there. How about a French trapper whose wife had run off with an aerobics instructor? That sounded just about right to him.

Clouds rolled in. They were lower than the Tetons, and blocked them from view. Pretty soon, rain started spattering down. Rain in June seemed perverse to someone from L.A., but Colin could deal with it. Besides, it would stop pretty soon, and then start up again whenever it felt the urge. He'd seen that on his drive up the day before—and on the drive down, and while he was in Yellowstone. Erratic weather was the price you paid for beating the crowds.

His older son, Rob, would have appreciated the empty highway. Rob spent much more time on the road than Colin did. He'd taken five expensive years getting an engineering degree from UC Santa Barbara. Since then, he'd made his living—when he'd made a living—playing bass in a band called Squirt Frog and the Evolving Tadpoles. "Best damn outfit nobody's ever heard of," was how he described it, not without pride.

Colin didn't hate the music. Some of the band's songs were funny. Some were clever. A few managed both at once. He did hope Rob wore earplugs at every gig and every rehearsal. Otherwise, his son wouldn't have any hearing left by the time he hit thirty-five. Squirt Frog and the Evolving Tadpoles liked turning it up to eleven.

The guys in the band liked smoking dope, too. They liked it a lot, Rob no less than any of the others. He didn't waste any time pretending he didn't smoke it, either. Hypocrisy wasn't in him, any more than it was in Colin. If such things came down through the gene pool, he'd got it from his old man.

"I could bust you for that," Colin had said the first time he smelled sweet smoke and walked in on Rob toking.

"Go ahead, then," his son had answered. He didn't yell *Fascist swine!*, but he might as well have.

And, of course, Colin had done no such thing. He'd woken up the next morning with a hangover at least as vicious as this one, though. Rob hadn't pointed out that pot didn't hurt you the morning after. For such small mercies, Colin was grateful. With a cop's cynical certainty, he was sure he wouldn't get the larger ones.

Several cars sat by the side of the road at an oxbow bend in the Snake River. People with binoculars and spotting scopes and cameras with long lenses peered out across the water. Colin kept going. He was only a halfhearted birder. A bald eagle he would have stopped for, but those seemed unlikely here. He couldn't get excited about some duck species he hadn't seen before.

Right now, he had trouble getting excited about anything. That was part of the reason he'd come here: the hope that being somewhere different, doing something different, would start him perking again.

He'd seen plenty of new stuff, all right. But none of it did much to distract him from the mess his family had turned into, or from the South Bay Strangler, the bastard who got his jollies raping and murdering little old ladies from Hawthorne down to Rolling Hills Estates. Over the past five years, he'd done in at least thirteen of them. Plenty of DNA evidence to put him away if he ever got caught, but no matches showed up with anybody who'd run afoul of the criminal-justice system.

"Probably a pillar of the fucking community—except when he goes hunting," Colin snarled, there in the Ford where nobody could hear him. He'd voiced the idea before, whenever the South Bay police met to coordinate the hunt. Nobody'd wanted to listen to him. He snorted. As if that were anything new!

It started raining harder. Colin fiddled with the windshield wipers, trying to keep them going just fast enough to wipe away the drops before the windshield got too spattered to see through . . . and no faster. Such relentless precision was a habit of his. It had driven Louise crazy. Crazy enough to shack up with a guy ten years younger than she was, evidently.

What did they call women who did such things nowadays? There was a word for it. Not being on the front lines of American slang, Colin had to go fishing inside his head. He caught it, though: "Cougars!" He felt good about remembering, then not so good because it was something he needed to remember.

A squirrel darted across the highway. It was smaller and redder than the squirrels in San Atanasio, but just as stupid and suicidal. He slowed down enough to keep from squashing it.

"Cougars," he repeated sadly. He wouldn't have figured Louise for one, not till it happened. But then, he hadn't realized his marriage was in trouble till it blew up in his face. Which proved . . . what, exactly?

Proves you don't know shit about women, that's what, he answered himself. *You were supposed to understand your wife better than any other woman, right?* Obviously, he hadn't. And he still didn't know why his daughter had dumped her longtime boyfriend three weeks after Louise bailed on him. Maybe Louise and Vanessa had plotted it together. Maybe it was just in the air, like swine flu.

Bryce Miller still came by the house every week or two. Part of that was bound to be misery loving company. Part of it . . . Colin clicked his tongue between his teeth: not a happy noise. The sad and sorry truth was, he liked Bryce better than Vanessa. Bryce had his head on pretty straight, even if he was writing a thesis about Hellenistic poetry. Vanessa . . . Vanessa got touchy. She snapped like a mean dog if things didn't go the way she wanted.

Colin's foot came off the gas pedal. *Did you just call your one and only daughter a bitch?* Unhappily, he nodded. He hadn't done it in so many words, but he'd done it. Yeah, that was the word for Vanessa. Not as in touchy-feely, either.

Here came the rangers' station at the south entrance to Yellowstone. It wasn't even nine o'clock yet. Not bad. This station was manned. Colin pulled up to one of the gates, stopped, and rolled down his window. A smiling ranger in what looked like a Marine drill sergeant's hat to Colin said, "Welcome to Yellowstone." That meant *Have you paid yet?* Colin held up his map and, stapled to it, the pass—good for a week—he'd bought the day before. Nodding, the ranger changed her lines: "Welcome back to Yellowstone."

"Thanks." Colin drove in.

The road up from the south entrance ran pretty straight for twenty miles. Colin held to a steady forty-five even so. A couple of cars and a monstrous SUV zoomed past him. The guidebooks warned that the rangers were fanatical about enforcing the speed limit, especially on this stretch of the Yellowstone highway system. Maybe that was pious bullshit. Or maybe . . .

He rounded a curve. A rangers' car with a light bar—now flashing—had pulled over the SUV. The guy behind the wheel looked righteously pissed off. Colin chortled. "Tough luck, sucker," he said.

You could still see what the big fires of 1988 had done to the park. Some dead tree trunks went on standing tall. Some lay scattered across the meadows that had replaced some of the old lodgepole-pine forests. And the lodgepoles that had sprouted since the fires ranged from the size of coffee-table Christmas trees up to twenty or twenty-five feet tall: about half the size of the burned ones.

When the road finally forked, you swung left to go to Old

Faithful and the swarm of famous geysers near it. Colin had done that the day before, his first day in the park. He supposed everybody did. They were Yellowstone's number one attraction, and he had to admit Old Faithful lived up to its billing.

If you swung right instead, you went to West Thumb, an arm of Yellowstone Lake. There was a geyser basin there, too, and an information station with a bookstore. And there were restrooms. With quite a bit of Bubba's coffee sloshing around inside him, that mattered to Colin. West Thumb Basin it was.

He pulled into the parking lot at half past nine. Not many cars in it yet. He'd beaten the rush to Old Faithful, too, but he suspected there was no enormous rush to beat here. The potholes scarring the lot argued that way. Had more people come, they would have kept things in better repair.

A round hot pool threw up clouds of steam by the entrance to the lot. It didn't have a sign or anything—just a wooden warning rail around it to keep idiot tourists from cooking themselves. He found a spot near the start of the boardwalk that let visitors go by the geothermal features in reasonable safety—no, the parking lot wasn't crowded. After he killed the lights and motor, he got out. Locking the car door as soon as he closed it was as automatic as breathing.

Signs in several languages warned people to stay on the boardwalk. The crust was thin. You could fall through. Right this second, boiling didn't seem so bad. He shivered despite sweatshirt and jacket; it had to be down in the forties. It had been in the upper eighties when he flew out of LAX. Well, he wasn't in L.A. any more. That was the point of this exercise, if it had one.

Blue Funnel Spring was . . . blue. The Thumb Geyser sputtered and blew out steam. The Fishing Cone sat a few feet out into Yellowstone Lake. You couldn't reach it from the boardwalk. Once upon a time, his guidebook said, people had steamed fresh-caught trout in there. Some of them had hurt themselves trying it. Now the Fishing Cone was off limits to a close approach.

Farther back from the shore, ice still covered much of the lake. That was just too weird for somebody who'd lived most of his life in Southern California. It made Colin think of *Uncle Tom's Cabin*. A lot of snow still lay on the ground, too.

It was beautiful—no two ways about that. The beauty and the snow were reason enough for some people to live in these parts. Colin shook his head. *In the forties, the week after Memorial Day? Forget about it!*

He worked his way around the boardwalk. A duck swimming in the unfrozen water close inshore eyed him, decided he was dangerous, and taxied along the surface, wings beating, till it got up enough speed to take off.

The Black Pool was a sickly green, not black. Colin had no idea whether the Abyss Pool, on the other side of the planked path, led to the abyss. By the sulfurous steam rising from it, though, he wouldn't have been surprised.

Somebody in a broad-brimmed hat, a rain slicker, and jeans was hunkered down on the narrow lakeside beach, back to Colin, intent on something he couldn't see. Not six feet away stood one of those *stay-on-the-boardwalk!* signs. "What the hell d'you think you're doing?" he growled, a line whose every intonation was honed by years on the beat.

The miscreant jumped and whirled back toward him. Only he—no, she: a woman in her mid-thirties, with short, honey-blond hair and attractively weathered features that said she spent a lot of time outdoors—probably wasn't a miscreant after all. She wore a picture ID on a lanyard around her neck, the way rangers here did. And she answered, "Checking a seismograph. Why? What business is it of yours?"

Colin felt like a jerk. He wouldn't have minded vanishing under the oh so thin, oh so hot crust that seemed to have no trouble at all supporting the woman's weight. "Sorry," he said, and for once he meant it. "I'm a cop back home. I saw you out there where I didn't think you were supposed to be, and I jumped to a conclusion, and I went splat."

She weighed that. On one side of the scales was something like *Okay, fine. Now fuck off, asshole.* He'd earned it, too. But a couple of other tourists were coming. Maybe she didn't want to cuss him out in front of an audience. All she did say was, "Mm, I can see that—I guess."

Then fate—or something—lent a hand. The ground shook more than hard enough to need no seismograph to detect. Colin staggered. He was glad to grab the handrail on the boardwalk. For ten or fifteen seconds, he felt as if he were standing on Jell-O. At last, the earthquake stopped.

"Holy moley!" said one of the approaching tourists. "Nobody told me it was gonna do *that*! Let's get outa here, Shirley!" He and Shirley did, at top speed.

Waves—not big ones, but waves—rolled up onto the beach. The ice farther out cracked with noises that made Colin think of what would happen if the Jolly Green Giant dropped a tray from his freezer. Darker streaks—water—appeared between the remaining chunks of ice.

Eyeing them and the direction from which the waves had come, Colin said, "That's gotta be a 5.3, maybe even a 5.5. Epicenter's *that* way somewhere." He pointed northeast.

One of the woman's eyebrows jumped. "I was going to ask you where home was, but now I hardly need to. Norcal or Socal?"

"Socal," Colin answered. "San Atanasio. L.A. suburb." Of course he had to come from California. Guessing the Richter scale was a local sport of sorts. "How about you?" he asked. That she knew it was a local sport, and that she used local slang for the two rival parts of the state, argued she was a Californian, too.

Sure enough, she said, "Some of both. I grew up in Torrance"—which wasn't far from San Atanasio—"but I'm finishing my doctorate at Berkeley. So I'm Norcal now."

In his mind, Colin prefaced Berkeley with *The People's Republic of*, the same as he did with Santa Monica. The university was good, though; Marshall, his younger son, had been bummed for weeks after he didn't get in. He'd followed Rob to UC Santa Barbara instead. He'd followed Rob into smoking pot, too, and still hadn't graduated. One more thing for his old man to worry about.

Not the most urgent one at the moment. "I didn't know you could get quakes that big up here," Colin said.

"Oh, yeah," the woman answered. "This is the second-busiest earthquake zone in the Lower Forty-eight, after the San Andreas. There was a 6.1 in the park in 1975, and a 7.5 west of Yellowstone in 1959. That one killed twenty-eight people and buried a campground. A landslide dammed the river and made what they call Quake Lake. You can still see drowned trees sticking up out of the water."

"A 7.5 will do it, all right," Colin said soberly. How many people would an earthquake that size kill in L.A. or the Bay Area? One hell of a lot more than twenty-eight.

"It sure will," she agreed. As Colin had before, she pointed northeast. "I think you've got the size just about right, too—"

"Practice," he broke in.

"Uh-huh." But she hadn't finished. "You got it right if the quake's from magma shifting in the Sour Creek dome. But if it's from the Coffee Pot Springs dome . . . That's farther away, so the quake would have to be bigger."

"Didn't feel that far off," Colin said. "The jolts were sharp, not roll-roll-roll the way they go when they're a long way out."

"Here's hoping you're right." She didn't sound—or look—happy. And she had her reasons: "The Coffee Pot Springs dome literally just showed up on the map a little while ago, and it's swelling like a stubbed toe. It's like the magma's found some new weak area that gives it a path up toward the surface."

Colin knew what magma was: the hot stuff that spewed out of volcanoes. Here in Yellowstone, it was also the canned heat that kept geysers boiling and hot springs bubbling. He had trouble putting those two things together, though. "What would happen if it did?" he asked.

"Did what? Get to the surface?"

"Yeah. Would it be . . . a volcano, like?"

"Mm, kind of." Now the look on her face said he'd disappointed her. He'd known something about earthquakes, so she'd hoped he would know something about volcanoes, too. That shouldn't have bothered him. If anybody'd had practice disappointing women, he was the guy. But, obscurely, he didn't want to disappoint this one. She went on, "Like a volcano the way a Siberian tiger's like a kitten, maybe."

"Huh?" he said brilliantly. To try to salvage things, he added, "I'm not staring at your chest. I'm just trying to read your name badge."

That got him a crooked grin. "Well, it's a story. I'm Kelly Birnbaum." He gave her his own name. She came up and shook hands over the boardwalk railing. He'd known police sergeants with a less confident grip. She looked west. "I bet you went to Old Faithful before you came here."

"Well, yeah." Colin hated being predictable. Sometimes he was—sometimes everybody was—but he still hated it.

"Don't worry. People do that. It's what the thing is there for, you know?" Kelly said. That made him feel worse, not better. Then she asked, "After you looked at all the stuff there, what did you do?"

"I had lunch." He'd testified in court too often to be anything but literal-minded.

This time, she stuck out her tongue at him, which made her look about twelve. "You sound like a cop, all right. Let's try it again. What did you do after lunch? Did you drive up to the Black Sand Basin?"

"Yes, your Honor," Colin answered, deadpan.

"Okay," Kelly said in now-we're-getting-somewhere tones. "You can see the caldera wall—the edge of what fell in the last time the supervolcano erupted—really well from there. I think they've got a sign about it, too. Do you remember that?"

"Uh-huh. As a matter of fact . . ." Colin took the camera out of his jacket pocket, powered it up, and thumbed back till he found the pictures he wanted. One was of the sign she'd mentioned. The other was of the caldera wall itself: an almost vertical cliff of solidified lava, several hundred feet high, with lodgepole pines growing up out of it here and there.

Kelly leaned forward to look at the photos in the viewfinder. She nodded. "That's it, all right. That's what's left from the last time it went off, I mean, maybe 640,000 years ago. It shot out about two hundred and forty cubic miles of ash and lava and rock—say, a thousand times as much as Mount St. Helens."

"How about compared to Krakatoa?" Colin asked. "Or the earlier one in the 1800s—I forget its name, but the one that made the Year without a Summer?"

"Mount Tambora." She beamed at him. People did that when you surprised them by knowing more than they'd expected about what they were interested in. "That was about thirty-five cubic miles. Krakatoa was only a squib next to it: six or seven cubic miles."

"Wow." Colin didn't need a calculator to do the math. "So this eruption was a heck of a lot bigger than either one of those." By himself or with his colleagues, he was as foulmouthed as any other policeman. He didn't like to swear in front of women, though. It wasn't the only reason he often felt like a dinosaur these days.

"Right," Kelly said. "But this one went off 1.3 million years ago, too. Only sixty-seven cubic miles that time."

"Only," Colin echoed. The word seemed to hang in the cold, moist, sulfurous air.

"Only," she repeated. "'Cause it went off 2.1 million years ago, too, and that was the big one. Something like six hundred cubic miles of junk—enough to bury California twenty feet deep. For real, the ash reached from the Pacific to Iowa and from Canada to Texas."

There was a thought alongside which even a hangover didn't seem such a big deal. Colin did some more math in his head. "Um, 2.1 million years ago, 1.3 million years ago, 640,000 years ago . . . Seems like it's about due. Is it?"

"Nobody knows," Kelly answered. "And even if it is about due, that might mean it's ten thousand years away instead of a hundred thousand. Or it might not. But people here and people back in Berkeley don't like the way the Coffee Pot Springs dome is bulging all of a sudden."

"What would it be like," Colin said slowly, "if it did go off for real? I mean, the way it did the biggest time?"

He wondered if she'd say it would be indescribable. But she didn't: "Take Rhode Island. Blow out lava and ash all around the edges. Then drop it half a mile—maybe a mile—straight down onto molten rock." She cocked her head to one side, waiting to see what he'd say to that.

What he said was, "Best thing that could happen to the lousy place."

"Huh?" Whatever she'd expected, that wasn't it.

"For my sins, I got stationed in Providence when I was in the Navy," Colin explained. "If America ever needs an enema, that's where you'd plug it in."

"Oh." Kelly laughed—nervously. "I've heard the same thing about Buffalo and Syracuse."

"Only from people who've never been to Providence." Colin spoke with complete assurance.

"If you say so." Kelly hurried on: "Then we'd get the ashfall all over the place, like we did before. And bunches of particles would go twenty or thirty miles up into the stratosphere and block off sunlight. Best estimate—"

"Guess, you mean," Colin broke in.

"Guess. You're right. It's not like we can make the experiment. Best guess is, global temps go down about five degrees Celsius—nine degrees Fahrenheit. For years. Ten? Twenty? Two hundred? Nobody knows."

Colin thought about that. L.A. nine degrees cooler would be more like Portland or Seattle—different, but not too bad. But Seattle nine degrees cooler would be more like Anchorage. Brr! And Anchorage nine degrees cooler would be like the North Pole. So would London and Stockholm and Moscow and lots of other places. The North Pole would be more like the South Pole. The South Pole . . . He didn't want to contemplate what the South Pole would be like.

"Start of a new Ice Age?" he asked.

"There doesn't *seem* to be any cause-and-effect between supervolcanoes and glaciation," Kelly said. "But it sure wouldn't be fun. Back seventy-five thousand years ago, Mount Tabo in Indonesia blew up. It's Lake Tabo now—that was even a little bigger than the biggest blast here. And, about that same time, genetics studies show *Homo sap* almost went extinct. We got squeezed down to a few thousand people. Why? The bad weather from the supervolcano makes the best sense."

"Happy day. Happy, uh, bleeping day." Colin almost slipped. "That'll give me sweet dreams tonight."

"If it makes you feel any better, you're standing in the middle of the last big caldera," Kelly said cheerfully. "And there's another caldera—a smaller, newer one—under the water in the West Thumb. There are little calderas all over the place in Yellowstone, if you know where to look."

"Oh, boy," Colin said. An aftershock rattled the boardwalk. Another tourist who'd just set foot on it decided this was a hell of a good time to go somewhere else. She hustled back toward the parking lot.

"Nothing much." Now Kelly sounded disdainful. "That wasn't even a 4.0."

"Nope. Not even close," Colin agreed. He realized he'd just spent fifteen minutes or so talking with a reasonably attractive woman without getting shot down in flames. That was one of the more pleasant novelties he'd run into lately. He asked, "Where does somebody doing research at Yellowstone stay?"

"In the employee housing at Lake Village, near the Fishing Bridge you can't fish from any more," Kelly said. "Not the Black Hole of Calcutta, but not the Ritz-Carlton, either. Makes dorm rooms look good."

"Ouch! I'm sorry for you." Colin remembered the UCSB dorms Rob and Marshall had lived in before they moved to off-campus apartments. (Vanessa had commuted to Long Beach State till she decided she knew it all and quit halfway through her junior year. She'd made a living ever since—he gave her that much.) He also remembered what student housing had given his sons to eat. "I hope the food's better, anyhow."

"Not so you'd notice." Kelly made a face. Then she asked, "How about you? Where are you staying while you're visiting here?"

"Jackson," he answered. He saw that surprised her. You could go through cash in a hurry in Jackson if you were so inclined, and plenty of people were. *What? I don't look like I just finished a term as ambassador to the UN?* he asked himself. Himself answered, *You bum, you look like you just started a term for drunk and disorderly*. He wasn't that bad, not after caffeine and painkillers, but Himself could be rougher on him than anyone else. With a sheepish grin, he added an explanation she could hear: "Motel 6."

"Oh. Okay." She laughed. "So you're not gonna sweep me off my feet, drive me away in a gold-plated Mercedes, and fund my research for the rest of my life?"

"Now that you mention it, no," Colin said. But if that wasn't an opening, he'd never heard one. (If that wasn't an opening, she'd do unto him as the waitress had the night before.) Trying his best for suave, he went on, "If you've got a phone number or an e-mail, though . . ."

He waited to see if he'd wind up with egg on his face. She pulled a little imitation-leather card case out of a jacket pocket, extracted a card, and started to hand it to him. Then she said, "Hang on." Second thoughts? She scratched out the phone number on the card and wrote in a different one. "This is my cell. The one that's printed here is my office back in Berkeley. I won't be there till fall, and they're liable to kill all the landlines anyway, to save money. Budgets." It wasn't a four-letter word, but she sure made it sound like one.

"Thanks." He'd rarely been so sincere about what sounded like ordinary politeness. "And let me borrow that pen a sec, would you?" He scratched out not only the phone number but also the e-mail address on his card. "Here. This is my cell, and this e-mail doesn't go through the official police system."

"Thank you." She looked at the card before she stowed it away. "You just said you were a cop, not a lieutenant."

He shrugged. "All it means is, I wear a suit more often than a uniform. No gold-plated Mercedes. Not even tin-plated."

"Oh, it means more than that. It means you've spent a lot of time working hard," Kelly said quietly. "Later on, if either one of us decides this wasn't such a good idea . . ." She didn't go on, or need to.

To show she didn't need to, Colin gave back a quick nod. "No harm, no foul. Sure," he said. If he figured she wasn't young enough or skinny enough or whatever the hell, he wouldn't write or phone. If she thought he looked too weather-beaten to stand or that he really was a lush coming off a bender, she wouldn't call back or return his e-mail. It would all be very clean and civilized.

He had zero intention of not getting in touch with her again. A drowning man didn't push away the spar he'd just grabbed, did he? Not likely! What she'd do then . . . Again, he could only wait and see. And if she didn't decide he was too strange to deal with, he could only wait and see how they got along, or if they got along at all.

For now, Kelly said, "You'll want to do some more exploring, and after the quake I really need to check that seismograph. I got more data than I thought I would." As if to underline her words, another little aftershock rattled the boardwalk.

What Colin wanted to do was hang around right here and get to know her as well as he could as fast as he could. But he saw she'd given him a test question. Between the lines, it said *If you come on too strong, you blow it.* If he couldn't work that out, he flunked.

So he said, "Sure. Glad to meet you," and went on his way. He drove up to Dunraven Pass, which he might have done anyway, and looked south across miles and miles (more than thirty of those miles, he later figured out) to the distant mountains on the far side of the caldera (*the middle-sized caldera*, he reminded himself). Then he left the park altogether, which he wouldn't have done if he hadn't talked to Kelly Birnbaum.

He drove into the town of West Yellowstone, up US 191 to US 287, and west on 287 to Hebgen Lake and on to Quake Lake. The visitors' center there perched high on the debris that had slid down from the far side of the Madison River and dammed it after the 1959 temblor. The rangers at the center seemed impressed he'd ever heard of the quake. They didn't worry about the supervolcano. Maybe it was too big to worry about. Hoping the world stayed lucky seemed a better way to go.

II

Not far from Marshall Ferguson's apartment in Ellwood was a historical marker. It said a Japanese submarine had fired twenty-five shells at the oil refinery there in February 1942. No need to worry about subs now. The refinery was long gone, too.

Marshall, by contrast, intended to stay in Ellwood as long as he could. He'd started out at UCSB as an engineering major, the same way his brother had. Rob had stuck it out. Marshall switched to history in the middle of his sophomore year. Calculus was tougher than he was. It landed him on academic probation, but he didn't quite flunk out.

He hadn't stayed a history major long. Ancient Greece interested him most. But if you were going to study ancient Greece in any serious way, you needed ancient Greek. As far as Marshall was concerned, foreign languages were even more poisonous than calculus. He'd counted himself lucky to get a B- in Spanish at San Atanasio High. They held your hand every step of the way in high school. If you fell on your face at the university, that was your problem, not theirs.

And so . . . film. Vanessa'd been sweet as usual about it. "That kind of bullshit is what you're good for, Marshall," she'd told him.

"It's very, um, creative. It'll put you more in touch with your inner self, your feelings. The right side of your brain—or is it the left?" his mother had said when he told her the news. That would have made him happier if he'd taken Mom more seriously. Getting in touch with her inner self eventually meant walking out on Dad. Marshall might have rolled with it more easily had she acted happier afterwards. But she just seemed confused—more confused than usual, even.

Rob said, "You help us make videos for the band, you'll get your fair cut." The way Squirt Frog and the Evolving Tadpoles were doing then, that would have been a fair cut of nothing. He didn't need calculus to understand how much a fair cut of nothing was.

Dad was the one who worried Marshall, though. For one thing, he was hard to snow. For another, he wrote the checks. He eyed Marshall the way he would have looked at someone he'd busted for running a Ponzi scheme. "I told you I'd support you till you got your bachelor's," he said.

"Uh-huh." Marshall had just nodded. Sometimes the less you said, the better off you ended up. With Dad, anything that came out of your mouth could be used against you.

"I didn't figure the sheepskin would take twelve or fifteen years," Dad went on, an ominous mumble in his voice.

"Yeah, well—" Marshall spread his hands. But that wasn't good enough. Dad kept staring at him, willing words out of him. He had to be a hell of an interrogator. Marshall found himself saying, "I didn't exactly expect it would work out like this, either." That held . . . some truth, anyway.

Dad grunted. "I don't like to go back on my word. I'll keep footing the bills—for a while. But I don't like getting taken for a ride, either. I'm getting tired of these new majors. You hear me?"

"Sure, Dad," Marshall said. Arguing with his father was a losing proposition, and not just because Dad wrote the checks. Colin Ferguson had never smoked, but owned a deep, raspy voice that suggested two packs a day for thirty years. Marshall had a tenor—nothing even close to a baritone. His mom's voice was high and thin, and so was his. Hard to sound serious about stuff when you squeaked.

It wasn't that Marshall didn't or wouldn't work. He'd glommed on to the usual part-time jobs at groceries and fast-food places and retail outlets. Those were great for pocket money and gas money and the like. They didn't come within miles of making him self-supporting, not in Santa Barbara. It had some of the highest real-estate prices in the country, which made apartments similarly scream-worthy.

He had no idea how he would make his living once he did get that sheepskin. Did anybody hire people with film degrees? Or would he still be going *Do you want to supersize that, ma'am?* when he hit fifty? That wasn't what he thought of as the American dream.

And so he tried to finish as slowly as he could. UCSB was a good school for that, and Goleta an even better town. If it wasn't the party capital of the USA, he didn't know what would be. The student newspaper listed a cocktail of the week—for people over twenty-one only, the pious disclaimer always said. One of the spring rituals was couch burning: getting publicly rid of furniture too beat up for even students to stand. The Goleta Fire Department did not approve, which probably worried nobody who didn't work for the Goleta FD.

Another ritual was going home for summer, or at least part of summer. Going home, for Marshall, meant the house where he'd grown up, the house where Dad still lived. He'd see Mom, sure, but he couldn't stay with her. The condo she shared with Teo Acosta didn't have room for guests, and they'd made it plain they wouldn't have wanted any anyhow.

Marshall didn't know what to make of his folks' breakup. What kid ever does? His father said as little about it as he possibly could. When he had to say something, his jaw clenched even tighter than usual. Mom would talk at the drop of a hat, or without one. But Marshall had seen long before she left Dad that you couldn't count on everything she said.

When he came home after finals this summer, he found his father reading a book about the geology of Yellowstone Park. In a way, that wasn't too surprising. Dad had gone there on vacation, after all. The card he'd sent Marshall featured something called the Fishing Cone, and was postmarked at Old Faithful Station. That was kind of cool. Even so . . .

"Geology?" Marshall pointed to the book, which had an aerial photo of some colorfully steaming pool on the cover.

"It's interesting—a hell of a lot more interesting than I thought before I went there," Dad said. "And besides, I've read everything there is to read about the South Bay Strangler. None of it does any good, or we'd've caught the son of a bitch by now. And—" He stopped short.

"And?" Marshall prompted.

"Nothing." By the way his father said it, it was definitely something. Marshall didn't have Dad's experience at questioning suspects, but he didn't need it to know that.

"C'mon. Give," he said. "Who am I gonna tell? The tabloids? *Entertainment Tonight*? The Huffington Post?"

Dad despised the Huffington Post—and, to be fair, its rivals on the right. He chuckled: uneasily, if Marshall was any judge. "I hope not," he said.

"Well, then? C'mon!"

"I, uh, met somebody." Yeah, Dad was uneasy, all right. What did he think Marshall would do? Tar him and feather him and ride him out of town on a rail? Tell the Huffington Post for real? Worse, tell Mom? Mom had always said she wanted Dad to be happy, but no, she wasn't always a reliable narrator.

"Cool! How'd you meet her? What are you doing about it? Does she live around here?"

If not for the *Cool!* in front of them, all those questions asked at once would have made Dad clam up for sure. "We met during an earthquake at Yellowstone," he answered after a pause to decide if it was okay. "She goes back and forth between there and Berkeley. We've talked on the phone a few times, and sent e-mails and texts back and forth. That's about it." He shrugged, as if in apology it wasn't more.

It was more than Marshall had expected, even as things were. "Cool!" he said again. "But what's up with the geology?"

"She studies it," Dad said, which took him by surprise. "She was checking a seismograph when the quake hit." Another chuckle. "Got more than she was looking for then."

"I guess," Marshall said. "So you're getting into it because she is?"

"Maybe some." His father was relentlessly honest—even about himself, as much as anyone could be. "But it turns out to be pretty interesting stuff."

"All the geysers and hot springs and whatever." Marshall knew he sounded vague. He'd never been to Yellowstone, and what he knew about the place came from some half-remembered *National Geographic* documentary. Or was it Ken Burns? One or the other.

"Yeah. All that," Dad agreed dryly.

"Would you still care about it if you didn't find out about it from—?" Marshall stopped. "You didn't tell me her name."

"Kelly," Dad said. "You know what? I would. I really would.

I don't see how you could *not* be interested once you knew what was—what is—going on there." He sounded convinced. Just because he sounded that way, of course, didn't mean he was. And even if he was, that didn't mean he was right.

"Idiot!" Vanessa Ferguson said, her *voce* not nearly *sotto* enough. The idiot in question was her boss. Mr. Gorczany had written *between you and I* in a letter soliciting a bid on the widgets his firm produced. Vanessa wondered if she was the last person alive who could actually use English grammar these days. She changed the boner to *between you and me*, fixed a couple of other clumsy phrases, and printed the letter for his signature.

Even if he wrote like a baboon, he owned the company. He lived on an acre and a half in Palos Verdes, and he bought himself a new BMW every year. Vanessa's job title was technical writer, which translated into *hired keyboard*. She had a cramped one-bedroom apartment and an eight-year-old Toyota Corolla with bad brakes. Where was the justice in that?

"Thanks, Vanessa." Nick Gorczany looked over the letter before inscribing his John Hancock. He was very blond, about thirty-five, and putting on weight. Because he knew all about widgets, he thought he knew all about everything. He pointed to *between you and me*. "Are you sure that's right?"

"Yes, Mr. Gorczany," Vanessa said. Braining him with the softball trophy on his desk would only get her talked about. Besides, who said any brains lurked inside that skull?

"I dunno. It looks funny," he said, frowning.

"The object of a preposition takes the accusative—the objective, if you like that better." All she had to do was reach out, grab the ugly trophy, and . . . "If you don't believe me, see what the Word grammar checker says." She never bothered with the Word grammar checker, but it wasn't—quite—dumb enough to make the moronic mistakes Mr. Gorczany did.

"Maybe you know that, but I bet Don Walsh over at Consolidated doesn't," he said. "Change it back to *you and I*. I don't want him thinking we're a bunch of yahoos."

"But it's wrong that way," Vanessa said helplessly.

"If he doesn't know it's wrong, then it's not wrong for him," Nick Gorczany told her.

She rolled her eyes. "Good God in the foothills! Why do I bother?"

"That will be enough of that, Miss Ferguson." Now Mr. Gorczany spoke with some snap: the snap of a boss putting a third-tier employee in her place. He sometimes looked at her in a way she found mildly annoying—not enough to call him on, even for her, but annoying even so. The way he eyed her now scared her, as it was meant to do. "I begin to see why you've worked at so many different places the past few years. If you can't get along with people, you're going to have problems. Now fix that letter, please."

By *get along with people*, he meant *do as you're told*. She almost choked on the injustice of it. She also almost told him to fold the letter till it was all corners and shove it up his wazoo. But the economy, not to put too fine a point on things, sucked. If she punted this job, how long till she snagged another one? Longer than her savings lasted? It might be close.

And so she contented herself with stalking out of his office, head high, back stiff. The look on her face made a software engineer who was coming in to show him some printouts flinch. It also made a couple of people talking by the coffee machine stare. That didn't bother her; it wasn't as if either one of them knew anything.

Changing *between you and me* back to *between you and I* took only a few seconds, printing out the letter only a few more. They would have gone even faster if she hadn't done them through a red mist of fury. *This* was what the world was like?

Too right it was! You got along better if you were one more smiling moron than if you gave a rat's ass about doing things right.

The phone rang. As Vanessa reached for it, she thought how tempting it would be to scream *Fuck you!* and slam down the receiver. Or to imitate Marshall and answer with *Yankee Stadium—second base*, and let the jackass on the other end go from there.

Tempting? God, how tempting! But no. She'd just reminded herself she needed the paycheck. "Gorczany Industries, Vanessa Ferguson speaking." If she sounded like a slightly constipated robot, well, Mr. Gorczany couldn't can her for that.

"Hello, sweetheart." Hagop Nersessyan had a voice like a lion's rumbling purr. It was the first thing that attracted her to him. She'd rapidly found out there were others. He knew things in bed poor lame Bryce didn't even suspect. She wondered how she'd got tangled up with a loser like Bryce to begin with. The same way she'd ended up working here, she supposed. It had looked like a good idea at the time.

"Hello," she said, but even Hagop's voice didn't cheer her up as much as she thought it should have.

"I will see you tonight," he said confidently. "I will close up shop early, and I will see you tonight." He bought and sold fine Oriental carpets.

"I don't know," Vanessa said. "Work's pretty crazy right now"—which was putting it mildly—"and I may not be fit company for anybody."

"I will see you tonight," Hagop repeated. She knew what that meant: he was horny. He had definite rhythms. Well he might—he was a year older than her father. Bryce seemed to be turned on all the damn time, and he'd expected Vanessa to feel the same way. She didn't just want to screw; she wanted to be wanted, to be seduced. No wonder they hadn't lasted, even though she'd thought about marrying him.

"Well . . . okay." She wasn't happy with herself for giving in. She never was. She'd find some way or another to get even. Now she hurried on: "Listen, I can't talk. I've got to get this document to Mr. Gorczany."

"Tonight, then," Hagop said. He meant after dinner, of course. He wasn't offering to take her out. He had a good deal of cash, but he was slow about parting with it. She'd wondered if he was married. That would explain why he didn't want to be seen in public with her. She didn't necessarily mind being a mistress, but she wanted to know if she was one. Some Internet work convinced her that wasn't the issue. Hagop just didn't like to spend money.

She waited outside Mr. Gorczany's office till he stopped speaking in tongues with the software engineer. Then she brought in the letter and set it on his desk. "Here it is—the way you wanted it." Her words might have been carved from ice.

He scanned it to make sure she wasn't saying one thing and doing the other. She'd thought about that, but hadn't figured she could get away with it—a good thing, too. Nodding, he scrawled his signature at the bottom. "Take it to the post office. I want to make sure it gets today's postmark. We could have taken care of this sooner if you hadn't gotten foolish about it."

She got off at half past four. It was 4:27 now, by the digital clock on his desk. The trip and the wait in line would cost her anywhere between ten minutes and half an hour, depending on how retarded the Post Awful clerks were. And he was waiting for her to complain about it—she could see that. So she just said "Right" between clenched teeth and carried the letter out with her fingertips, as if it stank of manure. As far as she was concerned, it smelled worse than that.

The line at the post office was long, and moved slowly. As soon as Vanessa saw the plump blond woman at one of the two open stations, she knew it would be bad. That gal couldn't count the fingers on one hand and get the same answer twice running.

They talked about employees going postal—how about customers who gathered dust waiting their turn?

She collected a receipt when she handed off the letter. She wasn't about to pay postage for Gorczany Industries. Then back to her car and back to her apartment. She picked up her mail—junk and a cable bill. The cat gave her a big hello when she came in. Pickles always did. A day in there with nothing but two fish tanks to watch wasn't very exciting. Vanessa petted the fat-bottomed marmalade tabby and fluffed its fur. Then she fed it some kitty treats. After that, it stopped caring about her. She'd performed her functions, which made her superfluous till the next time the beast wanted something.

Cats were more honest than people.

Vanessa nuked a Jenny Craig frozen dinner. It was . . . better than going hungry, anyway. She ate a yogurt for dessert. Hagop would have liked her plumper than she was. Had she thought she'd stay with him . . . She wondered why she didn't. Whatever the reason, she stuck with Jenny Craig.

She tossed her silverware into the sink. The apartment had no dishwasher. She did dishes when they started getting stinky or when she ran out of clean ones. That appalled her old man, not that it was any of his business.

The buzzer sounded. There was Hagop, waiting for her to pass him through the building's security system. She did. A few seconds later, she heard his shoes on the stairway up to the second floor. She had to remind herself she was supposed to be glad to see him.

Spokane wasn't a big city. With Washington State there, though, it had plenty of little clubs. This one had been around a long time. The joint's name—Harvey Wallbanger—proved as much. Lots of things had come back into style over the years, but not drinks with Galliano in them. As far as Rob Ferguson was concerned, a Wallbanger was a nasty thing to do to a perfectly good screwdriver.

But Squirt Frog and the Evolving Tadpoles had played here the year before. Rob and his bandmates were glad to be back. The sound and light guys—the guy on lights was a girl, actually—knew what they were doing. The management didn't try to stiff acts as a matter of principle, the way so many clowns who ran clubs did. And the crowd was lively and enjoyed the show. They had last year, anyhow.

Which meant . . . they were the same kind of weirdos as the ones who played in the band. And if that wasn't a judgment on them, then it was a plate of spaghetti and meatballs. Or something.

Rob turned to Justin Nachman, who would have been Squirt Frog if the band were set up like that. Justin played lead guitar, did most of the singing, and had as much fame as anyone in a resolutely unfamous band could claim. "What *would* you call the kind of stuff we play?" Rob asked.

"Beats me," Justin answered cheerfully. "I don't put labels on it. I just play it. Long as you don't call me late for supper, you can call it anything you want." He meant it, or near enough. Nobody in the band was on the wrong side of thirty, but Justin had a good set of love handles.

They'd gone round that barn before, of course. They'd been going round it since the band formed—*congealed* was the word Justin used—in Santa Barbara. Rob and Charlie Storer, the drummer, were the analytical ones. Justin and Biff Thorvald, who played rhythm guitar, didn't sweat it. They did what they did, and hoped they did it well enough to keep them from needing to look for honest work.

Charlie said, "We're probably somewhere between Frank Zappa and Al Stewart."

He'd said that before. Arguments came and went like tides,

and almost as regularly. Rob sighed. "What's wrong with this picture?" he asked, a rhetorical question if ever there was one. He answered it, too: "For one thing, most of the people who listen to us have never heard of Zappa *or* Al Stewart."

"I think you'd be surprised," Charlie said. "Al Stewart still gigs at places like this. Zappa would, I bet, only being dead makes it harder."

"Maybe a little," Rob agreed in tones he'd picked up from his father. In some ways, they were like water and sodium, and caught fire whenever they touched. In others—most of them ways Rob never thought about—they were very much alike.

"That's what I said." Charlie's brown hair frizzed out in a perm that looked as if he'd stuck his finger in an electric socket. It bounced when he nodded, which he did now.

"Yeah, yeah." Rob wasn't about to be sidetracked, in which he also took after Colin the cop without noticing it. "The other thing I was going to say is, I don't think there *is* any place between Al Stewart and Zappa."

"Sure there is," Charlie said. "They both write interesting, off-the-wall lyrics. Only Zappa stopped caring about whether he sounded like a rock-and-roller after a while, but Al Stewart still does. Well, as much like a rock-and-roller as you can sound with just a couple of acoustic guitars."

Rob pondered that. It wasn't one of Charlie's usual comebacks. Biff bailed him out before he had to respond to it, saying, "C'mon, you guys. Give it a rest, okay? Let's do the sound check and hit the greasy spoon next door. We dick around much longer, my belly'll growl louder'n my axe." He brandished his guitar.

The so-called greasy spoon next door was an outstanding Vietnamese place. Rob remembered it fondly from the last time they were in Spokane. You couldn't get better pho in Santa Ana's Little Saigon. And the only place you could get better Vietnamese food than you could in Santa Ana was Ho Chi Minh City (which had been Saigon, and was likely to be Saigon again one of these years).

An idea tickled the back of his mind. "Maybe we could do something with places that've had more than one name. Tsaritsyn, Stalingrad, Volgograd. St. Petersburg, Petrograd, Leningrad, back to St. Petersburg."

"We've done songs about Russia," Justin said.

"Not just Russia. Saigon's Ho Chi Minh City—I was just thinking about that—and Constantinople is Istanbul nowadays. And is it Strassburg or Strasbourg?" Rob tried to make one of those last two Germanic and guttural, the other nasally French.

Justin's frown warned him he wasn't the most cunning linguist running around loose. But the lead guitarist said, "Well, write it and we'll see what it looks like." Most bands came up with tunes and found lyrics that went with them. Not Squirt Frog and the Evolving Tadpoles. With them, words usually came first. That had to be one more reason they wouldn't hit the jackpot any time soon.

"Al Stewart already did a song about Constantinople," Charlie pointed out. "And They Might Be Giants did 'Istanbul (Not Constantinople).' Does the world really need three?"

"It wouldn't be the same kind of song as those," Rob said. "Give me a break, man. Doctor Seuss used Constantinople, too."

"See? Everybody does." Charlie could be relentless.

"Enough, you guys." Biff sounded more forceful this time. He struck a ringing chord to emphasize the suggestion.

They tuned up. They'd played in Pasco two nights before, and in Portland two nights before that. They'd been on the road together since forever—it sure seemed that way, anyhow. They didn't need long to get ready for what they would be doing later that night. Then it was off to the place next door. "Fee, fie, pho, fum," Rob said happily. Not even Charlie called him on that one.

Pho had to be the best comfort food in the world, even better than chicken soup. You could put almost anything into it. Rob's favorite was beef tendon. Before he started eating pho, he wouldn't have imagined you could boil beef tendon long enough to make it meltingly tender. He wouldn't have imagined it turned so delicious when you did, either.

The waiter and the cook and the proprietor were all the same little guy. He had a wispy mustache and iron-gray hair. His English was good, but no one would ever mistake it for his native tongue. Had he got out of Saigon just before it turned into Ho Chi Minh City? Rob wouldn't have been surprised.

"Not many Americans like that one," he said. "Round-eyed Americans, I mean. They see it on the menu, they make a face." When he made a face, he showed more wrinkles than he did with his features in repose.

"They've never tasted it, then," Rob said. He left a big tip, although the place was so cheap it was a big tip on a small bill.

They went back to the dressing room and passed joints around. Rob couldn't prove using weed made him play better, but he sure thought so. Time slowed down when he was loaded. There seemed to be more of it between the notes, so he had as much as he needed to nail them one by one. And he could hear—he could almost see—how they fit together ever so much better than he could straight. Everything sounded better stoned, too.

Justin stepped into the corridor and checked the house. A few shouts out there said people spotted him doing it. He came back with a grin on his round face. "We'll make enough to go on to the next gig," he reported. They'd been doing that for a few years now. As far as Rob was concerned, it beat the hell out of a day job.

A local band played a short set before they went on. The locals got the kind of hand an opening act could expect. Rob remembered getting that kind of hand himself, and remembered being pumped about it. Now . . . A guy with a booming baritone shouted, "Here they are—the band you've been waiting for! Let's give a big Spokane hello to . . . Squirt Frog and the Evolving Tadpoles!"

And damned if they didn't. Applause was a drug, too. Anybody who didn't think so had never tasted that particular high. It was one of the reasons Rob came out here and waved to the people beyond the house lights. The other two were oldies but goodies: to piss off his old man (he'd sure done that) and to get laid till he couldn't even stand up (not so easy when you were on the withdrawn side, but Rob had no complaints).

They started out with "Pleasures," not least to bring along people who were hearing them for the first time. Always a few newbies in the crowd. Why not let 'em think they were listening to regular rock 'n' roll, at least for a little while?

> *"I would bed you,*
> *I would head you,*
> *I'd do anything that's right*
> *For your body's sweet delight."*

Justin sang. Rob strummed and found chords without conscious thought. A good thing, too, right this minute. Yes, he seemed to have all the time in the world. He knew he didn't, but he seemed to, and that was all that counted.

After the song ended, they got another hand. Somebody in the front row squirted Justin with one of their namesakes: a piece of made-in-China plastic madness from Archie McPhee. Somebody else called out, "I don't believe in evolution!"

"Well, if you find a band called Squirt Frog and the Created Tadpoles, maybe you should latch on to them," Justin answered easily. He was fast on his verbal feet. He got a laugh. It was still fading when he went on, "If you didn't like that last song, you really won't be able to stand this next one."

They swung into "Punctuated Equilibrium." Not everybody could make a song out of Stephen Jay Gould's attack on classical Darwinism, but Justin Nachman wasn't everybody. He was wasting a master's in biology even more thoroughly than Rob was squandering his engineering degree. Well, they were having fun . . . weren't they?

They were tonight. They got called back for two encores. Afterwards, they sold CDs and signed them for the people who thought autographs proved reality. They plugged the new single on their Web site. They did all the other necessary things that separated music-as-business from music-as-fun.

Then they went back to the motel, not completely alone. A little sleep, or something, would be good. They'd play in Missoula, Montana, tomorrow night. Another long haul, another university campus. With luck, another crowd. Another paycheck. Sometimes this gig looked an awful lot like work. But only sometimes.

Colin Ferguson took notes on the things he read. He found that helped him remember them better. He often kept the scribbles to himself. When they held nothing earthshaking, he didn't bother.

Cops are no less nosy than other people. Cops, in fact, are nosier than most other people; if they weren't, they'd make lousy cops. And so Colin wasn't particularly surprised when Sergeant Gabriel Sanchez pointed to a sheet of paper on his desk and asked, "Who the hell is Huckleberry Tuff?"

"Not who, Gabe. What," Colin said.

"Oh, yeah?" Sanchez said. He had a bushy black mustache just beginning to get gray flecks and sideburns a good half an inch longer than the San Atanasio Police Department's dress code allowed anyone not on undercover drug duty. He reached for the pack of Camels in his breast pocket.

"Naughty, naughty," Colin said. The San Atanasio PD had

gone smokefree the year before. Colin's father had died of lung cancer, one bad inch at a time. He had his share of bad habits and then some, but cigarettes weren't one of them.

"Ah, fuck," Sanchez said without heat. "I'll go outside when I'm done bugging you, then. Okay, *what's* Huckleberry Tuff? Sounds like a gangbanger who's read Mark Twain."

Colin chuckled. "Kinda does, doesn't it? But it's this layer of rock the supervolcano under Yellowstone Park laid down when it went kablooie two million years ago and change. There's lots of it—I mean lots—in Wyoming and Montana and Idaho."

"O-kay." Whatever Sergeant Sanchez had expected, that wasn't it. "And how come you give a rat's ass about this super-watchamacallit?"

Normally, that would have been an altogether reasonable question. As things stood, though, Colin had a reasonable answer: " 'Cause this gal I've got interested in is studying the supervolcano. Geologist, I guess you'd call her."

"Oh. I gotcha." The medium-brown skin on Sanchez's hands had a lighter streak on his ring finger that testified to his own recently deceased wedded bliss. Caution—police work may be hazardous to your marriage. They didn't issue warning labels like that, but they should have. The sergeant leered and laughed a dirty laugh. "Geologist, huh? Long as she gets your rocks off . . ."

"Har-de-har-har." Colin had heard that one before, from almost every cop who knew what a geologist was. Before he could say so, his telephone rang. He picked it up. "Ferguson." He listened for a moment, then seemed to sag in his seat. "Shit," he said heavily. "Are they sure? What's the location?" He wrote down an address on the sheet that held the words *Huckleberry Tuff*, then slammed the handset into the cradle.

Gabe Sanchez might not make original jokes, but he could sure read between the lines. "Another one from the Strangler?" he asked.

"Looks that way. Mildred Szymanski, seventy-seven, found dead in her place. Nobody saw her, she didn't answer her door for three days, and the neighbors finally called us. Bedroom's a mess—looks like she put up a fight. She's naked from the waist down."

"Jesus." Sanchez reached for his smokes again. If he had lit up, Colin wouldn't have said a word. But he jerked his hand away instead. "Mildred. Nobody's named Mildred any more. Who the fuck gets his jollies raping little old ladies?"

"This guy does," Colin answered. "It's in one of the apartment buildings near San Atanasio Boulevard and Sword Beach Avenue. Wanna come with me?"

"Sure. We can damn near walk," Sanchez said. Colin nodded. The scene of the crime was only a few blocks from the cop shop.

As soon as they got outside, Sanchez did light a Camel. He smoked in quick, furious puffs, and stamped on the half-smoked cigarette when they got into one of the department's unmarked cars: a Plymouth that had seen better years. It wheezed to life when Colin turned the key.

The Sunbreeze Apartments had seen better years, too. They'd probably been a cool place to live when they went up in some 1970s real-estate boom. Now they looked more like the Sun-bleached Apartments. Lots of serious armor, added on as things went downhill, secured the entrance and the gateway to the un-derground parking garage. Two black-and-whites were parked in the no-parking zone out front, their red and blue lights flashing.

Colin pulled in behind one of the cop cars. A uniformed of-ficer started to wave the Plymouth away, then recognized him. The guy grinned sheepishly. "Sorry about that, Lieutenant."

"No sweat, Malcolm," Colin said as he and Gabe Sanchez got out.

When reporters talked about San Atanasio these days, they called it "working class." That meant most of the chatter Colin heard from looky-loos was in Spanish. Some was in Tagalog, some in Korean. And some was in English. The people who used English as their native tongue were up near the late Mildred Szymanski's age. They'd lived here a long time, and hadn't let all the changes to their town push them to places like Torrance and Redondo Beach.

An ambulance arrived, with the coroner's car right behind it. Dr. Ishikawa and a photographer climbed out of the car. The guys in the ambulance sat tight. They wouldn't be able to take the body away till the police and the coroner finished their jobs. Ishikawa waved to Colin. "Another one?" he called in a harsh, grating voice.

"Haven't been inside yet," the lieutenant answered. "I just got here, too. But that's what the call sounds like."

A tall, skinny bald man with tufts of white hair sticking out of his ears stumped up to Colin. "You catch the son of a bitch who done this, you hear?" he said.

"Sir, I'll do my best," Colin told him. What else could he say? A TV news van started sniffing for a parking space. "Keep those clowns outside," Colin growled to Malcolm. He hurried into the apartment building, Gabe Sanchez at his heels. He hated scenes of violent death. But he hated dealing with the blow-dried vultures who gorged on them even more. And he was given to telling the truth as he saw it, which endeared him to neither reporters nor his superiors.

A glance at the mailboxes told him Mildred Szymanski had lived in apartment 251. A glance at the body on the bedroom floor in the apartment told him the South Bay Strangler likely had struck again. Sooner or later—probably sooner—he'd have to talk to the newshounds after all.

III

"Well, we're here," Colin said as he pulled into the driveway. San Atanasio was only a few minutes away from LAX. Colin despised the airport. Who in his right mind didn't? But the trip back and forth was easy enough.

Rain drummed on the roof of his middle-aged Taurus and splashed off the windshield. In the passenger seat, Kelly Birnbaum grinned a crooked grin. "Why don't we ever meet when it's sunny?"

"Hey, it's February. Even L.A. gets rain in February. Sometimes, anyhow," Colin said.

"I know," she admitted. "It was coming down even harder in Norcal, I'll tell you that."

He thumbed the trunk button. "Head for the porch. I'll grab your bag."

"Such a gentleman." Her eyes twinkled.

Several raindrops nailed his bifocals before he could get under cover himself. He wasn't wearing a cap now, the way he had in Yellowstone. He wiped off most of the water with a hankie and undid the dead bolt and the regular lock. Then—a gentleman—he held the door open for Kelly. "Go on in."

She did. "It's so big," she marveled.

"It's just a house."

"When you've lived in dorms and grad-student apartments and tents as much as I have, a house looks humongous. I freak out when I visit my parents down here, and their place is smaller than this. You've got it all to yourself, too."

"Yeah," Colin said tightly. "Marshall visits sometimes. His room still has his junk in it. The rest . . . It's mine, all right, such as it is."

Kelly caught the edge in his voice. "Sorry. I've got foot-in-mouth disease."

"Don't worry about it. If I didn't have this place all to myself, I wouldn't have pried your phone number out of you when we started talking there by the lake, and I'm darn glad I did." He set a hand on her shoulder.

She moved closer to him. "Me, too." She looked around some more. "Everything is so neat. Books, DVDs, CDs—they're all where they belong. I have to paw through piles of trash to find anything."

"Navy hangover," he said with a shrug. "Want something wet?"

"A beer, I think. But give me the tour first."

"Okay. You've got to remember, most of the stuff on the tables and the shelves and all is Louise's taste." That taste ran to sad-faced icons, enamelware boxes, and figurines that nested one inside another. Colin didn't know why his ex had wanted to make the place look like a cheap imitation of the Hermitage, but she had. Thinking back on it, some of the pieces hadn't been so cheap. Way too late to worry about it now.

"Well, Russian art is something different, anyway," Kelly said diplomatically.

One upstairs bedroom had a closed door with yellow tape reading POLICE LINE—DO NOT CROSS! running from the top left corner to the bottom right. "Marshall's," Colin said dryly.

"Duh!" Kelly winked at him.

Colin's study was next door, with his computer and more bookshelves. It looked out on the backyard. Some wet sparrows and mourning doves pecked seed from a tray feeder.

"I like this," Kelly said. "It feels like you."

"No saints on the wall here," Colin replied, which might have been agreement. He also had a work niche in the master bedroom, the next stop. He'd been using it more since he didn't need to worry about waking up Louise by turning on a light at odd hours. Kelly didn't seem to care about that. She was looking at the bed. Colin needed no grad school to work out why. "If it bothers you, there's still a bed in what used to be Vanessa's room. All the bedclothes are new since—well, since. Same old mattress, though."

She thought about it for a few seconds. Then she said, "That should be okay. Now what about that beer?"

They went downstairs. The kitchen was also humongous, at least if you listened to Kelly. As Colin poured a couple of Sierra Nevada Pale Ales (he'd drunk Bud, but going with Kelly had opened his eyes to the notion of good beer), he said, "I know why you say that all the time."

"Say what all the time?"

"Humongous. It's what you guys call the top end of eruptions. A real technical term, like perpetrator or something."

"You've been reading books again." Kelly sounded amused and accusing at the same time.

"Guilty. I didn't know it wasn't in the rules." Colin raised his glass. The pale ale was several shades darker than Bud, which was, now that he thought about it, the color of piss. This brew had real ingredients in it. "Here's to us." They solemnly clinked, then drank. The pale ale had real flavor in it, too. A damn shame it cost as if it did.

"To us." Kelly glanced around the kitchen, which was as

clean and tidy as the rest of the house. "I still get nervous saying that."

"How come?" Alarm bells jangled in Colin's mind. He was pretty sure he'd found a good one, a keeper. Was she having doubts she'd found one? If she was . . . He didn't know what he'd do if she was.

"Because people who go through divorces are usually crazy for a couple of years afterwards," she answered seriously. "God knows I've watched enough grad-school marriages explode."

God knew Colin had watched enough cops' marriages explode, including Gabe Sanchez's and his own. If you were crazy, did you know you were crazy? If you knew you were crazy, did that mean you weren't really crazy after all or only that you couldn't do anything about it? A DA would argue one way, a defense attorney the other.

He'd seen people do some pretty nutso things after their marriages crashed and burned—no two ways about that. He'd seen guys date women and women hook up with guys they never would have looked at twice if they were in their right minds. Most of them regretted it soon enough. One or two made it work. He'd also seen one guy smash his truck and end up in a wheelchair with gazillions in medical and legal bills because he hopped in while he was drowning his sorrows. And one pretty good cop had got buried in a closed coffin because not even a mortician could make him presentable after he ate his gun.

Suicide scared cops shitless, not least because it sometimes seemed contagious. If one guy did himself in, it could happen that a couple of weeks later someone else, someone nobody'd thought had any big troubles, also took the long road out. Spooky.

Colin didn't want to feel spooky right now, which was putting it mildly. Kelly hadn't flown down from the East Bay to make him feel spooky. He hoped like hell she hadn't, anyhow. He put his hand on her shoulder again. She smiled and moved closer to him, the way she had before. That eased his mind.

"So how's the supervolcano doing?" he asked casually.

Her smile winked out like a blown candle flame. Maybe *he'd* spooked *her*. "My chairman doesn't like what it's doing," she said, the way Colin might have said *The chief wouldn't like that*. She went on, "And I *really* don't like what it's doing."

"I've seen stuff in the papers," he said, nodding. "More quakes over 5.0, the geysers' schedules all fouled up . . ."

"Yeah, the tourists get upset when Old Faithful doesn't go off right on time." Kelly didn't bother hiding her scorn. "But that's only part of what I mean—the part that makes the papers and sometimes even the TV news. The worst things don't. They only show up in surveyors' records and satellite radar readings."

"How do you mean?" Colin asked.

"The magma domes are bulging. Pushing up. Especially the new one, the one under Coffee Pot Springs," Kelly said. "Moving up by feet where they moved by inches even just a couple of years ago."

That led to the obvious question, so Colin came out with it: "Is it getting ready to blow, then?"

"Nobody knows. We've never observed a supervolcano eruption before, so how can we tell for sure what we've got?" The way Kelly knocked back a big gulp of beer said she sure didn't like what they had. "Something's going to happen, though. Maybe it'll go back down again. It could. Maybe there'll be ordinary volcanic eruptions. We haven't had any for seventy thousand years, give or take, and they might relieve the pressure. Or maybe you can drop Rhode Island half a mile straight down."

"Your chairman will know people—people in the government, I mean," Colin said slowly. "So will the other scientists who study this thing. Are they jumping up and down, trying to make the Feds pay attention in case Yellowstone does go kaboom? There ought to be . . . contingency plans, they call 'em in the service."

"I know the geologists are talking to people in the Interior Department," Kelly answered. "And I know they're having trouble getting anybody to listen to them. It's a—" She broke off, groping for the word. "A question of scale, I guess you'd say."

She paused again, plainly wondering if she'd have to explain. She didn't. "The South Bay Strangler's murdered fifteen little old ladies now. That's a story. People understand it. It gets splashed all over CNN Headline News," Colin said, his voice thick with disgust. "But what Hitler did, and Stalin, and Mao—you can't take in numbers like that and what they mean. A good thing, too. Anybody who could *feel* all those millions of murders would have to go nuts, wouldn't he?"

"You'd hope so," Kelly said.

"Uh-huh. You would," Colin agreed. "So the Interior Department guys can't wrap their heads around the supervolcano?"

"Not even close," Kelly said. "They see the studies, and they go, 'It can't be this bad.' And what our people give them is always cautious and careful and conservative. Even that's enough to make them not take it in. Or they say, 'If it really does what you say it'll do, what's the point of planning for it? It's too big.'"

"Bend over and kiss your behind good-bye." Colin wasn't quite old enough to remember drop-and-cover drills in school, but he knew plenty of people who were.

"Yeah. Like that. Except the supervolcano is so much bigger than an H-bomb, it's not even funny," Kelly said.

"It isn't radioactive," Colin pointed out. "No fallout."

"Well, no," she allowed. "Not like you mean. But it would put so much ash in the air. . . ." She laughed, shakily. "We sure have cheerful things to talk about, don't we? Stranglers and supervolcanoes. Oh, my!"

"They're what we do. And it's better than not talking," Colin said. After the kids got out of the house, he and Louise had hardly said anything to each other for days at a time. She didn't care about policework. She'd cared that he hadn't been chosen chief, but that was because she'd lost face through his failure. And he hadn't worried about how she got through her days. With any brains in his head, he would have noticed that that was a bad sign. Aerobics class? Hey, why not?

Kelly held up her empty glass. "I think I could use a refill."

Colin's glass was empty, too. He didn't recall finishing the beer, but if he hadn't a drunk pixie was hiding in one of the cabinets. "Motion seconded and passed by acclamation," he said, and opened the fridge.

She gave him a quizzical look. "You talk funny sometimes, you know?"

"Too many City Council meetings. They'd make a penguin go jogging in the Mojave, honest to God they would."

Kelly snorted. "You *do* talk funny."

He'd heard that before from his fellow cops. He'd also got dressed down by his superiors for writing reports in English rather than police jargon. *Jesus! No wonder I never made chief,* he thought. *If anybody ever came out and just said what goes on in a cop shop, they'd ride him out of town on a rail. They'd have to.*

Some of his bitterness at getting passed over went away. The administrative part of the job would have been a piece of cake. Knowing which asses to kiss and when, on the other hand . . . Even if he'd tried, he would have made a hash of it. A police chief had to be a pol, too, and that just wasn't part of his makeup.

The second beers vanished faster than the first ones had. "What do you want to do now?" Colin asked.

"Could I take a shower?" Kelly said. "You go through the airport and you sit on a plane, you feel all grubby even if the flight only lasts an hour. And after that, well, who knows?" She grinned at him.

"Sounds better than anything else I can think of," Colin said.

She came out of the bathroom off the master bedroom naked. Colin lay on the bed waiting for her. She grinned again. "Oh, good," she said. "You turned up the heat."

"We aren't wearing clothes. No insulation," he said gravely. And he knew damn well that any woman ever born would shiver at temperatures he thought fine. He had no idea why things worked like that, but they did.

She got down beside him. It felt a little strange, a little awkward—the more so for him because it was their first time here, in this bedroom full of memories. He'd gone up to Berkeley a few times before, but they were still learning what floated whose boat. With Louise, after all those years, he'd known.

Or he'd thought so. If he were as smart as that, how come she'd bailed on him? If people generally were as smart as they thought they were, they'd be a hell of a lot smarter than they really were. Cops learned that fast. Most crooks—not all, but most—were crooks because they were dopes.

All of which went through his head in odd moments when he wasn't otherwise distracted. Before long, he stopped having moments like that. Much too soon, or so it seemed, he lay on his back, holding an imaginary cigarette between his first two fingers and blowing an imaginary plume of smoke up toward the cottage-cheese ceiling.

She laughed. The rain tapped softly at the roof. Then, suddenly, there was a much bigger noise up there—something alive running from one side of the house to the other. "What the devil was that?" Kelly said.

"Squirrel," Colin answered. "Just a rat with a pretty tail. You can hear crows up there too sometimes. Wildlife." He made a face. "Not like Yellowstone, even if we do get coons and coyotes and skunks every once in a while. Possums, too."

"Yeah, we have possums in Berkeley," Kelly said. "A guy I dated a few times—grad student in biology—called 'em junk mammals."

"Pretty good name," Colin said, and let it go right there. Of course she'd gone with guys before him. He didn't want to know all the gory details. He snooped for a living. He didn't care to do it on his own time. The way she relaxed beside him, just a little, showed he'd passed one more test.

Was he going to stay crazy for another year and then some? If he was, present company seemed pretty good. He started to tell her so. Before the words came out, he noticed her eyelids had slid shut. He lay there quietly. In a few minutes, her breathing said she'd fallen asleep. He sometimes thought sleeping—really sleeping—with someone was more intimate, more trusting, than merely going to bed.

And he could tease her for doing what everyone said guys always did. Or he could have, if he hadn't started softly snoring himself about ninety seconds later.

If I jump, God, will You catch me? Louise Ferguson remembered wondering about that a few days before she finally nerved herself to walk out on the emptiness that had been her marriage. Which was pretty funny, when you got right down to it, because most of the time religion meant Easter eggs or Christmas presents or a wedding or a funeral. Except for those last two, she couldn't remember when she'd set foot in a church.

But you needed to think of something outside yourself—didn't you?—when you turned your life upside down and inside out. Back in the day, she would have been a scandal. Prominent police officer's wife runs away with younger man! People would have cut her dead on the street—except for the ones who wished they had the nerve to bail out of their dead marriages, too.

She rather missed being a scandal. One of Colin's unendearing endearments for her was *drama queen*. These days, though, anybody who couldn't stand living with somebody else another second went ahead and quit, and no one got up in arms about it.

She might even have been a role model for Vanessa, who'd dumped her live-in boyfriend (even having one, much less dumping him, would have been another scandal back in the day) not long after the breakup with Colin. Louise sighed. Now she had a companion fifteen years younger than her daughter's.

Louise wasn't inclined to judge. *I'm not a judgmental person,* she often told herself. It was an odd way of asserting autonomy, but it worked for her. Colin not only was judgmental, he was proud of it, too. She'd never known a cop who wasn't, and she'd known a lot of cops.

Vanessa was also judgmental, and competitive, and several other things her father was. When she set her chin and looked stubborn, she might have been Colin reborn. She'd always had that air, even when she was only three years old.

Louise's cell phone rang. Actually, it started playing "Addicted to Love." The old word stuck, though, even if the noise the phone made had nothing to do with a landline's boring, squawky ring. She fished the phone out of her purse, which sat on the severely modern couch in Teo's condo.

"Hello?"

"Hi, Mom."

"Hello, Vanessa. I was just thinking about you." Louise wasn't going to tell her one and only daughter how she'd been thinking about her. *Keep it nice if you can* had been drilled into her when she was a little girl. She'd tried to drill it into Vanessa, too, but she hadn't had much luck. "What's going on?" Something had to be; Vanessa didn't call her to pass the time of day.

"Hagop's moving to Denver." Her daughter couldn't have

sounded more tragic if she'd just watched a crowded orphanage go up in flames.

"Is he?" Louise tried to hold her voice as flat as she could. She didn't know why Vanessa had taken up with a man old enough to be her father. Well, she knew some of the reason: Hagop wasn't Bryce Miller and wasn't anything like Bryce Miller. She made no effort to tell that to Vanessa. She knew useless when she saw it.

"Yeah," Vanessa said. "The business climate is better there. That's what he says. Lower taxes, fewer hassles, the whole nine yards." She paused. *Now she's going to tell me whatever she really called to tell me,* Louise thought. Vanessa let the pause stretch long enough for the thought to form very clearly. Then she said, "So I'm going with him."

"To Denver?" Louise exclaimed. "To live?" Vanessa had lived in or near San Atanasio her whole life. She thought a shopping expedition to South Coast Plaza in Orange County was like a safari in Burkina Faso.

But she said, "That's right. I've already started looking for jobs online. I'm sick of working for this idiot, anyway—am I ever."

Are you sick of your paycheck? Louise had had some sudden, painful lessons about money since she'd stopped banking Colin's checks on the tenth and twenty-fifth of every month. But Vanessa was good with computers. She'd find something with more certainty to it than arranging dried flowers. Louise was liable to have to find something like that herself, dammit.

"I thought I should probably tell you," Vanessa said, and by her tone of voice she'd been in some doubt.

"What does, uh, Hagop"—funny name!—"think about you packing up and moving to be with him?"

"He was surprised," Vanessa said. *I'll bet he was,* her mother thought. She went on, "But he got used to the idea okay."

"Did he?" Louise had wondered if the older man was leaving town not least to get away. Maybe not. Something else occurred to her: "Have you told your father yet?"

"Oh, sure," Vanessa said carelessly. "He doesn't want me to do it."

"I know he's not crazy about Hagop. . . ." Louise wasn't, either, but didn't want her opinions associated with Colin's.

"It wasn't that." Now her daughter sounded impatient. Vanessa was good at that. "He kept going on that Denver was too close to what's cooking under Yellowstone Park. Is he okay? He sounded kind of, I don't know, loopy about it."

"Oh." Now Louise understood what was going on. "You don't need to lose any sleep about him, I don't think. He's got a, ah, lady friend who studies volcanoes, so no wonder he's all excited about them."

"But there aren't any volcanoes in Yellowstone, are there?"

"I don't know. But that's what this woman, girl, whatever she is, studies." Louise's spies—people from the old neighborhood—were sure about that. Come to think of it, Marshall had said something about it, too. Louise hadn't put it together with the other till now.

Vanessa went on with her own train of thought, the way she often did: "Besides, Denver's, like, four hundred miles from Yellowstone. More, even. I looked on a map. Dad must not have. He doesn't usually freak out over nothing, but he sure did this time."

"Okay." Louise was thinking about Denver a different way. It was one more milepost marking how the family was fragmenting, with all the people going their own way. Modern families did that. It was part of how things worked. Rob spent so much time on the road with his silly band, he was like a stranger when he did drift back into town.

"Listen, Mom, I've gotta go. Break's about over," Vanessa said. "I'll try to come by before I move, or maybe we can have lunch or something. 'Bye."

" 'Bye," Louise echoed, but she was talking to a dead phone. She sighed again and stowed hers in her handbag. She'd spent upwards of twenty years—*the best years of my life*, she thought, sincerely if not originally—raising the kids. And for what? To see them scatter to the winds, the way kids did. From their point of view, it was as if she hadn't done a goddamn thing.

Which meant . . . what? She frowned. Thinking about What Stuff Meant—in capital letters—wasn't something she did every day, or every week, either. Her style had always been more along the lines of *do whatever you do, then see what happens next.*

Besides, frowning wasn't a good plan, not if the man in your bed was younger than you were. Wrinkles stayed. Deliberately, she made her face relax. Teo was so sweet. He said he appreciated all the things she knew, all the things she did with a lack of inhibition that amazed her when she noticed it. Had Colin ever noticed? Had he cared? Not likely!

Well, if she wasn't going to live for her kids, who was she going to live for? She surprised herself by answering the question out loud: "For me, that's who. And you know what else? It's about time!"

She started to pull the compact out of her purse, then stopped. To scope herself out at close range with that teeny-tiny mirror, she'd have to put on her reading glasses. She didn't want to be reminded that she needed reading glasses, not right now she didn't. She walked into the bathroom instead.

Yes, that was better. She could inspect herself here at a distance her eyes were able to handle on their own. Okay, she had fine lines at the corners of those eyes. Okay, some of the lines on her forehead weren't so fine. Time went by, no matter how little you wanted it to. And she'd spent a lot of afternoons tanning when she was younger. She'd looked terrific then. Her skin would be smoother and softer now if she hadn't.

Her hair was perfect. That was a line from an old song, but

she couldn't come up with the rest of it. She was, by God, still a honey blonde. If she had some gray roots, that was between her and the Clairol people. And she kept the bottle with her tampons and pads, where Teo wouldn't stumble over it.

What she really hated was the sag under her chin. It wasn't *bad*, not yet, but it was there. And her upper arms flopped sometimes. She'd had a high-school English teacher whose arm did the shimmy whenever she wrote on the board. The kids, heartless with youth, had laughed at her. It didn't seem so funny any more.

"My boobs sag, too," Louise said sadly. With a bra, it didn't show. But there were times, important times, when you weren't wearing a bra. And Teo's mouth and fingers would know her flesh was less resilient than it had been when Colin started pawing her. Nurse three kids and that was what happened.

She turned around and looked back at herself over her shoulder. Her ass was too damn wide. That also came from having three kids . . . and from having all the years she did her best not to think about.

She was what she was. Most of the parts still worked most of the time. With as many miles as she had on her, and some of the bumpy roads her life had banged over, how could she ask for more? How? Simple. She wanted everything to work the way it had when she was Vanessa's age. That wasn't gonna happen, but she wanted it anyhow. Who didn't?

When she went back to the front room, she turned on the Food Network. She wasn't a great cook—Colin had once accused her of being able to burn water—but she liked watching whizzes put meals together. *I could do that*, she'd think, even if she was one of the people for whom God created Hamburger Helper. They made everything look so easy, though. If TVs came with smell attachments . . . Wow!

After a while, she punched the remote. She didn't flip through channels the way a man would, but she wasn't locked in. MSNBC said the Iranians were doing something or other the President didn't like. Louise went back to the Food Network, and then on to Oxygen. The Iranians had been doing things Presidents didn't like for, well, for ever.

Footsteps on the stairs. Louise brightened. She knew those light, bright steps. A key went into the lock, and then into the dead bolt. The door opened. In bounced Teo, as fresh as when he'd left this morning—literally, because he'd showered again at the gym.

Louise smiled a thousand-watt smile. "Darling!" she said, and all but threw herself into his arms.

"So how are those Greek poets?" Colin asked Bryce Miller. They sat across the dining-room table from each other, a chessboard between them. Colin had a cup of coffee in front of him; Vanessa's ex-boyfriend, a Coke.

"I'm getting there—diss'll be done next year, maybe year after next," Bryce answered. He was tall and skinny and pale almost to translucence, with curly red hair and a wispy little beard. After due consideration, he pushed a pawn.

Colin took it. He played chess the way he approached most problems: with straightforward aggression. He simplified ruthlessly and tried not to make too many dumbass mistakes. Against a lot of opponents, that was plenty good enough. Against Bryce, he won maybe one game in five: enough to keep him interested, not enough to let him imagine they were in the same league.

Bryce moved a knight. Colin wagged a finger at him. That nasty horse would fork his queen and a rook if he didn't do something about it. He moved the queen to threaten the knight and the forking square. Bryce covered it with a bishop.

Okay, Colin thought. *Now I can get on with my own attack.* He moved a bishop of his own, over on the other side of the board.

Bryce had long, thin fingers. He picked up the knight the way a surgeon might lift a scalpel. He took a pawn with it. "Check," he said regretfully.

One of Colin's pawns could wipe it from the board. But as soon as he did that, Bryce's bishop would assassinate his queen. He eyed the board for a moment, considering his chances after losing the queen. He saw only two, bad and worse. He tipped over his king.

"You got me good that time," he said. "I saw the bishop defending, but I didn't see it would turn to attack as soon as you unmasked it. And the check meant I couldn't just ignore the lousy knight." Everything was obvious—after the fact. It usually worked that way.

"Uh-huh." Bryce nodded—a spider encouraging a fly. "Want to play again?" He tried not to look too hopeful.

But Colin shook his head. "Not right now. That one kinda stings." He leaned back in the dining-room chair. Something in his shoulder crunched. Bryce could sit forever in any position and never get uncomfortable. Colin hadn't been able to do that even in his twenties. He tried a different tack: "How's the world treating you these days?"

"Oh, fair to partly cloudy, I guess you'd say," the younger man answered. "Maybe a skosh better than that. Writing your thesis leaves you hostile. And having a relationship blow up in your face doesn't exactly make you want to go out and party, either."

"Tell me about it!" Colin said with more feeling than he'd intended.

Bryce nodded. "Yeah. You know what I'm talking about, all right. So I ought to be down in the Dumpster, right?"

"Hadn't heard anybody put it like that before, but it seems like a possibility," Colin said. "You aren't, though?"

"I aren't," Bryce agreed. "I had another poem accepted by a pretty good journal. Theocritus updated, you might say."

Theocritus was one of the 2,000-plus-years-dead poets he studied. Colin knew that much, and not a nickel's worth more. Still, he brought his hands together in one silent clap. "Not bad," he said. "That's two in a few months."

As soon as the words came out of his mouth, he wondered if he should have left them in there. Bryce had got the first acceptance just before Vanessa threw him out. Cause and effect? Jealousy? Vanessa made a hell of an editor. She had all the tools she needed to be a writer herself except the nerve. She would rather submit to a root canal without Novocain than to an editor.

Bryce said "Uh-huh" again. He owned a pretty fair poker face. Colin couldn't tell what he was thinking. That might have been just as well.

"They pay you anything for this one?" Colin asked.

Now Bryce snorted: derision for a silly question. "Copies." By the way he said it, he figured he was lucky not to have to buy them. "My mom will be happy—she'll have something to put on her shelf and show my aunts and uncles. But you can't make a living as a poet. Or I sure as hell can't, anyway, not with the kinds of things I write. So I do 'em as well as I can, for me. If anybody else likes 'em, cool. If nobody does, I can live with that."

Colin wondered whether he was kidding himself or knew he was blowing smoke. You didn't sit down and write poems if you didn't want other people to see them. You probably wanted to end up on the *New York Times* bestseller list. Bryce was right about one thing, though: if you modeled your poems on ones from some ancient Greek, you damn well wouldn't.

"Other thing is . . ." Bryce hesitated, perhaps almost as carefully as he would have while building and polishing one of his poems. He usually wasn't shy about telling Colin what was on his mind. Which meant . . . No sooner had Colin realized what it meant than Bryce confirmed it: "I've met somebody I like. She seems to like me, too. We'll see where it goes, that's all."

"Good for you!" Colin was glad he could say it quickly. He didn't want Bryce thinking he liked him only because he'd been attached to Vanessa. "So have I—but you've heard about that."

"Right." Bryce raised an eyebrow. "We'll all run for the hills when the super-duper volcano pops its cork." Said in a different tone of voice, that would have made Colin want to punch him in the snoot. As things were, and accompanied by a disarming grin, it wasn't so bad.

"Something's gonna happen there. I don't know what. I don't know when. Neither does anybody else, including Kelly," Colin said. "Nobody knows when the Big One'll hit, either. I've got an earthquake kit in the steel shed out back, though, and a little one in my trunk. Don't you?"

"I have one in the car. Harder to put one in the shed when you're in an apartment," Bryce said.

"Could be," Colin admitted. "So who's your new friend? What's she do? How'd you meet her?"

"Her name's Susan Ruppelt. She was moving into the TA office I was clearing out of. We got to talking, and I got her e-mail, and one thing kind of led to another. She's working on the Holy Roman Empire. Tenth-century stuff, maybe eleventh-."

"AD, you mean, not BC."

"That's right."

"Too modern for you, then."

"Hey, what are thirteen hundred years between friends?" Bryce grinned again. He looked as happy as a cat lapping up cream. He hadn't looked that way while he was with Vanessa, not after the first few months. Maybe it would last longer this time. Or maybe not. Even if it did, things might fall apart years later. Colin had learned more on that score than he'd ever wanted to find out.

"Luck," he said, and meant it.

"Thanks. You, too." Bryce's mouth twisted. "It's as much as

you can hope for, isn't it? Luck, I mean. You grow together, or else you grow apart. I think Susan's on the sheltered side, you know? Otherwise, she'd have more sense than to mess with a guy on the rebound."

"Well, bring her by here one day," Colin said. "If I can't scare her away from you, nothing will."

"I may take you up on that," Bryce said. "You have been warned."

IV

Between two and three million people came to Yellowstone every year. In July and August, they all seemed to be there at once. Cars and RVs and tour buses clogged the roads till they made California freeways at rush hour look wide open by comparison.

Kelly Birnbaum knew how to beat the crowds. Go a quarter of a mile off the asphalt and you shed way more than nine-tenths of the visitors. Go a couple of miles from the highways and you were pretty much on your own. That was bad news as well as good. Cell-phone reception in the vast park was spotty at best. If you got into trouble, you might not be able to let anybody else know.

The idea, then, was not to get into trouble. Kelly was a city girl. She didn't hike the wilderness because she particularly loved hiking the wilderness. She went out there because that was what you did if you were a geologist working in the field.

What did the gravedigger in *Hamlet* say? Something about familiarity lending a quality of easiness. That was as much as she remembered. Considering that she hadn't needed to worry about

Hamlet since her undergrad days, she was moderately pleased to come up with even so much.

One of the basic lessons was never to hike alone. Since she was part of a team of researchers trudging out to Coffee Pot Springs, that wasn't an issue. Ruth Marquez came from the University of Utah. Daniel Olson, who was younger than she was, had just landed a tenure-track job at Montana State, in Missoula. Kelly didn't know whether to be jealous or to remember it was Missoula. And the calm, unhurried fellow who needed to buy a vowel was Larry Skrtel. He'd been with the U.S. Geological Survey the past twenty years, and headed up the team.

He enjoyed hiking. "The critters are less likely to bite you or run over you than the damn tourists are," he declared.

"Except for the bison, maybe," Daniel said. "They're as dumb as the morons who bought Hummers when gas was cheap." He was at least six-three, but Kelly had seen his car: a fire-engine red Honda the size of a roller skate.

"Keep your distance and they won't bother you," Larry said. "Well, usually."

"Famous last words," Daniel said. The other hikers laughed, as if he didn't mean it. Bison knew they were the biggest critters in the neighborhood, and expected everything else to get out of their way. Some of the males weighed as much as Daniel Olson's little car. They were dumb as rocks, and lots of those males had testosterone poisoning. Not a good combination.

The geologists had set out from Indian Pond. One of their colleagues took the car that brought them that far back to Lake Village. A train led towards Astringent Creek, which guided them most of the way north. Indian Pond was a good place to start. It lay near the northernmost edge of Yellowstone Lake. It was about a quarter of a mile across, and round as Charlie Brown's head. A hydrothermal explosion had gouged it out of the ground about 3,000 years before—that was what the radiocarbon dates said, anyhow.

A bigger hydrothermal explosion had formed Mary Bay, the nearby part of the lake. Down below Mary Bay, the temperature got up over 250 degrees. The hot spot under Yellowstone might still sleep, but it was a long way from dead. Kelly shivered, though it was a nice day.

She was slathered in Deet. Mosquitoes buzzed around her just the same. Repellent or no repellent, she knew she would pick up bites. She'd even been bitten through thick socks. Now she sprayed her ankles, too. But all you had to do was miss a couple of square inches anywhere, and the mosquitoes would find them.

Larry Skrtel pointed to half a dozen lodgepole pines that lay tumbled like jackstraws. When his hand went up, a woodpecker that had been drumming on one of the trunks flew away. "Those trees weren't down two years ago," Larry said in a voice that brooked no argument. "Five gets you ten one of the quakes knocked them over."

No one did argue with him. Kelly wouldn't have dreamt of it. Arguing with somebody who was obviously right was a loser's game.

Up the eastern side of Astringent Creek they went. They were near the eastern edge of the caldera. Kelly shook her head. *Of the last caldera,* she corrected herself. This one stretched most of the way across the park. The eastern edge of the one from two million years ago was also somewhere around here. That one's western edge, though, lay well over into Idaho.

Quakes . . . Was that a brief rumble underfoot? Kelly had almost convinced herself she was imagining things when Ruth Marquez laughed self-consciously and said, "Did the earth move for you, too?"

Everybody groaned. But Daniel said, "Yeah, I think so. That was only a little one—maybe a 3.3." Larry nodded.

Kelly smiled, remembering Colin guessing the magnitude of the stronger quake the year before. They might never have got together if he hadn't. Life could be seriously strange sometimes.

"Harder to be sure when you're outdoors," she said. "Not as much stuff to rattle and shake. When you're indoors somewhere, there's less room for doubt."

Larry paused thoughtfully. "I'm not sure I've ever been indoors for an earthquake," he said. Daniel and Ruth both nodded.

"Only proves you guys aren't from California," Kelly said. As far as the other geologists were concerned, that made them lucky. They teased her. She sassed them back.

As the crow flies, Coffee Pot Springs was between twelve and fifteen miles north of Yellowstone Lake. There were more ravens than crows in Yellowstone, and the land route was longer than the aerial one would have been. They hadn't got an early start. They weren't hurrying, either. They were fit enough, but none of them except possibly Daniel was really *fit*. Kelly guessed they wouldn't get there before nightfall, and she turned out to be right.

Along with the Deet, she smelled of her own sweat and the sunscreen she'd also used liberally. Up around 8,000 feet, sunburn came easy. She also smelled the chemical odor rising from Astringent Creek. Yellowstone was full of such hellish reeks. Fire and brimstone had shaped this land, and were a long way from gone even now.

Freeze-dried food could have been worse. That was as much as she could say about it. But a million stars blazed in the night sky, and the Milky Way glowed bright and ghostly. You never saw—you never imagined—the heavens like this in L.A. or Berkeley. Too much air (too dirty, too), too many lights. Too many people, was what it boiled down to.

Kelly would have enjoyed the view more if she'd stayed up longer. But she soon sought her sleeping bag, and she wasn't the only one. Her last conscious thought was *I hope the bears stay away.*

They must have. She woke up undisturbed just before sunrise. Almost undisturbed: an itchy bump on the inside of her left wrist said at least one mosquito had found a place to eat.

Larry had real coffee, and was willing to share. Kelly and Ruth were glad to partake of his bounty; they'd only brought instant. Daniel declined. "I don't drink it," he said.

"My God!" Kelly exclaimed. "How did you get through grad school?"

"Crank," he answered calmly. She didn't know him well enough to tell if he was kidding.

They buried their trash, doused the fire, and went on. "I want to put in for a new set of legs," Ruth said as she worked out the kinks.

"Oh, good. I'm not the only one," Kelly said. Neither Daniel nor Larry complained. Maybe they weren't feeling it the same way. Then again, they were guys, so maybe they were just being macho. Testosterone didn't addle male bison alone.

Here and there, hot springs fumed and mud pots bubbled. A lot of them didn't even have names. There were more features like that in Yellowstone than in the whole rest of the world. A couple of dozen hot spots burned through the earth's crust. One of them raised the Hawaiian Islands, another the Galapagos chain.

But most of them lay under the oceans. The lava that came from those was smooth-flowing basalt. The Yellowstone hot spot alone sat under continental crust. Rhyolite was like granite, only with bigger crystals. When it melted, it didn't spread out easily, the way basalt did. It was too viscous. It just sat where it was till the pressure got too great. Then . . . Then the supervolcano went off.

They tramped along Shallow Creek, getting close to the

springs. A coyote eyed them from the edge of the pines, then drew back. Larry said, "If it was along the road, half a dozen cars'd stop so the jerks inside could photograph a wolf to wow Aunt Martha back home."

He was right once more. Kelly had seen it happen. She knew the difference between the two. Most people these days, though, grew up—and stayed—so isolated from nature that any wild animal seemed exotic to them.

That was one of the things that made Yellowstone so precious. Here was a great big, not too badly disturbed chunk of what North America had been like before Europeans arrived. You couldn't find anything like this elsewhere, and not just on account of the wildlife.

And if the hot spot sitting under it discharged, then what? Then you'd gone and dropped thousands of square miles of unspoiled wilderness into what was literally the world's biggest barbecue. You'd never see your bison or your wolves or your grizzlies again.

The really bad news was, that would be the least of your worries.

Steam rose ahead. A small swell of ground kept the geologists from seeing the springs themselves for a little while. Kelly remembered them from the last time she'd come this way, not long before she met Colin. They'd been, well, hot springs. If they'd been anywhere close to a road, people would have stopped and snapped pictures of them and queued up to use a couple of odorous outhouses. They weren't so showy as the ones in Black Sand Basin or Biscuit Basin, northwest up the highway from Old Faithful, but they weren't half bad.

They lay within a rough circle of sinter: the grayish white silica that precipitated out of mineral-laden water as it cooled. All things considered, they reminded Kelly of zits on the face of the earth. On a larger scale, that was what the Yellowstone supervolcano was. She wished she knew where she could get her hands on a dab of cosmic Clearasil.

"Remember, folks—watch where you put your feet. No boardwalks here," Larry said. Fair enough: he had more field experience than the rest of them put together. "Stay off the sinter crust. You can break through. You won't like it if you do—trust me. Don't count on animal tracks, either. I've seen more parboiled critters than I like to think about. Most places, I'd say the grass was pretty safe. Here, with everything that's been going on, I'm not sure how good a guide it is."

"That doesn't leave much," Daniel observed as they climbed the low rise. "Maybe we should walk three feet off the ground."

"Don't let me stop you," Larry said. Daniel gave him a sour smile.

Going uphill made Kelly's thighs and calves ache. Walking gave you great legs. (Better legs, anyhow; Kelly feared hers would never be great.) But you paid a price. Everything you did came with a price. The older she got, the more sure of that she became.

As if defying time (no, not as if—if only!), she pushed the pace the rest of the way. The others didn't mind letting her forge ahead. They'd all come to Coffee Pot Springs before. It wasn't as if she were stout Cortez (well, Balboa, if you wanted to be picky—Keats would have got a C- in Western Civ) on that peak in Darien, staring at the newfound Pacific.

Except she was. Coffee Pot Springs had gone nuts. A brand-new geyser threw water at least a hundred feet in the air. Some of the other springs weren't just pools any more. They boiled and raged, blorping water eight or ten feet high, trying to find their inner geysers, too. Several of them, she was convinced, blorped from places that hadn't boasted springs before.

Ruth and Daniel and Larry came up beside her. As she had done, they stopped and stood there gaping. "Holy shit," Ruth said. Larry nodded. Recovering faster than the rest of them,

Daniel pulled a camera from a pocket of his windbreaker and started snapping away.

Kelly started to reach for her own little Canon. She knew earthquakes messed with the plumbing systems under Yellowstone. After the Hebgen Lake quake in 1959, Sapphire Pool at the Biscuit Basin went batshit. It erupted so ferociously, it wrecked whatever subterranean channels that supplied it with water. Then it went back to being a pool.

Knowing about such things was all very well. Seeing Coffee Pot Springs totally transformed . . . that was something else again. And, as Kelly's fingers closed on the digital camera, yet another sharp but mercifully short quake rattled the ground under her feet.

A voice said, "I'm scared." Kelly needed a second or two to recognize it as her own.

Marshall Ferguson gripped one end of his sister's coffee table. He hardly knew the guy on the other end—a shlub named Lemuel Something. Lemuel! Vanessa had dated him for a while in high school, and even in college till she met Bryce.

He did know that, if he weren't her brother, he wouldn't have done this for less than a blowjob. The table was about the size of a carrier's flight deck, and solid wood, with planks at least three inches thick. It weighed as much as a rhino. All her furniture was like that. Why couldn't she have bought cheap, flimsy crap, the way most people did?

"Ready?" Lemuel asked. He didn't even go by Lem. Definitely a shlub.

"No, but let's do it anyway," Marshall answered. Lemuel needed a few seconds to process that. They lifted more or less together. Marshall swore. The table was even heavier than it looked. *And they said it couldn't be done!* he thought. To make matters worse, they had to tilt it sideways to get it out the door.

Dad was here, and a couple of other, younger, guys Vanessa had lured with one blandishment or another. No sign of Bryce, of course. No sign of Vanessa's current old-fart boyfriend, either. He'd already gone to Denver. And no sign of Rob, dammit. The band was gigging in some college town in—was it Montana?

Since Marshall was taller than Lemuel, he took the bottom position as they lugged the coffee table down the stairs. That kept it more nearly level. It also left him bearing more of the weight. *Lucky me*, he thought.

Vanessa had been carrying boxes into the U-Haul parked outside. Pickles was already in his plastic cat carrier, and yowling as if he expected them to start vivisecting him any second now. He probably did. Marshall wouldn't have wanted to drive to Denver with a cat in a carrier on the seat beside him. Vanessa didn't seem to worry about it. She also wasn't too busy to play sidewalk superintendent when the coffee-table haulers came up. "Careful," she said. "You don't want to ding it."

"Says who?" Marshall inquired.

"Says me," his sister snapped. She liked dishing it out. She'd never been so good at taking it.

"C'mon," Lemuel said—to Marshall, not Vanessa. "Let's get this fucker into the truck before my arms fall off."

"Okay." Marshall was on the bottom again when they toted it up the U-Haul's ramp. At least the truck was big enough to have one. Getting the table into the cargo space by lifting it wouldn't have been much fun. Come to think of it, nothing about moving was much fun.

Marshall wondered how Vanessa would like driving this monster to Colorado. Even without Pickles and his editorials, she would have needed a special trucker's license to get behind the wheel of anything bigger. God, and the gas it would burn through! And . . .

"Who are you gonna get to move you in?" he asked her.

"Will, uh, Hagop help?" He knew a guy who said that helping somebody move was a proof of true love. He'd met Vanessa's new squeeze a couple of times, but he wasn't convinced the rug merchant had a whole lot.

"He's got a bad back," she answered.

"So do I—now," Marshall said as he eased the table down. Lemuel covered it with a dropcloth, then shoved it into a corner of the cargo bed and stacked boxes on top of it. That made good sense. Marshall wouldn't have guessed Lemuel had it in him.

"Funny. I'm laughing my ass off," Vanessa said. "You don't have to be here, you know. If you want to go back to Santa Barbara and your bong, be my guest."

He almost flipped her the bird, hopped into his car, and roared up the Harbor Freeway to the 101. Pissing her off didn't bother him one bit. But Dad wouldn't be happy, which was putting it mildly. And his father already had too many reasons to be unhappy at him and at most of the world.

"Anyway," Vanessa went on, "from what I hear, there are almost as many wetbacks in Denver as there are in L.A. Getting unloaded'll cost me a few bucks, but not that much."

"If you say so." Marshall turned back to Lemuel. "Ready for the next exciting episode?"

"If you say so," Lemuel replied. Not a bad imitation of Marshall. Maybe he was less of a dud than Marshall recalled. Or maybe he'd grown up some since. Who the hell knew?

Just after noon, Vanessa made a food run. She came back with enough Burger King burgers and fries—and, to her credit, onion rings, too—to sink a battleship, and enough Cokes to float it again. The moving crew plowed through the chow like Sherman plowing through Georgia, and left little more behind. "Grease, sugar, and caffeine," Marshall's father said, engulfing a Double Whopper with cheese in a couple of chomps. "Can't go far wrong like that."

"Amen, Dad," Marshall agreed. His Double Whopper was lasting a little longer, because he was scarfing onion rings between bites. He patted his stomach. "I feel like I swallowed a bowling ball."

"Yup." His father nodded and sucked up Coke through a straw. "I'm really gonna feel it in my back and shoulders tomorrow. I'm getting too damn old to play stevedore."

Marshall was half his dad's age. He knew he'd be sore come morning, too. Who wouldn't, except somebody who really was a mover? He was also amused to watch Dad look around to make sure Vanessa couldn't hear before he cussed. Who was Dad kidding? Himself, most likely. Vanessa swore whenever she felt like it, and she didn't care who was in range when she let fly.

Dad looked around again. Then he swiped a couple of Marshall's onion rings. "Grand theft!" Marshall said. "You're busted, dude."

"No evidence," his father said with his mouth full, and chewed harder to make sure he'd got rid of it all. After a heroic swallow, he changed the subject: "I wish like hell your sister wasn't doing this. I've told her so, too, but she's kinda hard of listening." One of his patented dry chuckles followed. "You may have noticed."

"Who, me?" Marshall's wide-eyed innocence made Dad chuckle again. He went on, "You really have no use for the rug merchant, have you?" Now he glanced around warily and kept his voice down. When it came to critiques of her love life, Vanessa wasn't sweet reason personified.

"As a matter of fact, no. DMV records say he's two years older than I am." Dad had the grace to look faintly embarrassed. "I mean, I'm seeing a younger woman, too, but nowhere near *that* much younger." His eyes slid toward Marshall's sack of onion rings again. Too late—they were gone. He sighed and ate French fries instead. Marshall thought he'd said everything he was going to for a while, but turned out to be wrong: "But Hagop isn't what I'm worried about."

"Huh?" Marshall said. Then he remembered what Dad's new girlfriend (who, from one brief meeting, seemed nice enough—he sure liked her better than Teo) did for a living, or wanted to do for a living, or however the hell that worked. He clapped a greasy hand to his forehead. "Oh, for God's sake! Don't do the sky-is-falling dance again! Like Vanessa will pay attention to that. Tell me another one!"

"Well . . . she didn't," his father admitted. "But the sky isn't falling. The ground's getting ready to blow up. That's worse. You have no idea how much worse. Nobody has any idea how much worse."

Marshall cocked his head to one side. "Only you, huh? Only you and Kelly, I mean?"

To his surprise—no, to his astonishment—Dad walked right into it. "That's right." His father stuck out his chin and looked stubborn. *Heredity*, Rob thought. Anybody could see where Vanessa—and Rob, too—got it. He didn't see it in himself the same way. But then, who ever does?

That was beside the point, though. He rubbed his father's nose in it the way you rub a puppy's nose right after it pisses on the rug: "You know what you sound like? You sound like you're ready for a rubber room—or else for a really rancid TV movie, one. Only you and your sweetheart know The Truth"—he made the capital letters painfully obvious—"and you can't get anybody to pay attention to you. Give me a break!"

Dad winced. "It's not like you make it sound," he mumbled.

"I understand, Lieutenant Ferguson. Please tell me how it is, then." Now Marshall did his best to impersonate a shrink.

His best must have been good enough. He wasn't made to be able to do what his father suggested. Dad was laughing when he made the suggestion, though. A good thing he was, too. Marshall didn't want to mess with him. It wasn't just training, though Dad had it and Marshall didn't. Marshall didn't want to hurt anybody. There were times when Dad did.

Once again, Vanessa got it from him. Marshall might be no threat to make Phi Beta Kappa at UCSB—not as long as the weed held out, anyway—but he was plenty smart enough to keep his big mouth shut on that particular pearl of wisdom.

"Come on, you lazy bums! Get busy!" Damned if Vanessa didn't make as if to crack the whip.

She had lots of boxes of clothes, which weren't bad to carry, and of books, which were. Paper seemed to defy the laws of physics. A 1 x 1 x 2 box definitely weighed more than twice as much as a 1 x 1 x 1. Lemuel played macho and carried a 1 x 1 x 1 box of books in each arm—once. After that, he used two arms for one box.

They finished loading about three. Vanessa hugged them all and kissed everybody on the cheek. "Thanks, kiddo," she told Marshall. Pickles squalled mournfully in the background.

"It's okay. That's why you've got brothers and other beasts of burden."

"Yeah, you're beastly, all right." She pressed an engraved portrait of Ben Franklin into his hand. "I want to get going. You guys can use this for dinner."

He started to say they wouldn't be hungry for a week after all the fast food they'd killed at lunch. He started to, yeah, but he sure didn't finish. He'd been working hard enough that his appetite was already coming back to life. By dinnertime, he'd be ready to make a pig of himself. A C-note wouldn't buy prime rib for the crew, but they could do better than Burger King.

He did ask, "Will you have enough to keep you going till you land something in Colorado?"

"One way or another, I'll make it," she answered. She went over to their father. He also got a hug and a kiss. He said something, too low for Marshall to catch. Then Vanessa tossed her head, the way Marshall had watched Mom do a million times. That meant Dad had come out with something dumb—again. Was the toss heredity, too, or had Vanessa just watched Mom till she imitated her without even knowing she was doing it?

Asking her wouldn't be so real smart, either. Again, Marshall kept his mouth shut.

Besides, he could make a shrewd guess about the subject line on that hair-flipping head toss. Five got you ten Dad was going on about the time bomb ticking under Yellowstone. Marshall had poked around online. It wasn't that he didn't believe the super-volcano was there. Whether it was likely to go off day after to-morrow—or a week from Tuesday at the latest—was liable to be a different question.

That was how it looked to him, anyhow. He knew how much he didn't know about volcanoes in general and the Yellowstone supervolcano in particular. By what Google and Wiki told him, though, nobody knew much about supervolcanoes. Not one had gone off in the past umpteen thousand years.

And if none went off in the *next* umpteen thousand years, that would suit him fine.

Vanessa stuck Pickles on the U-Haul's front seat and fas-tened the belt around his carrier. Then she climbed into the cab. She started the truck. It sounded like the beater it was. How far from L.A. to Denver? A thousand miles, plus or minus. After so many thousands already on the odometer, why worry about one more?

Another clunk meant she'd released the hand brake. The emergency brake, Dad still called it. Hardly anybody younger than Dad ever did. But the way the U-Haul farted as it rolled off made Marshall think that wasn't such a bad name after all. If you needed to use the hand brake in that truck, you might be in an emergency.

He displayed the hundred. "Do we eat dinner, or do we drink it?"

What they did was spend the next ten minutes knocking it back and forth and then splitting the difference. Kirin and cheap tempura went mighty well after moving, and they were all grubby enough that any place fancier than a Japanese greasy spoon wouldn't have wanted their business anyhow.

"Could be worse." Marshall didn't remember he was echoing a book his folks had read to him when he was little. The sentiment seemed to hit the spot as well as the food and the beer.

It did to him, anyhow. His father said, "That's what I'm afraid of."

You knew you were starting to make it in the music business when you couldn't fit the whole band and everything you needed for your show into one big old SUV. The members of Squirt Frog and the Evolving Tadpoles were all bemused to be traveling with two, but there it was. Rob Ferguson knew he was the band cheapskate, but not even he'd said boo when they bought the second vehicle. When it was railroad time, it was railroad time, and that was all there was to it.

They didn't go out of their way to look outrageous or even flamboyant; Squirt Frog and the Evolving Tadpoles wasn't that kind of band. They were just four tired guys in their twenties when they pulled off I-90 and drove south toward the place where they'd crash tonight.

Rob was sitting in the lead SUV's front passenger seat, which made him navigator and lookout. "There it is!" he said, pointing to the sign on the west side of the street. "Ruby's Inn."

"Sweet," said Justin Nachman, who was driving. The band tried not to stay at the big national chains. With them, you knew what you were getting, all right. That was the good news. More to the point, it was also the bad news. Justin slowed down. Then he muttered under his breath: "Where'd they stick the stupid driveway?"

Rob was about to suggest where they *could* stick it when Justin found it. Ruby's turned out to share an entrance with the next motel farther south. The little convoy pulled into the lot.

One of the girls behind the desk, a blonde who'd be porky in another five or ten years, had not a clue concealed anywhere about her person. The other, a skinny brunette, not only knew about the band's reservations but whistled the start of "Impossible Things Before Breakfast," one of the tracks from the new album.

Michael Jackson or Mariah Carey would have committed *seppuku* if an album sold the way *Out of the Pond* was doing. Well, Michael Jackson was already dead, but you get the picture. For a band like Squirt Frog and the Evolving Tadpoles, numbers that would have been disastrous for a big act looked terrific instead. They were making more money on sales from iTunes and the physical CD than they were from live shows, which had never happened before. They'd be able to afford to take some extra time getting their next release just right.

So maybe it wasn't an enormous surprise that the registration clerk knew one tune or another from *Out of the Pond*. Nice, yeah. Egoboo, for sure. But maybe not an enormous surprise. "Impossible Things Before Breakfast" wasn't a single, though. Never had been, never would be. If you knew that one, you not only had the album but you really liked it.

"Are you going to the show tomorrow night?" Rob asked her.

She shook her head. "Can't afford it," she said regretfully.

"What's your name?"

"Tina Morton."

He wrote it down. "Show up at will-call. They'll have a seat for you."

"Thanks!" She beamed at him. That might turn into something promising later on, or it might not. He wouldn't worry about it now. Tickets were only twenty-five dollars, but he wasn't far from the days when twenty-five dollars weren't *only* himself. And if the next album tanked instead of taking off from what *Out of the Pond* was doing, he'd go right back there again.

The rooms, next door to each other, were, well, rooms. Rob had been in a lot of different rooms in a lot of different places. He'd had some that were better than these, more that were worse. These were on the ground floor, as the band had requested. They wouldn't have to shlep stuff up and down stairs.

After everything was out of the cars, Justin stretched and grimaced, miming an unhappy back. "We're gonna be too old for all this hauling one of these days. One of these days *soon*," he amended, so maybe he wasn't faking the sore back. "What do we do then?"

"It's not what we do then. It's what we do in the meantime. We've gotta make ourselves a big enough deal so we can pay roadies to take care of all the heavy, sweaty shit for us," Rob said. "What I want to know is, where do you go for dinner when you're in Missoula, Montana?"

"Go ask Tina at the desk," Justin answered. "Or I will if you don't want to. She's not half bad."

"My old man always tells me *Never volunteer*, but I'll do it. *Not half bad* is right," Rob said. "And she knows 'Impossible Things Before Breakfast'! How impossible is that?"

"Pretty much so, most places, but every once in a while they do let the brain-damaged ones out of the Home for the Terminally Inane," Justin said. Rob shot him the bird and went back to the front desk to chat up Tina. When he came back, Justin gave him a sardonic hand. "Twenty minutes, man. What were you doing?"

"Like, talking."

"Like, right! I've never heard anybody call it that before. That long, you probably did it twice."

"I wouldn't have," Rob replied with dignity. "Some people don't blow their load too quick the first time. Anyway, about dinner—"

"You mean you remembered dinner, too?"

Rob took no notice. It wasn't easy, but he managed. "Back toward the Interstate half a block is something called the Stone of Accord. 'Where the Gaelic meets the garlic,' it says on the menu—she showed me one."

"Corned beef and linguini! Cabbage pizza! Oh, boy!"

"Menu looked pretty good. And they've got Moose Drool on tap. Maybe a block and a half the other way is the Montana Club. If you haven't lost all your money gambling, you can eat dinner there." Rob knew about poker clubs that doubled as restaurants; San Atanasio had several. When he was little, they'd paid the town a lot in tax revenue. Now, thanks to the big Indian casinos, they'd fallen on hard times. And, without that tax loot, so had San Atanasio.

"Which is better?"

"Stone of Accord is a couple of bucks cheaper. Tina says the food's better, too."

"Okay. We'll blame her if it turns out to be crappy." Justin set a hand on Rob's shoulder. "But don't worry. We'll blame you, too. If it's good, though, she gets all the credit."

"Have you been talking with my father?" Rob asked, not altogether in jest. The band walked up to the Stone of Accord. The food proved pretty good. The other three guys drank toasts to Tina. Draft Moose Drool stout was as good as anything this side of Guinness. And if you wanted Guinness instead, all you had to do was ask for it.

The waitress recognized them. "You look just like you do online!" she exclaimed, as if that were some kind of surprise.

"Not me," Rob said gravely. "I wouldn't let 'em photograph my tail."

"We made him climb out of the formaldehyde bottle, too," Justin said. The girl just kinda looked at him, which meant she didn't know what the hell formaldehyde was. *Fancier than informaldehyde*, Rob supposed. He also got his low taste in puns from his old man.

"You guys are playing at the Civic Stadium, right?" she asked.

"No, over at the Golden Sluice, near the university campus," Rob said.

"I've been there. No way it's big enough!" she said. "People will be jammed in there. Lined up around the block, like. You guys are the hottest band to come to town in a long time."

God help Missoula, in that case, Rob thought. Aloud, he said, "I like the way she talks."

"Me, too," Biff Thorvald agreed loudly. He sounded as if he liked it a lot. He got her name, and promised her a ticket. If they were gonna sell out the place, why the hell not? Rob liked Tina better—she got the jokes—but the waitress was a long way from terrible. No guarantees, but sometimes life on the road could be a lot of fun.

V

"Oh, Christ. Another one," Colin Ferguson said mournfully. Not all the little old ladies who died in San Atanasio went on the South Bay Strangler's page in the ledger. Not even all the little old ladies who got murdered in town did. Just the week before, a punk ransacking a house for shit to steal so he could feed his habit put three slugs into seventy-four-year-old Lupe Sandoval when she got back from Safeway sooner than she might have. One of them blew out the back of her head. The punk sat in a cell, awaiting arraignment. Colin had questioned him; he still had no clue he'd done anything wrong. It made you wonder why you bothered sometimes. Meanwhile, the widow Sandoval's family was scrambling for the cash they'd need to bury her.

Maria Peterfalvy, though . . . She'd got out of Hungary in 1956, one jump ahead of Russian tanks. A framed black-and-white photo on her dresser showed her not long afterwards. She'd been a beauty; no other word for it.

She wasn't beautiful now, lying there on the bedroom floor in the cramped little tract house where she'd lived for upwards of forty years. First with her husband and kids; then, after he died and they got on with their own lives, by herself.

She wasn't living now, either. Gabe Sanchez looked out through the window. Filmy curtains kept people on the outside from seeing in, but not the reverse. Sanchez said, "Here's the first news van."

"Happy fucking day," Colin answered. Mrs. Peterfalvy wouldn't mind his language, not any more she wouldn't. He patted his hair with his hand, though he couldn't imitate a newsie's perfect coif. He held his fist—an imaginary mike—under Sanchez's nose. "Tell me, Sergeant, why haven't you been able to catch this Strangler son of a bitch when he's knocked off—what is it? nineteen?—little old ladies now."

"Nineteen is correct, yes," Sanchez replied, as if he were really being interviewed. "And we haven't caught him because he doesn't leave fingerprints anywhere and his goddamn DNA isn't in any of our databases." He eyed Colin as if his boss truly were a brain-damaged reporter. "So why don't you fuck off and die and let me try and do my job?"

"But don't you realize you aren't protecting the public the way the public deserves to be protected?" Colin persisted, his eyes wide with innocent indignation (or possibly raw ignorance).

Gabe Sanchez started to say something, then stopped and shook his head. "Man, that's scary. You sound just like one of the shitheads. How d'you do it?"

"The more you repeat yourself, the better the imitation you do," Colin said. "I mean, if you only say something once, it can't be important, right? It can't have any real significance, either."

"That, too," Sanchez agreed. "And here comes another van."

"Where's the coroner?" Colin asked morosely. "He's the guy who needs to answer questions. Him and the DNA analysts, I mean."

"But you're the officer in charge of the investigation. That means you're the guy with all the answers," Gabe said. "You know you are, Lieutenant. It says so right here on the box."

Colin told him where to put the box, and how to fold it before he did. Sergeant Sanchez laughed. He could afford to; he *wasn't* the officer in charge of the investigation. Neither was Colin Ferguson, or not exactly. Even counting Mrs. Peterfalvy, only seven of the South Bay Strangler's victims lived in San Atanasio. Other poor harried cops were looking for him all over the region.

But Colin was the man on the spot right now. He walked out to face the wolves. He wished they *were* wolves. He might have thrown them raw meat. He might have shot them. If all else failed, he might have reasoned with them. Reporters were immune to reason, and there wasn't enough raw meat in the world to make them happy. Opening fire would have got him talked about.

He strode out onto Mrs. Peterfalvy's neatly kept front lawn. Sure as hell, the newsies bore down on him like the slavering beasts they were. The TV and radio reporters thrust microphones in his face. He disliked them more than the ones who worked for newspapers. The latter actually had to be able to write. TV people just had to know how to read, and they didn't even need to be especially good at that.

Video cameramen aimed the tools of their trade at him like so many bazookas. Unlike bazookas, though, video cameras could blow up an unwary man's reputation. The cameramen watched what they filmed with a certain ironic detachment. Unlike the pretty people they abetted, they actually had to know what they were doing.

Reporters' manners came straight out of preschool. Four shouted questions at the same time. They didn't go *Me!* . . . *No, me!* . . . *NO, ME!*, but they might as well have.

Like a playground monitor, Colin held up a hand. "If you all talk at once, I can't hear any of you," he said. That made them yell louder. But they started waving their hands, too. Colin pointed to a porky Hispanic guy from what he thought of as Eyewitless News. "Yes, Victor?"

"Is that the South Bay Strangler in there?" Victor asked, neatening his hair with the hand that wasn't holding the mike.

"No, sir," Colin answered, his face expressionless. "The victim is Maria Peterfalvy, age seventy-nine." He spelled the last name. Some of the reporters, as he had reason to know, couldn't spell their own right more than two times out of three.

Victor stamped his foot on the sidewalk. He pooched out his lower lip like a three-year-old working up to a tantrum. But he did manage to say, "No! What I mean is, did the South Bay Strangler strangle her?"

Then why don't you say what you mean? In Colin's experience, people who didn't speak clearly also didn't think clearly. Then again, if you expected a TV reporter to think clearly, you were much too naive to make a good cop. "We don't have anything back from the lab, of course," Colin said. "As a matter of fact, the lab techs aren't even here. So we can't be sure yet."

"But you do think so?" The redhead in the dark green suit couldn't have finished lower than third runner-up in the Miss California pageant six or eight years earlier. Had they hired her for her reporting skills or for the way she filled out that suit? Colin couldn't be sure about that, either, but he knew how he'd guess.

He also knew that, if he said no, most of the newsies would leave in a huff. The South Bay Strangler was sexy, especially during a sweeps month. Who cared about some dumb, ordinary murder, though? Poor Lupe Sandoval hadn't so much as made the news, even though she was just as dead as Mrs. Peterfalvy.

"Everything we see is consistent with what the Strangler does," the detective said reluctantly. "It could be a copycat case, of course, but that doesn't seem likely." Certain details about the Strangler's M.O. hadn't reached the media yet. (If they had, one TV station or another would have shouted them to the skies, with a big EXCLUSIVE! label pasted on.)

"How long will you let the Strangler continue his terror-ization of women throughout this broad area of Los Angeles County?" another TV reporter demanded, as if it were all Colin's fault. Colin had been positive that kind of question would come from somebody. It was one of the reasons he'd so looked forward to meeting the press.

"We're doing everything we can to catch this guy, Dave," he said. "If you can suggest anything we've missed, we'll listen. Be-lieve me, we will."

"That's not my place!" Dave sounded indignant. And well he might—the next idea he had would be his first. He went on, "What you've done hasn't helped Mrs., uh, Peterfalk much, either, has it?"

Colin might have known—hell, had known—he would get the name wrong, and probably wrong like that. "Peterfalvy," he corrected with cold politeness, and spelled it again. Useless, of course. The only time reporters were shown to be morons was when they came on with nothing to read—during a car chase, for instance. Otherwise, scripts from smarter people disguised their vapidity and foolishness.

"Any sign the Strangler's slipped up here?" asked Mort Greenbaum, who'd covered the crime beat on the *Breeze* for about as long as Colin had been a San Atanasio cop. Not quite long enough to have started out in a snap-brim fedora, in other words, but long enough to give the impression that he had.

"Well, like I said before, the lab hasn't turned the house upside down and inside out yet, so I can't say for sure," Colin replied. "Offhand, though, doesn't look that way."

"Gotcha." Mort had a recorder, but he took notes, too,

probably to organize his own thoughts. Looking up from the scribbles, he went on, "He's bound to sooner or later, isn't he?"

"Lord knows I hope so," Colin said.

"Or maybe he'll pick on a little old lady who sleeps with a .45 under the pillow."

"Maybe he will," Colin agreed. "I'm still hoping we catch him, though. We don't want to have to rely on civilians for do-it-yourself justice."

"Wouldn't you have a better chance if the San Atanasio Police Department—if all the police departments in the impacted area—weren't so incompetent?" Dave had finally figured out that Colin had mocked him for screwing up Mrs. Peterfalvy's name. Cops weren't supposed to do that to TV personalities: the natural order of things was the other way around. Now, stung, the handsome man in the Hugo Boss suit was trying to get his own back.

The TV news would be a hell of a lot better if you clowns weren't brain-dead, too. Colin didn't—quite—come out with it. You couldn't let them know what you thought of them. And the chief would ream him out if he got into another slanging match with a reporter. Life was too short. A damn shame, but it was.

"I already told you, we're doing everything we know how to do to go after him. State personnel and the FBI have given us a hand, too," Colin said. "We expect to succeed."

"How many more innocent victims will perish before you do?" Dave asked dramatically. He never knew how close he came to becoming one of them.

The coroner and the lab technicians pulled up then. Some of the reporters descended on Dr. Ishikawa for pearls of wisdom. He and the techs hadn't done anything or viewed the crime scene yet, but that didn't trouble the Fourth Estate. Other newshounds went after the neighbors for quotes about the late Mrs. Peterfalvy. If the neighbors didn't tell them she was a nice old lady who never bothered anybody, Colin would learn something new about human nature.

Sergeant Sanchez came up behind Colin. "Boy, that musta been fun," he said in a low voice.

"Always is," Colin agreed. "I want a cigarette, and I don't even smoke. I want a drink, too."

"I notice you aren't saying you don't drink."

"Good for you, Sherlock! But I don't. On duty I don't. Unless I really and truly need one. Or more than one."

"I'll never tell," Sanchez said.

"Somebody will. Or a surveillance camera will catch it. Or something else will go wrong. I don't need one *that* bad. Wouldn't mind writing a ticket for that cocksucker from Channel 2, though."

"Think their van's close enough to the hydrant there to write them up?"

Colin eyed it. "No," he said regretfully. "Besides, they'd have a cow if one of us did it. They'd say it was on account of they were asking questions we didn't like." *And they'd be right.* But he didn't say that.

"I didn't mean you or me. That's why God made the guys in the blue suits." Sanchez hadn't been out of a uniform so very long himself. By the way he talked, he'd never worn one.

Well, Colin had been that way himself. Most cops were. "Let it go," he said. "It's not like the dickhead would pay the ticket himself. TV stations, they've got money falling out of their assholes."

"Wish I did," Gabe Sanchez said morosely. "The bills my kids run up, they think I'm made of the stuff so I really can crap it." He eyed Colin. "Yours are pretty much grown. Do they ever stop scrounging offa you?"

"Eventually. Pretty much. The one who's still in college goes a long way toward making up for the other two, though. And there are the lawyers' bills, too, but you know about those," Colin said.

"Fuck, do I ever!" Sanchez winced. "Those mothers send their kids to Harvard, and it's, like, petty cash for them. No wonder they run the country."

"No wonder at all." Colin nodded. Gabe had that one straight, all right. Did he ever! Colin consoled himself by remembering that even lawyers' brats at Harvard fell foul of booze and dope. And some of them would decide they were more interested in discovering themselves than in getting a diploma. Some would figure they already knew it all, and again leave without the sheepskin. Some *would* graduate, and then try to make it as rock 'n' rollers instead of sensibly imitating Dad and Mom.

He knew all the verses to all those songs. Maybe, in the end, things evened out. Maybe. He wouldn't bet anything he couldn't afford to lose.

Dr. Ishikawa came out of Mrs. Peterfalvy's neat little house. "We won't be sure till the DNA results come in, but it sure looks like another one."

"Yeah, I figured the same thing," Colin said. "Will this guy *ever* fuck up?" He'd put on an optimistic face for the TV morons. Among his own kind, he could say what he really thought. Cops were like family. They didn't—usually—hold the truth against you.

Not that that did you a hell of a lot of good. But there it was, and Colin took what small advantage of it he could.

The Rockies. There they were, right out the apartment window. Vanessa liked that. On clear days, you could see mountains in Los Angeles, too, but they sat lower on the horizon, and they sure didn't march from north to south in one magnificent straight line. When it got smoggy, they disappeared.

Then again, the Rockies also disappeared when it got

smoggy. Till Vanessa moved here, she hadn't thought Denver could get smoggy. Surprise! Too many cars in not enough space could do that almost anywhere. Denver had so many cars, and so many people who'd moved here in the past twenty-five years to escape the crowding and pollution in wherever the hell they were from, that its freeway system was hopelessly overstretched. Morning and afternoon traffic crawls made Vanessa miss L.A.'s commutes. Before she moved, she wouldn't have imagined anything could.

Pickles was not a big Denver booster. He'd spent the first couple of days after he got here pissing and shitting on the apartment rug. She'd gone through a bottle of that Nature's Miracle enzyme junk, but the place still smelled of cat. Part of that was marking his new territory, of course. And part was expressing his opinion of anybody who could coop him up in a carrier for as long as it took to get from California to Colorado. He couldn't write angry e-mails, but he got the message across.

Vanessa's new job didn't pay as well as the one she'd left. But the apartment was bigger, newer, and cheaper than the one she'd had before. People in Denver bitched about the high cost of housing. Vanessa wasn't impressed. Even after a couple of market meltdowns, L.A. still cost more.

She didn't particularly like her new job. Amalgamated Humanoids made everything from crash-test dummies to fancy audio-animatronic robots. They competed for a lot of government grants, so they needed someone to write and edit proposals. Reading RFPs from the Feds proved that Washington did believe in capital punishment, at least by boredom. Reading what allegedly bright Amalgamated Humanoids engineers fondly imagined to be English proved some people grew up without a native language. That was the kindest explanation Vanessa could find, anyhow.

She hadn't liked the job she'd quit so she could move to

Denver, either. And she hadn't liked the one before that. She really hadn't liked the classes she was taking at Long Beach State, which was why she'd got a job instead.

She wasn't happy unless she disliked something, not that she'd ever put it like that. Bryce had, not long before she told him to hit the road. Cause and effect? She would have denied on a stack of Bibles that the crack had anything to do with the breakup. She would have said the same thing about the poem he'd had accepted. It was, when you got right down to it, a pretty goddamn stupid poem.

One thing she didn't love about Amalgamated Humanoids—she was starting a collection, the way she always did—was the wild up-and-down workload. Proposals had iron deadlines. If they had to go out by 3:27 p.m. Tuesday precisely, you made sure they did. If that meant pulling sixteen-hour days Saturday, Sunday, and Monday, you pulled them.

And if, after that, you spent the rest of the week counting paper clips and rubber bands and goofing around online, the boss didn't care. You stored up energy for the next crazy time.

Not everything in Denver was perfect, then. But it was no worse than L.A. As soon as Vanessa turned in her California license plates for ones stamped out by Colorado convicts, she felt more or less at home.

The one down spot—the place where she was unhappy without wanting to be unhappy, in a manner of speaking—was her love life. When she was in the throes of writing, or of translating into English someone else's godawful attempt at writing a proposal, she didn't have time for Hagop. And she soon started to wonder if Hagop ever had time for her.

"I am too busy," he would say when she called him. Not all the time, but often enough to be annoying. More than often enough: Vanessa had a low annoyance threshold.

He wasn't always too busy. Oh, no. When he woke up with a

bulge in his pants, he was charming and attentive and sweet . . . till she put out. Then the carpet business consumed him again.

Bryce had been horny all the damn time. He'd sulk and get pissy when she said no. And if she said no two or three days running, he'd play with himself instead. It made her feel she was just a convenience for him, maybe a little more enjoyable than a hand but not absolutely necessary. She'd told herself things would be different with an older man. He wouldn't keep bugging her the way Bryce did. And he'd be grateful when she gave herself to him.

Well, yes and no. Hagop wasn't horny all the damn time. Biology wouldn't let him be. But, when he was, he bugged her just as much as somebody half his age would have. Once he got what he wanted, he ignored her till the next time he started feeling the pressure again.

Vanessa had never been one to suffer in silence. As soon as she got irked enough—which didn't take long—she called him on it. "The only reason you want me around is so you can fuck me," she said one evening, after he'd done just that. The blunt language would have made her father flinch, so she hoped it would have the same effect on any man his age.

No such luck. Hagop leaned up on one elbow and looked at her, his heavy-featured face expressionless. He liked a light on in the bedroom; seeing what they were up to helped him get where he was going. After a moment, he said, "And this surprises you because . . . ?"

"If we're lovers, you're supposed to love me. Not just lay me. Not just make love to me. *Love* me," Vanessa said. *Or what the hell did I go and get rid of Bryce for?* She kept that part to herself: she had an accurate suspicion that Hagop wouldn't care why. Bryce sure hadn't cared why she'd dumped the guy she was living with before she met him. All he'd ever cared about was getting it in.

Hagop's face remained studiously blank. "I am afraid you may ask more than I am able to give."

"Oh, yeah? I'd better not." Vanessa glared at him. "I've got news for you—I didn't pack up and move to Colorado just to be your fuck toy."

"I did not expect you to move here at all," he answered with a shrug. "As long as you did, though, do you expect me not to enjoy it?"

Things were falling apart. Vanessa didn't need to be the King of Babylon to see the writing on the wall. "You *filthy* son of a bitch!" she snarled—not the ideal endearment when they were both naked in her bed and his seed still dribbled out of her to make a wet spot, but most heartfelt. "You moved here to get rid of me!" It was obvious now. Why in blue, bleeding hell hadn't it been while she was still back in San Atanasio?

With dignity, Hagop shook his head. "I moved here for exactly the reason I told you in California: I saw the chance to make more money."

"Rug merchant!" she jeered. "That's all that matters to you, isn't it?"

He got out of bed and started to dress. "I am going to pretend I did not hear that. Count yourself lucky that I am." His voice held . . . nothing.

Vanessa knew all about hot rages. Meeting a cold one gave her pause. She'd fight like a wildcat. All the same, it wouldn't be hard for her to end up dead in this apartment where she hadn't lived very long.

"So I did not move here for the purpose of getting rid of you," Hagop continued tonelessly, tucking his shirt into his slacks. "That, as they say in the trade, was an added bonus."

An added redundancy. But she didn't say that, either. She did say, "What am I supposed to do now?"

He shrugged again. "This is no longer my worry. You are old

enough to be an adult, unlikely as it sounds. You will land on your feet or on your back—whichever suits you. And then, before too long, you will find out that the next one, whoever he is, does not measure up to your imagination, either."

He walked out of the bedroom. Pickles meowed at him. He didn't answer the cat. The front door opened. It closed. It didn't slam—Hagop was still holding things in. His footsteps faded down the stairs. With the door closed, she couldn't hear them at all by the time he got to the bottom.

"You bastard! You stinking, shitheaded bastard!" she whispered. Then she all but ran into the shower. She'd used it not long before he came over, but so what? Now she wanted to scrub every trace of his touch off her body. She didn't usually use a bath sponge. Tonight she made an exception. She turned the water up as hot as she could stand, too.

Once she finally came out, she stripped the sheets off the bed. She wanted to throw them out. She *really* wanted to douse them in gasoline and make a bonfire out of them. Wasn't some ancient movie called *The Burning Bed*? If she could douse Hagop in gasoline and make a bonfire out of him . . .

But she couldn't. Oh, she could, but she was much too likely to get caught. The asshole wasn't worth doing hard time for. As a cop's kid, she knew better than most how godawful state prison was.

And she couldn't even toss the sheets. Replacing them wouldn't be cheap. After making this move—making this move for that worthless, reptilian turd!—she couldn't afford a lot of grand gestures. She'd just have to shove quarters into one of the building's machines and wash that man right out of her bed-clothes. Any of Amalgamated Humanoids' products had more in the way of warmth, more in the way of feeling, than he did.

So why hadn't she realized that when she fell for him after she gave Bryce the heave-ho? She shrugged. She'd been looking for a lifeline, and she'd found one. *Now* she discovered it had an anvil on the end, not one of those cork floats.

She pulled fresh sheets out of a cabinet in the hall. All the bed linen in there had been washed since Hagop's nasty sweat last polluted it. It would have to do. Grimly, she started making the bed. Pickles thought it was a game, and tried to help. In lieu of punting him, she tossed a couple of kitty treats out into the hall and bribed him to go away.

Bryce Miller wondered if he would ever see a job after he finally finished his thesis. The way the economy looked these days, odds were against him. He'd played the grad-school game as well as anybody could. He'd been a reader. He'd had research assistant-ships and TAships. He'd tutored high-school kids. He'd taught at a couple of community colleges. The proof of his success was that he could see the end of the dissertation ahead, and he wasn't broke. Yet.

Maybe if he'd chosen a sexier field than Hellenistic poetry . . . He shook his head. Wrong comparison. Hellenistic poetry could be plenty sexy. It could, here and there, be downright filthy. Maybe if he'd chosen a more practical field than Hellenistic poetry . . .

"But then I wouldn't be me," he murmured. He had his laptop set up on the table in the dining nook of the little one-bedroom place he'd hastily found after Vanessa decided change was in the air. Papers and books covered about two-thirds of the tabletop. When he needed to eat, he had to put the computer away.

If he hadn't found a secondhand copy of *The Persian Boy* when he was in high school, he might never even have heard of the Hellenistic age, much less ended up trying to make a living studying it. Somewhere out in the big, wide world, there might be people, possibly even English-speaking people, who could resist getting drawn in by Mary Renault's prose. There might be, but

Bryce wasn't any of them. He'd started trying to find out how much in the novel was real and how much she was making up. Most of it and not a whole lot, respectively, he'd soon discovered.

Writers were dangerous people. They could warp the lives of readers they'd never met, readers they couldn't meet because they were dead by the time some beat-up old copy of one of their books fell into the right—the wrong?—hands.

Bryce wondered if he would ever write a poem that affected even one person as much as *The Persian Boy* had changed him. He laughed at himself. Talk about setting your sights high!

Out in the courtyard, one of the poolside regulars did a cannonball that raised a splash like a young mushroom cloud. Three or four of the others gave forth with whoops and applause. Maybe a dozen people—more men than women—pretty much monopolized the pool here. There was no law that said Bryce couldn't swim in it. He didn't think they would have gone out of their way to make him feel unwelcome if he had.

But that was the point. They hung out there, and he didn't. The same kind of group, down to sex ratio and precancerous tans, had ruled the roost at the building where he'd lived with Vanessa.

He looked down at his own hands. He was pale almost to invisibility. No need for him to worry about melanoma, no sir. He'd probably die of some fungus infection he caught from an Egyptian papyrus of the second century BC, or else of pneumonia brought on by aggressive library air-conditioning.

Another cannonball, this one even bigger and wetter than the last. More cheers from the regulars. Bryce eyed the waves rolling across the pool and slopping over the coping on the far side. If you threw an asteroid into the Pacific somewhere near New Zealand, waves would swamp Los Angeles the same way.

"Cheery thought," he said. The longer he lived alone, the more he talked to himself. He would have worried about it more if Vanessa's dad (which was still how he thought of Colin Ferguson most of the time) hadn't told him he did the same thing.

Susan thought it was funny-peculiar that he'd stayed friends with his ex's father. It wasn't even that they both found themselves in the same boat at the same time (or that the boat was named *Titanic*). Dammit, Bryce liked Colin, and for some reason it worked both ways. Had the older man's life worked out differently, he would have made a good scientist instead of a good cop. He had that restless itch to know, to put pieces together till they formed a satisfying whole.

It probably wasn't an accident that his new lady friend was a geologist. Bryce wondered what he'd seen in Louise, back in the day. She was nice enough—she worked at being nice, in fact, worked hard at it—but she wasn't what you'd call long on brains.

"So what?" Bryce wondered, again out loud. Chances were Colin had been so happy he was getting laid regularly that he hadn't cared about anything else.

Kai su, teknon? Bryce wondered. That was Greek, and it was what Julius Caesar had really said when he saw that Brutus was one of the guys shoving knives into him on the Ides of March. It meant *You, too, kid?*

Bryce was aiming it at himself. Now that Vanessa was gone, he wondered what he'd seen in her past a pretty face, nice tits, and long legs that opened for him like the door into heaven. What more did you need? When you were first starting out, you thought everything was just like the movies and you were guaranteed to live happily ever after.

He knew what she'd seen in him. She'd been fighting with her then-boyfriend, and Bryce looked like an escape hatch. That she'd been fighting with the other guy should have been a red flag. But when you had a boner that wouldn't quit, it was easy enough to figure the fights were all the fault of the SOB she was ditching.

Did Hagop What's-his-name figure Vanessa's fights with Bryce were all his fault? Maybe, but then again maybe not. Hagop had a good many miles on the odometer. Chances were he'd seen that things were rarely as one-sided as the person talking about them made them out to be.

Of course, why would he care? When you landed a girl young enough to be your daughter, why would you care about anything? It might not last long, but wouldn't you have fun while it did?

When I'm in my fifties, will I troll for girls in their twenties? Bryce was sure he'd still look at girls in their twenties; that was one of the things they were for. But to touch instead of just look? He hoped to be happily settled with someone by then. He'd hoped to be happily settled with Vanessa. Whatever else might happen, that wouldn't, not now.

His phone rang. He picked it up, and smiled when he recognized the number. "Hey, Susan," he said. "I was just thinking about you." In a manner of speaking, it was true.

"Well, good. I was thinking about you, too," Susan Ruppelt said. German or maybe Dutch, Bryce guessed. One of these days, he'd get around to asking her. It wasn't urgent, not the way it might have been a lifetime earlier. In L.A. these days, any white whose first language was English counted as an Anglo. That cracked up Bryce and some of his Jewish friends, which didn't mean they didn't take advantage of it. Susan went on, "How crazy should you get before your orals?"

"There's an interesting question. You're going to, you know, whether you want to or not," he answered. She was scheduled to take them fall quarter. It seemed a long way off to Bryce, but it wouldn't to Susan.

"Tell me about it!" she yipped.

"I know. I know." He tried to sound soothing. He'd survived his exams almost three years ago now, and got blasted afterwards. "Listen, if your chairperson's worth the paper she's printed on—"

"She is," Susan broke in. "Claudia can drive me nuts sometimes, but she's one of the best in the country. That's why I came here."

"Cool." Bryce stayed in soothing mode. He still didn't call Professor Towers by his first name, and wondered if he ever would. But then again, Professor Towers' first name was Elmer, so chances were nobody called him by it. That was neither here nor there, though. "Like I was saying, if she's worth anything, she won't let you go up for exams unless she's sure you'll do fine."

"She told me the same thing. I don't know whether to believe it, though," Susan said.

"Believe it," Bryce said firmly. "When you look back on them, doctoral exams are more a rite of passage, like, than anything else."

"They don't feel that way when you're looking forward to them." Susan sounded fretful—and who could blame her? Disasters did happen. The year after Bryce passed his orals, a woman doing ancient Rome gruesomely flunked hers. No one but the profs who examined her was supposed to know what happened, but word got out all the same. The guy under whom she'd studied had retired a few months after the fiasco. UCLA was still searching for a full-time Romanist. With upcoming budgets looking as starvation-lean as the current one, the university might keep searching for a long time.

But Susan wasn't like poor underprepared Joanna. Bryce didn't know much about Western medieval history. He knew a solid scholar when he saw one. And he'd done a Roman minor field himself, as Susan was going to with whatever temporary lecturer held the slot come fall. He'd tutored her after they started dating, but not for long—she had a better grasp of the Romans than he did.

"Hey, you know your stuff," he said. "The only thing you have to fear is fear itself. You don't come down with stage fright, do you?"

"Not usually. But I'm not used to going up on this big a stage, either."

"They'll cut you slack for that. They've seen panicked grad students before. If *I* got through, you can do it. You're way more outgoing than I'll ever be."

"I'm just afraid I'll forget everything the second they start asking me questions."

"Won't happen. Honest to God, babe, it won't. They started me out with softballs so I could loosen up a little before they started hitting me with the tougher ones. From everything I've heard from other people, that's how they usually do it."

"They know so much, though." Come hell or high water, Susan was going to worry. "If they want to flunk me, they can."

"Sure they can. They can flunk anybody if they want to. They sure could've nailed me to the cross. But that's the whole point. They won't want to."

"Really?" Susan said in a small voice.

"Really. You'll do great," Bryce answered. They'd been through this before. If she needed a shoulder to cry on—or to fret on—he was glad to lend his. He'd got through what she was approaching; he knew the bumps in the road. He sometimes thought grad students were the only people fit to associate with other grad students. No one else understood the peculiar pile of shit they had to shovel.

He also sometimes thought people who'd gone through messy breakups were the only ones fit to associate with others of their kind, for similar reasons.

"Thank you, Bryce," Susan breathed. No messy breakups in her past, so Bryce hoped like hell he was full of it.

VI

A secretary dumped the latest pile of printouts on Colin Ferguson's desk. "Here you are, Lieutenant," she said.

"Thanks, Josie." Colin spoke Spanish after a fashion: small vocabulary, bad grammar, heavy accent. It often came in handy on the street, but he knew better than to trot it out with Josefina Linares. It would only piss her off. She went out of her way to show how American she was. Chances were he knew more *español* than she did. He also knew she'd had family in the States longer than he had.

He went through the printouts one by one. They were DNA records from convicted felons. Plainly, the South Bay Strangler had never been nabbed for anything that required him to give a DNA sample. But if someone who was closely related to him had, the near miss might point the cops toward the real perp.

It could work. It had worked. The LAPD had busted the bastard they called the Grim Sleeper after his son's DNA made them look in his direction. He'd got away with murder—and with a whole swarm of other crimes—for more than twenty-five years. But he sat in San Quentin now, going through the endless appeals that came with capital-murder cases.

Maybe one of these days he'd get the lethal injection he deserved. (Colin thought he did, anyhow; he'd met only a handful of cops who opposed capital punishment.) Or maybe he'd die of old age first—he was up around sixty. The way justice worked in California, old age seemed the better bet.

None of these DNA tests was even within shouting distance of the South Bay Strangler's genetic material. Except for rape and murder—details, details—the Strangler was a good citizen. He came from a family of good citizens, too. Or if by some chance he didn't, his relatives were also careful criminals.

Colin muttered darkly. You couldn't give up too soon. Just because none of these samples led anywhere, that didn't mean some other one wouldn't. Maybe it would come in the next batch. What was that song about tomorrow, tomorrow? You had to hope it looked better than today.

He'd had to try to convince himself of that too often lately. Sometimes it was true. He'd had that enormous hole in his life after Louise walked out on him. Kelly filled . . . some of it, anyhow. Did he love her? Did she love him? Even thinking the word scared him more than a crackhead with a shotgun. How long would he need to work up the nerve to say it?

And Vanessa had dumped (or been dumped by—she couldn't tell the story the same way twice running, which made Colin's bullshit detector go off) the old guy she'd been seeing. Colin came out with sympathetic noises whenever he talked to her, but he was anything but brokenhearted. The couple of times he'd met the guy, Hagop had been perfectly—almost greasily—polite. The Armenian didn't have a record; Colin had quietly made sure of that. But the notion of Vanessa sleeping with a man his own age had still given him the willies.

So he didn't need to worry about that any more. What she'd

do next, whether she'd stay in Colorado or come back to L.A. . . . Whatever she would do, she hadn't done it yet. So he didn't need to worry about it yet. So he wouldn't.

Unless, of course, he did.

He still had plenty to worry about here at the cop shop. Not just the South Bay Strangler. His thoughts about a crackhead with a shotgun weren't free association. *Somebody* with a shotgun had blown the head off a Korean who ran a liquor store near the corner of San Atanasio Boulevard and New Hampshire. That was only a couple of miles east of the station, but it was anything but a prime part of town.

Most of the time, people robbed liquor stores to get money for drugs. Most of the time, they started shooting because they were already amped to the eyebrows. That made crack and crystal meth the two leading candidates. A surveillance camera showed that the perp was African American, so crack seemed more likely. No guarantees, but more likely.

Three different news shows had run the surveillance video— including what happened when a charge of double-aught buck caught the luckless so-and-so behind the counter square in the face. "This footage may be disturbing," they'd all said, or words to that effect. It was a hell of a lot worse than disturbing, as if they cared. If it bleeds, it leads.

With luck, somebody out there would recognize the asshole with the scattergun. With more luck, whoever did recognize him would have the nerve or the moral indignation or whatever else it took to call the police. It did happen. Not always, not even often enough, but it did.

No matter what the TV shows claimed, though, that wasn't why they ran their "disturbing footage." They ran it for the same reason they preempted things to show car chases: it made people watch. Once you'd said that, you'd said everything that needed saying, as far as they were concerned.

The phone rang. Colin picked it up. "Ferguson—San Atanasio Police."

"Hey, Colin. Nels Jensen here." Jensen was a Torrance police captain also chasing the South Bay Strangler. "Any luck on the DNA profiles?"

If there was, Nels would find some way to take credit for it. He was a pretty fair cop, but he liked seeing his own smiling face in the paper and on TV. He'd be a chief one day, and probably of a department bigger than the Torrance PD. Because he was a glory hound, Colin might have been tempted to tell him no even if the answer were yes. If he wanted yes so much, he could do the work that produced it instead of scrounging off other people.

As things were, though, Colin could say "Diddly-squat" with a perfectly clear conscience.

"Ahh, shit," Jensen said. "I've got one of my sergeants plowing through them, too, but he hasn't found anything close to a match. I was hoping you'd do better."

Because I'm a lieutenant, not just a chickenshit sergeant? Colin wondered. At least Nels had somebody in his department checking through them. But if that hardworking sergeant did find a DNA close to the Strangler's, two guesses who'd announce it. Not the guy who did the work. The captain who'd assigned it to him.

"I always hope," Colin said. "I don't expect too much, that's all."

"Yeah, I know that tune," Jensen agreed. He *was* a cop. "Okay, I'll check with you later—and I'll let you know if we come up with anything juicy."

Uh-huh. I'll believe that when I see it. Colin kept his mouth shut there. It was usually the best thing you could do. "Right," he answered. "Thanks." He hung up. From the desk next to his, Gabe Sanchez raised a questioning eyebrow. "Jensen," Colin said.

"Oh, boy." Gabe silently clapped his hands together. "He's got everything wrapped up in a pretty pink bow, I bet."

"Yeah, right," Colin said. "Torrance is looking at the DNA, too—I will give them that much."

"Yippy skip." The sergeant was good at curbing his enthusiasm. "I notice you aren't saying Jensen's doing it himself."

"Nah. He gave it to a sergeant. Not like it's important or anything."

Sanchez flipped him off. "So what was his High and Mightiness doing instead? Getting his teeth whitened for the next time he goes under the lights?"

"He didn't tell me, but it wouldn't surprise me a bit."

"One of these days, the guy will fuck up," Gabe said. Colin wasn't sure whether he was talking about the Strangler or Nels Jensen till he went on, "Assholes almost always do. They never think they will, but they do. It's part of what makes them assholes."

"Yeah," said Colin, for whom that was also an article of faith. "I just hope to God he does it soon."

When he got home that night, he grilled a couple of lamb chops with paprika and garlic powder and nuked a package of frozen mixed veggies. It wasn't exciting cooking. It was an imitation of Louise's, and she wouldn't show up on the Food Network any time soon even if she did watch it. After they broke up, at first he'd eaten out almost every night. That got expensive fast, though. This saved him money, and it was more what he was used to.

Half the veggies went into a plastic icebox dish, then into the refrigerator. He wrapped half a chop in aluminum foil and stuck it in there, too. It would do for lunch when he had a day off. When he was done eating, he washed the dishes and left them in the drainer to dry—he hated drying dishes. The kitchen had a dishwasher, but using it for one person was another money-wasting joke.

He pulled out a mystery after dinner. Most of the time, he

read them to laugh at them. What the authors didn't know about police procedures would fill fatter books than the ones they'd written. Every once in a while, he had the pleasure of finding a good one.

This one seemed betwixt and between. Not silly enough to laugh at, not good enough to keep him turning pages. He tossed it aside and grabbed the remote. ESPN was showing the World Series of Poker. Poker was a fine game—he'd won several grand in his Navy days—but it was not a goddamn sport. Colin changed channels.

A talking head on Fox News bellowed his opinions to the world. Colin changed again, just as fast. He had opinions of his own, and didn't figure he needed anybody else's secondhand ones.

CNN was showing . . . What the hell *was* CNN showing? A long-distance shot from a helicopter. Snowy ground, with dead pine trees sticking up through the snow like whiskers on a corpse's cheek. A big plume of black smoke climbing high in the air. Mountains in the distance.

"Fuck," Colin said. "That looks like Yellowstone." He shook his head. What could be going on in Yellowstone in the middle of November? It looked like a forest fire—a big old forest fire, like the one they'd had back in the last century. But that was crazy. How could you have a big old forest fire this time of year? Wouldn't the snow on the ground and the snow on the trees control a fire's size?

Then a graphic appeared in the lower left-hand corner of the screen. YELLOWSTONE ERUPTION, it said.

"Holy shit!" Colin yanked the phone out of his pocket. Kelly was in Yellowstone, doing more seismic research. When he dialed her number, he got voice mail. That didn't surprise him; cell-phone reception in the park was spotty at best. "Hey, hon, it's me. Just saw the news. Call when you get the chance. Hope you're okay. 'Bye."

The anchor had started yakking while he was delivering his message. "—eruption in the Lower Forty-eight since Mount St. Helens in 1980," he was saying. "It began this afternoon in Yellowstone National Park, near Ranger Lake."

"Where the hell is Ranger Lake?" Colin asked—he didn't remember hearing of it.

As if on cue, a map of Yellowstone replaced the eruption shot. Ranger Lake lay in the far southwestern part of the park, about as far away from a paved road as you could get this side of the Canadian border. A big red X near the lake presumably marked the spot where the volcano was going off.

"Geologists tell us that Yellowstone National Park was formed by ancient volcanic activity," the anchorman went on. "The last known eruption there, though, took place some seventy thousand years ago." By the way he said it, that was long enough ago to be sure the fire down below was out now. The story he was reporting gave his tone the lie. He went on, "With us earlier today was Kelly Birnbaum, an expert on the geological peculiarities of Yellowstone."

And there she was on Colin's TV, in a heavy jacket and a wool stocking cap kind of thing with her hair sticking out underneath. "No, the eruption isn't a big surprise," she said. "What's probably a surprise is that it's been so long since the last one."

"How will this impact attendance at our most popular and most beloved national park when summertime rolls around again?" asked the reporter who was holding a mike up to her face.

"No way to tell yet," she answered. "Also no way to tell whether this eruption is a stand-alone, so to speak, or a forerunner to something bigger."

Instead of letting the reporter find out what she was talking about, CNN cut back to the anchorman and the shot of the eruption. He started going on about the ash the new volcano was spewing into the air, and about how it would impact—that seemed to be CNN's favorite word tonight—air travel in America.

Commercials came on. Colin went back to Fox News, hoping to see something different. The talking head there was trying to blame the eruption on the administration. Swearing, Colin switched to MSNBC. *Their* talking head was blaming the volcano on Congress.

No one on any of the news channels said anything about the supervolcano under Yellowstone. They couldn't all be that ignorant . . . could they? After weighing it, Colin decided they couldn't. So why weren't they talking about it? Because they hoped this wasn't the beginning of the big blowup? Because if they talked about it and this turned out not to be the big blowup, they'd look even more like fools than they commonly did? Because if this was the start of the supervolcano eruption, nobody could do anything about it anyway?

After a little more weighing, Colin decided any or all of those reasons might be good enough. He wished like hell Kelly would call him back.

Kelly had never been on a snowmobile before. If God was very kind, she told herself, she'd never be on another snowmobile again. Noisy, bouncy . . . If you combined the worst features of a motorcycle without shocks on a crappy road and a chainsaw motor, you were within screaming distance. And screaming was what she felt like doing.

Screaming was also what she had to do if she felt like talking with Larry Skrtel. The USGS geologist was driving the hideous contraption on which she found herself a reluctant passenger. Daniel Olson piloted another one, with Ruth hanging on to him for dear life. The only way she could communicate with them was by shooting off a flare.

The scenery was beautiful. Most people never got to see Yellowstone like this. Then again, most people never had to worry about whether the ground would give way beneath their feet in the biggest goddamn volcanic eruption since the Paleolithic. Knowing too much could be worse than not knowing enough.

And her colleagues gave her a hard time before they climbed aboard the snowmobiles. *Teacher's pet*, they called her, and went on from there. "They should have interviewed Larry—he really knows what he's talking about." Ruth was grinning when she said it. Kelly felt the needle even so.

"Hey, c'mon, they're CNN. You can't expect them to know who to grab," Daniel put in. "We're all probably lucky they didn't talk to that guy who analyzes leftover nutrients in bison feces."

"Nah, they know bullshit when they see it," Kelly said. Everybody groaned. She added, "They crank out enough themselves."

Now she was zooming past half a dozen bison. The big, shaggy beasts pawed at the snowy ground with their forelegs, working their way down to the dead but still tasty grass under that blanket of white. They didn't like the noisy snowmobiles. A couple of them trotted away from the mechanical contraptions. That was good. If they'd charged instead, they could run faster than the machines were going.

Then again, maybe the snowmobiles' flatulent buzz wasn't the only thing spooking the bison. Kelly needed a little while to realize exhaust from the machine Daniel and Ruth were riding wasn't all that was fouling Yellowstone's crisp, cold, clean late-autumn air.

You could smell sulfur almost anywhere in the park if the wind was blowing the right—or the wrong, depending on how you looked at it—way. Some of the ancient Greeks had said quakes were caused by what amounted to earthfarts. Put one of those robed and bearded philosophers here in Yellowstone and he'd be sure he was right.

But what Kelly smelled now seemed harsher—hotter?—than the usual brimstone reek from hot springs or fumaroles. The wind was blowing to the southwest, at a right angle from their approach route toward the eruption, but the new volcano made itself known all the same.

And the farther they went, the less pristine and white the snow seemed. Volcanic ash had started pattering down from the big column of dust and ash ahead. The prevailing wind would sweep more of it across Wyoming and down into Colorado—and who could guess how much farther than that? Nobody could, not yet.

The ash still floating in the air could prove an even bigger nuisance. The eruption in Iceland had screwed up air travel between the States and Europe and from one part of Europe to another on and off for weeks. If little bits of grit chewed up jet engines on routes between one American coast and the other, that wouldn't be so good—which was putting it mildly.

Airplane travel in this day and age sucked. Not being able to travel by airplane would suck even harder in a country as big as the United States.

But that wasn't all that was rattling Kelly's cage. So far, this seemed like a normal volcanic eruption, the kind Yellowstone often had—even if *often* didn't mean *lately*. Nobody knew how a supervolcano worked, though. All the evidence pointed towards everything happening at once. If lava spurted up all around and most of what was now the park fell toward the center of the earth . . .

It would all be over in a hurry, anyhow.

Larry steered a little closer to the Bechler River, which ran in the direction of (though not into) Ranger Lake. The river hadn't frozen up yet. Ducks rose from it, wings beating swiftly as they got airborne. They liked snowmobiles no better than the bison had.

Something ahead was burning. Larry waved to Daniel. They stopped side by side. At first, Kelly thought she was seeing lava oozing up from some new crack in the earth's crust that led down to the magma pool under Yellowstone. But no. The lodgepole pines were burning, which was pretty goddamn awe-inspiring in its own way. Snow stifled wildfires. That was a rule as old as the park.

Well, there were older rules. How hot did the lava flow heat the trees? Hot enough to steam the snow off them, and off the ground between them. Hot enough to dry them out and set them blazing. Some of what was going up into the air was genuine, honest-to-God wood smoke.

Silence slammed down after the engines cut out. It seemed all the more quiet because Kelly's ears were on the stunned side. Through it, Larry said, "I don't think we ought to get a whole lot closer, y'know?"

Daniel spread his gloved hands. "You're the boss. If you don't think it's a good idea, we won't. But it's a shame to come this far and not be able to go the rest of the way."

"It'd be a shame to get into trouble we can't get out of," Larry said, and Kelly knew they wouldn't be going any farther.

"I wonder what it looks like from space," she said. "What are the satellites picking up?"

"Dust. Ash. Smoke," Ruth said.

"Oh, more than that," Kelly said. "They're bound to have infrared sensors to look through all the crap and see exactly where the hot stuff is coming out."

"No doubt about it," Larry agreed. That made Kelly feel good, the way a nod from one of her profs at her doctoral orals had. She'd understood something clearly. Very few things outside the bedroom were more satisfying.

Inside the bedroom . . . Did Colin know what was going on? If CNN had somebody in Yellowstone, it was bound to be making the headlines, but was he watching TV or listening to the radio? She hoped he was. She wanted him to see her. He'd be proud of her if he did, and having him proud of her mattered.

It mattered a lot, in fact. Was that love? If it wasn't, it sure felt like a stop on the way. They'd known each other for a year and a half now; they'd been lovers for more than a year. Colin hadn't said the word, not once. Kelly hadn't, either. She didn't think it was her place to start talking about love. He was the one who'd been burned. He needed time to work that through.

How long did he need? Kelly shrugged inside her anorak. This wasn't the time or place to worry about that.

Something not far enough ahead went *Boom!*—a sub-sub-bass, a noise felt more than heard. Kelly felt something else, too: the ground shook under her feet. Ruth pointed into the sky. "Whoa!" she said.

Whoa! was right. A chunk of rock about the size of a school bus flew through the air with the greatest of ease. For a bad second, Kelly thought the parabola it was describing would end right on top of her. Then she realized the volcanic bomb would fall short.

It did, by a couple of hundred yards. The ground shook again at the impact. How much would a flying boulder that size weigh? Plenty. And how hot was it? Hot enough so the snow went *sssss* when it came down. That was just steam rising into the air.

"I've never seen anything like *that* before." Daniel sounded deeply impressed.

"I have, in Hawaii. No snow there, of course," Larry said. "But that was too close for comfort. I think we're like Kansas City right now—we've definitely gone as far as we can go, or maybe a little farther. Move we adjourn. We probably shouldn't waste much time doing it, either."

Daniel still looked disappointed. He didn't argue this time, though. That enormous boulder still steaming in the snow was a potent argument all by itself. Adjourn they did.

Marshall Ferguson wanted to talk to an academic advisor at UCSB about as much as he'd wanted to have his wisdom teeth pulled. The dentist had knocked him out beforehand. He'd got to eat ice cream and milk shakes for a couple of days afterwards, and the Lorcets the quack prescribed for pain weren't the least enjoyable drugs he'd ever swallowed.

No anesthetic here. If he wasn't careful now, he not only wouldn't get the shift in majors he wanted, but he might end up with a bachelor's degree at the end of next year. Back in the old days, people said, you could flit from major to major like a butterfly in a botanical garden.

Times had changed. They wanted you out the door, diploma clutched in your sweaty fist, ready to turn into cannon fodder for the big, wide world. Marshall, on the other hand, liked living in Santa Barbara. He liked the weed and the booze and the girls. He liked the very idea of a town where they had a Couch-Burning Day. He even liked some of his classes.

Whatever the big, wide world held in store, it wouldn't be as much fun as he was having now. He was all too sure of that. And he was also sure his old man wouldn't keep subsidizing him once he said farewell to the university. He wasn't allergic to work, but he vastly preferred partying. Sooner or later, it would have to end. He was also too mournfully sure of that. Later was better, though.

Rob was still partying, the lucky so-and-so. He hadn't let an engineering degree get in his way. But Marshall had seen that playing in a band you wanted to take somewhere was also a hell of a lot of work. Besides, unlike Rob, he was hopelessly unmusical himself.

He'd thought without much hope about landing a Hollywood job with a bachelor's in film studies. But, like history, it seemed more likely to lead to your working in retail the rest of your life. That looked like hell on earth to him.

Then again, there was no guarantee he'd ever get any kind of job at all with a film-studies degree. The way the economy bit the big one, nobody was hiring anybody these days. One more reason not to pile up enough units to make them throw you out. If you probably couldn't get a job any which way, staying in school looked great by comparison.

It sure did to Marshall. Convincing Dad wouldn't be so much fun, but he'd done it before. He'd be able to come through one more time.

A girl walked out of the advisor's office. She was kind of cute: a brunette with a button nose and perky tits under a tight blouse. Marshall smiled at her. You never could tell. But she didn't smile back. Whatever the advisor'd told her, it wasn't what she wanted to hear.

"Ms. Rosenblatt will see you now," the secretary told him. Her nameplate said SANDE ANKENBRANDT. Her hair, by coincidence or design, was sandy, too. "Go on in."

"Uh, thanks." Marshall did.

Selma Rosenblatt—her first name was on a plaque on the door—was a little older than his mother. She'd let the gray in her hair show, which made her seem older yet. The way she eyed him warned that he was the eleventy-first student she'd seen today, and that she wasn't delighted to have him here.

"Take a seat," she said. "Give me your name and your SIN." From her name, he'd guessed she would sound like a New Yorker. She didn't. By the way she talked, she was a Valley girl. Only she wasn't a girl any more, and hadn't been for quite a while.

Sit he did, on the vinyl-covered, badly padded chair in front of her desk. Behind it, she was snuggled by a leather armchair.

They let you know who was who, all right. "I'm Marshall Ferguson—two *l*s," he said, and rattled off his nine-digit Student Identification Number. Some bureaucrat, his ass in a fancy chair like the advisor's, must have come up with the acronym, never noticing what he was doing. By now, it was too entrenched in UCSB life to be replaced.

Ms. Rosenblatt wrote it down as he gave it to her, and used the number pad on her keyboard to enter it into her computer. He knew what she'd see on the monitor: his academic career, in all its occasional splendor.

One of her sharply penciled eyebrows jumped a quarter of an inch. "Well, well," she murmured. The admiration might have been reluctant, but it was real. "We don't see a transcript like yours every day."

"My interests keep changing," Marshall said. That was true, and then again it wasn't. His interest in staying right where he was had been remarkably constant ever since his sophomore year. The proof of that was how far behind him his sophomore year lay now. But here he was, still an undergrad.

Selma Rosenblatt studied the transcript more closely. She clicked her tongue between her teeth. "You know," she remarked, with the air of a literary critic approaching an interesting novel, "if you'd taken Introduction to Geology two years ago, they would have had to turn you loose."

She's on to me! Marshall thought. How many losers sitting in front of his father had felt that same stab of panic? Hundreds, maybe thousands. Marshall did his damnedest not to show it. "I wanted to," he lied, adding, "but I couldn't," which was true. "That was the year the Legislature and the Governor didn't agree on a budget till November, and everything went to, uh, the dogs." Sarcasm from his old man—and an occasional whack on the behind—had taught him not to cuss in front of people of the female persuasion.

"Oh, yes. I remember," Ms. Rosenblatt assured him. "I didn't say you could have taken the course, then. I just said, if you had. Then you switched majors, of course, and your breadth requirements changed. You timed it well."

"Huh?" Marshall aimed to play innocent as long as he could.

"You timed it well," she repeated, with no rancor he could hear. "And what have you got in mind for today?"

Encouraged, he answered, "Well, I was thinking of changing majors again."

"To what?" Again, only curiosity in the advisor's voice—Marshall hoped.

"Creative writing," he answered brightly.

"Well, let's see how that would work. We'll stack the requirements up against what you've already taken. . . ." Ms. Rosenblatt punched a few keys. Marshall didn't have her software, but he'd already gone through the same arcane calculations. Now he had to hope he'd done them right. She studied the monitor. A slow smile spread across her face. It didn't seem to want to take up residence there, but there it was. "Yes, that may keep you enrolled a couple of quarters longer than sticking to film. I gather you're not paying for your stay here?"

"Uh, no," Marshall admitted. He was chuffed—he'd worked it out exactly the same way her program had.

"We do try to get people on their way. Some students are more diligent in their efforts to stick around than others, though," Ms. Rosenblatt said. "And it may be better for the state's poor, abused balance sheet to have you here paying in rather than out there collecting unemployment or welfare." She studied Marshall. "Who knows? Maybe you will turn into a writer . . . and maybe the horse will learn to sing."

"Herodotus!" Marshall exclaimed. He remembered the story, read in translation. If only he weren't such a hopeless goof at languages.

"Very good. I was a history major once upon a time, too—and look where I ended up." Ms. Rosenblatt hit a few more keys. "The change is recorded. Now get out of here so I can take on someone who really needs advice."

"What do I need, then?" Marshall asked.

"You need your head examined. But then, that's one of the reasons you come to a university. Or you're missing something if it's not." Selma Rosenblatt pointed to the door. "Scoot. You'll probably piss off your folks doing this, but then you're probably doing it to piss them off."

Marshall left. Another more than reasonably pretty girl was sitting there waiting for the advisor. UCSB could spoil you that way. But she also ignored his experimental smile as she went in to do whatever she was going to do.

Every once in a while, adults made you wonder if maybe they did know what they were up to after all. Marshall's dad could pull that off sometimes. And Ms. Rosenblatt had the same kind of mojo. She saw right through him. How many college kids had traipsed into her office, to give her the knack of reading at a glance what made them tick?

She was damn good at it. Damn good, but not quite perfect. Mom wouldn't care that he had a new major. Mom cared about Mom, and about Teo, and, now and again, about Vanessa. Mom and Vanessa were going through the same adventures at the same time, which gave them a bond they hadn't had before. Sons? Mom remembered she had them and everything, but all they did was remind her of Dad. The way things were there, that was news as bad as it got.

Even Dad wouldn't be too bent out of shape. After all the other changes Marshall had made, Dad would just roll his eyes and wonder out loud if his kid thought his initials were ATM. (Marshall did think so, but he'd learned long before he got to UCSB that saying as much was one of the really bad ideas.) Dad would also wonder—pointedly—if Marshall thought he could get a job with his new major in the unlikely event that he graduated. Marshall could hear the whole thing already, inside his head. He didn't even need to go home for it.

He hustled down the stairs and escaped air conditioning and fluorescent lights. The sun smiled on him. The sun smiled on all of Santa Barbara almost all the time. It was May. L.A. was sweltering under a heat wave. Even San Atanasio, which caught a lot of sea breeze, would be up in the eighties. The Valley, Riverside, places like that . . . Marshall didn't want to think about them.

Here, he didn't have to. It was seventy-three, maybe seventy-four. It might climb to eighty on the hottest days of summer. It might sink down to sixty on the coldest days of winter. The campus had its own lagoon, full of reeds and ducks and shorebirds. How awesome was that?

Guys and girls went by. Some wore shorts and T-shirts, some jeans and T-shirts. About one in three was talking into a cell phone or texting and trying not to bump into anybody. Bicycles wove in and out among the people on foot. Some of the riders were talking on cell phones, too. And yes, some of them were texting. Even Marshall didn't think that was exactly brilliant. It wasn't that he'd never done it, but he didn't do it a whole lot.

A girl smiled at him. He waved back. They'd been in a class together . . . last year? Year before? He couldn't remember, any more than he could remember her name. She wasn't anyone special, just someone vaguely nice. He supposed she thought he was somebody vaguely nice, too.

He was a creative-writing major now. What kind of story could you make out of a couple of people, each thinking the other was vaguely nice? How would you even start? Or maybe that was the wrong question. How would you end the story? What would you be trying to say? You had to say something about life, the universe, and everything, didn't you? Otherwise, why would you bother to write?

Those all struck him as pretty good questions. He didn't have answers for any of them. How did you find answers for questions like those? By writing? Would you—or somebody—see what was wrong with what you did and how to fix it? Wouldn't you get awful tired of turning out crap? Sooner or later, you were supposed to stop turning out crap, weren't you? But how?

Those struck him as good questions, too. The person he knew who came closest to being a writer was Vanessa, and cranking out reports and proposals and editing other people's garbage didn't seem awful goddamn creative to him.

Maybe I'll learn, he thought. *Or maybe I'll switch majors again, even if Ms. Rosenblatt does laugh at me.*

VII

Berkeley. Colin Ferguson always felt he needed a passport when he came up here. The People's Republic of Berkeley, cops called it. Cops called Santa Monica, the L.A. beachside suburb, the People's Republic, too. Damn few cops had an idealistic view of human nature. Jerks and assholes—that was what their world boiled down to.

"Holy shit!" he said happily. That was a parking space, right around the corner from Kelly's apartment building. Parking spaces in Berkeley were even harder to find than Republicans. He had to parallel-park to get into this one, but he did it. It wasn't even a two-hour zone; he could stay as long as he wanted. He put on the Club and got out.

There wasn't any secure entrance at her building. People just went in and out. Most of the ones who did looked like college students. That didn't automatically make them princes among mankind, as Colin had reason to know. But Kelly said she'd never had her apartment broken into, and her car only once. Plenty of folks in places with better security had worse luck.

A girl—well, she was around Vanessa's age, which made her

a girl to Colin—coming down the stairs gave him a curious look as he climbed them. She didn't say *What's an old fart like you doing here?*—her eyes did it for her. But as long as Kelly thought Colin belonged, he could suffer the slings and arrows of outrageous near-adolescents just fine.

He knocked on her door. She did have a little spy-eye so she could see who was there. And she had a dead bolt. It snicked back. Then she threw the door wide. The smile on her face was bottled sunshine. "Hey!" she said, and threw her arms wide, too.

They hugged with the door open. Then he went all the way in, and she closed it behind him. Phone calls and e-mails and texts kept them up on what they were doing. But not being able to get together all the time made the times when they could that much sweeter.

In between kisses, they went through variations on *How are ya? How ya doin'?* for some little while. Colin bragged about his parking *fu*. Kelly looked suitably impressed. She knew how lucky you needed to be to cadge a space anywhere in the Bay Area.

Kelly's place looked quite a bit like Bryce's—quite a bit like most grad students' apartments, Colin suspected. Books and papers and printouts were scattered everywhere. She wasn't compulsively neat about things the way he was. That didn't mean she couldn't find whatever she needed, though. He'd seen her pluck a journal out from under a blizzard of papers so she could check something in an article. He had no idea how she knew it was there, but she did.

She pulled Anchor Porters out of the refrigerator. They clinked bottles. "What's the latest on the park?" he asked. Unless you had to fly cross-country, the volcano was old news by now. It wasn't on CNN much any more. Even the late-night talk-show hosts left it out of their monologues.

"Still massively fucked," Kelly answered—she was much easier swearing around him than he was around her. "I mean massively."

"Is the road down to Jackson still closed?"

"Oh, you bet. The whole Pitchstone Plateau is going back to being a lava field," she said. Colin must have looked blank, because she explained: "When you drive down—drove down—from Yellowstone Lake to the park's south entrance, you were driving across the Pitchstone Plateau. It's what happens to a lava field after it weathers for a hundred thousand years or so."

"Pines," he said, remembering. "Lots and lots of lodgepole pines."

"Uh-huh." Kelly nodded. "They can grow on almost zero nutrients, so they spring up first. Of course, a gazillion acres of them burned back in 1988, and now they're burning again."

"I bet they are," Colin said. Even after all these years, the charred lodgepole pines, some still upright, some fallen and more than half hidden by their upspringing descendants, others lying out in the middle of what was now grassland, remained a big part of what you saw—had seen—at Yellowstone. "What's the Park Service going to do when tourist season rolls around again?"

"Cry," Kelly answered, which startled a snort of laughter out of him. She went on, "They ought to close it up completely, but that'd cost 'em God knows how many hundred million dollars."

"How much would getting tourists swallowed up in a big eruption cost 'em?" Colin asked, not altogether ironically. Governments and corporations did risk-benefit analyses all the time, weighing whether lawsuits from a foul-up were likely to cost more than not fixing what was wrong. Of course, they couldn't fix it here, but they could hope it didn't get any worse.

"That's what they're wondering, all right," Kelly thought along with him. "From what I hear, right now the plan is to let people in to see Mammoth Hot Springs and the other stuff way at the north end of the park, but to keep the rest of it off-limits."

"Maybe that's far enough away," Colin said. You didn't think about Yellowstone's immensity till you were actually there. It was bigger than some of the little states back East.

"Maybe." But Kelly didn't sound convinced.

"You're worrying about the supervolcano."

"You bet I am. If it goes, Mammoth Hot Springs aren't far enough away. Jackson isn't far enough away." She took a long pull at her beer. You weren't supposed to drink porter like that, which didn't stop her. "Hell, Denver isn't far enough away."

Colin grunted.

Kelly looked at him in surprise. Then she nodded. "Oh. Your daughter's in Denver. I forgot."

"Yeah. She is."

"Can you tell her to come back to Socal?"

"I can tell her all kinds of things. Whether she'll pay any attention—that's a different story. What I say about Vanessa is, she's hard of listening. She goes her own way, no matter what." Most of the time, Colin would have thought that was a good thing. Rob did, too, and Colin admired him for it—reluctantly, but he did. Here, though . . . "What are the odds it'll blow?"

"The odds? Nobody has any idea. A lot of geologists hope the Ranger Lake eruption will take off some of the pressure down below."

"You don't believe it." Colin had listened to too many people telling too many stories to have any doubts on that score.

Kelly shook her head. "No. I don't. I wish I could, but I don't. Remember how Coffee Pot Springs started going nuts? Things there are crazier than ever. More geyser eruptions there than at the Upper Geyser Basin with Old Faithful and all the rest. Swarms of people would go to see 'em if the place weren't miles from the nearest road."

Picturing a park map in his head, Colin remarked, "That's a long way from Ranger Lake."

"It sure is," Kelly said, and left it right there.

Maybe Colin should have, too, but what kind of cop would he have made if he believed in letting well enough alone? "If there's a serious risk it will blow, shouldn't they make some kind of plan?"

They'd gone around that barn before. Kelly, he realized too late, would have spent a lot more time brooding and talking about it than he had. It was . . . It was her South Bay Strangler, was what it was. "I used to think so. I really did. For a long time," she said slowly, and spread her hands. "Now? I just don't know any more. It's too damn big. How do you make a plan that says *We need to evacuate the whole Midwest—and that's just for starters*? You don't. You can't. The best you can do is hope it doesn't happen. Pray, if you think praying helps. It won't hurt."

"Like not being there when the H-bomb goes off," Colin said.

"Well, yeah." She barely gave him the benefit of the doubt. "Only this is so much bigger than an H-bomb, it ain't even funny."

She meant it. He'd grown up at the tail end of the Cold War. Imagining something that dwarfed mankind's finest warlike foolishness took mental muscles he wasn't used to exercising. "The biggest thing ever, huh?"

"Not *ever*," Kelly said seriously—he might have known better than to say something like that to a geologist. "A really big supervolcano will blow out maybe six hundred cubic miles of rock."

"Yeah, you've said so before." He nodded. "That's a lot of rock."

"It sure is. But 250,000,000 years ago the Siberian Traps let loose a thousand times that much lava—enough to bury about ninety percent of the Lower Forty-eight. And sixty-odd million years ago, the Deccan Traps coughed up enough lava to bury

Alaska, pretty much. So the supervolcano's small potatoes next to those, even if it's plenty big enough to screw us to the wall."

"Sixty-odd million years ago," Colin echoed. "Isn't that when the dinosaurs went under? I thought an asteroid was the number-one suspect for doing them in."

"An asteroid sure hit then. Whether that was what finished them or whether the Deccan Traps had more to do with it . . . People are still writing papers. And the Siberian Traps happened about the same time as the even bigger extinction between the Permian and the Triassic."

"How about that?" Colin said tonelessly. In the scale of things she considered, the South Bay Strangler wasn't worth noticing. He couldn't think so big, much as he wished he could. Even—even!—the supervolcano was beyond his comprehension. "You have any other good news?"

"Well, the sun could go nova and fry the whole planet like a pork chop." She sounded cheerful, of all things. And she told him why: "But it won't go supernova. It's not massive enough, poor thing."

"Aww," he said, which got a laugh out of her. "You start thinking about stuff like that, what can you do about it?"

"Not one goddamn thing. So why don't we get drunk and screw?" Kelly said. He wondered if she knew that was a country song from before she was born. He doubted it like anything; her taste in music didn't run that way. But it struck him as a terrific idea even so.

Justin Nachman charged into the dressing room at Neptune's Resort waving a *New Yorker* around as if he intended to swat a fly with it. The dressing room was tiny and cramped and hot, and several flies were buzzing around. As far as Rob Ferguson could see, everything in New York City was tiny and cramped—except for the stuff that was enormous and mind-blowingly magnificent.

Every bit of it, squalid and stupendous alike, was insanely over-priced.

The cover of the *New Yorker*, as Rob finally discovered when Justin stopped brandishing the magazine, was a photorealistic painting of an entrance to Yellowstone Park, with a brand-new volcano with a Fujiyama-style perfect cone sending up smoke and fire in the background. The sign at the entrance read CLOSED NEXT 1,000 YEARS. A long line of cars and motor homes stretched away in disappointment.

Seeing it reminded Rob of his father's girlfriend. He shied away from that. He wanted things back home to be the way they were supposed to, which to him meant Dad and Mom together. He understood that what he wanted wasn't about to happen. He'd understood that maybe even before Dad did. Understanding it was a long way from liking it, though.

"What are you doing with that thing?" he asked Justin.

Before the band's front man could answer, Charlie Storer added, "It's last week's, anyhow." The drummer actually read the *New Yorker* sometimes. Justin rarely read anything but e-mail and texts these days. He'd got over his biology degree bigtime.

Now, though, he opened the magazine to the front section in smaller type. "We're in 'Night Life—Rock and Pop'!" he burbled.

That got his bandmates' attention, as he must have known it would. "Well, what's it say?" they chorused, or words to that effect. Biff Thorvald might have been the loudest of them. Then again, so might Rob or Charlie.

"'Squirt Frog and the Evolving Tadpoles bring a musical sensibility that mixes Cowboy Bebop with Bebop Deluxe from Oxnard, California, to Manhattan,'" Justin read.

"Oxnard!" Biff exclaimed in disgust. Oxnard was a gritty, grimy, working-class town closer to L.A. than to Santa Barbara, and had about as much in common with the latter as Passaic,

New Jersey, did with the Hamptons. Charlie made gross-out noises, too.

"Yeah, I know. It all looks the same from this side of the country," Justin said.

Rob thought of an old surreal map he'd seen: the USA from New York City's viewpoint. About half of it was this side of the Hudson. Then there was upstate, Pennsylvania, Texas, and California, with a palm tree sticking up out of the Pacific to show Hawaii. Evidently, that kind of attitude lived on.

"I wasn't done yet," Justin said. He took a deep breath and read some more: "'Under his Brillo fright wig, lead singer Justin Nachman effectively puts across the up-and-coming band's quirky lyrics.'" He patted his Yiddishe Afro. "Me and Dylan, right?"

"In your dreams," Charlie said sweetly.

"Your wet dreams," Biff agreed.

Of course Rob razzed Justin, too. No responsible band member could do anything else. But at the same time he chewed on the *New Yorker*'s assessment. *Could* you mix animé and one of the stranger British outfits from the 1970s? If you could, did Squirt Frog and the Evolving Tadpoles do it? That wasn't altogether impossible, he supposed. But it struck him as more likely that the music writer was just getting cute.

Justin's thoughts went in a different direction. They often did. He started waving the magazine around again. "Not the cover of the *Rolling Stone*, but as close as we're likely to get," he said.

The others nodded. Rob would have loved to make the cover of the *Rolling Stone*. That implied serious success; serious sales; with luck, even serious money. He knew it wasn't in the cards. The music writer nailed the reason why, too. *Quirky* could get you to up-and-coming. To serious success? Not likely.

"Does the notice talk about Snakes and Ladders, too?" Charlie asked. That was an important question, all right. If the

New Yorker didn't mention the opening act, they'd get pissy about it, and who could blame them?

"I think so. Lemme check." Justin opened the magazine once more. Hadn't he already looked? If any of them was going to go all rock star, he was the guy. He was the one the *New Yorker*'d mentioned by name, after all. But nobody'd put his ego ahead of the band yet. They'd been good about that, better than a bunch of outfits that had fallen apart for the sake of somebody's usually aborted solo career. Justin read again: "'With them is another California band, Snakes and Ladders, with a distinctive twang.'"

It was a mention, yeah, but not one that would thrill the other band. Their lead guitarist wanted to be Robin Trower, or maybe Hendrix (a man's reach should exceed his grasp, or what's a heaven for?). No, *a distinctive twang* wouldn't make Lenny turn handsprings.

"Put that thing somewhere," Rob said. "If they haven't seen it, don't show it to them. Don't talk about it, either."

By all the signs, Justin wanted to blow up the little notice till it was about the size of the tablets the Lord had given Moses on Mt. Sinai. He wanted to carry it around with him the way Moses had carried the tablets down the mountain, too. No, nothing wrong with his ego, not a bit. But he wasn't to the point where he needed another chair for it. He might nod reluctantly, but nod he did. And he opened the case of a guitar he wasn't planning on using tonight and stashed the *New Yorker* inside.

The way Snakes and Ladders played showed that they, or at least Lenny, *had* seen the notice. He tried to coax licks from his guitar that should have been illegal, or more likely impossible. And sometimes he did, and sometimes he sounded like a man trying to strangle a cat that didn't feel like getting strangled.

It must have been an exhausting set to play. It sure as hell was an exhausting set to listen to, for Squirt Frog and the Evolving Tadpoles and for the crowd that packed Neptune's Resort. The applause that followed it seemed more like relief than anything else.

A voice spoke from the heavens: "Now welcome Squirt Frog and the Evolving Tadpoles!" If God had been a classic-rock FM DJ, He would have sounded a lot like that.

More relieved applause came as the band walked out on stage. Some of the relief, Rob judged, was that they weren't Snakes and Ladders. You didn't always know what you would get with SF and the ETs, but brooding angst wasn't a big part of the mix.

Rob waved as he took his place behind Justin. He looked out over the crowd before the lights went down, scouting for cute ones. Who didn't do that? Cute ones were a main reason for joining a band to begin with. And New York City offered a variety he hadn't seen since the last time they played in Socal.

Justin waved, too. "Good to be here," he said, sounding calm and sane—to anyone who knew him, an illusion, but a soothing one at the moment. "I always wanted to play Carnegie Hall."

He got a laugh. The club was packed with people in jeans and T-shirts, not the fancy-dress crowd Rob imagined at Carnegie Hall. They sat on metal folding chairs. Carnegie Hall would have had better, softer, wider seats. Something in the air said a good part of the crowd hadn't showered any time lately. Once upon a time, tobacco fumes—among others—would have added to the fug. Nowadays, New York City's public antismoking rules were as ferocious as anybody's. Which, of course, didn't stop the band from taking a few tokes before going on.

Being an engineering major, Rob had lately designed an experiment to see if he played better stoned. He'd listened to recordings of himself both wasted and straight. There didn't seem to be much difference one way or the other. He still liked getting loaded, though, so he did.

Other guys who'd played New York had warned that fans

there were different from fans in Indiana or Idaho. "If they like you, man, they *really* like you," somebody'd said in wonder. "They know your shit better than you do."

After two songs, three people in different parts of the room shouted for "Brainfreeze" at the same time. Squirt Frog and the Evolving Tadpoles hadn't played "Brainfreeze" in at least two years. Rob had written the song, and even he didn't like it any more. It appeared on no album. As far as he could recall, it had never been recorded. How did these dudes—no, one was a gal—even know it existed?

Justin shook his head. His poufy perm wobbled. "We aren't taking requests yet," he said firmly.

Other guys who'd played New York also said fans there didn't want to listen to shit like that. They soon proved right. The crowd yelled requests between songs and even during songs, which got old real fast. But the band had Marshall stacks and the audience didn't. The guys on the stage could play over the crowd; the converse wasn't true. A murmur to the sound man let them do just that.

And the crowd didn't seem to mind. New York bands had attitude. Maybe they expected their fans to show attitude, too. They damn near brought down the low ceiling when they whooped and hollered after the set, and again after the encore.

Then the band set to huckstering. CDs and posters sold briskly. "I already downloaded the music," one girl told Rob as she bought a disk, "but I can't download your autographs."

"Darn right," he agreed, scribbling his on the cover insert with a Sharpie. She paid cash, too. He approved of that. So did all his bandmates. They split the greenbacks into four equal piles after every gig. What Uncle Revenue didn't find out about wouldn't hurt him one bit.

Over on the other side of the anteroom, Snakes and Ladders were shilling, too. They were trying, anyhow. But next to nobody went over to them. Lenny'd put the fear of God in people, all right. That was fine for a fire-and-brimstone preacher, not so good for a rock 'n' roller.

The other guys in his band seemed to be trying to talk some sense into him. He tossed his head. His mane flew. He didn't want to hear it. The more they talked, the angrier he got.

He finally lost it. "Will you assholes just shut the fuck up!" he screamed, loud enough to make everybody stare at him. Hideously uncomfortable silence slammed down.

"Well," Justin said after a moment, "isn't showbiz fun?" Enough people chuckled—some nervously, but even so—to let Squirt Frog and the Evolving Tadpoles, if not Snakes and Ladders, get back to the serious business of separating customers from their money.

"We're supposed to go to Connecticut with them, and Massachusetts, and on up into Maine," Rob whispered to Charlie Storer. "What do we do if they break up?" It happened all the time, which didn't mean it didn't screw things up when it did. Divorces were usually expensive and inconvenient. Rob thought of his folks again.

"What do we do?" The drummer considered, but not for long. "We damn well do *without*, that's what."

Rob grunted. Charlie was much too likely to be right. Maybe they could hook up with some local band that wanted to swing through New England. That might work . . . if they could find a band that felt like touring . . . if the two outfits didn't clash like plaid and paisley . . . if . . . if . . . if . . .

Then Rob stopped worrying about it. The young woman who set down a CD cover insert to be signed was so pretty, she should've been against the law. No hulking boyfriend loomed behind her, as happened much too often. When Rob found out her name was Jane, he instantly wanted to be Tarzan.

He wasn't dumb enough to tell her that. Instead, sounding as

California cool as he could, he said, "Why don't you hang around if you're not doing anything else later on?"

About half the time, a girl would say she couldn't possibly because her hamster had the heartbreak of psoriasis. The other half . . . Jane gave back a megawatt smile. "You mean it?" she breathed. "For sure?"

"For sure," Rob said solemnly. "Cross my heart and hope to . . ." Dying wasn't what he had in mind right then. The little death, maybe—no, definitely—but not Mr. Big. "C'mon around to this side of the table. We'll find you a chair or something. Or what the hell? You can just sit on my lap."

It wasn't quite *You can just sit on my face*. But it also wasn't a line most guys could try on a girl whose last name they didn't know yet. Damned if Jane didn't, though. She started running her fingers through his hair, which distracted the hell out of him when he tried to sign the next autograph.

Yeah, he thought, setting a hand on her leg while kind of pretending to steady her. *Oh, fuck, yeah. This is why I do this stuff. What better reason was there?

Louise Ferguson took her sorry office skills to a sorrier job at one of the sorriest offices she'd ever seen. It was the American headquarters for a company that imported Japanese ramen into the States. When she'd first married Colin, Braxton Bragg Boulevard had been one of San Atanasio's main drags. These days, steel-barred fencing topped by coils of razor wire surrounded the ramen importer's parking lot. Fencing like that could have kept out the Taliban. The importer needed a full-time security guard along with it. Even so, as soon as Louise walked into the building, a woman hissed at her in a harsh farm-belt accent: "You didn't leave anything out there you care about, didja?"

She shook her head. "Nope." She usually thought of her years being a cop's wife as a total waste. But they'd left their mark on her, all right, often in ways she didn't even notice.

She wasn't much surprised when the inside of the office proved as big a Wild West show as the parking lot. Her boss was a Mr. Nobashi. He was about as inscrutable as a fireworks display. He spent most of the time talking to the home office in Hiroshima in impassioned Japanese interspersed with things like "Ohh, Jeesus Kerrist!" and "goddamma son of a bicha!"

When he wasn't swearing, he spoke tolerable if schematic English. He showed Louise the spreadsheets she was supposed to ride herd on. Her heart sank when she saw them. They were enormous and complicated, and Excel had always disagreed with her every chance it got. She had the feeling it would get plenty here.

"Well, I'll try," she said doubtfully. If Mr. Nobashi didn't get his hopes up real far to begin with, he wouldn't be too disappointed later on. She could hope not, anyhow.

"You no try! You do!" he declared.

She nodded. What else could she do? *You do* was what she was here for. If she couldn't do, what was the worst thing that would happen? He'd fire her, and she'd have to try to land another job somewhere else. Somewhere better than this? Maybe, but the odds were against it. This seemed to be the kind of place where jobs lived these days.

The first thing she did after sitting down at the computer was copy her spreadsheets. If she screwed up the copies, she'd have undamaged originals to fall back on. How much good that would do her . . . she preferred not to dwell on, not right this minute, thank you very much.

"Here." The woman who'd asked her if she'd left anything in the car plopped a pile of printouts down in front of her. "You're supposed to plug these shipping invoices into the inventory system."

"Oh," Louise said: a word full of gloom if ever there was one.

"Want me to walk you through it the first time?" the woman asked. She added, "I'm Patty. If you don't learn it from me, Nobashi-*san* sure as hell won't be able to explain it to you."

"Thanks! Would you, please?" Now Louise knew she sounded pathetically eager, but she didn't care. Maybe there was a cork ring on this ocean of trouble after all.

"Here. What you gotta do is . . ." Quickly and deftly, Patty did it. When she noticed she was working on copies—Louise hadn't even renamed them yet—she let out a wry chuckle. "You ain't so dumb, are ya, sweetie?"

"If I'm not, what am I doing here?" Louise asked in return.

This time, Patty laughed out loud. "You see how I set up the inventory transfer?" she asked. When Louise shook her head, Patty did it again, slower this time. "Okay," she said, rising from the chair. "Now you try it."

With no enormous hope, Louise did. Damned if it didn't work! Louise clapped her hands together in amazed delight. She just missed cheering out loud.

"See? It ain't so tough," Patty said. "Now e-mail the spreadsheet to the boss and go on to the next one."

Before Louise could, the phone rang. Answering it was part of the job. When she did, somebody started gabbing at her in excited Japanese. "One moment, please," she answered in English, and pressed the HOLD button. Then she fumbled her way through transferring the call to Mr. Nobashi. Patty also helped her there.

"You're a lifesaver," Louise exclaimed, remembering her thought of a few minutes before. "Why didn't you get this slot?"

" 'Cause I didn't want it," Patty answered calmly. "I'd sooner just crunch numbers most of the time. Nobashi pretty much leaves me alone, on account of he knows goddamn well I'm good at what I do. But you—you're gonna have to deal with him, you poor thing, you."

"Does he try to get his girls to go to bed with him? Is he one of those?" Louise asked. "I'll knock his block off if he does."

"Nah." Patty shook her head. "He knows better'n that. Guy he took over for two, three years ago thought he could get away with that crap, like he would've in Japan. The gal he hit on didn't slug him. She sued the company instead—won a pile of dough, too. So Nobashi keeps his hands to himself."

"What's so bad about him, then?"

Mr. Nobashi chose that minute to yell "Coffee!" from his inner sanctum. "Coffee and sweet rolls!"

Louise rapidly discovered that he ran on coffee and sweet rolls. Tea? Rice? Sashimi? Ramen, even? When sugar and caffeine weren't enough to rock his world, he sent her down the street to pick up big boxes of drumsticks and thighs at Popeyes Chicken & Biscuits. So grease was definitely one of his basic food groups, too.

He also guzzled bottled water by the case. He didn't go to the refrigerator to grab a bottle himself. God forbid! That would have been beneath a boss' dignity. He yelled for Louise to fetch and carry instead. No matter what else she was doing, bringing his supplies was more important.

By midafternoon that first day, Louise understood exactly why Patty wanted nothing to do with the position she now occupied herself. Mr. Nobashi might not be a lech, at least on company time. A pain in the ass he definitely was.

But the ramen company paid pretty well. The woman that other exec from Japan had sexually harassed hadn't taken them for every nickel they owned. Besides, as long as there were college students, no ramen outfit would ever go broke. Marshall sometimes seemed to live on the stuff. So had Rob, in his college days. Vanessa . . . From what Louise remembered, ramen was beneath Vanessa's dignity.

As soon as it got to be half past five, Patty said, "I am so outa here. If you've got sense, you'll bail, too. Otherwise, they'll think you want to make like a salaryman and they'll keep you here 24/7. Sometimes I think Mr. Nobashi lives in that crappy little office of his."

Bail Louise did. A different rent-a-cop was guarding the parking lot: a burly Hispanic guy who might have been an ex-Marine. He tipped his Smokey Bear hat to her as she slid into her car.

Teo was home before her. Better yet, he'd brought back Thai takeout so she wouldn't have to mess with ground round or chicken. "You're so sweet!" she said. Colin would never have done anything like that. He expected to be fed. *Just like Mr. Nobashi*, Louise thought, a little surprised at herself.

"Hey, it's your first day," her younger lover said, opening packages. The smells of spices and coconut filled the condo. "How did it go?"

"It's not exciting, but I coped. One of the gals there is showing me the ropes, so that helps. The Japanese guy in charge is a real piece of work." Louise was checking out the plastic and styrofoam package. "Oh, you got that squid salad I like!"

"I thought that was the one." Teo made a point of keeping in mind what she liked and what she didn't. Even though they'd been together for almost three years now, Louise still wasn't used to that. What had she ever been to Colin but a convenience?

He was still hanging out with that geographer or geologist or whatever she was. That vaguely irked Louise, who hadn't expected him to make anything last. After all, if she couldn't put up with him anymore, what halfway-sane woman would be able to? Well, from what she'd heard, her ex's squeeze was a lot younger. Odds were she didn't have standards of comparison.

Louise did. She knew just how lucky she was. Teo'd barely had to lift a finger to sweep her off her feet.

"How was *your* day?" she asked him as she spooned food

onto a paper plate. If she wasn't going to worry about cooking tonight, she wasn't going to worry about doing dishes, either.

"No sweat," he answered. It made her laugh, the way it always did. For Teo, sweating—and making other people sweat—was making a living. It was also what made him look so good. Colin was like a brick with soft corners. She'd forgotten what a man ought to be like till she signed up for the aerobics class. She knew now, by God, and she'd never forget again.

"How many girls want your special program?" she teased. She knew she hadn't been the first one he'd attracted. She just hoped—and kept hoping—to stay interested enough to keep ahead of the competition.

He grinned at her. He knew what she was thinking. Sometimes he sassed her about it. Always gently, though—a younger man didn't want to set an older woman worrying. A younger man with a heart didn't, anyhow. "Nobody you've got to worry about. Believe me," he said now.

And Louise did believe him. She brought the paper plate over to the table and sat down beside him. No police scanner farted out calls. The TV wasn't on, tuned to the news. Nothing but the two of them and dinner. Who needed more?

Sitting by Teo, she had no trouble forgetting Mr. Nobashi, either, or her anxieties about Excel. And if that wasn't magic, what would be?

VIII

Colin Ferguson tried to carry around in his head a map of everything the San Atanasio Police Department was doing at any given moment. The city grid was easy enough. He knew the routes the patrol cars took, and when each car would be where.

He also knew where the detectives were working, and about the meth buy the drug squad was trying to arrange. Before long, though, something always screwed up his perfect picture. There'd be a big accident, or a knifing outside a strip club on Hesperus, or a shooting in one of the Cuban bars at the north end of San Atanasio Boulevard. Like splashes in a calm pool, the ripples from something like that would distort the picture for a while.

He didn't need to do any of that. He'd been passed over for chief, the one slot where such an encyclopedic grasp of what was going on really mattered. He wasn't a hundred percent sure of making captain, even. He'd annoyed enough people that simply passing the exam might not do the trick. He carried around the mental map anyway. He'd started making one back in the days when he still rode a patrol car himself. He could no more stop now than he could stop breathing.

The telephone rang. "Ferguson," he said into the mouthpiece.

"Stu Ayers, down in Palos Verdes," said the voice on the other end of the line. Ayers was also a lieutenant, and a pretty good guy. Like Colin, he was chasing the South Bay Strangler.

"What can I do to you today, Stu?" Colin asked.

"To me, huh?" Ayers plainly didn't miss many tricks. Chuckling, he went on, "Could you shoot me the lab reports from your latest Strangler case?"

"Will do. What's your e-mail?"

Instead of giving one connected to the city of Palos Verdes, Ayers offered Colin a gmail.com account. Half apologetically, he explained, "My captain thinks I'm spending too much time on this. Let's keep it private, huh?"

"Sure," Colin said. After he hung up, though, he thoughtfully rubbed his chin. He called up the fat folder of documents, but didn't e-mail it right away. He looked up the Palos Verdes Police Department's phone number, called it, and asked to be connected to Lieutenant Ayers.

"Who's calling, please?" Whoever the gal handling the PVPD's calls was, she owned one hell of a sexy voice.

"This is Lieutenant Ferguson, from San Atanasio."

"Please hold, Lieutenant. I'll put your call through."

The music Palos Verdes played while you were on hold was different from what San Atanasio used, but no more interesting. Fortunately, Colin didn't have to listen to it for long. "Stu Ayers here. What's cooking, Colin?"

"Did you just call me a minute ago and ask for the electronic file on the latest South Bay Strangler killing?"

"Not guilty," Ayers responded answered at once. No, it wasn't the same voice as before. Not too different, but definitely not the same. The authentic Lieutenant Ayers went on, "Somebody just did, huh?"

"Yup. Dunno if he's a snoopy ordinary civilian or a reporter or what, but he wanted that file."

"You didn't give it to him?"

"Nope. I'm not always as dumb as I look—only sometimes," Colin said. Ayers laughed. Colin went on, "My bet's on a reporter. He knew to use your name and everything. So he could have taken some wild-ass guesses for the *Times* or the *Breeze* or whoever's paying him."

"Like those cocksuckers don't do enough of that anyway," Ayers said.

"Tell me about it. Well, thanks. I'm glad I thought to stop and check." Colin exchanged good-byes with his opposite number, then got off the phone. He eyed the folder front and center on his monitor, the one he'd almost e-mailed. A nasty smile crossed his face. He created another folder with an almost identical name. He filled that one with subfolders and subsubfolders, and on down for several levels. All of them bore titles that had to do with the case. All of them led nowhere—except to other interestingly named folders nested within.

Well, all but one. If Mr. Snoop out there was persistent enough, he would eventually find a deeply buried folder called *Evaluation of Case*. That one did have a document in it, one with Colin's three-word assessment of the situation. *Nice try, asshole*, he typed. He sent the spurious folder to the no doubt equally spurious gmail.com address.

That done, he deleted the folder from his own hard drive and leaned back in his chair till it creaked. He felt he'd accomplished more than he did on some days when he cracked a case. The SOB on the other end, whoever he was, would have to open all those folders one by one. With all that horseshit around, he was bound to find a pony in there somewhere . . . wasn't he?

Now that you mentioned it, no.

For the rest of the afternoon, Colin was actually interested every time his phone rang. Would it be the fellow he'd thwarted, calling to tell him where to head in? Or would the so-and-so come up with some new scheme to seduce information out of him? No and no, respectively, but anticipation did keep Colin in the game.

He knocked off at five on the dot. That didn't happen every day—or every week, either. He put on his jacket and drove home. The L.A. basin was sweltering through a late-summer heat wave. Weathermen bleated that it might hit 110 in the Valley. Newsmen said the brushfire danger was extreme.

All of which meant jack diddly in the South Bay, which reliably got the sea breeze. It had topped out in the mid-eighties at San Atanasio City Hall, across the street from the cop shop. By now, it was at least ten degrees cooler than that. Whatever fires the Santa Anas blew up wouldn't come within miles.

As usual, the first thing Colin did when he got home was pull the mail out of the mailbox. A pile of catalogues—retailers could smell Christmas from months away—a cable bill, a bill from the pool guy, a statement from his lawyer . . . and a postcard from Rob. It showed a big apple, with a good-sized worm, iridescent green, sticking out his head and neck. The worm wore a toothy grin and a Yankees cap.

Colin snorted. That was his older son's style, all right. Glued to the back of the card was the little *New Yorker* notice about Squirt Frog and the Evolving Tadpoles' local appearance. The commentary below was in Rob's spiky script: *Still not famous, but we may make it in spite of ourselves. Love from your kid.*

That anyone could want to be famous still mystified Colin. As TV had trained him to do, he associated the word with divorces and court appearances and rehab and jail time. He knew more than he wanted about all of those except rehab, and that was the one famous people blew off anyway.

He went inside. He had a little steak waiting in the fridge. He'd broil that while he nuked a package of frozen mixed veggies. As usual, not exciting cooking, but functional. A hell of a lot better for him than the fat-and-sodium bombs that masqueraded as frozen dinners. He'd eat the rest of the vegetables tomorrow with whatever meat he defrosted then.

He thought about a beer. Not without regret, he shook his head. It wasn't that he never drank alone. But he didn't do it very often. A drink had a way of turning into a few drinks. A few drinks had a way of turning into a drunk. He'd done too many drunks for a while right after Louise left. He remembered waking up hungover in that Motel 6 in Jackson goddamn Wyoming.

He'd met Kelly that day. If he'd scored with the waitress the night before . . . He didn't think he'd be as happy as he was now. The way things had worked out, he counted himself pretty lucky. If Kelly'd been here now, he would have had a beer with her. But she was off in Yellowstone, keeping track of the new volcano.

Colin dusted the steak with ground pepper and garlic powder and put it in the broiler. The microwave buzzed as the vegetables spun round and round inside. In lieu of that beer, he poured himself water from a pitcher with a Brita filter in the refrigerator.

He turned on CNN to keep him company while he cooked. Indonesian pirates were saying they'd kill the crew of a Russian freighter if they didn't get a ransom big enough to suit them. Colin was sorry for the scared-looking sailors, whose images went up one by one. France or Germany might have come through with the cash. The Russians mostly didn't make payoffs like that.

A Congresswoman had been caught with her hand in the Federal cookie jar. She was loudly denying she'd done anything wrong, and claimed it was a sexist plot because the investigating committee happened to be all male. "Yeah, right," Colin said. In a way, it was reassuring to see that corruption crossed gender lines, too.

A radio commentator was in hot water for making slurs about GLBT people. Colin was a cop, so of course he'd never heard—or told—a fag joke in all his born days. Of course.

Commercials came next. He hit the MUTE button. The dough-faced brunette shilling for an insurance company was annoying even when he couldn't hear her, but she wasn't *as* annoying. But why did ad men seem convinced the American public had a collective IQ of 9—maybe 11 with a tail wind? Colin grunted as soon as the question formed itself. Like any other cop, he'd seen enough aggressive stupidity in his time to understand exactly why admen thought that way.

The news finally returned. The young woman reading it was another beauty contest runner-up, or maybe winner. That she was drop-dead gorgeous had nothing to do with her getting the job, of course. Again, of course.

"Mother Nature is showing off her power again," she said. "Take a look at this video from an already-beleaguered Yellowstone National Park." She must have been a college graduate: she didn't make a hash of *beleaguered* when it came up on the teleprompter.

He waited for her to explain how the eruption by Ranger Lake was screwing up air traffic over the Rockies this time. More to the point, he waited for her to explain how the eruption was impacting, or even being impactful of, air traffic. To his way of thinking, the only way the eruption could impact air traffic was by pitching a volcanic rock through an Airbus' windshield. But reporters loved the bullshit jargon even more than cops did, which was saying something.

She threw him a curve, though, and not one of hers. As he took the steak out of the oven, she continued, "*Another* new volcano has started blowing its stack in Yellowstone. This one is a good many miles away from the Ranger Lake eruption. It's located not far northeast of a set of geysers called Coffee Pot Springs."

"Oh, shit," Colin said softly. The video was taken from a helicopter. It showed the kinds of things he'd seen before: black smoke and ash and dust rising high into the sky while lava set lodgepole pines afire on the ground. After fifteen or twenty seconds, a map replaced the view of the new eruption

Most people, even people who regularly went to Yellowstone, didn't have the faintest idea where the hell Coffee Pot Springs were, so the map came in handy. Guidebooks didn't talk about them, because they were so far from the roads through the park and you had to hike across bear country to get to them. Colin, anything but a Yellowstone regular, would never even have heard of them if not for Kelly. But he had. Oh, my—had he ever.

The pretty newsie reappeared on the screen. She said, "Coffee Pot Springs recently showed a dramatic increase in activity. Hot springs turned into frothing geysers and blew boiling water more than a hundred feet in the air. A geologist CNN talked to this afternoon said this was probably related to the new volcanic outbreak."

Colin was pouring A-1 Sauce on his steak. He proceeded to pour it all over the place mat, too, because there was Kelly on TV again, a mike shoved in her face. She looked windblown and worried. "Yes, magma—melted rock—in the Coffee Pot Springs dome is moving up toward the surface," she said, as if she were TAing a Geology 1 section. "It heated the underground water in the springs, and now it's starting to break through here, the way it did earlier near Ranger Lake."

Would the reporter ask her about the supervolcano? How much panic could she sow if he did? He didn't; the picture cut back to the newscaster. "A porn star claims she's having a billionaire's baby," the woman said brightly. "We'll be back with the details after these messages."

Colin hit the MUTE button on the remote again. If that wasn't one of the great inventions from the tail end of the last century, he didn't know what would be. He patted up the spilled A-1 with a paper towel. After a couple of bites of steak and a forkful of the mixed veggies, he discovered his appetite had disappeared.

He pulled out his cell phone. He didn't get Kelly; he got her voice mail. He said "Shit" again, but he wasn't amazed. She'd be really, really busy. And Yellowstone had some of the crappiest cell-phone reception of, well, anywhere. At the beep, he said, "This is what you were worrying about, isn't it? Sounds like it's time to get out while the getting's good. Be careful. Be as careful as you can, anyhow. Love you. 'Bye."

For good measure, he sent her a text, too. *Get out. Now. Love, Me.* It lacked the voice mail's flavor, but it sure as hell got the message across. She'd check texts before she listened to her voice mail because she could do it faster.

Which didn't say word one about whether she'd pay any attention to him. She would if she felt like it. Otherwise, she'd ignore him. He didn't need to be Sherlock Holmes to figure that out. He wished he weren't upwards of eight hundred miles away from her. She might take him more seriously face-to-face. Then again, she might not. He couldn't go all caveman on her, bop her over the head with a club, and drag her away from danger by the hair.

Again, though, he wished like hell he could.

By the time he unmuted the TV, the commercials were gone. So was the story about the bimbo and the billionaire. Even in this high-flying Information Age, Colin couldn't be too sorry about staying ignorant there. The markets had dropped sharply. The man explaining why had to be in his late fifties, maybe even past sixty. He had wrinkles. He was losing his hair, and what he had left was gray. He'd never make anyone mistake him for a movie star. But here he was on TV anyway. From this, Colin concluded that he might even know what he was talking about without a teleprompter for backup.

He kept hoping Kelly would call him back. She didn't.

Another earthquake shook Yellowstone. Kelly had lost track of how many she'd felt the past couple of days. Some of them were barely there—just enough to startle you and disappear. Some were mean mothers, getting up toward 6 on the Richter scale. A quake that size would do considerable damage in a built-up area, even one with strong building codes like San Francisco or L.A. What was it going to knock down here? Trees? So what?

Oh, the Yellowstone Inn and the other fancy places in and around the park would never be the same. But that was the least of Kelly's worries right this minute. If the supervolcano went kablooie right this minute, the United States would never be the same, for crying out loud.

If the supervolcano went kablooie right this minute, she would turn into a tiny part of that kablooie, too, because she was at the West Thumb of Yellowstone Lake, smack in the middle of what would be the new caldera: a red-hot zit on the face of the earth big enough to see from the moon.

"That one was about a 5.0." As usual, Larry Skrtel seemed inhumanly calm.

"Feels about right," Kelly agreed. "The more often they come, the more rattled I get." She didn't see how you could avoid that. Human beings hadn't evolved to stay calm during earthquakes. Staying calm wouldn't help keep you alive while things were falling on you. Panicking might.

She sure felt like panicking now. Too many earthquakes took it out of anybody, the same way too many body shots made any boxer fold up. Maybe Larry wasn't anybody. Maybe he didn't have that *earthquake = panic* gene. He pulled out his phone, checked to see if he had bars—a better bet here than most places in Yellowstone, but no sure thing—and must have found he did, because he started dialing.

"I hope that's somebody who can get us out of here," Kelly said. She had Colin's messages, along with a slew of others that said the same thing in different words. They left her more annoyed than anything else. Didn't people think she could see it was sayonara time all by herself?

Maybe not. Maybe she'd given them reason not to. She didn't feel like worrying about that, so she didn't.

"I hope so, too," the USGS geologist answered. "I—" He broke off and started talking into the phone: "Heinrich? Larry. Listen, *mein Freund*, things are getting a little more interesting than I really like right now. I'm at the West Thumb Geyser Basin, and all the pools are going batshit like you wouldn't believe. . . . Batshit . . . It's a technical term. . . . *Fliedermausscheisse*, okay?"

Fliedermausscheisse? Kelly silently mouthed the word, and as silently clapped her hands. With a dictionary and patience, she could read scientific German. Thanks to fragments of Yiddish from her folks, she could make a better—not good, but better—stab at speaking it than most of her anglophone peers. But she knew she never would have come up with that particular *terminus technicus* in a million months of Sundays.

Not that it didn't fit. It did, like a skintight glove. The pools around here had just sat and steamed for as long as anyone could remember. They weren't sitting and steaming any more. At the moment, four of them were flinging water into the air like Super Bowl champs spraying one another with champagne. One was the Fishing Cone, out past the edge of Yellowstone Lake. The air, unfortunately, smelled of flatulence, not of bubbly.

Daniel Olson was on his phone, too, talking with somebody from Montana State. He didn't look very happy. No, scratch that—he looked about as unhappy as any one man could.

Whatever he'd been counting on, the person on the other end of the line couldn't or wouldn't deliver. That was bad news.

Standing where Kelly stood, there was no good news to see. Off to the southwest, the Ranger Lake volcano was still doing its thing. Prevailing winds blew most of the ash across Wyoming and down into Colorado and even Kansas, not up this way, but the relevant word was *most*. She and her geologist comrades wore surgical masks. Gray grit coated the pines. Your feet crunched in it when you walked across the parking lot here.

And, up to the northeast, the new Coffee Pot Springs eruption was also going great guns, sending another huge plume of volcanic ash high into the sky. Most of that was blowing away from Yellowstone Lake, too, but it blotted out another big chunk of darkening blue. Anybody would guess that those two eruptions marked opposite edges of what was liable to turn into a caldera any time now. And anybody could see that the passel of geologists were in the middle of the frying pan, waiting to drop into the fire.

Snatches of songs and poetry ran through Kelly's head. It was much too liable to be the end of the world as she knew it—the REM tune had been all over the radio when she was much younger—but she was anything but convinced that she felt fine. And if this was the way the world ended, it wouldn't be with a whimper. This would be a bang to top all bangs. TS, Eliot. You missed that one.

The earth shook one more time. Next thing Kelly knew, she wasn't standing in the middle of the potholed, ash-gritty parking lot any more. She was sitting on her ass. The involuntary yelp that came through her mask said she'd landed hard, too. Ruth Marquez also screeched as she went down. Kelly wondered how long her left cheek would be black and blue. Rending crashes from in amongst the trees said not all of them were standing any more, either.

Somehow, Daniel had managed to keep his feet. "Hello?" he

shouted into his phone. "Hello?" He put it away. "Shit. Some of the relay towers must be out."

"If that wasn't a 7 . . ." Kelly left it there. A 7 was very bad news. For a couple of horrifying seconds, though, she'd feared a massive earthquake was the least of her worries.

Did the Richter scale even begin to measure the magnitude of the quake there'd be if a state-sized chunk of crust collapsed? *Goes to eleven, man.* In spite of herself, Kelly giggled as she got to her feet. If she could think of *This Is Spinal Tap* now, she had to be well and truly deranged.

Well, of course you are, you idiot, she thought, slapping ash and random dirt off herself as best she could. *If you weren't, what would you be doing here?*

Aftershocks kept trying to knock her off her feet. She hoped like hell they were aftershocks, anyhow. If that big quake had been a foreshock, the one it was warning of *would* send her half a mile straight down.

Larry still had cell-phone reception. He could do a commercial for whichever wireless company he used. "Listen, Heinrich, that last one made all the others feel like love pats. We don't have a lot of time to waste. . . . Yes, I know it's getting dark. We've got flashlights. We'll set fires in trash cans to mark the parking lot. . . . Yes, I know that's against regulations. We'll do it anyway." He rolled his eyes and lowered the phone for a one-word editorial: "Germans!" Then he was talking into it again. "Come on. Get moving. My will says you can't have my desk if you let me cook instead of pulling me out. . . . Yes, Heinrich, of course I'm joking. You hope."

He lowered the phone again. "Any luck?" Daniel asked.

"Some," the USGS geologist answered. "Some time tonight or tomorrow morning, two helicopters will come and take us away from all this. If they can land. If Heinrich really can pull the right strings. If, if, if . . ."

"If this stretch of terrain is still in working order by the time they get here," Kelly put in.

"Yeah, that, too." Larry whistled tunelessly between his teeth. "Anything that can happen can happen to you. That's what they say. I wish to hell they didn't know what they were talking about."

"Fires in trash cans, you said?" Kelly looked around. There were plenty. The people who ran Yellowstone didn't like litter. Unlike volcanic eruptions, they could actually do something about that. "Let's start filling 'em up with dry branches and stuff."

"Drop zones," Ruth said. "It's like something out of a World War II movie."

"No choppers in World War II," Larry observed.

Ruth sniffed. "Okay. Fine. A Vietnam movie."

Kelly and Daniel said the same thing at the same time: "*Apocalypse Now*!" Kelly cocked her head to one side, listening for the strains of "The Ride of the Valkyries." She was half disappointed when she didn't hear Wagner's fierce, churning music.

"I love the smell of hydrogen sulfide in the morning," Daniel intoned. "Smells like . . . tenure."

"Hydrogen sulfide does smell a lot like tenure sometimes," Kelly said. The others laughed, so she must have got the tone right. A good thing, too. Was she jealous of Daniel? Oh, just a little.

"Wonder what happened to that CNN crew that interviewed you earlier in the day," Larry said.

"*They'll* have helicopters," Kelly said. Like most academics, she was positive corporations had more in the way of money and everything money could buy than they knew what to do with. That only proved she'd never worked for one.

"Sure they will," Ruth agreed—she was an academic, too. "But will they have the sense to use them?" Like most academics, she was convinced people who worked for corporations were none too bright in spite of all that money. Like Kelly, she'd never examined the paradox. And exactly how bright did that make academics?

Pine branches and old refuse made lovely fires. If another earthquake knocked over the metal trash cans . . . Well, they were on asphalt. If a grass fire started all the same, Kelly told herself she just wasn't going to worry about it. A grass fire was the least of what Yellowstone had to worry about.

Trail mix and beef jerky made an uninspiring supper. They beat going hungry, though. Kelly kept listening for thuttering rotors. She kept not hearing them. What if Heinrich hadn't pulled the right strings?

Then we're screwed, that's what. She wondered how big a traffic jam there was now, heading north from Mammoth Hot Springs into Montana. Park authorities hadn't been too smart, leaving the northern attraction open. They'd been greedy, was what they'd been. She'd thought so at the time. Had anyone listened to her when she said so? As if! Nobody listened to her, fucking nobody.

She stopped right there. Colin did. Sometimes he listened so hard, it got scary. He might have been listening to an interrogation. Nobody'd ever paid attention to her like that before him. Had she been ten years younger, and less jaded and abraded by the world, she would have been sure he listened to her with a lover's ears. And, being sure of that, chances were she would have got burned again. As things were, she knew he listened to her like a cop. So what? He listened.

Aftershocks kept right on coming. Some of them seemed almost as big as that 7, or whatever the hell it was. Both as a geologist and as a Californian, Kelly knew things worked that way. Knowing didn't stop each new quake in turn from almost scaring the crap out of her. The crashes and thuds as more trees went down didn't help, either.

Something very large and just barely visible ran past them. It ignored them—it was heading for the trees on the far side of the lot, no doubt hoping they wouldn't fall over like the ones it was escaping from.

"Was that a grizzly?" Ruth asked in a very small voice.

"That was a grizzly." Even Larry sounded less cool and collected than usual. If it had been a pissed-off grizzly instead of a terrified one . . . Bison might kill more people in Yellowstone than bears did, but one reason that happened was that people had an unfortunate tendency to treat them like cows: not really dangerous critters. A lot of years of natural selection warned that bears would chow down on people if they got half a chance.

Larry's cell phone went off. His ring tone was classical, but Beethoven, not Wagner: the opening bars of the Fifth. That would get your attention if anything would. "Hey, Heinrich. What's up?" he said. After listening for a while, he sighed and went on: "Fuck. Are you sure?" Another pause, shorter this time. Evidently Heinrich was sure, because Larry sighed again. "Well, if that's the best you can do, it's the best you can do. If we're still here in the morning, I'm sure we'll thank you for it. *Auf wiedersehen*—I hope." He killed the phone to give himself whatever small charge he got from the last word.

"Well?" Kelly, Ruth, and Daniel made like a Greek chorus . . . or, given the reputation scientists had these days, a geek chorus.

"No helicopter till morning," Larry said glumly. "Sorry, but that's the way it goes, or doesn't go. Heinrich's a good guy, but he can't get the government to get anybody airborne before then. Copter pilots don't like night flying to begin with. When you factor in two erupting volcanoes . . . It's hard to blame anybody, you know?"

Put that way, he had a point. The logical, rational part of Kelly's mind saw as much. The big aftershock that rocked the parking lot just then made paying attention to that logical, rational part a skosh harder than it would have been in the Geology Department conference room back in Berkeley.

"What do we do if . . . if the bottom falls out before sunup?" Ruth asked. Her logical, rational part was feeling the strain, too.

Larry's still functioned. Kelly supposed she should admire him for that. But then again, what was that parody of Kipling's "If"? *If you can keep your head when all around you are losing theirs, chances are you don't understand what the fuck is going on.* Something like that, anyhow. Larry proved he did, though, because he answered, "Remember all those liability waivers we had to sign before they'd let us back into the park to study the Ranger Lake eruption? Well, every one of the little bastards is still in force."

Kelly remembered that pile of paperwork much too well. What it boiled down to was, she'd admitted to the U.S. government and the Parks and Wildlife Service that she was out of her ever-loving mind for coming back into Yellowstone, and agreed that anything that happened to her was her own goddamn fault, not the Feds'. At the time, it had just seemed like more forms to sign off on. That was then. This was now. Now was a lot scarier.

Bleakly, she said, "After all that paperwork, I'm surprised the government will try to get us out of here at all."

"As a matter of fact, so am I," Larry answered, which did nothing to set her mind at ease. He went on, "God only knows how many markers Heinrich had to call in to get as much as he got. I owe him bigtime. Now I hope I last long enough to have a chance to pay some of it back."

Something out in the darkness went *boom!—splash!—*a new noise. It was large, but not very close. The ground shook yet again. "If that wasn't a hydrothermal explosion, I've never heard one," Daniel said.

"*Have* you ever heard a hydrothermal explosion?" Kelly asked.

"Well, no," he admitted.

"Good," she said. "Neither have I—till now, I mean." Somewhere out there, steam bursting through to the surface had just created a new pond near Yellowstone Lake, or maybe taken a new bite out of the lake's shoreline. With a shaky laugh, she added, "We'll have a fresh tourist attraction if this turns out not to be the supervolcano after all."

"We always wanted to study one," Ruth said.

"Sure, from a safe distance." Kelly pointed up at the moon, which the plume from the Ranger Lake eruption dimmed but didn't hide. "Right now, I think that would be a pretty safe distance. Nobody's messed around with the geology there for the past couple of billion years."

"Do you think it's going to blow?" Daniel asked.

She shrugged. A mosquito buzzed near her left ear. They weren't so bad as they had been earlier in the summer, but they hadn't disappeared. The supervolcano meant nothing to them. Probably even the earthquakes didn't scare them. Except perhaps for squashing one with a toppling pine, what could an earthquake do to a mosquito?

"I still don't think anybody know for sure," she said slowly. "We're like preachers studying Revelations, trying to figure out if these finally are the Last Days."

"If it goes now, these *are* the Last Days—for us, anyway," Larry said.

Kelly was old-fashioned enough to wear a watch in spite of carrying a phone. She brought her left wrist up close to her face to read the glowing hands. It wasn't even ten o'clock yet. "What do we do for the rest of the night?" she asked.

"Assuming we've got the rest of the night to do it in," Ruth said.

"If we don't, there's no point to worrying about it, so we may as well pretend we do." As usual, Larry made good sense. He continued, "We can try to sleep—"

"Good luck!" Daniel broke in.

"We can try," the older man said. "Or we can stay up and talk. Not a whole lot of other stuff going on." An aftershock contradicted him. Unfazed, he corrected himself: "Not a whole lot of other stuff going on that we can do anything about."

Kelly had sometimes slept through small aftershocks in California. If you were tired, a 3.2, say, might not wake you up, even if it was centered close by. Sleep through quakes that started at 5.0 and went up from there? Sleep through quakes that felt as if they started six inches under your shoes? In the immortal words of any New York cabby of the past hundred years, fuhgeddaboutit.

She learned more about her comrades that night—and they about her—than she had in all the time since she'd met them. How much she'd remember when the sun came up, if she was still here when it did, was a different question.

Telling when the sun came up was also a different question. Volcanic ash from the eruption northeast of Coffee Pot Springs darkened the eastern horizon. Little by little, the sky above that mass of tiny rock particles lightened. Somewhere beyond the ash plumes, the sun still shone. Kelly thought of that reminder in *The Lord of the Rings*, where Tolkien talked about Sauron's smokes and fumes. Unlike Sauron's smoke screen, this wasn't evil. It just . . . was.

She was gnawing on more beef jerky when, in lieu of Tolkien's eagles, two helicopters came down out of the sky and landed on the beat-up parking lot. They were louder than a Metallica concert. The wind from their rotors tried to blow the geologists away. The pilots both wore orange suits that made them look like animated carrots. They gestured frantically.

Along with Larry, Kelly got into one copter. Ruth and Daniel hopped into the other. The cabins didn't cut the noise at all. Kelly was still fumbling with her uncomfortable seat's safety harness when the copter took off again. They flew due north, which struck her as a good idea. If the supervolcano erupted, the plume would blow south and west. And . . .

"Try to put some mountains between us and the eruption," Larry bawled, over and over, till the pilot got it. "They may shield us from the worst of the blast." The pilot swore, but he did it.

IX

The helicopters flew like jinking halfbacks, using the peaks of the Rockies for blockers. But they were running from, not towards. And what they were running from would flatten them more mercilessly than any middle linebacker ever hatched. Kelly found a whole new reason to be glad she liked football; the comparison never would have occurred to her otherwise.

By the time they were zooming down the canyon between Prospect Peak and the slightly lower Folsom Peak to the west, she and Larry both wore helmets like the pilot's. They cut the din in the cabin a little, and let the geologists talk by shouting instead of by screaming. Most of what Kelly and Larry had to say amounted to variations on the theme of *Go like hell!*

"Don't get your knickers in a twist," the pilot said when they banged on that drum once too often. "I'm going flat out now, and there's no guarantee the sumbitch'll go off while we're airborne. There's no *guarantee* the sumbitch'll go off at all, right?"

Every word he said was gospel truth. But he hadn't spent the night on the ground in that potholed parking lot. He hadn't felt the earth shudder under him only God knew how often. He also hadn't been studying the Yellowstone hot spot for his whole career.

Maybe it wouldn't blow now. Maybe it wouldn't blow at all. Maybe the two eruptions would do whatever they did and then subside, leaving Yellowstone changed and damaged but still a place someone in his right mind—someone not a geologist, in other words—might want to visit. Maybe the big explosion wouldn't happen for another few thousand years or another few tens of thousands of years.

Maybe. But Kelly couldn't make herself believe it.

While she stewed, the pilot talked with people who weren't in the helicopter. At last, he said, "Okay. This is what I've cooked up. A car'll be waiting for you at the Butte airport. That's about as far as I can go on my fuel load. One of you people has a place in Missoula, right?"

Daniel was in the other whirlybird. Somebody out there had a feel for what was going on. Missoula was about 120 miles northwest up I-90 from Butte. If the supervolcano blew, most of what it blasted into the air would go in the other direction. Missoula might get some, but probably wouldn't get a lot.

And if the eruption held off, Kelly could head back to California. Ruth could go to Utah . . . assuming anyone would want to go to Utah in the shadow of the big blast. Larry mostly hung out in and around Yellowstone. Knowing him, he might be *meshuggeh* enough to head back if he got some kind, any kind, of excuse.

Meanwhile . . . "Thanks," she said, a whisker ahead of Larry. She had no idea what Daniel's place was like. If they couldn't crash on him . . . Well, Missoula was bound to have motels. Hotels, even. Times like this were why God made plastic. She might even get the Berkeley Geology Department to reimburse her. Then again, given California's never-ending budget woes, she might not.

One more thing she could worry about later, if she was still alive *to* worry about it.

Once they got over the Gallatin Range, they were out of the mountains and forests and roaring along above ranch country. The copter flew much lower than the airliners that had been Kelly's only source of views of the ground from on high. She could see individual cows and even sheep from the herds, and individual cars scattered along the pale asphalt of country roads that hadn't been repaved in a long time and got so little wear that they wouldn't need to be for quite a while yet.

There was I-90 up ahead. Kelly had wondered if it would be packed solid with cars and RVs full of people fleeing Yellowstone, but it wasn't. Probably weren't that many left to flee any more.

The Interstate was two lanes wide in each direction. But for the lack of traffic lights, that would have been a boulevard in L.A. or the Bay Area. When your whole state was almost the size of California but held fewer than a million people, you could have a four-lane main highway and go like hell instead of sitting stuck in traffic on a freeway twelve lanes wide.

"Bert Mooney Airport coming up," the pilot said in due course. Kelly idly wondered who Bert Mooney was or had been. The pilot did things with his stick—with the collective, he called it, as if it were a farm in the extinct Soviet Union. The helicopter descended. Not far away, so did the one carrying Ruth and Daniel.

Whoever Bert Mooney might have been, the two helicopters were his airport's only current business. Kelly was used to airports like LAX and San Francisco and Oakland. That green Ford sitting there near the terminal couldn't be the car they'd take away . . . could it?

"There's your wheels, I expect," the pilot said, pointing to it. Sometimes simplicity had advantages.

Touchdown on the tarmac a moment later was surprisingly gentle. The other chopper landed three or four seconds after Kelly and Larry's. A fuel truck pulled up and waited for their rotors to stop spinning.

Kelly took off her helmet. Now, with the motor cut, it wasn't deafening in here. "Thanks more than I know how to tell you," she said.

"Amen," Larry agreed.

"Not a big deal. Might not've been anything at all," the pilot answered. "Sometimes you'd sooner be safe than sorry, is all. Good luck to you guys."

"You, too," Kelly said as he opened the canopy and she scrambled out. Larry followed her. Ruth and Daniel got out of the other helicopter. They all started dogtrotting across the tarmac toward the car. Kelly presumed it was a rental. She didn't know for sure, but that was one more thing she could worry about later. After they got to Missoula seemed a pretty good time.

Halfway to the green Ford, Larry suddenly stopped. Intent only on getting to the car and getting onto I-90, Kelly sent him an annoyed glare. "What's the matter with you?" she snapped.

Instead of answering with words, he pointed southeast, over the top of the low, flat-roofed terminal building. Kelly's gaze automatically followed his index finger. That great, black, swelling, leaping cloud hadn't been there when they touched down a minute before. It grew every second. Even across a couple of hundred miles, Kelly could see the lightning bolts lashing around its edges. Which meant they were how big? How bright? Some questions either answered themselves or didn't really need answering, one.

"Oh, my God," Kelly whispered. Ruth crossed herself. Kelly hadn't known she was Catholic. With a last name like Marquez, it was a good bet, though. Maybe Ruth hadn't thought about being Catholic herself any time lately. Seeing . . . that ahead was the kind of thing that would remind you.

"Why isn't there any noise?" Daniel asked. "Why isn't the ground shaking?"

"Don't worry. We'll feel it. We'll hear it, too," Larry answered. "The earthquake waves and the sound waves haven't got here yet. But they will." He looked as grim as a phlegmatic person could. "Oh, boy, will they ever. People heard Krakatoa two thousand miles away, and Krakatoa was only a fart in a bathtub next to this."

"What would have happened to us if we'd been in the air when the sound wave or shock wave or whatever you want to call it hit us?" Ruth said.

Kelly looked back at the helicopter pilot. He was staring toward Yellowstone, too. Even through the chopper's Plexiglas canopy, she could see his mouth hanging open. "What happens to a fly when the swatter comes down?" she said. If you hit a fly with a swatter the size of a house, that probably came closer to describing the force matchup.

None of them went any closer to the car. Out here in the open, they were about as safe as they could be. Even if the terminal building fell over, it wouldn't fall on them. "I think we ought to get down," Larry said. "You guys are too young to remember 'Drop!' drills, but you know about 'em, right?"

An officious fifth-grade teacher from days gone by would have yelled at Kelly for bad form, but she didn't care. She assumed the classic position on the pavement, which was much smoother than the parking lot where she'd spent the night before—the parking lot that was now one tiny puff in that insanely huge mass of smoke and dust. Drop drills were designed to protect you against Russian H-bombs. What did you do when something way, way bigger than an H-bomb went off not nearly far enough away?

"Whoa, Nelly!" Larry yelled when the shaking started. Getting down was a good idea, because Kelly knew she couldn't have stayed on her feet. She'd wondered what the Richter reading for a supervolcano would be. It was enormous, or whatever one step higher than enormous was. She'd put all this distance between herself and the epicenter, and she was still getting tossed around like a rag doll.

It didn't want to ease up, either. Like the Energizer Bunny, it kept going and going and. . . . *How* much energy was being released all at once? The calculator inside her head said TILT.

Windows in the airport terminal broke. One of the helicopters that had flown the geologists out of Yellowstone went over onto its side. Luckily, the pilot was still in his safety harness, so he might be okay. Even more luckily, neither copter had started refueling. Everybody'd stopped to gape at the cataclysm off in Yellowstone.

The ground was still shaking when the wind came. Blast from an atomic bomb could wreck things far away from the actual explosion. The roar came at the speed of sound. It had had plenty of distance to attenuate, and had gone around and over a couple of mountain ranges on the way. That meant it was just far and away the loudest thing Kelly had ever heard in her life.

Somewhere she'd read that artillerymen yelled to help equalize the pressure on their ears. She tried it. It couldn't possibly hurt. And she felt like screaming any which way. She blew twenty or thirty feet down the runway, picking up more bumps and bruises and scrapes. If she hadn't had her hands up to her face, that would have been worse, too.

Part of the terminal did fall in on itself about then. Knocked down by the wind roaring around and through it? Flattened by the unending quakes? Wrecked by nothing more than the vibration from the great roar? Kelly would have checked *all of the above* on a multiple-choice test.

The green Ford didn't flip over. That was something. How much, she wasn't so sure. Could they make it to Missoula? She'd traveled I-90 before. As she did in many parts of the country, she'd noticed how spindly the supports for the overpasses were. Building codes hereabouts didn't mandate anything like the quake resistance required in California. So what would happen when something bigger than the Big One hit, even if it was a long way off? They'd find out.

That cloud in the sky swelled and swelled. It hadn't blotted out the sun—not yet, not here. But how much of Wyoming and Montana and Idaho had seen night fall in the middle of the day? More every minute, as the long, long shadow went on stretching. It reminded Kelly of the blast from Mount Doom when the Ring went into the fire in *The Return of the King*.

But Sauron proved impotent in the end. The hot spot under Yellowstone was anything but. How many millions—or was it billions? probably—of tons of pulverized rock did that cloud represent? Not all of it would be thoroughly pulverized, either. How far could the biggest explosion in the past 75,000 years throw boulders big enough to squash houses and cars? How far could it throw rocks big enough to smash skulls? People in a broad swath of the Rocky Mountain West were finding out right this minute, sometimes the hard way.

And, for the ones too close to the supervolcano, flying boulders and ash in the sky would be the least of their worries. Good, old-fashioned lava was pouring out of the caldera along with all the junk going straight up. So were pyroclastic flows—mud and boiling water mixed into a hellbrew. When Vesuvius blew in 70 AD, a pyroclastic flow was what buried Pompeii. But, like Krakatoa, like Mt. St. Helens, like, well, everything, Vesuvius was only a hiccup next to this.

West Yellowstone, Montana, a tacky tourist town, would be gone, off the map. So would Gardiner, Montana, at Yellowstone's north entrance, and Cooke City and Silver Gate, Montana, to the park's—the ex-park's—northeast, and Cody, Wyoming, a little farther east. South of Yellowstone, the Grand Tetons were going to get another layer of volcanic tuff pasted on. And it would be tuff—and tough—on Jackson, Wyoming, too.

And all that, of course, was only the beginning. Only the tiniest fraction of the beginning.

Larry managed to make it to his feet. His denim jacket had a hole in one elbow. His jeans were out at both knees. One knee was bleeding into the blue denim. He didn't seem to notice. Well, Kelly had hurts she hadn't started reviewing yet, too. One thing at a time.

The ground went on rolling under them. Normally, you wouldn't feel aftershocks from a quake that far away, but that was a *big* quake, and these were big aftershocks. Still, they did roll instead of jerking, as they would have done closer to the epicenter. You could—Larry could—stand up while they were going on. The wind blasting out from the eruption was still fierce, too, but not fierce enough to knock him over.

He could even yell through it and make himself heard: "Let's haul ass while we can. The farther we go before ash starts falling on us, the better. I don't know how the car's air filter will like all that grit, and I don't know how the engine will like the crud the filter lets through."

Kelly had known him for a while now. He was low-key, unexcitable. She translated what he'd said into what would have come from most people. He figured the air filter wouldn't like volcanic ash for hell, and the motor would go queep and die once it inhaled enough grit.

How many cars—and trucks, and fire engines, and ambulances—across how many states would go queep and die when their engines seized up from overdosing on ash? One more interesting question, in the Chinese sense of the word.

She'd seen the maps that showed how far the supervolcano threw ash in previous eruptions. Most of the Midwest and big pieces of the West were in deep, deep kimchi. And all that also was only the beginning.

Can I stand up, too? she wondered. Only one way to find out. Ruth had already made it to her feet by the time Kelly did. Daniel also did it, though he limped as he went over to the Ford. Knee? Ankle? Whatever it was, he could, after a fashion, walk on it. That would do for the moment.

Larry tried the driver's door. It opened. He looked inside. "Key's in the ignition," he reported. "The pilot wasn't lying to us."

They got in. The guys took the front seats; the women sat in back. It was fair—Larry and Daniel were taller than both of them. As Kelly fastened her belt, she noticed she'd barked her right palm. Ruth had a nasty scrape on her forehead and a bloody ear. All that was stuff they could worry about later.

Only after the belt clicked tight did Kelly start giggling. Ruth, who was also buckling up, sent her a curious look. She explained: "It's the end of the world, and I'm fastening my stupid seat belt. So are you."

"Oh." Ruth managed a sheepish nod. "Force of habit."

Larry started the car. He'd also used his belt. So had Daniel, who said, "We may need them. If it is the end of the world, people will be driving like bats out of hell."

If that wasn't a mixed-up metaphor—well, simile—Kelly'd never heard one. Being mixed up sure didn't make it wrong, though.

Larry drove around the battered terminal building. People, some of them bleeding, were coming out through windows and doors. "I don't like to pass them by, but. . . ." he said. No one tried to change his mind.

By Montana standards, Butte was a good-sized town: it held about 35,000 people. It had banks and offices and apartment buildings and fast-food joints, just like a real city. Some of them had stayed up; some had fallen down. Glass from countless broken windows sparkled in the sun like snow. Some of the glass sparkled on Harrison Avenue, the street that would take them up to the Interstate. That wind hadn't been fooling around.

"A flat would be all we needed right now, wouldn't it?" Ruth said.

"Bite your tongue," Kelly said sweetly. "Hard."

Some of the locals were helping others who'd been hurt. But lots of men and women stood on the sidewalks—or sometimes in the middle of the street—staring and pointing at the cloud swelling up and up and out and out from the supervolcano. Kelly couldn't blame them. She kept twisting to stare back at it herself. How high? How wide? How close? More of each every second— that was the only thing she was sure about.

Larry turned on the radio. Hiphop blared out of it: no doubt the station chosen by the last guy who'd serviced the Ford. He punched buttons. Before long, he found someone solemnly saying, "The President has declared a state of emergency in Wyoming, Montana, and Idaho. The governors of those states have also declared emergencies, and have called out the National Guard."

"Well, that's a relief," Daniel said. "We're all safe now."

"Will you sock him, please?" Kelly said to Larry. "It's a long stretch for me."

"Consider yourself socked," Larry told Daniel as he swung the car onto the westbound I-90. He pointed. "This overpass is okay, anyhow."

"That makes one," Kelly said. Ruth made as if to sock *her.* Kelly dipped her head in apology.

"Loss of life in and around Yellowstone Park is believed to be heavy, as is property damage," the newscaster intoned. Obviously, he was in Washington or New York City or some place like that, some place where this seemed like one more natural disaster that didn't have anything to do with him or his well-connected way of life. And so it was.

For the moment.

He went on, "For the time being, we have no direct reports from the impacted area."

All the geologists in the Ford hooted and hollered. "No shit, Jackson!" Ruth yelled, which was among the more coherent editorials.

"1-800-BUY-CLUE," Kelly added.

She and Ruth both kept twisting around to look back through the rear window. Every time, the cloud from the supervolcano looked bigger and blacker and closer. They were making Interstate speed. How fast was it going? How far would it come? Right about to Missoula, if past eruptions were any guide—and they were the only guide anybody had. How far the ash would blow in the other direction was an altogether different, and much bigger, question.

Every so often, the car would kind of lurch for a little while, as if a tire were low on air. Then it would straighten out and fly right again. "Didn't they put any shocks on this hunk of junk?" Daniel asked.

"It's not the shocks," Kelly said. Being a Californian, she had more direct and more varied experience with earthquakes than any of the others. "It's the aftershocks. This is what an earthquake feels like in a car."

"Oh," Daniel said in a small, sheepish voice.

Larry hit the brakes. Kelly had to look forward instead of back. A pair of Montana Highway Patrol cars had their light bars flashing red and blue. An officer from one of them waved traffic towards an off-ramp. Sure as hell, an overpass was down. Half a car stuck out from under it. Kelly's stomach lurched like the Ford in an aftershock when she thought about being in the other half. It would have been over fast, anyway. All that concrete falling . . .

The Highway Patrolman—no, Patrolwoman: she had boobs under her khaki shirt and a ponytail—waving cars to the ramp wore a mask like the ones the geologists had used in Yellowstone. That was smart. Whether it would be up to the challenge ahead . . . Whether the whole country would be up to the challenge ahead, let alone one crappy mask . . .

Larry finally got around to asking Daniel if his place would hold four. "For a little while, anyway, if you don't mind sleeping on the couch," Daniel answered. "Kelly and Ruth can have the bed, and I've got a spare sleeping bag in my closet. I'll use that."

"Should work," Larry agreed. In musing tones, he went on, "I wonder whether Missoula gets gas and food and things shipped in from the east or from the west."

That was another fascinating question. Kelly hadn't started thinking in those terms, but she realized she'd start needing to. Supplies might be able to reach Missoula from Idaho. Nothing much would be able to cross Montana for God only knew how long. Ash—and probably boulders, too—would already be raining down on Livingston and Bozeman. I-90 would be impassable. Stretches of it might end up under hundreds of feet of volcanic debris. Maybe some secondary routes farther north would stay open. Maybe—but Kelly had trouble believing it.

What would Missoula and lots of places like Missoula do when a whole bunch of what they depended on for daily living didn't—couldn't—get through? They'd damn well do *without*, was what. And what would come of that?

Kelly knew the question really mattered. She knew she ought to be worrying about it. But she couldn't, not right now. Thanks to that helicopter pilot, she hadn't been smack in the middle of ground zero when the Yellowstone caldera fell in on itself. She was still here. She was still breathing. She still had a chance to go on breathing a while longer. She still had the chance to find out the answer to her important question, and perhaps to some others as well.

Right this minute, she figured that made her one of the luckiest and, in a way, one of the richest people on the face of the globe. And she wasn't going to worry about a single goddamn thing.

The powers that be at Amalgamated Humanoids didn't mind if people listened to the radio at their desks. Every so often, there was a little dustup when somebody listened to something the person at the next desk couldn't stand, and turned it up instead of down when the allegedly injured party complained. But that didn't happen as often as Vanessa Ferguson would have guessed. Not everyone was as touchy as she was, though she didn't see it that way.

She bounced from NPR to the classical station to political talk. She would have liked to bring her iPod, but the powers that be did frown on headphones—even earbuds. They claimed people got too distracted using those. It sounded like bullshit to Vanessa, but she hadn't been there long enough to stick in her oar on something like that.

She sure as hell needed something to take part of her mind off the proposal she was editing. If she gave the wretched document her full attention, she'd grab a paperweight or something and chuck it at her monitor. Uselessly long words in uselessly long sentences that twisted and writhed like worms on a sidewalk after a rain . . .

Would the engineers write better if they learned English the way they learned programming, however they learned that? They couldn't very well write worse.

An announcer broke into a Bach harpsichord concerto. If

that wasn't a hanging offense, it damn well should have been. "I do apologize for the interruption," the woman said, "but an important news bulletin has just reached us. There is a major—I repeat, a major—volcanic eruption in Yellowstone National Park. This is on a scale far larger than anything previously known. There is some concern that Denver may be adversely affected. Please stay tuned for any further developments. Thank you." Bach returned, cool and pure.

As far as Vanessa knew, she was the only person here who listened to classical music. But exclamations floated up from several cubicles, so the bulletin must have gone out on a bunch of stations. Vanessa remembered her dad pitching a hissy fit because she was coming here.

That was just too ridiculous, though. Volcanic ash could screw up flight schedules, sure—Denver politicos had been pissing and moaning about revenue reversals for months now. Even so, Yellowstone was . . . well, how far from Denver was Yellowstone, anyhow? Vanessa had checked once, before she moved here, but she'd forgotten.

She hit Bing.com to find out. Most people would have Googled it, but she was Microsoft all the way. From Yellowstone to Denver was about 430 miles. She laughed. Ridiculous to think that anything so far away could possibly do much here. Reporters got you to keep listening by exaggerating bulletins, and the poor woman at the classical station had to read whatever they stuck in front of her. She wouldn't have any way of knowing what bushwah it was.

Nodding to herself, Vanessa closed the Bing window and grimly returned to the proposal. She tried to tell herself it wouldn't seem so bad with Bach lilting out of the radio. She tried, but she didn't have much luck.

At first, she hardly noticed the rolling motion under her. But it built and built and kept on building. A rolling motion rather than a sharp wham meant a quake was a long way away—all her California experience taught her so. A quake a long way off that was this big was a lulu, though.

A file cabinet somewhere not far enough away went over with a crash. Next thing Vanessa knew, she was under her desk, trying to bunch her legs up under her so it would protect them, too. The rolling went on and on. Screams—soprano and baritone—rang through the office. "Make it stop!" somebody yelled, but it wouldn't stop.

Little by little—after several more tall files fell—it did ease up. A final shake sent Vanessa's keyboard clattering down. She supposed she was lucky the monitor didn't slide off the desk, too. And acoustic cottage cheese drifted from the ceiling like indoor snow.

She scrambled out from under the desk. She was one of the first to emerge, maybe because she was a Californian and more used to quakes. Several cubicle partitions had gone down along with the file cabinets. She could see much farther across the office than she'd been able to before. *Lucky the power stayed on*, she thought.

Which must have tempted fate or something, because a doozy of an aftershock almost knocked her off her feet. She squawked and grabbed for the edge of the desk to steady herself—and as she touched it the lights went out. For a few seconds, everything went as black as the inside of a mortgage banker's heart. People started screaming in earnest. Vanessa didn't join them, but she didn't miss by much.

Then a few wan emergency lights came on. Somebody spoke from ceiling speakers that she hadn't known were there: "Evacuate the building! Immediately evacuate the building!"

She couldn't remember hearing an idea she liked better. Pausing only to grab her handbag, she hurried toward a red EXIT sign glowing over a door. The office was on the second floor.

Along with everybody else, she went down a gloomy hallway to the stairs. Several people limped. A small man had his arms around the shoulders of two bigger guys. As Vanessa squeezed past, the smaller fellow said, "Goddamn file cabinet smashed my ankle. Hurts like a motherfucker, pardon my French."

"I've heard the word," she answered. He chuckled before he went back to swearing.

The stairwell was dark except at the bottom, where dim daylight beckoned. Vanessa had done plenty of things she'd enjoyed more than trying not to trip and break her neck, or even an ankle of her own. If anybody above her fell, everybody on the stairs was liable to go ass over teakettle.

She made it. She hurried to the front entrance. It had those glass doors that automatically slid sideways when anyone approached. Printed across them was the legend IN CASE OF EMERGENCY, PUSH OUTWARD. Vanessa had seen it a million times without ever paying much attention to it. But someone had pushed, and the doors had indeed opened outward.

Yet another aftershock hurried her into the parking lot. How much could the building take? What kind of quake standards did Denver have? Out in the open, she didn't have to worry about that so much. She really had wondered if the ceiling would come crashing down.

People in the lot were aligning like iron filings scattered across a paper on top of a magnet. They were all facing a little west of north. Vanessa turned that way, too, before she quite realized what she was doing.

She liked Denver's western horizon, with the Rockies shouldering their way up into the sky as far as the eye could see—if air pollution let the eye see them at all. This was a clear, bright day; the morning had been downright chilly. She could see the mountains just fine.

And, towering far above them, she could see what all the

other people saw: that enormous column of smoke growing, swelling, every second. "That can't be Yellowstone. It can't," someone said, with the plaintive tones of a man hoping to be contradicted. "It's too far away . . . isn't it? I mean, a little ash at the airport, that's one thing. But this . . ." His voice trailed away.

Vanessa wanted to believe it was much too far to be Yellowstone. She couldn't. You could see the Rockies most of the way to Kansas in good weather. That cloud, obviously, was a hell of a lot taller than the mountains. For all she knew, her father could see it back in San Atanasio.

"It's getting bigger," a woman said. "It's heading this way."

Plenty of crap from the little eruptions—though they hadn't seemed little till now—had headed this way. That was why flights into and out of the airport had been hit-and-miss for so long. Not all of this titanic cloud was heading toward Denver, obviously. Oh, no. There'd be plenty to go around and then some. But what would happen when Denver's share landed? Nothing good. Vanessa could see that right away.

"Go home, folks." That was Malcolm Talbott, who ran Amalgamated Humanoids. "We're not going to get anything done today. Go home," he repeated, louder this time. "We'll see how things are tomorrow. If they aren't so bad, we'll work. If they are . . ." He shrugged. "We won't be the only one with troubles. You'd best believe we won't." One more earthquake put a rolling period under his words.

Nobody needed to tell Vanessa twice. She made a beeline for her car, fumbling in her purse for the keys. She'd just unlocked the door when the bellow from the blast tore through Denver. Yellowstone was over 400 miles away—she'd found that out. Sound took forty minutes or so to get from there to here. She wondered what that bellow would have been like if she were only, say, fifty miles away. She didn't wonder long. It would have torn her head off.

She jumped into the car and slammed the door. That helped a little: less than she would have wished. The car rocked under her. She started it anyway, and punched the radio buttons till she found news. For once, it didn't take long.

"—gigantic disaster," someone was saying in a high, excited voice. "Several states are sure to be severely impacted."

Vanessa started a reflexive sneer, then cut it off. Things were going to come down on several states, sure as hell. Things were already coming down on several states. When you used *impact* as a verb, that was what you were supposed to mean. Maybe this yahoo meant *affect*, but for once he was literally correct.

"We'll be right back after this important message," he said. The message proved to be important only to the male-enhancement company that put it out and to the radio station's bottom line. Vanessa hit another button.

"—will undoubtedly blanket Denver," an educated-sounding woman was saying. "How deep the ashfall will be, and how serious its effects, no one can yet predict. It is already obvious, though, that removing it will be more challenging than clearing a heavy snowfall. Where can we take it that isn't also already covered in ash?"

Wasn't that also true of snow? But snow eventually melted, and you just had to get it out of the streets. Snow on lawns and parks was beautiful. Volcanic ash would be anything but.

"How will volcanic ash affect people with respiratory ailments?" a man asked.

"The only thing I can say right now is, it won't be good," the woman answered. "It won't be good for anyone. And it won't be good for livestock, and stockraising is particularly important in the eastern half of the state."

Colorado had always been uneasily divided between agriculture and mining. Tourism added a third leg to the stand, but now everything was knocked for a loop. Who besides geologists would want to come visit a city blanketed—how deep?—in volcanic ash? Escaped lunatics, maybe.

"Some of this dust—maybe a lot of it—will reach the upper atmosphere and be blown around the world," the woman added. "Global climate change may be severe."

That didn't sound good. The hugely towering black cloud off to the west of north didn't look good. The earthquakes that kept rolling through Denver didn't feel good. Nothing seemed good—except Vanessa had the rest of the day off.

X

Colin met Gabe Sanchez at a familiar spot: in front of the coffeepot. As Colin loaded up more instant brain cells, Gabe said, "Well, it's finally gone and happened."

"What's gone and happened?" Colin asked, adulterating his java with cream and sugar. He stood aside so Gabe could get at the pot.

"That superwaddayacallit in Yellowstone went kapow," Sanchez answered. "I just saw it on a news feed from the Net. . . . Hey, where you going, man?"

"To find out what's going on for myself," Colin said grimly. "Kelly's still up there, or she was last night."

"Oh. Hell. That's not good," Gabe said.

"Tell me about it."

"I hope everything turns out okay." Sanchez crossed himself.

Raised a hardshell Baptist, Colin had long since lost his religion. Most of the time, he didn't miss it. Most of the time, in fact, he forgot he'd ever had it. It was easy not to believe in God, especially a merciful God, when you were a cop. Colin often wondered how guys like Gabe managed. Every once in a while, he envied them the solace their faith could bring. This was one of those times.

The first thing he did was check his phone. He breathed again when he saw a text from Kelly: *On helicopter. On my way out.* "Thank you, Jesus," he muttered. It was as close to a prayer as he'd come in God knew how long.

One thing the cop shop could boast, and that was fast Internet. When Colin turned to CNN.com, he got live streaming video from a weather satellite. There was a hell of a lot of smoke, and under it patches of fire. The headline was simple: YELLOW-STONE CATASTROPHE! When he noticed the computer-added state boundaries on the video, he realized that was an understatement, but English didn't come equipped with words to describe anything this big. No language did. No language since the primeval *Ook!* had ever needed to cope with anything like this.

There was a story under the video. The great collapse had happened only forty minutes earlier. He shook his head in wonder. The world was a connected place these days, all right.

Then he remembered he'd had a coffee cup in his hand when he ran back to his desk. He reached for it . . . and discovered the world was a connected place in more ways than the information superhighway. That gentle rolling motion under his swivel chair could only be an earthquake. By the way it went on and on, it was one doozy of an earthquake, too. Cops and secretaries started exclaiming—he wasn't the only one who felt it. But it stayed mild, so it was a long way off.

"Holy crap!" he said. "That's got to be the supervolcano."

Back more than a hundred years before, they'd felt the San Francisco earthquake in Los Angeles. But Yellowstone was a lot farther away than San Francisco. Didn't that argue that the quake that went with the supervolcano eruption was bigger than the one that had flattened the city by the bay? How much would this one flatten?

He wondered what had happened to Denver. Central Colorado suddenly seemed much too close to northwestern Wyoming. He called Vanessa. He got her voice mail, which might mean anything or nothing. At the beep, he said, "You okay? Give me a call and let me know. 'Bye." He'd done what he could on that front.

A little fiddling on the computer told him how far from San Atanasio Yellowstone was. It also told him how fast earthquake waves traveled, even if the Wiki article did say they "propagated" (he tried to imagine fornicating earthquake waves, but his mind rebelled). San Atanasio would feel an earthquake in Yellowstone about forty minutes after it happened, assuming it felt such an earthquake at all. *Yeah, assuming*, he thought.

His cell phone rang. He always answered the landline on his desk with some variation on *Ferguson*. Here he said, "Hello?"

"Hi, Dad." It was Vanessa. "I just got home. Could you feel the quake there?"

"Sure could. What's it like where you are? You just got home, you said?"

"Yeah. The building where I work stayed up, but power's out. It's out here, too. I don't know when it'll come back." She hesitated, then added, "I don't know if it'll come back. And the sky . . . Oh, my God, the sky! The cloud's coming this way. You can tell. Pickles is under the bed, and he won't come out. He's scared shitless—I cleaned it off the rug."

"I believe that. Should you get out now, while the getting's good?" Colin asked.

"I don't know. I'm thinking about it. Will you let Mom and the brothers know I'm okay? I don't want to run my battery any more than I have to—I don't know when I'll be able to charge it again."

"Okay," Colin said, though he looked forward to calling Louise the way he looked forward to losing a tooth. "Take care."

"You, too. 'Bye."

He started to add *Good luck*, but she'd hung up by then. Sighing, he called Louise's cell. Maybe he'd luck out. Maybe he'd get her voice mail and not actually have to talk to her.

But no. That familiar voice, once loved, now . . . not, said, "Hello?" in his ear.

"Hi. It's me." His own voice was hard and flat. "I just talked to Vanessa. She's okay, but it sounds like the quake hit Denver a lot harder than it did here."

"The same quake?" Louise said incredulously, so she wasn't with it at all.

Colin filled her in in words of one syllable. "Power's down in Denver, and the ash cloud is heading that way," he finished. From what Kelly'd said, the ash might even dust Los Angeles. Louise didn't need to worry about that right now, though.

"Good God!" she said. "I'd better call the poor baby."

"Don't," Colin said sharply. "She's trying to save her battery till power comes back, if it does. She told me to call you. She's being sensible." *For once in her life.* He didn't say that. What good would it do?

What good would anything do? "She talked to you instead of me, Mister High and Mighty? How did that happen?" Louise demanded.

"Because I found out what was going on and called her," Colin answered. "That's more than . . ." He was talking to a dead line again.

He powered off his own phone. Chances were Louise *would* call Vanessa, just to show him. Chances were she'd talk the kid's ear off, too. Well, Vanessa could tell her to shut up. Vanessa could try, anyway.

He scrolled down the story under the wound in the earth. It said the ash plume would top out at over 100,000 feet. *Twenty miles*, he thought. None of the Rockies was even three miles high.

You couldn't see the Rockies from L.A. Even imagining you could was silly. But something seven times as high? He didn't know. He didn't think he had enough trig left to find out, either. His long-ago high-school math teachers would be pissed off that he didn't, but that was how the cookie bounced or the ball crumbled. His high-school math teachers had been a bunch of bores.

Rob was on the other side of the country, touring with his band. If anybody was okay, he was. Marshall was up in Santa Barbara, getting ready for a new quarter and another new major. The eruption wouldn't trash Santa Barbara. Colin didn't think trashing Santa Barbara was possible. The only thing that convinced him Santa Barbara wasn't heaven on earth was the real-estate prices there. Heaven wouldn't have been anywhere near so expensive.

The CNN news feed said the President was urging everyone to stay calm during the present emergency. How calm could you stay when a quake knocked down everything you had or when boulders or ash fell out of the sky on you? Colin routinely despised Democrats in the White House, and Republicans routinely disappointed him. But hadn't this clown's advisors briefed him about what a supervolcano eruption would mean?

Or maybe they had. As Kelly'd said, some disasters were just too big to plan for. You hoped they didn't happen. If they happened all the same, what could you do but duck and cover and roll with the punches and try your best to come out the other side, if there turned out to be any other side to come out to?

Half the country must have felt this punch, maybe more. And the eruption itself was only the first part of the combination the supervolcano would throw at civilization. Under those circumstances, urging calm on people might not be so bad. It wouldn't hurt, and it might do a tiny bit of good.

Something rumbled outside, and went on rumbling. During the big war, the Germans on the Eastern Front must have heard noise like that when the Russians shelled them before sending in the tanks. Colin knew about naval gunnery, but it was never this continuous. For this, you'd have to line up guns of every caliber hub to hub, shoot them all off at once, and have enough ammo to keep shooting and shooting and shooting.

Or you'd have to have a supervolcano go off eight hundred miles away. This sound had been traveling for more than an hour, and it was still loud enough to shake the building almost as hard as the earthquake had. In another hour or hour and a half, the President would hear it in the Oval Office.

And, three or four hours after that, they might hear it in Europe. They'd heard Krakatoa a couple of thousand miles away, and this thing made Krakatoa look like Vanessa's Pickles next to a sabertooth.

"Gabe!" Colin said through the rumble that wouldn't quit.

"Waddaya need?" Sergeant Sanchez answered.

"C'mere a sec," Colin said. Gabe got up from his own desk and ambled over. Colin went on, "We had better secure a supply of gasoline for the department, and I mean right now. This thing will screw transport like you wouldn't believe."

"So why are you telling me? Why aren't you telling the chief, or else the mayor? Have we got the money in the budget to do anything like that? Can the city get it for us if we don't?" Gabe was full of reasonable questions.

Or rather, he was full of questions that would have been reasonable a little more than an hour earlier. The chief and the mayor would be full of it, too. Colin had no doubts on that score. The difference was, he could—or he hoped he could—make Gabe see sense. His superiors wouldn't want to listen . . . as if they ever did.

"This has to be unofficial," Colin said. "No refineries in San Atanasio, but there are some over in El Segundo and down in Lomita. Talk to the managers there. Tell 'em we're gonna have problems. Tell 'em the whole state's gonna have problems. Do it now—get there ahead of their own cops. Show 'em we're on the ball. See what you can do to get 'em to lend us a hand."

"I got you," Gabe said. "You want 'em to think we know more about what's going on than their local people do."

"Uh-huh." Colin nodded. Thanks to Kelly, he *did* know more about what was liable to go on than most of the local competition. The problem with that was, the more you knew, the worse things looked. You could tell a refinery manager that California would have problems for a while. You couldn't tell a guy like that that the world had just walked into a sucker punch. If he didn't already know it for himself—and chances were he wouldn't—he wouldn't believe you.

"Okay. I'll do it," Sanchez said. "Better get moving, while those guys're still shook up by the quake and the boom and shit."

"Good plan," Colin agreed. The refinery managers would be shaken—literally and otherwise. They might be more inclined to listen to bulky, imposing Sergeant Sanchez. Colin would have bet his last quarter that things would get worse, not better. But you didn't want to tell civilians too much too soon. They couldn't always handle bad news.

And he knew he was a cynical cop, ready to look on the gloomy side both by training and by temperament. He had to put that in the equation, too. Kelly might not understand supervolcanoes as well as she thought she did. It wasn't as if geologists had ever had a live one to study.

So maybe this wasn't a catastrophe after all, CNN.com notwithstanding. Maybe it was just a disaster. Colin laughed at himself. Only a cynical cop could have a thought like that and actually find consolation in it.

Bryce Miller had a window seat on the flight from O'Hare back to LAX. He couldn't stand LAX. He didn't know anyone who could. O'Hare was even busier. It seemed to run more smoothly, though.

Or maybe that was just his imagination. The conference on the Hellenistic world at the University of Chicago had gone as well as he'd dared hope. He hadn't given a paper, but he'd critiqued one. He thought his remarks were to the point. The professors who'd listened to him seemed to think so, too.

Something might come of that. No guarantees—there were never any guarantees—but something might. If he could get his thesis done . . . Or why think small? They did hire people who'd done all but the dissertation. There was even a name for them: ABDs. They got paid less, of course, but after a TA's money any real salary looked terrific.

The guy in the middle seat wiggled. He wasn't deliberately annoying, but he was there, right there. And the woman in front of Bryce had reclined her seat as far as it would go. She wasn't trying to kneecap him, which didn't mean she wasn't doing it.

He got out the pastrami on rye and the big chocolate-chip cookie he'd bought in the airport. The bastards weren't about to feed you. He counted himself lucky the flight attendants had doled out a Coke. Such extravagant generosity had to be bad for the bottom line.

Somebody somewhere in the plane was eating something smellier than airport pastrami. Bryce was forcibly reminded of the modern fable about the Stinky Cheese Man. You'd think whoever was chowing down would have more regard for everyone else trapped in the flying cigar with him. But no.

And even that minimal regard might be too much to hope for. Going with a cop's daughter and getting to know the cop himself had made Bryce look at his fellow humans with a freshly jaundiced eye. Getting dumped by Vanessa hadn't done anything to improve his attitude, either.

He took a bite from the sandwich in self-defense. While he

chewed, he looked down out the window: about seven miles down. The landscape was flat and green and gold, and laid out in geometric patterns. The Midwest, from on high.

It wasn't great pastrami. No way you'd find great pastrami at an airport sandwich shop. But it wasn't lousy pastrami—all fat and peppercorns—either. And the cookie honest to God was pretty good. It made a better lunch than American would have given him once upon a time—but also a more expensive one.

Bryce slammed the tray into place again. Let the bitch who'd shoved her seat way back feel it. After one more look at the fields far below, he leaned against the bulkhead and tried to sleep.

He'd just dozed off when . . . "This is the captain speaking." Bryce's eyes jerked open. He was surprised he didn't bleed out through them. The airline's customer-prevention program was going full blast.

Or so he thought till he saw one of the flight attendants. She looked pale and stunned, like the gal he knew who'd flunked her orals.

"This is the captain," the slightly Southern voice repeated. "We've just got word of . . . an emergency ahead. We are not going to be able to continue to Los Angeles. We will have to turn around and head back towards O'Hare. I am very sorry for the inconvenience, but this is unavoidable. I don't know yet whether we'll land in Chicago or somewhere between here and there. When I find out, be assured I will inform you pronto."

The PA system crackled into silence at the same time as the cabin exploded into noise. An emergency ahead? What the hell was that supposed to mean? What would make them turn around and head for Chicago again? A replay of 9/11? That was the first thing Bryce thought of.

As the plane began to turn, the guy in the seat next to his fired up his iPhone. You weren't supposed to do that in flight, but Bryce would have bet gold against gallstones his seatmate wasn't the only one breaking the rules right now. People wanted to know what the hell was going on. If the pilot wouldn't tell them, they'd find out for themselves.

Not thinking anything of it, Bryce looked out the window again. His eyes started to track across it, but then stopped as if physically seized. They had to be bugging out of their sockets.

He'd flown between anvil-topped thunderheads that towered higher into the sky than his airliner. Not often—most of the time, you stayed well above the weather—but he had. Those had been goddamn bumpy flights, too.

But those clouds'd gone up a little higher than his plane. That black column off in the distance ahead . . . If he hadn't seen it with his own eyes, he would have been sure it was impossible. Even seeing it, he thought it should have been. Not knowing how far away it was, he couldn't say how high up it went. He could say, though, that it went one hell of a lot higher than anything he'd ever imagined, let alone seen.

The guy next to him was staring at the iPhone as hard as Bryce was staring out the window. "Supervolcano," the man muttered to himself. "The fuck is a supervolcano?"

No one could possibly have dropped an icicle down Bryce's back. But that was how he felt. He knew what a supervolcano was. He might not have if not for Colin's new lady friend, but he did. Colin had taken Kelly seriously even before Yellowstone started bubbling over. Bryce hadn't known how seriously to take her, not then, especially since he was hearing her message delivered through Colin. He knew now, by God!

Other people in the window seats on his side of the plane were seeing that colossal—and seemingly expanding, too—cloud. The word *supervolcano* started rippling through the whole cabin. Not everybody seemed sure what all it meant, but it obviously wasn't good news.

"Does this mean we won't get to have dinner with Uncle

Louie tonight?" a woman said. Some people were not overburdened with brains.

"This is the captain one more time. If I could have your attention, please . . ." The man in the cockpit had to know the passengers were seething. "If I could have your attention, *please* . . ." He waited for them to settle down a little before continuing, "Some of you on the starboard side will have seen a large cloud of ash and dust rising into the upper atmosphere."

Naturally, all the people who hadn't seen it craned their necks in that direction, trying to get a glimpse. Bryce admired the pilot's power of understatement. A lesser man would have been incapable of it.

"That is why we're turning around," the pilot went on. "We can't fly over it, we don't dare fly through it—grit does bad things to turbine blades—and it doesn't look like we can go around it. There is some turbulence associated with this eruption. And I'm going to ask all of you who turned on your smart phones to for God's sake turn 'em off again. Getting our electronics screwed up right now would be the last thing we need. Thanks very much, folks."

Bryce would have hit the flight-attendant call button if the guy in the middle seat hadn't turned off the iPhone. Maybe he was worrying about the hazard too much. But if the captain was getting up in arms about it, he figured he was also entitled to.

Up ahead a few rows, somebody didn't want to squelch his BlackBerry. He loudly and profanely didn't want to, in fact. Aided by two other passengers, a flight attendant dispossessed him of it. That brought on more profanity.

"You can have it back when we land, sir," the stewardess said sweetly. Sweetly still, she added, "Then I hope you ram it up your stupid ass."

That startled the foulmouthed passenger into silence. You didn't expect someone in a service industry to shoot back at you with your own weapons. Bryce hadn't expected anything like that, either. Hearing it made him wonder how much trouble the flight might be in.

Up till then, he'd worried what the dickens he would do in Chicago once they got back there. He had nowhere to stay, he had a carry-on's worth of clothes, and he had no more money than any other grad student. Now he wondered whether they'd make it back. If that flight attendant felt she could let fly at a passenger, she was wondering the same thing.

Some turbulence associated with this eruption. The captain's bloodless phrase came back to Bryce. Suppose you dropped Rhode Island into a frying pan big enough to hold it—a figure of speech Colin liked, since, as Bryce had long known, he couldn't stand Rhode Island. What kind of shock wave would go through the air after you did that? How fast would it go? What would it do to any old airplane it happened to meet?

Those were all fascinating questions, weren't they? They sure were, especially that last one. Bryce's current perspective aboard one of those old airplanes made it even more intriguing.

He could do exactly nothing about it. He'd never felt helpless in this particular way before. The guy sitting next to him must have made the same kind of calculation, because out of the blue he said, "I did two tours in Afghanistan. When the mortars start coming in, you just hope you're lucky. After I got out of the Army, I didn't figure I'd ever have to worry about that kind of shit again, y'know?"

"Uh-huh." Bryce managed a nod. He wanted to freak out, but not in front of a bunch of strangers. How much of what got labeled bravery was really just fear of embarrassment?

He couldn't see the cloud any more; the airliner's turn meant it was behind them now. But he could imagine the shock wave tearing through the air and gaining on them every second. A bell chimed in the cabin. The seat-belt warning lights came on. "The captain has directed that everyone should return to their seats and remain there," the boss flight attendant declared on the PA. "This is due to safety concerns for all on board, and will be enforced as necessary."

That sounded tougher than airline personnel usually talked. Bryce thought of the Coke he'd had with his sandwich. Sooner or later, it would make itself known again. What was he supposed to do then if he couldn't get up? Pee in his airsick bag? Maybe. And men had it easier there than women did.

The engines changed note once more. They were working harder. If that meant the plane was going faster, Bryce was all for it. The intercom came back to life: "This is the captain speaking, folks. We have been cleared to land in Lincoln, Nebraska. We will be approaching from the northwest, and I will have you down on the ground just as soon as I possibly can. Do please stay in your seats, with your belts securely fastened. This may not be real pretty, but I will make it work."

One more piece of news that didn't sound so good. Bryce looked out the window again. They were coming down like mad bastards. No leisurely landing descent today. When the pilot said he wanted to get down fast, he wasn't kidding. Bryce's physical eyes saw farms and ponds and roads swell beneath him. His mind's eye saw a red needle on an altimeter sliding from right to left. Altimeters probably didn't look like that these days— everything now was bound to be digital. So his mind's eye wasn't as precise as it might have been. So what?

Lincoln. The University of Nebraska was there. What did he know about the University of Nebraska? They had a good football team and a good university press. Who was their ancient historian? What kind of classics department did they have? He'd talked with some of their people in Chicago. Now he might try to crash on them for a little while—they were as close to family as he had this side of Youngstown, Ohio.

He didn't want to think about crashing on right now, or crashing into, or crashing anything. When you analyzed poetry, you always had to remember the difference between literal and figurative language. Bryce was fully aware of it here. He still didn't want to think about crashing just now.

They weren't that far off the ground any more. If something went wrong, could they try landing on one of these country roads? They were long and straight, and most of them looked as if they took maybe one car a week. Not ideal runways, but better than nothing.

"Please raise your tray tables and return your seat backs to the fully upright position," the boss flight attendant said. "We may be a little early with this announcement, or—" She broke off, one word too late.

How many people noticed? The Afghan vet beside Bryce muttered "Fuck" under his breath, so he did. Some passengers still had no clue about how bad things were liable to be. A middle-aged woman—Bryce thought she was the gal who'd miss dinner with Uncle Louie—was indignantly complaining that an attendant had no right to keep her from getting up and going to the bathroom.

"I haven't got time to argue with you," the frazzled attendant snapped. "But if you even touch your goddamn seat belt, I'm gonna crown you with my solid-steel coffeepot. You hear me? You better, 'cause I mean it."

"I'll get you fired for this!" the passenger said shrilly.

"Now ask me if I care," the stewardess answered, and hurried to her own seat.

"This is the captain one more time." The drawl came out of the PA again. "I suggest you take a brace against your seat backs. We have some turbulence coming up behind us, and it may get kind of severe. Once the wind event is past, we'll take a look around and see where we're at then. Hang on, folks."

See where we're at then could only mean *see if we're still flying.* The veteran said "Fuck" again, more sincerely this time. It might have been a prayer. Across the aisle, a Hispanic woman was telling her rosary beads. Bryce Miller, a secular, bacon-scarfing Jew, wondered if she had some consolation he didn't. Too late for him to start praying now. He knew more about the dead religions of ancient Greece than about the one he'd been born into.

Then *something* gave the plane a kick in the ass. Bryce said "Fuck!" himself, very loudly. He couldn't even hear the obscenity through everybody else's chorus of screams and curses and prayers. He waited for the wings to come off or the skin to peel away from the fuselage. The only thing he hoped for in that moment was that it would all get over with in a hurry.

But the plane didn't come to pieces, though booms and crashes said carts were going cattywumpus no matter how well they'd been stowed. Oxygen masks deployed from the panels he'd never seen open before. Half the overhead luggage compartments flew open, too. They were stuffed so tight, though, that surprisingly few pieces flew out and clobbered people. It was the first advantage he'd ever found to charging for checked bags.

Someone in the cabin had thrown up and missed the airsick bag. Someone else—maybe more than one someone else—had shit him- or herself. Bryce hadn't, though he didn't know why not. In ultimate emergencies, human beings turned back into the animals they were beneath civilization and intelligence.

It wasn't quite so bad after the first big boot. The plane kept shaking, but on a lesser level. *Watch out for that first step,* Bryce thought dazedly. *It's a doozy.* In fact, as the screams eased off, it was as quiet as he'd ever known it to be inside a plane in flight.

Then he realized why. All the engines were out.

Which meant this wasn't an airliner any more. It was the

world's most expensive glider. The most expensive, not the best. It was way too heavy to be the best. Someone had once said the space shuttle glided like an aerodynamic brick. The airliner would do better than that. How much better? Bryce didn't know, but he was about to find out. The hard way.

"This is the captain." The man still sounded absurdly calm. Maybe that was attitude, maybe training. Whatever it was, Bryce admired it. Still easily, the pilot went on, "Some of you will have noticed our descent is now powerless. The turbulent airflow snuffed out our engines. We have not been able to get a restart. I'm sorry to tell you that we won't make it to Lincoln."

He paused. Perhaps he was human after all. "That means I am going to have to find a place to put this aircraft down. The best place we've got is dead ahead, a reservoir called Branch Oak Lake. I am going to try and pull a Sully. As he had, I've practiced this on the simulator many times. Now I get to do it for real, just like he did."

Another pause. "All I can do is give it my best shot. If you all stay as calm as you're able to, it'll help. I have radioed ahead to Lincoln. They will help us as quick as they can, and so will the folks around the reservoir. We'll be going in in about a minute and a half. You folks in the exit rows, you'll have a job to do. Listen to the flight attendants. Good luck to everybody, and God bless you all."

Seat cushion may be used for flotation, it said on the back of the seat in front of Bryce's—and on all the others. At least it didn't say *floatation*, the way it did on some airlines. For some idiot reason, the idea of going into the drink with a misspelled safety device weirded Bryce out.

He was four rows behind the exit. *I've got a chance*, he thought—if the plane didn't smash itself to smithereens hitting the water, if it didn't sink like a chunk of concrete, if, if, if . . .

"One more thing," the captain added from the speakers. "If

anybody goes for anything in the overhead bins, clobber the jerk and then step on him. This isn't the time to worry about your stuff. You've got enough other things to worry about, right?"

Both Bryce and the veteran beside him nodded. He looked out the window again. Here came the lake or reservoir or whatever the hell it was. It was mostly quiet in the cabin now. People had gone through panic and, with luck, come out the other side. The plane flashed past a bird, almost as a car might have on the 405. One more look . . . They were over water, closer by the second.

"Here we go," the captain said. "Take your brace again."

The airliner's belly smacked the smooth surface of Branch Oak Lake. The plane skipped like a stone, then almost instantly smacked again. This time, it stayed on the surface. The splash made Bryce's window useless. He didn't care. At least he hadn't got smashed to strawberry jam right away.

"Open the exit doors!" the boss flight attendant shouted, and then, "Passengers, remember your flotation devices! Help anyone near you who is injured!" One more afterthought, reminiscent of recess at elementary school: "Take turns!"

And damned if they didn't. A mad rush would have hopelessly clogged the exits. But the passengers moved toward them in an orderly hurry. Bryce paused at the edge of the aisle to let a woman go up ahead of him. "Thank you," she said.

"You're welcome," Bryce answered. He supposed there'd been scenes of such civility aboard the *Titanic*, too. The chilly water streaming in through the exit doors made the comparison much too apt. But it wasn't even up over his shoetops yet. He had no trouble moving against it.

When he got to the open door, a flight attendant and one of the big men from the exit row were standing on the wing helping people come out. "You all right?" the attendant asked.

"Shit, I'm alive," Bryce blurted.

She smiled. "There you go. Now off the wing and into the water. Get as far from the plane as you can."

He put his arms through the straps on the seat cushion and went into the lake. It didn't feel too cold once he got used to it. He'd been in pools that were worse. What it would feel like come February was bound to be a different question, but it wasn't February, thank God.

Kicking was awkward in his Adidases. He pulled them off. The plane settled behind him as he moved away from it. He hoped the captain would get out. Damned if the guy *hadn't* pulled a Sully. If the passengers had anything to say about it, he wouldn't be short of drinks or anything else he happened to want for the rest of his days.

"Some fun, huh?" The Afghan vet bobbed in the water a few feet away.

"I've had rides I liked better," Bryce replied. The other guy laughed.

The sky looked a million miles away from down here, even though Bryce had been flying a few minutes before. The ugly black cloud rearing over the western horizon had to be the same thing he'd seen up there.

Buzzing noises swelled from distant mosquitoes to up-close Harleys in a matter of minutes. Everybody who had a boat by Branch Oak Lake must have put it in the water. Corn-fed Cornhuskers started hauling people out of the drink. Bryce waved to make sure they saw him. When a guy in a baseball cap in one of the boats waved back and gave him a thumbs-up, he knew rescue was only a matter of time.

The Nebraskan picked up the veteran first, then put-putted over to Bryce. Strong, sunburned arms helped him out of the lake and into the bottom of the boat, where he lay like a just-caught bluegill—except he lacked the energy to flop around. "You okay, man?" his rescuer asked. "Everything in one piece?"

"I . . . think so," Bryce answered after taking stock. "Thank you."

"Yeah!" the Afghan vet said. "Thank you! Amen!" He sounded as if Bryce had reminded him of something important he'd been too rattled to remember on his own. And that was probably what had happened.

"I'm gonna see how many more folks we can get aboard," the local said, and got the boat going again. Bryce didn't care. He'd made it . . . so far.

XI

Squirt Frog and the Evolving Tadpoles were on I-95, heading north toward Portland, Maine, when the boom from the supervolcano roared over their van. They weren't taken by surprise; by then, NPR was tracking the progress of the enormous sound wave. "The biggest noise this poor old planet has heard in tens of thousands of years," one of their correspondents declared.

"Yeah—except for Congress," Rob Ferguson said.

Justin Nachman followed a snort with a reproachful look. "Piss and moan, piss and moan. Five minutes ago, you were bitching about paying the toll before they let us onto this stretch of the Interstate."

"Well, it sucks," Rob said.

"It's how they pay for keeping the road up," Justin said, as if reasoning with a possibly dangerous lunatic.

The van chose that moment to bounce on a pothole. Rob, who was driving, said, "They do a great job, too. We manage okay back home without this toll-road bullshit."

The lead guitarist rolled his eyes. "Give me a break, man.

How many years in a row is it that the California budget's been fucked up?"

Rob didn't know how many consecutive years it had been. He did know he couldn't remember a year when the budget hadn't been a disaster area. And he could remember further and further back as he got older: close to twenty-five years now, though he hadn't cared about the budget when he was a little kid. Twenty-five years seemed a hell of a long time to him. He'd never had the nerve to say anything like that to his father, though. He had what he was all too sure was an accurate suspicion the older man would have laughed in his face.

Since he didn't have a good comeback for Justin, he concentrated on making miles. Charlie and Biff were in the other van, right behind this one. They were on their own. Snakes and Ladders *had* dissolved in New York City, and they hadn't booked another opening act.

Rob wondered what his bandmates thought of the supervolcano. They knew about it: everybody'd been talking about it when the band stopped at a roadside Hardee's for lunch. Seeing the star on something called Hardee's weirded Rob out every time he came East. In his part of the country, the chain that served those same burgers went by Carl's Jr. Well, Best Foods mayonnaise was Hellman's back here, too. Bizarre, all right. He wondered if there was a song in it.

"Devastation continues to spread across wide stretches of Wyoming, Idaho, and Montana," the NPR newsman continued gravely. "There are as yet not even the vaguest estimates of lives lost or property damage. Nor is there any way to stop the spreading ash cloud. An astronomer has calculated that the supervolcano eruption might well be observable from the planet Mars."

"Wow," Justin said. "Can you imagine the Martians going, 'Bummer, man! The Earth is screwed big-time!'"

Rob could imagine it. "Write that down," he said. "We should be able to do something with it." It sure as hell made a better song idea than artery-cloggers with the wrong names.

The band always took *Write that down* seriously. Stuff that was supposed to stay in people's heads too often didn't. Justin produced a notebook and wrote. Better than even money nothing would come from the jotting, but at least it wouldn't get lost.

They had reservations at a motel not far from the airport. Rob had spent enough time on the road that he was good at it, which didn't mean he got off on it. There were times when he'd wake up cold sober, not wasted on anything, but still without the faintest idea of where the hell he was. The feeling didn't always disappear right away, either. Rooms rarely gave a clue. Cable stations were the same everywhere, pretty much. If a paper was shoved under the door or waiting outside, odds were it would be *USA Today*. Hotel management types commonly felt it was better than the local rag. The sad thing was, they'd be right more often than not.

By the time he got down to breakfast, he'd usually have things figured out—usually, but not always. He liked playing. He liked performing. He liked the small-scale celebrity status being in a halfway successful band brought. Travel . . . He wasn't so sure about travel.

There were guys older than his father who'd play a gig, hop in a car, and play at another club five hundred miles away the next night. Some of them had been big once upon a time and were still hanging on. Some had made a career out of being second-stringers. They had their fans—not enough to get rich from, but enough to pay the bills. Most of them. Most of the time.

That seemed to be about what Squirt Frog and the Evolving Tadpoles had to look forward to. *Do I want to wake up wondering where I am when I'm fifty?* Rob asked himself that question, and another one, every time he checked in somewhere. The other question was, *Do I want to wake up wondering where I am when I'm seventy?*

So far, he hadn't found anything else he wanted to do more. He hadn't found any place where he wanted to grow roots, either. So tonight here he was in Portland, Maine. He'd played in the other Portland, too.

Justin sometimes got sick of life on the road, the same way he did. As far as Rob could tell, Biff and Charlie didn't care where they were. For guys in a band that needed to stay on tour—and, in this age of MP3s and iTunes, how many bands didn't?—that was the right attitude.

After they checked in, Justin asked the desk clerk, "Where can we get some dinner around here? Doesn't have to be fancy. Just, y'know, food."

She named a place, adding, "They've got the best lobster rolls in Portland, I think."

"How do we get there?" Rob asked eagerly. He was in favor of lobster and shrimp and crab. If the rest of the guys weren't, well, the menu was bound to have other stuff on it they could eat.

Directions didn't sound too complicated. The band kept talking about getting GPS. God knew the systems were cheap these days. But Rob and Justin both liked to navigate. Finding a place on your own made arriving mean something it didn't when a computer held your hand all the way there. Even getting lost could be interesting. Rob thought so, anyhow. Charlie and Biff thought their bandmates were full of it. But they'd never missed a gig because they'd got lost, so the rhythm guitarist and drummer didn't grumble. Much.

A roll, split in half. A little mayo, even if under an assumed name. Lobster—lots of lobster. A lobster roll. A Maine specialty. The finest invention since the wheel, as far as Rob was concerned. Maine was one of the few places where lobster didn't cost an arm and a leg. Rob was happy to pay a mere arm for such concentrated deliciosity.

Justin had a big bowl of clam chowder—creamy, of course, with not a tomato in sight. Tomato chowder was a New York City thing, not a New England one. The divide was as fierce as Yankees and Red Sox. Rob actually liked both kinds, which made him either a neutral or a heretic, depending.

Charlie got a chicken pot pie. You could do that anywhere. Biff ordered the burrito. Rob didn't think he would have chosen a lobster roll in Phoenix. A burrito in Portland, Maine, struck him as an equally bad idea. But it wasn't his stomach. Sometimes the less you said to the guys you played with, the better off you were.

When they walked out of the restaurant, the sun was going down. It looked like . . . a sunset. The only screwy thing about it, as far as Rob was concerned, was that the Atlantic was at his back and the sun was sinking toward land. He was conditioned to think of the sun coming up over land and going down in the Pacific. This felt wrong—wrong enough for him to say something about it.

The other guys were all Californians, too. They nodded. "Hadn't thought about it, but you're right," Biff said.

"I read somewhere that after Krakatoa blew up, sunsets were spectacular for a couple of years because of all the dust and ash in the air," Justin said. "I was kind of hoping for something fancier than—this." He waved across the parking lot at the ordinary red ball going down into the ordinarily reddening western sky.

"Give me a break, man!" Rob exclaimed. "It just happened a few hours ago, you know."

"Yeah, yeah." Justin had the grace to sound sheepish. "But this thing is a lot bigger than Krakatoa, too. This thing is a lot bigger than, well, anything. I mean, it happened in fucking Wyoming, and we heard it here."

"Instant gratification, that's all you want, dude." Rob wanted to bite his tongue. Damned if he didn't sound like his father. If you played in a band and your old man was a cop, what did that say about you? Nothing good, for sure.

"Hey, who doesn't want gratification?" Charlie said. "We'll pick up some girls after we play."

"There you go!" Justin and Biff said the same thing at the same time in the same enthusiastic tone. Rob didn't, but it wasn't as if he hated the idea. It wasn't as if he didn't do it himself, either. What was the point of even fairly small celebrity, after all, if you didn't take advantage of it?

Why this is hell, nor am I out of it. Vanessa remembered that was a line from a play, but not which one or who'd written it. Things she was interested in, she remembered—and she'd hit you over the head with the details, too. What she didn't care about was as one with Nineveh and Tyre . . . which was also a line from something or other. From what? Who cared? If she ever needed to find out for some reason she couldn't imagine now, she could always Bing it.

If she got the chance, she could. Denver was also becoming as one with Nineveh and Tyre. She'd never dreamt it could happen so fast. Ash started raining down on the city—Jesus Christ, ash started raining down on the whole goddamn state—the day after the supervolcano went off.

Vanessa got up that morning intending to go back to Amalgamated Humanoids. There hadn't been any earthquakes big enough to wake her up during the night. She had power again; her digital alarm clock buzzed her at a quarter past six, as she'd set it to do when the electricity came on again. So, volcano or no volcano, everything should have been pretty much back to normal.

Well, almost everything. Pickles remained one freaked-out

kitty, and who could blame him? Cats and cataclysms didn't mix well.

She soon discovered she didn't mix so well with cataclysms, either. When she opened the blinds after she got dressed, everything was grayish brown: the walkway outside the apartment, the stairs, the grass in the courtyard, the air, everything. She could barely see across the courtyard to the apartments on the other side—there was that much crap in the air. The breeze made it drift and billow, now thinner, now thicker.

"Fuck!" Vanessa said, which exactly summed up how she felt. She'd looked forward to watching snow fall in Denver. It was something she'd never seen before; she was an L.A. kid, all right. What was out there now seemed like a filthy parody of the genuine article.

Somebody across the courtyard opened his door and headed for his car. He took about three steps before he started coughing and frantically rubbing his eyes at the same time. His shoes kicked up ghostly clouds of dust and ash. He turned around and went right back into his place as fast as he could.

How much volcanic ash did he bring in with him? Enough to keep him coughing and rubbing for the next week? Vanessa wouldn't have been surprised. She was glad she'd seen him. Otherwise, she would have charged out there herself. All of a sudden, that didn't look like such a great idea.

Instead, after coffee and some oatmeal, she went back into the bedroom and turned on the TV. She'd already given Pickles his usual morning kitty treats. Now he jumped up beside her on the bed and meowed for more. The world had broken routine, she'd broken routine—why shouldn't he? She fed him. If food made him happy, or at least happier, fine.

Then she opened up the bedroom blinds. The Black-and-White Fairy—actually, the Shades of Grayish Brown Fairy—had touched that side of the building, too. Dust drifted the vacant lot next door. The house on the far side of the house was painted a pink hotter than Vanessa would have used for anything but lipstick. You sure couldn't prove it now.

A couple of cars chugged by on the street. Their lights speared through the dust as if it were fog. They kicked up enormous, plumy wakes of ash as they went. One of them stopped before it got to the corner. The driver popped the hood and got out. Then, like the fellow in the apartment across from Vanessa's, the gal got in again and slammed the door. Only dimly visible, her hazard lights came on.

"This sucks. Big-time," Vanessa said. Pickles meowed again. If that wasn't agreement, she'd never heard it from the cat.

She turned on the TV. A talking head on CNN was going on about the climatic implications of the eruption. That wasn't what Vanessa needed to hear. If you were somewhere else, somewhere far away, you could afford to talk about such things. Vanessa wanted to know what to do about the mess she was in the middle of.

She grabbed the remote again and fired an infrared beam at the set. CNN gave way to local news. It was news for morons, but the other local morning news shows were news for imbeciles. If not good, this was better.

It wasn't the usual morning crew, but the gang who'd done the eleven o'clock news the night before. They were in the same clothes. They looked tired. One of them sipped from a styrofoam cup.

"If you're wondering where Jud and Mariska and Meteorologist Mark are, they were advised not to come in today," she said, setting the cup down. "Everyone in the Denver area is advised not to travel today—or for the foreseeable future—unless it's absolutely necessary. This is an emergency the likes of which we've never known."

Newsies usually laid things on with a trowel, to say nothing of a shovel. Vanessa began to think that they weren't exaggerating this time. Looking out the bedroom window again, she wondered if anybody could exaggerate this.

The advice the night newswoman gave was simple. *Don't go outside. If you have to go outside, for God's sake don't breathe.* That was fine for the moment. What happened when you ran out of food, though? If you had a choice between filling your lungs with crud and going hungry, which should you pick? If it wasn't *Don't know whether to shit or go blind*, what would be?

"Ash continues to fall," the weary-looking blonde said, brushing back a lock of hair that had come loose in spite of spray. News for morons, sure as hell. "Some geologists believe it may get three feet deep all over the Denver metropolitan area before it lets up. Roof collapses are probable, especially in case of rain."

"Urk!" Vanessa said, a dismayed noise she'd got from her old man. She hadn't thought of that. How much would a layer of volcanic ash three feet deep on a roof weigh? How much would it weigh after absorbing as much rainwater as it could hold? How much weight would a roof be designed to take? Some, sure, because roofs here had to hold up against snow. But that much?

Every time she heard a creak overhead, she was gonna freak out. She could see that coming like a rash. You weren't supposed to go outside into the ash. They'd made that abundantly clear. But what if the ash decided to come to you instead? It was a good question. Vanessa wished she, or somebody, could come up with a good answer.

After commercials—this didn't seem to be an urgent enough emergency to dispense with selling the product—a newsman whose boyish charm had worn thin by this hour said, "No one is sure yet whether mandatory evacuation of Denver and the surrounding areas will become necessary. The Governor, who was in

Lamar at the time of the eruption, has ordered out the National Guard to assist in protecting Colorado lives and property."

A newcomer to the state, Vanessa didn't know where the hell Lamar was. A road atlas showed her: out in the southeast, in cow country near the Kansas border. The governor was one lucky stiff. That put him a couple of hundred miles farther away from the eruption. Things might not be so bad out there.

Since the nighttime sports guy was still in the studio, he came on the air. The end of the Rockies' season and the early part of the Broncos' season had gone on indefinite hold. Vanessa despised baseball and football impartially. The only thing she wondered was which wasted more time.

Then the worn-looking newsman came back and said, "Snowplows are doing their best to keep the Interstates open south and east of the city to facilitate evacuation in the event that the authorities decide to implement it. No one knows how long the big machines' air filters can continue to protect them from the grit in the air. By the same token, no one knows how long the volcanic ash will keep on raining down from the sky, either." He added something he might not have been reading off his teleprompter: "Right now, nobody seems to know much of anything, folks."

Vanessa loathed *facilitate* and *implement* almost as much as she hated *impact*. They were stupid and pretentious. People used them to sound important and knowledgeable, and ended up sounding like pompous assholes instead.

But if I-25 and I-70 were open, at least partway . . . Shouldn't she get the hell out while the getting was possible even if not exactly good? If they were already thinking about evacuation, Denver was really and truly screwed. In the way of bureaucrats, the authorities were nerving themselves before doing what they plainly needed to do.

She looked out the window again. That car was still stuck there, with others easing around it and kicking up more dust and ash as they went. How long would her own elderly Corolla last? Wouldn't she be worse off if she got stuck somewhere in the middle of nowhere—which, to her, defined all of Colorado outside Denver—than if she sat tight?

Not necessarily. If the plows couldn't keep the highways open, how long would the town still have food? How would anybody bring it in? What would happen if—no, when—the waterworks stopped working? Or when the roofs started buckling and people discovered they couldn't breath indoors, either?

She was a cop's kid. Spinning out disaster scenarios came easy. So did knowing that most people would sit tight till it was too late, then start running around like chickens that had just met the chopper. That was what most people did. She'd seen it for herself; she didn't need to remember her father's scorn for the common run of civilian.

And since that was what the common run of civilian did, it behooved her not to do likewise. Her mind made up, she threw some clothes and pills and tampons and a couple of books into an overnight bag. She added bottles of water, granola bars, and anything else edible she could grab that wouldn't go bad right away. She also threw in kibbles and treats for the cat. If she slung the bag over her shoulder and carried the cat carrier in one hand, she'd be able to keep the other one free, and she needed that.

Pickles hated going into his carrier any old time. He knew going outside meant trouble—the vet and other notorious cat-torturers. And he particularly hated it when he was all jumpy anyhow. He scratched her but good before she finally stuffed him in there. "You'd better be worth it, you stupid fuzzhead," she snapped before she sprayed the wounds with Bactine. That little bottle went into the overnight, too.

Then she soaked a towel in the kitchen sink and draped it over the cat carrier. She soaked another one for herself.

"Are you sure you want to do this?" she said aloud in a voice whose calm surprised her. As a matter of fact, she wasn't remotely sure. *Damned if you do, damned if you don't* was another old phrase that fit much too well. She might be worse off bailing out; she might be worse off staying. The swirling gray-brown grit outside warned that she might be in over her head no matter what she did.

You could die out there. Or right here. That was what it boiled down to. Vanessa had always been the kind who *did* something when she had a choice between that and sitting tight. She wouldn't have given Bryce the heave-ho if she weren't. She wouldn't have followed Hagop to Denver, either.

Yeah, and look how well that turned out, her mind jeered. L.A. wouldn't be catching it like this.

But she wasn't in L.A. She had to do what looked best where she was. "Fuck," she said one more time, and lugged her chattels to the apartment door. Pickles yowled mournfully. "Shut up," she suggested. He yowled some more. Ignoring him, she shouldered the overnight bag and draped her own wet towel over her eyes and nose and mouth. It didn't want to stay, so she secured it with a rubber band.

The next little while would have to be in Braille. She opened the door, got the cat carrier out, and closed it behind her. She groped till she grabbed the iron railing that would take her to the stairs and followed it till she found them. *Left turn*, she reminded herself. Sixteen stairs down to the courtyard, right? Take 'em slow. You can't watch what you're doing.

At what she thought was the bottom, she felt around with her foot. Concrete, sure enough—concrete with a bunch of new grit on top. The stucco wall that led to the parking garage would be over to the right. To her vast relief, her hand brushed rough plaster. Okay. She knew where she was again.

Anyone who could see her was probably laughing his ass off. Too damn bad. Anyone who could see her was inside an apartment, which meant the sorry son of a bitch had his own problems. She patted the wall every step or two to guide herself along. She didn't want the stucco ripping up her fingers, especially after the number the cat had done on the back of her hand.

She patted again—and felt nothing. "Ha! Found it!" she exclaimed in triumph. Here was the opening for the stairway down to her car. Some more groping got her to the rail attached to the stairway wall.

Down she went. How many stairs till she got to the bottom? Sixteen from her place to the courtyard, but how many going below? She couldn't remember. She guessed it would be sixteen again, and slammed her foot against flat concrete flooring, hard, when that proved one too many. Taking a stair that wasn't there was almost as bad as missing one that was. But she didn't fall.

After a couple of steps away from the stairwell, she adjusted the rubber band and let the towel drop away from her eyes, though not from her nose and mouth. She had to see to get to her car, and she had to see to drive. Things weren't so bad here as they were up top. The air was still dusty, and there was grit with footprints going through it on top of the smooth concrete. It wasn't already hideously thick, though, the way it was in the courtyard.

She chucked her bag into the car, then stuck Pickles on the passenger seat. She draped a blanket on the overnight bag so nobody peering in could see it was there. At another time, she would have stashed it in the trunk. Not today. The less she got in and out, the better. She was just glad the tank was almost full.

As soon as she started the motor, she turned on the lights. You wouldn't normally need them during the day in Denver, but what did *normally* mean now? Nada, that was what. She backed out of her space. "Good-bye, God. I'm going . . . someplace," she said. Kansas? New Mexico? Some place where things like this didn't happen, like the frogs in *Cannery Row*.

She didn't have to open the window to use a card to open the gate. A beam sensed the car coming up. The gate slid back. Was it her imagination, or did the thing sound creakier, squeakier, than usual? What was all that volcanic grit doing to its mechanism? How long would it keep working? That wasn't her worry. As long as the thing had opened this time . . .

Vanessa drove slowly and carefully. A good thing, too. Somebody'd already rear-ended the car that crapped out down the street from her building. She skirted the fender-bender and went on. When she tried the radio, all she got was static. She pulled out her phone. No bars. She swore. What the hell was going on? TV back at the place had worked.

Sure it had. It was cable. But how many zillions of tons of crud were fouling the air right now? How much of that crud was tiny bits of iron? Some small fraction, no doubt. But a small fraction of a zillion was still a jillion: plenty to jam radio and phone signals. Vanessa cussed some more. She hadn't figured on that.

She hadn't figured on any of this. Who had? Who could have, except for a handful of crazy geologists? Only they'd turned out not to be so crazy after all, hadn't they?

Traffic lights were still working, but you couldn't see them till you got right on top of them—if then. She drove around more dead cars, and around a couple of more accidents, too. One of them looked bad: an SUV had broadsided a car at an intersection. Maybe the driver hadn't seen the light till too late.

Here was Mississippi Avenue. She turned left, ever so warily. Buckingham Square Shopping Center was only a couple of blocks east. Not far past it, she could get on the 225, and it would take her down to I-25 or up to I-70: whatever her little heart desired.

Her little heart desired to be back in L.A. The 225 wouldn't give her that, not directly. But it would get her started.

Kelly Birnbaum was four-hundred-odd miles from the center-piece of her academic career. She'd passed her doctoral orals not least by explaining in great detail what might happen if the Yellowstone supervolcano ever went off. Looking back on that terrifying morning in the Geology Department conference room, she'd done pretty goddamn well.

Only one trouble left: she couldn't get any closer, to see for herself just how smart she'd been. Ash had dusted Missoula, but only dusted it. The coating here was thicker than the ash from a bad brushfire would have been in California, but not a whole lot thicker. Missoula lay almost straight upwind from the eruption. Both surface winds and the jet stream blew stuff away from here. And Missoula got dusted anyway.

You could go fifty miles down the Interstate if you had a super-duper air filter on your car. If you had a vehicle with a super-duper air filter and caterpillar treads, you might make a hundred miles from Missoula. If you were real lucky, you could get to Butte.

Farther than that? No way, José. Wasn't gonna happen. The ash was too thick. The wind had already started blowing it into drifts that were thicker yet. I-90 was buried deeper than alas poor Yorick had been before they started playing catch with his skull.

Planes and helicopters were even more fugheddaboutit than cars. If your car's air filter clogged past survivability, you were stuck, yeah, but at least you were stuck on the ground. If your aircraft's filter died, so did you. It was a long way down.

She was still living at Daniel's apartment along with Ruth and Larry. Daniel had got a cot so he wouldn't spend all his nights on the floor in a sleeping bag. He'd offered the cot to

Larry, but the older man actually liked the couch. Kelly and Ruth shared the bed. The one-bedroom place was crowded. The geologists got on one another's nerves. Nobody complained too much, though. They all knew things could have been worse.

Refugees packed Missoula. Everyone who'd managed to escape from places farther east seemed to have stopped right here. No apartments or hotel rooms were to be had for love or money. People who'd never met till they got here found themselves living together as intimately as the geologists were. Plenty of people were sleeping in their cars or in tents—and living like that in Missoula as fall replaced summer and warned of winter ahead was not for the fainthearted.

Kelly would have been glad to get out. Her own small Berkeley apartment took on the aura of the earthly paradise in her memory. But no flights came into or went out of Missoula International. They were near the edge of the no-fly zone, but they were in it—the air was too foul. She couldn't afford a car, even a one-trip beater. Prices had skyrocketed because so many people wanted to get away. Not even trains were coming into town. She was stuck.

She did what she could with her cell phone and with Daniel's computer. He'd created new user accounts for her and Ruth and Larry. They took turns on the machine and tried not to hog it. But walking away from the apartment and talking on the phone where no one else could hear her was the biggest pleasure she got most days.

If she'd had her druthers, she would have talked Colin's ear off. But he was still working, and had his own worries. If you had to be somewhere when the supervolcano erupted, L.A. wasn't the worst place. Something within shouting distance of normal life still went on there . . . not that a cop's so-called normal life was anything to write home about.

Even so, it had to beat Missoula. "There's nothing fresh in

the stores," Kelly complained. "No fruit, no salad fixings, no vegetables—well, a few potatoes."

Across the miles and the wireless link, Colin chuckled. "You're right next door to Idaho, remember. Spud paradise, right?"

"I guess," Kelly said. "Next to no fresh meat, either, and no fish at all. Most of what we're getting is canned goods, stuff that keeps."

"It makes sense, you know," Colin said.

"That doesn't mean I've got to like it," she answered.

"Nope. Prices are way up here. There's talk about doing something to stop profiteers," Colin said. "What's it like there?"

"About the same—through the roof," Kelly told him. "People bitch like you wouldn't believe."

"Who says I wouldn't?"

"Okay, maybe you would. They wouldn't complain so much if they could get what they wanted. There isn't even much fresh bread here. Noodles and rice and flour take up less space and last longer, so that's what they ship in."

"What do you do with flour if you don't have much in the way of anything to bake it with?" Colin asked.

People in Missoula were starting to ask the same question, only louder. Kelly had an answer, though not one she'd offered the locals: "Matzos, what else?"

"Huh." In multicultural Los Angeles, Colin would know about matzos. He clinched it by saying, "Will that get you converts or a bunch of raving anti-Semites?"

He took Kelly by surprise—so much so that she laughed out loud. She laughed loud enough, in fact, to make an unshaven guy in a sweatshirt and ratty jeans give her a funny look. Despite his shabby appearance, he might have been anything from a wino to a bank president. Missoula was a funky place these days. Kelly didn't care what he was, as long as he didn't bother her. "I love you, Colin!" she said.

"Well, I love you, too, babe," he answered. They didn't throw the word around like a Frisbee. He was chary about using it at all. Considering how he'd been burned, Kelly had never blamed him for that. She wished she heard it more, though; it warmed her every time she did. Stuck in Missoula, Montana, in autumn, she needed all the warming she could get.

And this was only the beginning. The very beginning of the beginning, in fact.

Colin added, "I sure wish you were here and not there."

"Jesus, so do I!" Kelly said. "No way, though. Not even the Greyhounds are running yet. I'll escape sooner or later."

"Sooner, I hope. Let me see what I can do from this end," Colin said. "I've been working on a couple of things, but they haven't panned out yet. I'll keep trying. Didn't want to say anything about it, 'cause I can't promise. All I can do is try, same as you."

"O-kay," Kelly said. How many strings could a Socal police lieutenant pull in Montana, or maybe Idaho? What kind of connections did Colin have, to make him think he could pull any at all? Had he, say, spent ten years working alongside somebody who was now a county sheriff up here, or chief of police in some little town near the state line?

Kelly realized she had no idea. It didn't seem impossible, or even unlikely, but she couldn't have proved it one way or the other. There was a lot she didn't know about this man whose company she longed for.

She could have asked him, but what good would it have done? Either he'd finagle something, or he wouldn't. Or maybe the trains or buses would start up again, or she'd be able to find a ride heading west, or . . . something.

She said her good-byes and went back to Daniel's apartment. It had a TV, and it had books she was interested in reading. Stacked up against the rest of Missoula, that made it seem like heaven on earth, even if this particular version of heaven was on the crowded side.

Daniel was out when she got there: probably at the university. They were trying to get the fall semester going, though the odds seemed poor. She envied Daniel his place here. He fit in. It made a difference.

Larry and Ruth were there, though, and greeted her with long faces. "What now?" Kelly asked, wondering if she really wanted to know.

"The gas is out," Ruth answered. "I was going to heat up some corned-beef hash"—more stuff in cans—"but the stove doesn't work. Nothing's coming through the burners—you'd smell it if it was."

Kelly found the next reasonable question: "Have you called the gas company yet?"

"No, the gas is really out. As in, there is no gas in Missoula any more," Larry said. "The big pipeline that brings it into town comes from the east, through Montana. I don't know how much ash and rock the supervolcano put down on top of it, but enough to finally squash it or break it, looks like."

"That's . . . not so good," Kelly said. The other geologists nodded. No gas for stoves, no gas for heating water, no gas for heating houses? That was about as *not so good* as it got. Missoula was a place where you needed to be able to heat houses. Did you ever! And the weather wouldn't get *better* on account of the Yellowstone eruption. Oh, no.

"I was thinking, what happens if the electricity goes next?" Ruth said.

There was a cheery notion. "Welcome back to the nineteenth century, that's what," Kelly said. Only the twenty-first-century world wasn't ready to fall back more than a hundred years. Not even close. Unfortunately, the supervolcano didn't care whether the twenty-first-century world was ready. Ready or not, here it came.

XII

It was a quiet Saturday afternoon in Ellwood. There were times when Marshall Ferguson didn't appreciate his dad for getting him an apartment here rather than in Isla Vista, which was right next to the UC Santa Barbara campus. But his old man the cop had learned of Isla Vista's many bars and of couch-burning and other quaint native rituals, so Marshall was out in the boonies instead.

Nothing exciting had happened in Ellwood since that Japanese submarine shelled the place. But living here wasn't *so* bad. Marshall didn't mind riding his bike to school, or hopping on the bus on the rare days when the weather was bad. He had a car—of course!—but campus parking cost two arms and a leg. He could get anything he needed at the big shopping center on Hollister, just a few blocks away. And it wasn't as if Ellwood had no bars; it just didn't have quite so many. It was still a student town, but a quieter student town for quieter students.

No, not so bad. It wasn't as if Marshall never drank. Oh, no—not even close. Like his father was a teetotaler. As if! Like his mother had never got up on a Sunday morning making a beeline for the Excedrin. Yeah, right!

But he wasn't smashed on this Ellwood Saturday afternoon. He could have been. The quarter was still new. Nothing needed turning in Monday morning. So, yeah, he could have been, but he wasn't. He was stoned instead.

The apartment faced west, so he could sprawl on the ratty but unburnt couch in his front room and watch the sun go down through the Venetian blinds' half-open slats. Sprawled next to him was a little dark-haired girl named Jenny. They weren't touching right now. Sooner or later, he expected they would. No hurry, though. No hurry at all.

Not hurrying, he passed her the pipe. "Thanks," she said. He liked the way her lips closed on the stem as she inhaled. The apartment was already fragrant with smoke. It got a little more so.

She gave the pipe back. He took another hit himself. It was all good: the dope, the company, the half-dark room, the sun slowly sliding down between the slats. Thanks to the dope, it seemed to slide slower than usual.

"Wow," Marshall said. Jenny giggled—if that wasn't *the* stoner cliché, what was? Even wasted, Marshall was embarrassed. But he pointed out through the blinds and defiantly said "Wow" again. This time, he amplified it: "That's quite a sunset, you know?"

Santa Barbara sunsets, like a lot of Santa Barbara life, often spoiled you and made you feel every other place in the world was tacky and not worth living in. Clouds and soft, moist Pacific air painted the sky in red and orange and gold. Could nightfall in, say, Omaha come close? Not a chance.

This one was outdoing itself, even by Santa Barbara standards. Marshall blamed the good weed he'd got from a grad student in the creative-writing program. It made him feel pretty goddamn creative himself, though he would have been too languid to write even without a little dark-haired girl within arm's reach.

But seriously, would he have seen all those wild colors if he weren't baked? Reds and maroons and tangerines and carmines and lemons and lavenders and magentas and fuchsias and how many others the Crayola people had never heard of? He didn't think so.

"This is *good* dope," he said seriously.

"It is," Jenny agreed. She held out her hand. Marshall's fingers brushed hers when he gave her the pipe. They both smiled. They had time. When you're young and wasted, time stretches like taffy. She sucked in more smoke. After a while, she blew it out. She admired day's decline for a while. Then she said, "It's not just the dope."

"Huh?" Marshall said.

"It's not just the dope," Jenny repeated. "It's the volcano thing in Yellowstone, too. It's, like, put a lot of stuff in the air. Sunsets all over will be special for a while."

"Oh." Marshall nodded. "Cool." He seemed to remember that big volcanoes did that. The one they'd made the old movie about . . . He tried to come up with the name. It was on the tip of his tongue, but chasing it down seemed like more trouble than it was worth. A lot of things seemed like more trouble than they were worth.

A lot of things, but not all. He slid the palm of his hand along the warm, smooth skin on the inside of Jenny's forearm. It felt something like velvet, something like electricity. Some of that was normal, healthy horniness. Some of it was the dope, too. Girls were wonderful any old time. They got wonderfuler after a few bowls. Hey, what didn't? And he was sure the volcano had nothing to do with it.

Jenny made a noise down deep in her throat that sounded more like a cat's purr than human noises had any business doing. Her eyes sparkled. Dope definitely made it better for people of the female persuasion, too. She slid toward him.

They kissed for a while on the couch. Then they went into the bedroom. Marshall's bed was narrow for two, but that just meant they had to press together tighter. The amazing sunset played itself out in the front-room wall, forgotten.

The gig at Bar Harbor turned out to be a mistake. The club crowd there didn't get Squirt Frog and the Evolving Tadpoles, and it worked both ways. New England seaside vacation towns seemed different from their Pacific equivalents. Rob Ferguson tried to figure out what made these people tick. It wasn't easy.

Some of the crowd were leftover summer people. Not all of them went back to Boston and New York City right after Labor Day. Some stuck around and kept partying till . . . what? Till their money ran out? Not likely—they weren't the kind whose money ever seemed likely to run out. Till the cows came home, was the way it looked to Rob.

The rest were Maine townies. Summer people and townies. It reminded him of Eloi and Morlocks in *The Time Machine*. And why not? Wells had been talking about the class system in Victorian England. The class system remained alive and well on the East Coast of the modern USA.

For the summer people, the band was just background noise. The townies saw amplified instruments and expected—hell, demanded—straight-ahead, raucous rock. Neither was what Squirt Frog and the Evolving Tadpoles was all about. You needed to pay attention to the band, and it wasn't about head-banging or about ears that stayed stunned three days after the show.

A good time was had by few.

Afterwards, Justin put the best face on things he could: "Maybe Bangor will be better."

"Or Orono," Rob said. "Orono's got a University of Maine campus. Our kind of people will be listening to us."

"Stoned freaks and geeks, you mean?" Biff Thorvald said.

Rob made as if to bow to the rhythm guitarist, but there wasn't room in the cramped dressing room. "Precisely," he said.

"You know what the real trouble is?" As Justin often did, he answered his own question: "The real trouble is, there aren't enough stoned freaks and geeks running around loose to support us in the style we'd like to get accustomed to."

"If you mean we ain't gonna get rich like Miley Cyrus and Justin Bieber, why don't you come out and say so?" Charlie Storer demanded.

"We ain't gonna get rich like Miley Cyrus and Justin Bieber," Justin said obligingly.

"We don't have some corporate dickhead telling us what to do next, either," Rob said.

"Of course not. We know what to do next: go on to the next town," Charlie said. "Play there, then head for the one after that."

Rob remembered his own uneasy thoughts of not too long ago. Did he like doing this enough to keep at it the rest of his life? Could he make a living at it if he did? If he didn't, what would he do instead?

They got to stay in Bar Harbor; with most of the summer people gone, prices dropped like a stone. The desk clerk at their motel said, "We've had a Secretary of Labor stay in one of your rooms."

"Not after Labor Day, you didn't," Rob answered. She gave him a dirty look, but didn't try to tell him he was wrong. Afterwards, he was sorry he'd pissed her off; he'd seen plenty worse. As usual, afterwards was too late.

Summer weather seemed to have gone home with the summer people. The sun came up in blood-drenched splendor from the Atlantic, tinting the stacked clouds every shade of red and purple and red and pink and orange imaginable. Sunsets had been just as spectacular since the supervolcano let go. When TV pundits weren't bemoaning everything else about the disaster—deaths were well up into six figures, and damage estimates heading toward the trillions—they talked learnedly about particulate matter.

Eyeing the sunrise, Justin put it a different way: "My grandfather went to sea in freighters for a few years when he was about the age we are now. He always used to say, 'Red in the night—sailors' delight. Red in the morning? Sailors take warning.'"

"A bunch of nervous sailors out there, then," Rob predicted.

"I wouldn't be surprised." Justin shivered in the parking lot. "Brr! That's one nasty wind."

"Yeah. Well, welcome to Maine," Rob said. But nervous sailors wouldn't have surprised him, either. He wished he'd put on something heavier than an old UCSB sweatshirt. The wind seemed to have taken a running start from Baffin Island.

"How soon does it start snowing here?" Justin asked. Sure as hell, other cloud fortresses, these more ominous gray and less pretty pink, were stacking up to the north and west.

"I'd say tomorrow, or maybe this afternoon," Rob answered. "We've got chains for the vans, right?"

"Uh-huh," Justin said without enthusiasm. They weren't practiced at putting them on. They weren't practiced at driving in snow and ice, either. They were California kids. What did they need to know about that kind of stuff?

Trying to cheer up the lead guitarist—or something—Rob said, "Bangor and Orono are north of here, right?"

"Fuck you," Justin explained. He pointed to the diner across the street. They'd had dinner there the night before. It was okay. "C'mon. Let's go feed our faces."

"You don't want to wait for Charlie and Biff?"

"Nah. Let 'em sleep if they want to. They'll eat sooner or later. And Bangor's not that far north from here." Justin used the word with more irony than Rob had. "Even if we leave later than usual, we'll make our next date."

Breakfast was pretty good. You never could tell with local

places. They were like the little girl with the little curl. With Denny's, you always knew what you were getting—which was both the good and the bad news. This proved a step, even a step and a half, up from that. The potatoes that went into the hash browns were fresh, not frozen, and not too greasy. The same with the sausage, which had a hint of something—fennel?—you didn't taste every day. And the over-medium eggs came to the table hot and exactly over medium.

Biff and Charlie ambled in when Rob and Justin were getting close to done. Biff ordered coffee. "You never do that, dude," Rob said.

"Unless you got some meth, I hafta get my heart started some kinda way," the rhythm guitarist answered. Rob shook his head. Crank was not his drug of choice. Neither Charlie nor Justin volunteered any. Biff spread his hands. "See?" he said. When the coffee came, he poured in lots of cream and sugar so it wouldn't taste like coffee any more. Then he gulped it. The sugar rush would help wire him for the morning, too.

The waitress brought Rob and Justin more toast to give them something to nibble on while their buddies chowed down. Rob smeared strawberry jam on his. It came in the same little foil-topped plastic package you saw everywhere. Oh, well. As he ate, he stared out the tinted window and across the street at the motor lodge they'd just come from.

After a while, he said, "Is it the glass, or is the light funny?"

"It's the light," Charlie said. "I noticed it when I was coming over here. Did you, Biff?"

"Huh?" Biff said. Rob didn't need to be Hercule Poirot to figure out that Biff hadn't noticed much of anything till he surrounded his coffee.

They paid for breakfast and walked out. A guy about their age coming down the street on a bike stopped and said, "Hey, I was at your show last night. I don't know about anybody else, but I liked it."

"Thanks—I think," Rob said. Not enough people had. The guy gave a vague wave and pedaled off.

"The light *is* funny." Justin was looking at the sun. No clouds were close by or in front of it, but he looked at it anyway. Rob could do the same thing. The sun was uncommonly weak, uncommonly white, as if seen through fog. But there was no fog. You could see for miles without channeling the Who. Rob turned and looked at his shadow. He had one, but not the kind he should have had on a sunny day.

They all started across the street. Not much traffic in Bar Harbor, not after the end of the season. "Is this, like, Maine weather or volcano weather?" Charlie wondered.

"Volcano weather." Rob heard something peculiar in his own voice, something he didn't think he'd ever found there before: a sad certainty. A doctor might have had that tone after seeing a chest X-ray with a dark spot on the lung.

All of a sudden, *particulate matter* wasn't just a pompous phrase to Rob. There wasn't any fog down here, no. But way the hell up there? That was liable to be—no, that was bound to be—a different story. How much crud had the supervolcano flung into the stratosphere? How much sunlight was it blocking? How bad would that screw up the weather? And for how long?

He shivered. The old Gaucho sweatshirt felt even thinner and rattier than it had when he pulled it on. He wanted something warmer: an ankle-length polar-bear coat, maybe, or a goose-down sleeping bag with sleeves.

Charlie hopped up onto the curb. "Boy, you sounded like a judge passing sentence there," he said.

"You totally did, man," Justin agreed. Even Biff nodded. That wasn't quite how Rob had thought of it, but wasn't so far removed, either. Out of the blue—the pale blue, the almost icy blue—Justin asked, "You ever hear anything from your sister, the one who moved to Denver?"

"No," Rob said tightly. "Cell phones are down for God knows how far. I've been hoping she could get to a landline or send me an e-mail or . . . something. But no."

Justin set a hand on his shoulder for a second. "That's hard, man."

"Nothing I can do about it. I keep telling myself there's more to Vanessa than you'd think. She can get out of there if anybody can."

Rob wished he hadn't added the last three words. They helped remind him how enormous the catastrophe was. Denver was hundreds of miles from Yellowstone. But Denver was also not far from the middle of the area the eruption had screwed, blued, and tattooed. The TV said volcanic ash was coming down in Alberta, in Texas, in Iowa, even in California.

He didn't want to think about that, so he turned to Biff and Charlie and asked, "Are we ready to rock?" He knew he and Justin were; they'd cleaned out their room down to the last dirty sock.

Charlie nodded. "Didn't leave the drums behind, honest." That made Biff snort. It would be easier to forget an elephant than Charlie's kit, even if the elephant would be harder to disassemble.

"Let's go, then," Justin said. They piled into the SUVs. Under that pale, unnatural sunlight, they started up the road toward Bangor. Pretty soon, all the sunshine disappeared. Rob turned on his headlights. It started to rain. By the time they got where they were going, the rain had turned to snow. Maine weather or volcano weather? What difference did that make? It was here, and they were stuck in it.

The first thing Colin Ferguson did after sitting up in bed was check his cell for voice mail and texts from Kelly or Vanessa.

Nothing this morning from either one of them—nothing at all from Vanessa since the eruption. Had anything in his own bailiwick gone wrong, the folks at the cop shop would have called on the landline and woken him up.

After he took a leak, he went downstairs to fix coffee. He didn't have to go in today unless something hit the fan. If Kelly weren't stuck in Missoula . . . But she was, dammit. So instead of enjoying himself with good company, he'd try to catch up on some around-the-house stuff. His Navy-trained soul was dismayed by how much he just let slide.

It's not like I don't work, he thought defensively, but his internalized CPO knew bullshit every time.

He always looked out the window while he waited for his water to boil. This morning, he looked and then he *looked*: a double take Harpo Marx would have been proud of. Even with on-and-off water rationing, he kept his lawn green. He was proud of it, the same way he was proud of his well-organized filing system.

Only the lawn and the flowers weren't green any more. They were about the color of cement dust. So were the leaves on the orange tree and the lemon tree and the magnolia. So was the cinder-block wall, which had been pink. So was just about everything in the backyard. The supervolcano had come to L.A.

The microwave chimed. He absently took out the water and poured it into the brown plastic cone that held the Melitta filter—the coffeenose, the kids had called it when they were little. A cat (also grayer than it should have been; he recognized the critter, which lived down the block) left almost-green footprints on the grass. It didn't like what was going on. It would take a few steps, stop and wash, walk on a few more steps, then wash some more. How much grit was it swallowing? What would that do to its insides? Nothing good, Colin was sure.

Rationing rules said he wasn't supposed to water the lawn on

Saturday. He'd spent most of his life enforcing rules. Now he broke one. He ducked under the sink to fiddle with the sprinkler controls. Nozzles popped up and started spraying. The cat levitated, then teleported. The lawn turned green again—except for patches still streaked with ugly brown sludge.

Thoughtfully, Colin put on slippers before he went out to get the *Times* and the *Breeze*. He didn't want to walk barefoot through that crud, not even slightly he didn't. It scrunched under his crepe soles and came up in little puffs. The front lawn was gray: almost the same color as the sidewalk. The street, which should have been asphalt-dark, was doing a sidewalk impression, too, one slightly spoiled by a few tire tracks.

His car was gray. All the cars he could see were gray—windows, mirrors, the whole deal. All but one: right across the street, Wes Jones was breaking some more rules by hosing his Nissan back to its original blue. Wes was a retired aerospace engineer who spent most of his time gardening. Like everybody else, he'd be playing catch-up for a while.

Colin waved to him. "Some fun, isn't it?" he called, and grabbed the papers. They were both wrapped in poly bags, as if against rain. Volcanic ash slid off the plastic.

"Fun? Oh, you bet." Wes pointed east. "Even the sun's gone nutso." Anything he disapproved of was nutso. But Wes didn't disapprove of much; he was an easygoing guy.

"Huh?" Colin hadn't paid any attention to the sun, past noticing that the daylight looked wan and washed out. Now he did. It sat low in the sky, still red as if closer to its rising than it really was. A hellacious halo surrounded it, with a pair of sundogs—false images of the sun—on the halo. He'd seen a sundog once, while in a destroyer off the coast of Greenland, with a sky full of ice crystals. The sky above San Atanasio had a different kind of junk in it. He delivered his verdict: "Holy crap!"

"Yeah, that's about what I was thinking," Wes replied. "Anything from Vanessa?" He'd watched her grow up; he'd been an honorary uncle.

"Nope." Colin left it right there.

Wes grunted. "Well, I'll tell Ida she needs to pray harder." He was at least as skeptical as Colin, but his wife went to a Methodist church every Sunday and did good works during the week. She didn't try to ram it down anybody's throat, even her husband's; she just did what she did. They'd had their fortieth anniversary the year before. Colin remembered no more than a handful of cross words between them.

Now he said, "It can't hurt."

"I expect you're right. And I expect I'm going back in the house." Wes scuffed at the ash on his driveway. Some of it was wet, but some came up the way it had under Colin's slippers. "Breathing this crap has to be hazardous to your health—to my health, even."

"Wouldn't be surprised," Colin said, which only gave him more reason to worry about his cross-grained daughter. Like Missoula, the L.A. area was getting only a light dusting of volcanic ash. But the shit was practically burying places like Salt Lake City . . . and Denver. You could foul up your lungs inhaling sawdust at a furniture factory. What the supervolcano spat out was bound to be a hell of a lot nastier than sawdust.

If Vanessa had listened to him—she wouldn't have been Vanessa. He hadn't wanted to listen to anybody when he was her age, either. Come to that, he was none too good at listening to other people even now.

But what Wes said made good sense. Things Wes said usually did. And Colin had that coffee waiting for him back on the kitchen counter. It wouldn't be too cold yet. Wes was already making for his own front door. Colin followed his lead. He paused at the doorway and left the slippers outside. The less ash he tracked in, the better.

His bare feet left gray prints on the dark brown foyer tiles. He'd kicked dust up into the slippers. Well, 409 and some paper towels would take care of that. Coffee first, coffee and the newspapers.

A notice on the front page of the *Breeze* said *We will keep printing as long as we can. Our paper supplier is in Minnesota. The supervolcano eruption has disrupted communication with areas to the east. Even when things come closer to normal, we fear paper will have a lower priority than food and fuel. But, at least temporarily, we may be compelled to go to Web-only publication.*

Harder to have a cup of coffee and check your computer or your smart phone. Not impossible, but harder. And what happened if L.A. lost power? So much for Web-only publication, that was what.

The *Times* didn't talk about a paper shortage. Maybe it got its newsprint from the Northwest, which was still reachable. Or maybe the editor didn't believe in borrowing trouble. The headline there said SENATORS FROM AFFLICTED STATES APPEAL FOR FEDERAL AID.

Afflicted. Colin slowly nodded as he considered the word. It was one you seldom met outside the Bible, but no denying it fit here. If the Children of Israel had ever met anything as overwhelming as the supervolcano eruption, the Old Testament failed to mention it.

He did wonder what Washington was supposed to do for Wyoming and Montana, where the very geography had been pretty drastically revised. How many feet of dust lay on Idaho and Utah and Colorado and Nebraska and Kansas? Not just here and there in those states, but all over everything, or as near as made no difference. How many bulldozers and trucks and years would you need to clear hundreds of thousands of square miles? More than even the USA had in its back pocket: he was sure of that.

Colin also noticed the irony in the *Times*' headline. L.A.'s leading newspaper had leaned left for longer than he'd been alive after an even lengthier spell of leaning hard right. Had the headline writer chosen his phrase with malice aforethought? Colin wouldn't have been surprised. Those Senators appealed for Federal aid, did they? Before the supervolcano went blam, they would have found Federal aid about as appealing as HIV. It all depended on whose ox was being gored, didn't it?

Almost all the Senators—and Representatives—from the afflicted states were Republicans. That didn't stop them from sticking their hands out. If Washington couldn't help them, nobody could. To Colin, it looked very much as if nobody could.

Which raised other interesting questions. Was anybody at all left alive in Wyoming? Western Montana was hanging on, but barely. Idaho and Utah were in pretty bad shape, too. So was Colorado, though maybe not quite to the same degree. The farming states farther east had also taken a big hit. Almost all those states were red as Rudolph's nose. If they got depopulated, what would that do to American politics? Nothing good, not as far as Colin was concerned.

He grabbed the *Daily Breeze* again. Yes, that was what he'd read. *Paper will have a lower priority than food and fuel.* "What food?" he wondered out loud. America's breadbasket had just taken one right in the breadbasket. How could you bring in or move the harvest when volcanic ash smothered the fields and blanketed the roads and choked the life out of tractors and harvesters and trucks (to say nothing of farmers)? One more thing that wasn't gonna happen.

The United States had been the world's larder since the nineteenth century. That was out the window, too. How was the USA going to feed its own people, let alone the many, many hungry beyond its borders? Who would—who could—take up the slack? Anybody? If no one did, what would happen then? Colin couldn't see the details, but the broad outlines seemed plain enough. Nothing good would happen—that was what.

How much of the country's grain was stored in areas suddenly ungetatable on account of the eruption? How many cows and sheep and pigs and chickens were dying right now? He'd read a newspaper squib about a yak farm in the Colorado Rockies. Was anybody saving the poor goddamn yaks?

Yeah, the country was screwed. The part of the world that depended on the USA was screwed, too. And so was everybody else. He was still only on his first cup of coffee. He hadn't even started worrying about climate change yet. He got up and put some more water in the microwave. If he was going to do that, he'd definitely need more.

The knock on the door was loud and somehow official-sounding, as if the guy doing the knocking had a hell of a lot of practice. Daniel had gone to the university, which left Kelly and Ruth and Larry sitting around his apartment waiting for something to happen. Well, now something had.

Larry went to the door. He was the man. That wasn't exactly twenty-first-century thinking, but neither Kelly nor Ruth made a move to get there ahead of him. Kelly didn't even think about it till afterwards.

When Larry opened the door, standing there in front of it was the most cop-looking cop Kelly'd ever seen. Yes, he'd know how to knock on doors, all right. Shoulders. Chin. Khaki shirt with badge. Pistol on hip. Olive-drab pants, sharply creased. Shiny black boots. Gunnery sergeant's hat. Mirrored sunglasses, even.

"Yes?" Larry said, in a tone that couldn't mean anything but *You've got to have the wrong apartment.*

But the cop rumbled, "Is Miss Birnbaum here?"

"That's me," Kelly squeaked in surprise. About the most nefarious thing she'd done was smoke dope every once in a while, and she hadn't even done that since she'd started dating Colin. He made no bones about hating it, it *was* still mildly illegal, and she didn't get off on it that much anyhow. Quitting hadn't been hard.

"Miss Birnbaum, I'm Roy Schurz," the cop said. "I'm chief of police in Orofino, Idaho."

"Yes?" Kelly said blankly. "And so?"

"And so I used to be a cop down in San Atanasio, California," Schurz answered. "Colin Ferguson's a buddy of mine. He asked me to see what I could do about getting you out of here. Are you ready to go?"

Colin had said he might be able to pull some strings. He must have meant it. Colin, Kelly had discovered, commonly meant what he said. That was so far out of the ordinary, she was still getting used to it. "Am I ready?" she echoed.

"Yes, ma'am," Chief Schurz said. "I've got a Humvee with a desert air filter parked out front. It's what I came here in." *In case you think I bounced in on a pogo stick or something.* The mirrored shades kept his face from showing how big a jerk he thought she was.

"Let me grab my purse," Kelly said. All at once, she believed. It wasn't as if she had much more than that here. She hugged Ruth and Larry. "Tell Daniel thanks a couple of million for me."

"We will." Ruth Marquez sounded wistful, or more likely jealous.

Kelly followed Roy Schurz out to the Humvee. It *was* a Humvee, too, not a Hummer: a military vehicle, painted in faded desert camo. It mounted the biggest machine gun Kelly had ever imagined. A soldier sat behind the gun.

"National Guard," Schurz explained. "I borrowed the vehicle—and Edwards there—from them. Colin, he thinks you're something special." He didn't say *Hell with me if I can see why*, but it was in his voice.

"I think he's something special, too," Kelly managed.

"Good. When him and Louise broke up, he was mighty, well, broke up about it. Now he's more like his old self again." Schurz gestured. "Hop on in."

It was a tall hop; the Humvee had humongous tires. Kelly climbed aboard. The seat was severely functional. Chief Schurz got in on the driver's side. The engine might boast a desert filter, but it sounded raspy anyway. Of course, it probably had that filter because it had seen action in Iraq or Afghanistan. It wasn't new, or close to new. It was a Regular Army castoff good enough for the Idaho National Guard. Chances were it had sounded raspy for years.

Roy Schurz put it in gear. It rode as if it had left its shocks near Kandahar, that was for sure. "Do we really need a gunner?" Kelly had to shout to make herself heard.

"Well, you never can tell," Schurz shouted back. The Humvee kicked up its share of dust and then some. He pulled a surgical-style mask out of his shirt pocket and put it on with one hand. The Smokey Bear hat went into his lap for a second, no more. He extracted another mask and offered it to Kelly. "Your own air filter."

"Thanks." She put it on. When she turned around to look at the machine gunner—Edwards—she discovered he'd also donned one. The less volcanic crap you put in your lungs, the better. A lot could kill you pretty fast. Even a little wasn't good news. Twenty, thirty, fifty years from now, she expected mesothelioma cases to shoot through the roof. Not much of what the supervolcano belched into the air was asbestos fibers, but when you were talking about several hundred cubic miles of material there'd be plenty to go around.

A Missoula policeman with a shotgun stood guard at the edge of town. He was also wearing a mask. He waved to the Humvee as it got on US 12 heading south—Orofino evidently wasn't on the Interstate. Chief Schurz gravely waved back.

"What's he watching for?" Kelly asked. "Does he think somebody's gonna steal the highway?"

"Well, you never can tell," Schurz repeated. With the mask and shades, his face was almost completely unreadable. But the way he fidgeted in the hard, uncomfortable bucket seat told Kelly he realized he needed to say more: "People are starting to run low on all kinds of stuff. They're putting armed escorts on food and fuel convoys. We haven't had a lot of trouble yet, and nobody wants it to start, y'know?"

"I guess," Kelly said. How many folks couldn't get to a Safeway or a Mobil station so easily these days? How many couldn't get their hands on ground chuck or gasoline even when they did? How many of those folks had guns? In this part of the country, quite a few. And what would they do when they got hungry or otherwise desperate? If you had to take what you needed or starve, who wouldn't think about turning robber?

"I've got some jerrycans of gas in the vehicle here," Chief Schurz went on, as if she hadn't spoken. "That's one of the reasons I brought Edwards along. Nothing like a soldier on a .50-caliber to keep people honest."

"God, you sound like Colin!" Kelly blurted, all at once missing him more than ever now that she was actually heading toward him, not stuck in Missoula.

The Orofino (would that be *Fine Gold* in Spanish?) police chief chuckled. "Wouldn't be surprised if we rubbed off on each other some. You ride in the same patrol car a few years, that'll happen. Almost like being married, only without benefits."

Not knowing what to say to that, Kelly didn't say anything. They climbed toward the hills, which were covered with a light coating of ash, a little too dark and a little too brown to look like dirty snow. Most of the clouds in the sky were just clouds. It was a gloomy, chilly, lowering day. Her heart soared like a skylark anyhow. She was out, out, out of Missoula!

Hardly anybody shared the road with the Humvee. She didn't know how many people used US 12 on an average day, but this had to be way down from that. Just across the Idaho line, Schurz pulled onto the shoulder. Some grass showed through the ash here; they were right at the western edge of the throw line.

"Is the, uh, Humvee okay?" Kelly asked.

"As okay as it ever is," he replied. "Gotta throw in some fuel. It can do more than a jeep can, but Christ, it's a gas hog." He and the silent Edwards emptied two camo-painted jerrycans into the vehicle. Then he got behind the wheel again, fired up the machine, and drove on towards Orofino.

XIII

Things in Kansas were better than they had been in Colorado. Vanessa was convinced of it, even though she breathed through three masks worn one on top of the next and kept swimming-pool goggles on even when she slept. Her eyes itched all the time anyhow; she hadn't got the goggles soon enough. She couldn't take them off to rub or use Visine or anything. The air was still too full of fine dust.

Pickles was even less happy than she was. He couldn't wear a mask or goggles, poor thing. She didn't know what to do about him. She couldn't keep him in the carrier all the time, but she couldn't let him out, either. She still had nasty scratches from when she'd extracted him from under the Toyota's front seat. She had to get someplace where he'd be able to move around more—and where she would, too.

She carried a snub-nosed .38 revolver in her purse. Her father had taught her how to handle firearms when she was twelve. She'd never used what she'd learned; she always worried more about a moment of rage or stupidity or black depression than about blowing away a burglar. But the times, they were a-changin'.

She'd got the gun in Pueblo. Another hundred miles and a little bit away from the supervolcano, it hadn't been hit as hard as Denver. She stopped for gas and a fresh air filter. She paid ten bucks a gallon plus another fifty for the filter, and she didn't say boo. She could count the cost later. Now was a time for doing what she had to do.

The guy who took her money was already wearing goggles. "Where did you get those?" she demanded enviously.

He pointed across the street. "Walgreens is still open." She could barely see the sign through swirls of dust, but she stopped there as soon as he finished with her car. He used a mask, too, and had probably also got his hands on it at the drugstore.

Volcanic ash came in every time the automatic door opened, and would keep coming in as long as it kept working. Still, like the air inside her car, the air inside the Walgreens improved on the general run of things. There was a display of goggles with bright plastic straps.

Only three boxes of masks were left. "One box to a customer, ma'am," the clerk said when Vanessa tried to buy them all. "We want to spread 'em around as much as we can."

She could see the logic in that, even if she didn't like it. Unlike the man at the gas station, the Walgreens clerk didn't gouge her for what she bought. "How long will you stay here?" she asked him as she put on the goggles.

"I don't know. A while longer. I'll see if it looks like it's getting worse or better," he answered.

"It won't get better." Vanessa spoke with great conviction.

"Well, you may be right," he replied, which had to mean *I ain't paying any attention to* you, *lady.*

She put on one of the masks before she went outside again, too. Either it made a difference or her imagination was working overtime. That was when she noticed the gun shop between the Walgreens and a tropical-fish store. The fish place was dark, but a light burned in the gun shop. Out in the middle of—this—having a real weapon looked like a terrific idea. She went inside.

The man behind the counter looked like a shop teacher. He was leafing through—surprise!—a hunting magazine, but he put it down. "What can I do for you?" he said.

"I made it down from Denver," Vanessa answered. "I want to keep going. In case my car doesn't, I may need to take some chances. A pistol could come in handy."

He nodded. "If you know how to use one."

"My dad's a cop in California."

"Then you probably do," he allowed. "You'll have to fill out about five pounds of forms."

"As long as there's no waiting period," Vanessa said. "I'm not going to wait."

"Not in this state," he assured her. "I do have to perform a background check, though. Right now, the phones are out, and so is the Net." He rubbed his chin. "Turn around, please."

"Huh?" Mystified, Vanessa did.

"I liked your foreground," the man explained. "Your background will definitely do, too. I'll sell to you, and we'll sort everything else out later—if there is a later."

"Thank you," Vanessa said, more sincerely than she was in the habit of doing. She handed him her Visa card. "Here."

He took it, but he didn't do anything with it for a few seconds. Was he going to ask her for a blowjob, too, or something? If he did, she'd . . . She didn't quite know what she'd do. In normal times, she would have told him to go fuck himself. In normal times, though, she wouldn't have been standing here in a Pueblo, Colorado, gun shop. She needed a piece. If he decided he needed one, too . . .

But it didn't come to that. He just said, "You want to be careful on the road, Ms., uh"—he looked down at the little plastic rectangle in his hand—"Ferguson. A pistol can get you out of some tight spots, sure. Maybe you'd do better not getting into them in the first place, though."

She shook her head. "If I hadn't bailed out of Denver when I did, I would've been stuck there. If you don't get out of here pretty damn quick, you won't be able to leave, either."

"I'm still thinking about it," he said. Vanessa left it there; she was a refugee, not a missionary. He went on, "You'll want to buy a couple boxes of cartridges, too, am I right?"

"That's why God made plastic," Vanessa agreed.

As soon as she got back to the car, she loaded the .38. It was a double-action model; you could safely carry a round in every chamber in the cylinder. And she did. She felt better having it. She might have faced a nasty choice in the gun shop. Out on the road, there were bound to be sons of bitches who didn't believe in giving any choices.

If she got back on the Interstate, she'd end up in New Mexico. If she chose US 50 instead, she'd cross the Colorado prairie till she got to the Kansas prairie. Kansas held no appeal. Sometimes, though, you didn't get what you wanted. She hadn't been off I-25 very long, but when she went back cars were coming off at the on-ramp. That couldn't possibly be a good sign.

And it wasn't. A cop in a pig-snouted gas mask—which had to work better than goggles and a surgical job—waved what looked like an orange light saber. He yelled something at Vanessa. She couldn't make out what it was. Reluctantly, she cracked the window. Ash started coming in.

"Interstate's closed," the cop said, his voice sounding distant, almost underwater, through the mask. "Big old accident south of town. Worst mess you've ever seen, I swear to God."

Vanessa doubted that. She'd seen L.A. messes, after all. But then she had second thoughts. All the blowing dust might have done to I-25 what tule fog did in California's Central Valley—it could turn I-5 into Slaughterhouse Five, and did just about every winter. Twenty or fifty or eighty cars and SUVs and trucks all turned to crumpled sheet metal, some of them burning, with dazed and bleeding people wandering around coughing from the ash, every now and then a fresh, tinny crash as a new fool didn't spot the wreck up ahead soon enough. . . .

"Maybe I'll go east instead," she said, thinking *And to hell with Horace Greeley.*

"Good plan," the cop said in that otherworldly voice. "If there's wrecks on 50, they aren't close to Pueblo."

Which meant they weren't his problem. But which also meant she could put some more miles between her and the super-volcano. By Interstate standards, US 50 was old and shabby. It was also open, though, so Vanessa did her best to make lemonade. She might not be able to go as fast as she wanted to, but at least she was going. She tried to ignore Pickles' yowls, which was like trying to ignore a toothache.

A lot of cars were crapped out by the side of the road. She blessed the new air filter she'd got in Pueblo. Every so often, she'd come up on a car that had crapped out in the middle of the road. A couple of times, she almost rear-ended one. Was that how the giant pileup on I-25 had started? She wouldn't have been a bit surprised.

She was a little more than an hour—say, thirty-five miles—out of Pueblo when it started to rain. When the first big drops splatted down on her windshield, she let out a war whoop of delight. Rain would wash the ash out of the air. If she could see where she was going, she'd get there faster.

But the rain didn't wash all the grit out of the air—there was too much of it in the air for that. And when she turned on the wipers, they did as much harm as good. They pushed grit back and forth across the windshield; she could hear it, almost feel it, scraping first one way, then the other. And it was rock grit, some of it at least as hard as the glass it was grinding across. Arced scratches spread across the broad pane. That wasn't smeared dirt, the way she hoped for a moment; the windshield was marked for good.

Vanessa swore as loudly as she'd whooped, startling the cat into momentary silence. There was so much ash and dust on the highway that she soon began to feel she was trying to drive through mud. That was exactly what she was doing, too. She had to slow down even more instead of speeding up the way she wanted to.

A lordly Cadillac Escalade zoomed past her. Its giant tires splattered the side of her car—and her side windows—with muck. Then the supersized SUV cut in front of her. She had to hit the brakes to keep from smashing into it, or more likely going under it. More gritty mud splashed her windshield. The wipers did their best to shove it aside. Their best abraded the glass some more.

"You dumb fucking asshole!" she howled, and flipped the Escalade the bird. The imbecile behind the battleship's wheel probably couldn't see her do it, what with her filthy, scarred front glass, but she was most sincere.

Then she remembered the brand-new .38 in her handbag. She'd never understood road-rage shootings before. They'd always seemed the province of gangbangers with shaved heads and teardrop tats. Now she got it. Somebody did you wrong, so you went and made that sucker pay.

She imagined the Escalade slewing crazily off the road, flipping over—weren't all those stinking SUVs top-heavy as hell?—and bursting into flame. She imagined the jerk driving it toasting till he was overdone, along with Mrs. Jerk and all the little Jerks in their car seats.

And she let out a long, shuddering breath and made damn sure she didn't reach inside the purse. A moment of fury would be all it took, all right. You couldn't—well, you shouldn't—give in to something like that. But people did, all the time. Her old man wouldn't go out of business any time soon.

Thinking of him made her stick one hand in her purse after all. The only thing she took out was her cell phone. Maybe, with the rain scrubbing the dust out of the air, she'd finally have bars.

No such luck. She tried his number anyway. Again, no luck. Nothing coming in. Nothing going out. She turned off the phone and stowed it.

On she went, slowly. With the road the way it was and with her poor, abused windshield the way *it* was, slowly was the only way to go. Most of the people heading toward Kansas had sense enough to see things the same way. The jerk in the Escalade was no doubt still doing ninety. He was long gone in front of her. Even if she hadn't shot him, she wished him no good.

Every once in a while, Somebody listened when you made a wish like that. Less than fifteen minutes later, she drove past the Escalade. It was over on the shoulder with the hood popped. Mr. Jerk—who proved what he was by not bothering with a mask—stared forlornly at the engine. If he was waiting for AAA to come rescue him, he'd have a long wait.

Vanessa not only knew the feeling of *Schadenfreude*, she knew the word. Knowing the word sharpened the feeling. If only sex worked that way! The Escalade shrank in her rearview mirror and vanished into rain and dust.

Then she had to hit the brakes and crawl. Someone hadn't slowed down enough or had skidded in the new mud on the asphalt. The crash hadn't closed US 50—not yet, anyhow—but it sure had snarled traffic. If a jalopy in the backup decided this was a good time to overheat . . .

Why are you borrowing trouble? Vanessa asked herself. *Don't you have enough already?* In a way, those were questions without answers. In another, they were questions that hardly needed answers. She borrowed trouble because she was the kind of person who borrowed trouble. If she wanted to, she could blame that on her tight-assed father or on being the middle child or on Mrs. McKenzie, her neurotic—*make that nutso*, she thought, remembering Wes across the street from her folks— first-grade teacher. None of which changed things one goddamn bit. She borrowed trouble.

This time, she got to pay it back pretty soon. No steam plume ascended to the heavens from some old clunker's radiator. She inched along with everybody else, but she kept on inching. The accident involved four cars. Nobody seemed badly hurt. Men wearing wet clothes and glum expressions stalked around examining damage.

More gunk flew onto her windshield when the car ahead of her sped up as it found open road in front of it. Resignedly, she waited for the wipers to clear the smear, and to scratch up the glass some more. The only way she could have prevented that would have been to stay in Denver. This might be a bad bet, but that was a worse one—though poor Pickles would have disagreed.

She found more things to worry about. How much cash did she have left after that outrageous gas stop and air filter? Would it be enough to do her any good when she needed to fill up again? If it wasn't, would the station guy take plastic? Or could she find a working ATM? Odds were decent, she supposed. If a gas pump was working, an ATM ought to be. For now, with the needle well above the H, she kept making miles.

Making miles, these days, came with a price, though, or at least it did in a big part of the country, very much including the part she was in. By the time she got over the state line into Kansas, her car was starting to sound like hell, even with the new air filter. How much volcanic crud was getting in despite the filter? Jesus, how much had got in when she took off the gas cap to fill the tank in Pueblo? What was all that shit doing to her engine?

What was all the grit on the road doing to the rest of her moving parts? How long would they keep on moving? Long enough? She had to hope so.

In spite of the way the car sounded, she smiled for a second. She must have been about ten years old when Rob, a couple of years older, opened some atlas or other to a map of the USA. "They're gonna build a college right here," he'd said, pointing to the border between the state she'd just left and the one she'd just entered.

She remembered going, "Yeah? So?" Big brothers were obnoxious enough even if you didn't let them get the jump on you. When you did, they turned insufferable. She might not have known that word when she was ten, but she sure had understood the idea.

And she remembered his leer. He was just learning how to do it, which of course meant he overdid it. "So they're gonna call it the First United Colorado-Kansas University," he'd answered. "Only for short it'll be—"

Vanessa had understood the idea of acronyms, too, even if she might not have known that word yet, either. "FUCK U!" she'd shrilled, and laughed so loud, and in such delighted horror, that their mother had come into her room to see what the hell was going on. They'd both solemnly denied everything, of course. With no more than an open atlas for evidence, Mom hadn't been able to pin a crime on them.

Even then, you might have guessed Rob would end up playing in a band called Squirt Frog and the Evolving Tadpoles. Vanessa didn't much care for the music, though she had to admit some of the lyrics were clever. She had no idea where the band was right now—somewhere back East, if she remembered straight. If she did, the odds Rob was okay were good.

The odds on herself, or on Pickles, or on the Toyota . . . Red lights on the dashboard warned SERVICE ENGINE SOON. The car was running hot even though the eastbound US 50, heading away from the Rockies, tended downhill. If it crapped out, how far could she coast? Till the next hill, anyhow, and those were few and far between around here.

She drove through Coolidge, just over the border, almost before she realized it was there. If the place had ever had a hundred people, she would have been amazed. How many were still here, and how many had lit out when the supervolcano erupted? She'd never know.

US 50 paralleled the Arkansas River. The rain had washed some of the ash off the trees that grew alongside the river, so they looked a little more like their old selves. The river, by contrast, looked muddy and full and angry, even though it wasn't raining all that hard.

For a little while, Vanessa wondered why. Then the old metaphorical lightbulb went on above her head. The rain was washing volcanic ash off the trees, sure, and off the grass, and off the ground generally. And it was washing that ash . . . straight into the river. Where else could the stuff go?

How long till the Arkansas started flooding? The Missouri was a lot closer to the eruption, which could only mean even more ash would be going into it. So it would start flooding sooner, if it hadn't started already. The other rivers flowing from the Rockies toward the Mississippi would do the same thing.

They would also wash the volcanic ash toward and then into the Father of Waters. What would happen when the Big Muddy turned into the Big Muddier, and then into the Big Muddiest? Vanessa didn't know in detail, but this was one of those times when the big picture did fine. The big picture was lots of muddy water spreading out over lots and lots of land.

Her motor coughed. She forgot about the big picture. Somebody might have dropped an ice cube down the back of her shirt. A human being who sounded like that would have been dying of emphysema. The engine was dying, too. A mechanic wouldn't call it emphysema, but it amounted to the same thing.

Here came Syracuse. A roadside sign proudly proclaimed you could get gas there. It also said you could get food. Chances were you could get gas from the food, too, even if the sign didn't tell you that.

Go? Stop? Did she want to get stuck in the middle of nowhere if the car quit between towns? Wasn't this already the middle of nowhere? Was she better off with other people or as far away from them as she could get?

She kept going. Whether that made her an optimist or a pessimist was one more thing she'd think about when she had time. If she ever did. Which looked less and less likely.

After Syracuse, signs announced that the next town ahead was Garden City. By the way they announced it, Garden City might actually be something. It had hotels and motels and fast-food joints and meat-packing plants. Some of the signs for those were in both English and Spanish. She'd seen the like in L.A. and Denver, of course. Spanish was the language in which a lot of hard work got done in the USA.

But in a place like Garden City, Kansas? Evidently. It turned out not to matter to Vanessa. The engine coughed again. This time, it sounded more like Cheyne-Stokes breathing than emphysema. And, like somebody with Cheyne-Stokes breathing, her car died. All the red and yellow warning lights came on. As she'd figured she would, she rolled as far as she could. Then she steered over to the shoulder and stopped.

As soon as the motion ceased, Pickles quit sounding like an air-raid siren. Relishing the silence, Vanessa spoke out loud: "Well, what do I do now?"

Her basic choices were sitting tight or getting out and walking toward Garden City. If she sat tight, she was counting on somebody halfway decent rescuing her before she *had* to start walking to Garden City. If she got out, she'd feel like a snail without its shell. And she and Pickles—especially Pickles—would be breathing the outside air that had just killed her car.

In a TV show, they'd go to commercials. When they came back, she'd find the right answer with the greatest of ease. Or they'd cut away to her somewhere else, and she'd explain to an admiring friend how she'd got there.

Unfortunately, you couldn't cut away from life. She had no idea what the right answer was, or even if there was one. She hadn't come this far by sitting tight, though. She got Pickles and an abridged version of her stuff—iron rations, tampons, a few socks and panties, and an umbrella—and started walking.

She was glad for the umbrella right away. The rain was so mixed with ash that everything it touched got dirtier. That included her jeans from the knees down, but she couldn't do anything about it. She couldn't do anything about anything, except hope her feet didn't blister before she got to Garden City.

She almost slipped in the mud. A car going by splashed a little on her. If that went on, she'd look like someone made of muck by the time she got to the town. Another car sloshed past and splashed her some more. She kept walking.

Colin Ferguson begrudged the time he wasted doing the I-5 boogie from L.A. to the Bay Area. Even with all the security bullshit, flying would have been faster. But ash in the air kept planes on the ground. If you wanted to get anywhere, you drove.

He hoped the Taurus would make it. Driving was a crapshoot these days, too. California hadn't been buried under ash from the supervolcano, the way the Rocky Mountain states and much of the prairie had been. Ash lay on the ground, though, and the ash in the air wouldn't screw up airplane engines alone. It wasn't good for cars, either.

He'd made it over the Grapevine, anyhow. That long, tough climb getting out of L.A. County had worried him, but here he was, easing down the other side. He'd thought about taking Highway 1 up to Berkeley; there was supposed to be less ash along the coast. But, while the Pacific Coast Highway was breathtakingly beautiful, it was also slow and wearing. You couldn't just haul ass on PCH; you had to *drive*. He'd taken a chance for speed, he'd got away with it, and now he had his reward.

I-5 ran straight as a string through the Central Valley. It was the short way north, and it was the straight way north. As long as you didn't fall asleep at the wheel, you pointed the car and you went. Mountains off to either side, fields lying next to the unwinding road, occasional towns. The landscape didn't change, but the odometer did.

At one point, the atmosphere changed, and not for the better. Near Kettleman City (which wasn't one), they collected cattle to ship them to market. You breathed concentrated essence of bullshit for a few minutes as you went by. Then the air cleared again, and you were relieved you couldn't smell what had relieved the cows any more.

Except the air didn't completely clear. Oh, the stink went away. But a dust haze remained. It was worst near the Interstate, where tires and the wind of many cars' passage kept stirring up what the supervolcano had spewed all those miles away.

Sunlight still seemed wan. That wasn't only the ash in the lower atmosphere; it was also the finer-gauge crap—the particulate matter—the eruption had blasted into the stratosphere. Sunsets kept on being improbably gorgeous, showing every color of the rainbow. Sometimes the hues were splattered together in Jackson Pollock randomness, sometimes stacked as neatly as the layers in a poussé-café. They were never the same from one day to the next. Hell, they were never the same from one minute to the next. That ancient Greek who said you could never step into the same river twice knew what he was talking about. You could hardly step into the same river once.

It was chilly. Colin told himself that didn't necessarily mean anything. Fall didn't come to California the way it did to most other places. It could be hot or cold or hot and then cold. The only trees that changed colors were a few sycamores, and they didn't get around to it till Thanksgiving. So chilly weather now didn't have to mean the supervolcano was doing what Kelly had warned all along it would do.

It didn't have to mean that, no. But it sure was likely to.

Colin beat the darkness up to Berkeley. That was good. He knew the Bay Area well enough to sortakinda find his way around, but only sortakinda. Trying it at night would have been harder.

He made it to Kelly's street, and damned if he didn't find a parking space no more than two lengths away from where he'd snagged one the last time he drove up. It wasn't much longer than the Taurus, but it didn't need to be. There were plenty of things he couldn't do. By God, he could parallel park.

Her building had added a security door since the last time he was here. Nodding in approval, he pressed 274—her apartment number—on the keypad and buzzed. "That you, Colin?" Kelly's voice came out of the cheap speaker as if it were a tin-can telephone connected by a string that wasn't taut enough.

"Who else were you expecting?" He had to ask twice; the first time, he forgot to press the ANSWER button.

"You might have been the Thai takeout," she replied after he did it right. The door's lock clicked. He opened it, made sure it closed behind him, and hurried up the stairs like somebody half his age. If that wasn't love, it sure as hell was a reasonable facsimile.

Kelly opened the door while he was still walking towards it. He wished he'd thought to buy flowers. He wished he were the kind of guy who thought to buy flowers before it was too goddamn late. Of course, if he were that kind of guy, he might well still be married to Louise.

He was what he was. He was where he was, too, and damn glad of it. He grabbed Kelly and clung to her as hard as she was clinging to him. He wasn't usually touchy-feely, either—the opposite, in fact—but holding her was like finding a life ring in the North Atlantic after a torpedo hit your freighter.

"Jesus, it's good to see you!" he said hoarsely.

By way of reply, she tilted her face up for a kiss. Before he could deliver it, the buzzer in her apartment went off again. She made a face. "Sorry. Wait one," she said, and ran back inside.

This time, it was the Thai food. The short, skinny man who carried up the two big white paper bags had brown skin and a flat face, which probably made him a Thai. By his English, he hadn't been here long. Colin paid him. Kelly squawked. He ignored her. She was still squawking when they went back into the apartment. The dinette table was strewn with books and journals and papers, but Kelly shoved them back to make enough space for two people to eat. Colin set the bags down on the wood-grain Formica.

Then he held out his arms and said, "Where were we?"

"When we were so rudely interrupted, you mean?" Kelly stepped into the circle that closed around her. "Right about here."

A few minutes later, they spooned squid salad and larb and other good things onto paper plates. One of the bags also held two Thai iced teas, sweetened with coconut milk, in styrofoam cups. Colin slathered bright red chili sauce from little plastic containers onto everything but his iced tea.

"I'd have to eat flame retardant if I did that," said Kelly, who stuck to seasoning with soy sauce.

"I like it," Colin answered, and proceeded to prove as much by making his share disappear. As he took seconds, he said, "Lord, I'm glad to see you. I told you that once already, didn't I?"

"Uh-huh. But it's okay. I like to hear it. I'm glad to see you, too." Kelly's expression darkened. "I'm glad to see anybody. I was, like, three hundred miles from the supervolcano when it went off. Almost everybody who was—oh, God, I don't know—say, fifty miles closer is probably dead right now."

A circle five hundred miles across . . . Colin centered it on Yellowstone and laid it over a mental map of the United States. Salt Lake City wouldn't be far from the edge. Denver lay outside, but not far enough outside to suit him.

"Still nothing from Vanessa," he said, his voice harsh.

"I'm sorry," Kelly answered. "Still too early to know if it means anything, though. The whole middle of the country is fubar'd."

He stabbed a blunt, accusing forefinger at her. "That's what you get for hanging around with an old Navy guy."

"Why, what ever can you mean, sir?" She batted her eye-lashes fit to make Scarlett O'Hara gag. "It stands for *fouled up beyond all recognition*, right? Or something like that."

"Yeah. Or something like that." Colin aimed the forefinger again. "But nobody your age says 'fubar'd.' It's what you get for hanging around with an old Navy guy, like I said. Stuff rubs off."

"Suppose you let me worry about that," Kelly said, and a CPO couldn't have put more bite into it. She snapped the lids back onto the containers they hadn't emptied and stuck them in the fridge. Forks clattered in the sink. She nodded to herself. "The rest can wait."

"The trash?" Colin knew he sounded disapproving. Being an old Navy guy helped make him Felix, not Oscar.

But Kelly nodded again. "Yeah, the trash." For her part, she sounded defiant. "You keep telling me you're glad to see me. How are you gonna show me?"

After the long drive up and a belly full of Thai food, Colin hoped he *could* show her. He'd seen that occasional bedroom failures bothered middle-aged men more than their women, but he was a middle-aged man, dammit, and he especially didn't want to fail now.

He didn't. For a man, it's always terrific. Kelly didn't seem to have any complaints. She rolled over and made as if to go to sleep. "Hey, I'm the one who's supposed to do that," Colin protested. What with the drive and the big dinner and the exertions just past, he wasn't far from it.

She sat up. He put an arm around her. She leaned against him. "Everything works here," she said in wondering tones. "We had power in Missoula, but the gas went out. Landlines were iffy. So was the Net. My cell was iffier."

"I know. I wish I could've talked to you more," Colin said.

Kelly nodded, but kept following her own train of thought: "Everything works. I called for Thai takeout, and half an hour later it showed up. There's no problem with food here, not yet. And we're on the coast, so it'll keep coming in by ship. The weather here won't get *too* bad. California's lucky. I don't know what'll happen to Missoula once winter settles in." She bit her lip. "No. I do know. I just don't want to think about it. There's a difference."

"Maybe things won't be so bad," Colin said. "I was wondering about that on the way up here—right after I went past Kettleman City, matter of fact."

"Timing!" Kelly held her nose. Colin laughed. So did she, but she quickly sobered. "It will be that bad. It may be worse. This was a big eruption, even by supervolcano standards. Just about— maybe not quite, but just about—the size of the one over two million years ago, or the one that turned Mount Toba into Lake Toba."

"So we're in it for real?"

"We're in it for real," Kelly agreed. "Bigtime. The ash has already taken out most of this year's crops in the Midwest, and maybe next year's, too. After that . . . After that, it'll get cold. It's already getting cold—not so much heat from the sun can make it through the atmosphere. Things here seem fine now, but the whole world is running on momentum. When it slows down . . ."

"All we can do is all we can do," Colin said. "We'll pick up as many of the pieces as we're able to, and we'll try and keep 'em from getting any more broken than they already are."

"How come the politicians don't have that kind of sense?" Kelly asked.

"I'm a cop. Picking up pieces is what I do," he answered. "They sling bull. I get it slung at me. Nobody asks cops what we ought to do about this, that, or even the other thing. And when somebody does ask, he mostly doesn't pay any attention to what he hears."

"Nobody paid any attention to the geologists, either," Kelly said. "I mean, I'm nothing but a grad student. But there are people in my racket with clout. Nobody in Washington wanted to listen to them, though."

"Then they didn't have enough clout," Colin said.

"I guess not." Kelly laughed a singularly humorless laugh. "You want to know what else? Most of my research is obsolete."

"How do you figure that? You're an expert on the Yellowstone supervolcano. What's more important right now?"

"I'm an expert on what it did the three times it erupted before this one. I'm an expert on what that might have meant. I'm an expert on the complicated geology that used to be under Yellowstone, and on the geysers and hot springs and stuff. Well, the geysers are gone. So is a lot of the geology that made them possible. And now the supervolcano *has* gone off, and everybody can see what it means. And we don't need to worry about another eruption like this one for the next half-million years. If that doesn't spell obsolete, what does?"

"You're here," Colin said. "Too many people aren't." A circle five hundred miles across . . . "Like I told you a minute ago, all you can do is all you can do."

"Nobody can do anything. It's too big," Kelly said.

"Gotta keep trying anyway." Colin wished he could make love with her again. Back in the day, he would have managed a second round. But that was then. This was now. He had to comfort her with words, and words weren't such terrific tools for the job.

XIV

Another motel room in Maine. But till you opened the curtains—and sometimes afterwards—it could just as easily have been in Montana or Oregon or Arkansas. The road was simply the road once you'd been on it for a while. By now, Squirt Frog and the Evolving Tadpoles were veteran road warriors.

Justin sat at the desk, doing e-mail on his MacBook. Rob sprawled on the bed, channel-surfing with the remote. HBO was showing a prizefight. The movie on Showtime sucked. The stand-up guy on Comedy Central had only one thing wrong with him: he wasn't funny.

In a pop-culture course at UCSB, Rob had heard that people were calling TV a vast wasteland a generation before he was born. It hadn't got better since, only vaster. He checked the laminated guide on the nightstand. On this system, MSNBC was channel 23.

The President and Grand Ayatollah of Iran stood side by side in a mosque in Qom. The President was a skinny, swarthy little guy with black hair and a close-cropped graying beard. He wore a dark Western-style jacket, a dark shirt, and no tie. Omitting the tie was the only place where Rob—who wore them at weddings, funerals, and gunpoint—sympathized with him.

In turban, flowing robes, and even more flowing beard, the Grand Ayatollah looked like a man from another century. As the camera moved in for a close-up of the two of them, though, you saw his heavy-lidded, clever eyes. The President was doing the talking. The President, in fact, was pounding his fist into the palm of his other hand to make his point. The Grand Ayatollah didn't keep an arm behind the President's back or anything. But you could make a pretty fair guess about which was the ventriloquist and which the dummy.

Not that the crowd inside the mosque cared. They cheered the President's impassioned Farsi with passion of their own. To Rob, and to 99.9 percent of other non-Iranian Americans, Farsi was just guttural noise.

A translator who spoke almost unaccented American English spread the word to the wider world: "We have said for many years that the United States is the Great Satan. Now God is punishing the USA for its wicked war against Islam and for its poisonous support of the Zionist entity. It is a great punishment, and a punishment greatly deserved."

More applause from the crowd. The Grand Ayatollah nodded in approval. Rob got the idea that he might have smiled if he hadn't had his smile muscles surgically cut to make sure he couldn't.

"If only the Americans, mired in ignorance and disbelief, had had the wisdom to embrace the teachings of the glorious Prophet Muhammad, peace be unto him . . ." the President went on.

"Hey, Justin, you listening to this bullshit?" Rob asked.

"Now that you mention it," answered the band's front man, "no."

"Guy's been channeling Pat Robertson," Rob said, and summarized the President's remarks.

"Nice to see we don't have the loony market covered," Justin observed.

"There you go," Rob said. "You know we're screwed when the Iranians can laugh at us. When North Korea starts, it's *All hope abandon, ye who enter here.*"

"Yeah, that'd be something, wouldn't it?" Justin was about to say something more when his cell phone rang. He put it to his ear. "Hello? . . . Speaking . . . Yes, we're looking for gigs right now. The volcano's thrown everything for a loop. . . . In Greenwood, you say? . . . Green*ville*. Sorry. We're from the other side of the country, remember. Where exactly is Greenville? . . . At the south end of Moosehead Lake. Okay . . . When would you want us to play there, and what are you offering?"

They were in Orono now. They'd played several shows on and near the University of Maine campus here. Rob grabbed a Rand McNally road atlas. You couldn't get much more Maine-sounding than Moosehead Lake, could you? But Greenville was just a little dot on the map. He checked its population—a bit over 1,300. Greenville Junction, right next door, added another 850 or so. Given that the band was and intended to be caviar to the general, where would they find a crowd?

Rob circled Greenville and Greenville Junction in the atlas, then wrote *2100 people, total* next to them. He showed Justin the Rand McNally.

Justin nodded. He held out his free hand for Rob's pen. When he got it, he wrote a number with a dollar sign in front of it. It wasn't an enormous number, but it could have been worse. They'd done what they could do around Orono and Bangor. Money coming in instead of going out would be nice.

"We'll want cash up front when we get there—assuming we can get there," Justin said. "Like I told you, we're from California. I've never seen as much snow as this in my whole life before."

Rob nodded. It just kept coming down and coming down and coming down. It came down early enough and often enough to bemuse the locals, and if you weren't used to snow in Maine you had to be one of the loved-and-hated summer people. He'd heard people arguing about whether they'd ever seen so much snow so early in the season. Some said yes, and said it was just one of those things. The naysayers were inclined to blame it on the supervolcano.

No matter what caused it, it was real. Even people who'd been driving in snow since they'd got behind the wheel were having trouble. Snow plows had already started coming out. So had rock salt and grit to try to keep roads passable. And so had anguished howls from every agency that deployed snow plows and rock salt and grit. Doing so much so early, they wailed, would wreck their carefully crafted budgets.

Justin wrote a date beside the proposed fee: Saturday after next, ten days away. He put a question mark by it. Rob nodded without great enthusiasm. The lead time would let the people in Greenville promote the show—assuming they tried, assuming anyone paid attention.

"Well, Mr. Walters, we'll all give it our best shot, and we'll see how it turns out," Justin said. "Thanks for calling. So long." He high-fived Rob. "A gig!"

"Uh-huh." Rob still wasn't thrilled. "Biff'll love leaving Orono. That Nicole he's found . . ."

"How many girls have all of us left behind?" Justin countered. "It goes with what we do."

"I know." Rob nodded. "But sooner or later you meet a girl who counts more than the band. Even Lennon met Yoko."

"That goes with what we do, too," Justin said. "I don't think Nicole's the one like that for Biff. If she is, well, it's not like nobody on this side of the country ever played rhythm guitar."

"Mpf." Rob wouldn't give that more than a grunt. Squirt

Frog and the Evolving Tadpoles was what it was because of all four people who made it up. The band wouldn't be the same without Biff . . . would it?

If they could get along without him, could they also do without a bass player who wrote some of their quirkier songs? Rob really didn't care to contemplate that. It was too much like contemplating your own death after your best friend got killed in a car crash.

Instead of contemplating it, he looked at the practical side of things: "That's still a week and a half from now, you said? In the meantime, how do we make some money come in for a change instead of going out?"

"Good question," Justin said. "If this were the '90s, we could set up a free concert in a record-store parking lot. They'd sell their albums, we'd sell ours—for cash, too—and everybody'd be happy. But"—he sadly spread his hands—"where you gonna find a record store these days?"

"That's a good question, too. I wish I had a good answer for you," Rob said. "Which is a more endangered species, record stores or secondhand bookstores?"

"All of the above?" Justin suggested. "People get most of their music online nowadays."

"Especially the people who listen to us," Rob said. "Our bottom line would be better off if they didn't."

"Fuckin' tell me about it," Justin said. "And when they want used books, they hit Alibris or AbeBooks or even good old Amazon."

"So we don't play in a record-store parking lot, or in a bookstore lot, either," Rob said sadly. "We ought to play somewhere, though. You can still move CDs if you sign 'em when people buy 'em."

"Not in Orono. Not in Bangor, either. We've done all the business we can do around here." Justin had a keen sense for how much of Squirt Frog and the Evolving Tadpoles any given area could support—or stand, if you looked at it that way.

Maybe Rob believed the lead guitarist had that keen sense because he thought the same thing about these parts. "We already played Bar Harbor," he mused aloud. "We don't want to go back there. And there isn't much if we head north."

"There isn't *anything* if we head north," Justin said with relentless precision. "You end up in Canada, and not the part of Canada with lots of people—the part of Canada with lots of moose."

"How do you tell that from Maine?" Rob asked. They were going to play by Moosehead Lake (which, on the map, really did look like a moose's head), and they'd already seen one of the big critters lumbering across a road deserted by everything except the moose and their wheels.

But Justin knew what was what. "You head north from here, you end up in Quebec," he explained. "In Quebec, the moose—mooses? meese?—speak French."

"There you go." Rob clapped his hands. "I never would've figured that out on my own."

"I knew I was good for something," Justin said, not without pride.

Also not without pride, Rob answered, "Not me. I'm good for nothing. If you don't believe me, ask my father."

"Hey, at least your dad knows what rock is and probably likes some of it," Justin said. "My grandfather is like ninety-four. He's still got his marbles, but he's so old, he's on the other side of the line. He was grown up when rock 'n' roll started, and it's just kids' noise to him."

"Like my dad with hiphop," Rob said.

"Yeah, just like that," Justin agreed. "If you decide it isn't for you the first few times you hear it, you'll never get it."

"So where can we play between now and Greenville?" Rob

asked, reaching for the road atlas once more. "Some place where we haven't been, and where there'll be enough people who haven't heard us yet and might want to."

"Is there any place like that left in Maine?" Justin asked. "And if there is, can we get there and get back through the snow?"

"Boy, you ask a lot of questions," Rob said. "Come have a look—see what you think." They both bent low to study the small print that showed town names.

Bryce Miller gravitated to university campuses the way bees went for flowers. In Lincoln, Nebraska, the university dominated the town in a way UCLA couldn't begin to in Los Angeles. Too many other things went on in L.A. Without the University of Nebraska, though, Lincoln hardly had any reason to exist.

Not only that, Bryce had met a few of Nebraska's classicists and their grad students at conferences. They were the only people in the whole state he knew even slightly. He hadn't expected to end up here with only the clothes on his back. That he'd ended up anywhere at all alive and in one piece was something close to a miracle—and a testimony to the endless training pilots put in, getting ready for emergencies they might never see in their whole career.

The Red Cross had put him and the other passengers from the plane (minus a few who'd ended up in the hospital—but everybody'd got out alive) in a Motel 6 commandeered for the purpose. Colin Ferguson hadn't had many kind things to say about his stay in one a couple of years before. Now Bryce knew why. The place made getting away feel all the more urgent.

Getting away, though, wasn't so easy. Volcanic ash started falling on Lincoln three days after the supervolcano erupted. The sky went gray and hazy. The sun disappeared. It might have been fog. It might have been a sandstorm. It seemed to combine the worst features of both.

Red Cross workers handed out surgical masks. They were already wearing them. Some of them wore goggles, too. They didn't distribute those. Bryce's guess was that they didn't have enough to go around.

He took the bus to campus. A grad student with the fine classical first name of Marcus (his last name was Wilson, which was just—there) asked him, "Want to see something interesting?"

"Like what?" Bryce returned.

"Let's go over to the museum," Marcus said.

"Okay." Bryce was game. It would have air-conditioning. It would keep out the worst of the dust. He did wonder what Marcus reckoned interesting. Maybe the museum had a good collection of classical coins or Greek pottery or something like that.

If it did, they weren't on display. On display were the bones of a bunch of extinct elephantoid creatures. The L.A. County Museum of Natural History had some, too, but not so many. A placard declared that this museum boasted the finest collection of proboscidean fossils in the world.

But they weren't what Marcus wanted to show Bryce. Marcus took him over to a much smaller display of fossilized rhinos from something called the Ashfall State Historical Park. "Where's that?" Bryce asked.

"Northwest of here." Marcus pointed to a map on the wall above the display case with the bones. "Near a little town called Orchard. The text will tell you more about it."

The text told Bryce that the dead rhinos were almost 12,000,000 years old. They'd been buried by volcanic ash at what had been a pond. Many more of them remained *in situ* at the state park, along with the other critters that had been entombed by the ash at the same time.

That ash proved to come from a supervolcano eruption in Idaho, though that wasn't established till a generation after the fossils first got found. *This same geological hot spot*, the informative text went on, *is today responsible for the exotic geological features of Yellowstone National Park.*

Maybe the hot spot had been responsible for Yellowstone yesterday. Today, it was responsible for screwing up half the country—or the whole planet, depending on how you looked at things. Bryce went on reading. *Many of the bones on display here*, the text told him, *show the overgrowth typical of Marie's disease, or hypertrophic pulmonary osteodystrophy.*

Being a classics major let him translate the Greek and Latin medical jargon into ordinary English: bad bone overgrowth that had to do with the lungs. Sure as hell, the plaque continued, *Marie's disease is caused by slow suffocation. In this case, it was brought on by inhaling volcanic ash and dust. The rhinos and other animals probably came to this pond or waterhole to soothe themselves in the cool mud, since a high fever is another symptom of the illness. The ashfall that killed them also entombed them, and preserved them extremely well.*

"Hey, Marcus." Bryce jerked a thumb at the plaque. "Check this out."

The other grad student read it. He grimaced. "That's exciting," he said.

"Ain't it just?" Bryce used the bad grammar on purpose. "Remind me not to inhale as long as I'm here."

"Sounds like a plan." Marcus eyed the text again. "How many cows and sheep are dying like that right now? How many fossils will they dig up ten or twelve million years from now?"

"I don't know about the second part," Bryce said. "The answer to the first part is, all the sheep and cows—and pigs; don't forget about pigs—out there, minus three. Oh, and the chickens, too."

"We don't want to leave the chickens out," Marcus agreed gravely. "But what are we going to eat once they're all dead?"

"Well, the dust doesn't cover the whole country. Some of the livestock will live," Bryce said.

"Uh-huh. What will it eat, though? The corn and the wheat and the rye won't get, uh, Marie's disease, but they won't grow with a couple of feet of ash dumped on them, either. This is Nebraska, remember. TV shows about farming draw fat ratings here. They run commercials for tractors and things. Most of the country between the Rockies and the Mississippi is the same way. Wipe all that off the map, and what's left on the menu?"

"Crow," Bryce answered. Marcus gave him a funny look, but then nodded. And Bryce found a question of his own: "How many *people* are going to come down with hypertrophic pulmonary osteodystrophy?" He delivered the polysyllables with a certain somber relish.

"I don't know, and if anybody else does, they aren't talking," Marcus said. "It's liable to be everyone from here all the way to Vegas who hasn't got a dust mask."

How many million people was that? If they were all doomed, no wonder no one was talking about it. Not even CNN Headline News would want to lead with a story that went *Okay, Middle America, bend over and kiss your ass good-bye.* Bryce dared hope not, anyhow, which might have been the triumph of optimism over experience.

Then he remembered that Vanessa was living in Denver. He hadn't really thought about her since his plane ditched in Branch Oak Lake. How many people in Denver were coming down with Marie's disease right this minute? Wasn't it easier to wonder how many weren't?

He must have made some kind of noise as all that went through his head, because Marcus asked, "What did you say?"

"Nothing," Bryce answered. But it hadn't been nothing, or Marcus wouldn't have noticed. Awkwardly, Bryce explained, "I was just thinking about my ex. She moved to Denver a little while ago."

"Oh." The other grad student digested that. Then he delivered his verdict: "Bummer, man. Talk about timing."

"Yeah, no kidding," Bryce said.

"Ex?" Marcus said. "Ex-wife?"

"We weren't married. We were living together . . . and then we weren't." Bryce spread his hands. "You know how it goes? Well, it went."

"Uh-huh." Marcus nodded. Bryce thought he might be gay, but Marcus didn't make a big deal out of it if he was. After a few seconds' pause, he asked, "You still have feelings for her?"

"I'm going with somebody else who's a lot easier to get along with." For a moment, Bryce thought that was a responsive answer. When he realized it wasn't, he sighed and said, "Yeah, I've still got some. I sure as shit don't wish Marie's disease on her, or anything like that." He sighed again. "I'm not nearly certain it works both ways, though."

"So she told you to hit the road, not the other way round." This time, Marcus didn't make it a question. "Oh, well. Good luck to her and all that, but you can't do anything about it."

"I know." But now Bryce also knew he'd have to keep reminding himself of that. Everything that had gone on had driven Vanessa out of his thoughts ever since the shock wave hit his plane. Now she was back, dammit. Like a chunk of gristle wedged in between two molars, she wouldn't be so easy to dislodge.

After the display from Ashfall, the rest of the museum seemed an anticlimax to Bryce. He was relieved when Marcus was ready to leave. He carefully adjusted his mask before they stepped out into the open air once more. He might have been a little casual about it before. Not now. Never again. Hypertrophic pulmonary osteodystrophy sounded righteously horrible. And he noticed

Marcus taking pains to adjust the straps on his mask over his ears, too.

Everything out there was gray. Dust swirled through the air, now thicker, now thinner, but always around. It collected in drifts in front of fences that lay athwart the breeze. It was inches thick everywhere. Bryce's shoes scrunched and sank into it, so that he might almost have been walking on the beach. He left blobby, indistinct footprints.

"I wish it would rain," Marcus said. "That would clean the air—for a while, anyhow."

"It would, yeah." Bryce was a Southern Californian, used to wishing for rain and not getting it. He had to remind himself that things worked differently in the Midwest. He looked up to the sky. He could hardly see the sun through the dust still blowing east. "Come on, Jupiter Pluvius. Do your stuff."

Marcus laughed. "Jupiter Pluvius, Roman rain god known only to classics students and old-time baseball writers."

Bryce's ears pricked up. Baseball neep was meat and drink to him. "If you know about Jupiter Pluvius and sportswriters—" he began. For the next little while, he forgot all about the supervolcano. Here was somebody who spoke his language, and it wasn't ancient Greek.

Garden City, Kansas, was no garden, not these days. Vanessa didn't think any of Kansas was a garden these days. The only good thing you could say about Kansas was that it was farther from the supervolcano crater than Colorado was. It was still screwed. It just wasn't screwed quite so hard.

Nobody on the Interstate had stopped and tried to molest her. Nobody'd stopped and offered her a ride, either. She'd walked and walked and walked till her arms were about to fall off and her blisters bled.

And when she got into town at last, nobody seemed the least bit interested in heading west with her and fixing her car. "Sorry," said a mechanic in a gimme cap with PUROLATOR FILTERS in big letters on the front. He didn't sound sorry—not even close. "I got more work in town than I can handle. I take my tow truck out into that blowing shit—'scuse my French—and I ain't got but a fifty-fifty chance of comin' back with your vehicle." He put heavy stress on the *hick* in the last word, which seemed much too fitting to Vanessa.

She fixed him with her flintiest—hell, bitchiest—and most footsore glare. "What am I supposed to do now?" Pickles' yowl from inside the carrier underscored the question.

All the same, the mechanic remained depressingly unfazed. "Y'ought to thank the Lord you made it this far. Plenty of people ain't," he answered. That was true, but also infuriating. He went on, "Red Cross done set up a shelter at the high school. It's three blocks over from here and two blocks up." He pointed. "You can't hardly miss it, even with all the crap in the air."

He wasn't wearing a mask. He was smoking a Camel. The pack stuck out of a front pocket of his chambray work shirt. Written above the pocket in machine-embroidered red script was the name Virgil. *Hick is right*, Vanessa thought disdainfully. *And whatever happens to his lungs, he fucking deserves it.*

Lugging Pickles, she wearily limped over to the high school. Most of the time, *You can't miss it* warned that you'd get lost, but not today. She wasn't the only tired-looking person toting this, that, and the other thing converging on the school, either. A woman with a so-help-me beehive hairdo who looked pretty goddamn tired herself checked Vanessa in at the front office.

"Denver?" she said when Vanessa told her where she was from. A carefully plucked eyebrow rose. "We only have one other person from Denver here that I know of. Not many from there have been able to get this far."

"I got out the morning after the supervolcano blew," Vanessa said, now sounding proud as well as pooped. "I bet it just kept getting worse from then on."

"I wouldn't be surprised," the woman answered. "Before we check you in, though, either I'll take charge of your cat or you can let it go if you want to. No pets here. None. It's the rule." By the way she said it, even the idea of appealing against The Rule was unimaginable.

Vanessa did anyway: "You can't do that! I got Pickles all this way! I won't turn him loose now!"

"Then you can look for help somewheres else," the woman with the beehive said flatly. "Only there ain't no somewheres else in Garden City."

That struck Vanessa as much too likely to be true. "What happens if you take charge of him?"

"He goes to the pound."

"You kill him, you mean."

"He goes to the pound," the woman repeated, as if she didn't like to think about that.

Tears stung Vanessa's eyes behind the goggles. "You're mean. You're cruel. You're hateful. I'd feed him out of whatever you feed me."

"Where's he gonna piss? Where's he gonna crap? What if he bites a kid or scratches somebody up? What if he gets into fights with other cats and dogs? Well, he won't, on account of we don't allow any pets. Any. Like I said, that's the rule."

No matter how mean and cruel and hateful it was, it made sense in a bureaucratic way. Even though it made sense in a bu- reaucratic way, it *was* mean and cruel and hateful. Trying not to sob, Vanessa carried Pickles outside. He wasn't an outdoor cat. He wouldn't know what to do loose in the world. But it was better—she hoped it was better—than just killing him.

Even after so long in the carrier, he didn't want to come out.

When he finally did, he stared with big round eyes. The ash and dust on the grass made him sneeze. Then a noise or something made him scoot away. He slunk around the corner of the office building and was gone.

When Vanessa went back in, she'd lost her place in line. She had to work her way up to the front again. She wondered if she'd have to go through all the paperwork twice, too, but she didn't. The woman with the beehive said, "Let's see—where can we put you? The auditorium is full, and so is the gym. It'll have to be a classroom. . . . Susie, have we filled up J-7 yet?"

Susie was the next woman standing behind the counter. "Sure did, Lucille. They're packed in there like sardines. We're working on the K block."

"K-1 it is," Lucille said, and told Vanessa how to get there. "Here's your authorization card," she added. "It's good for rations and water and enough cot or floor or whatever they got for sleeping."

"Wonderful," Vanessa mumbled, still leaking tears. She'd had nothing to do with high school since escaping not so good, not so old San Atanasio High. Well, almost nothing: she'd gone to a five-year reunion with Bryce, and spent most of her time dishing the dirt on the local guy she'd lived with before him with other girls who'd also known that luckless fellow. The guy himself didn't come, which only made the stories better.

They'd done English in room K-1. Posters of Shakespeare, Walt Whitman, and Toni Morrison hung on the walls. A lesson plan for *Julius Caesar* covered one of the whiteboards. A bookcase in a corner of the room held more copies of *The Mill on the Floss* than anyone in his right mind would ever need.

All the desks were gone, including the teacher's. No cots—just people. The air inside was warm and stuffy, though less dusty than the stuff outside. Vanessa shed her masks and goggles. The room smelled of humanity, but not of raw sewage. Which probably meant . . .

"Do we go down the hall to use the bathroom?" she asked.

Half a dozen people nodded. "Sure do," a chunky guy said. "But you don't need no hall pass, anyways, and they don't hit you with detention if you smoke in there."

He was playing to everybody stuck in K-1 with him. He got his laugh, too, though not from Vanessa. She mourned poor Pickles. Maybe putting him out of his misery right away would have been better. But maybe someone would take him in before he starved or got eaten or choked on dust. She could hope. She had to hope. She made herself ask another question: "What do they feed us?"

"It was Del Taco last time. Gen-you-wine dogmeat Mexican," the chunky man said. He woofed, and got another laugh. If he hadn't been class clown when he was a skinny teenager with zits, Vanessa would have been amazed.

Asshole, she thought while Mr. Class Clown preened. She almost said it out loud. Old Porky wore thin in a hurry. But some of the other jerks who'd got here before her plainly liked him. She kept her mouth shut and staked out her own little patch of worn, dirty linoleum. Her purse would make a lumpy pillow, but better than nothing . . . maybe.

More people came in. The room got crowded, and even stuffier. The power was out, so the air conditioner didn't work. With all the blowing, drifting crud outside, opening a window seemed a doubleplus ungood idea. She was exhausted from her hike into town, and the bad air sure didn't help.

The door opened again. This time, it was two Red Cross workers. One pushed a wheeled cart with flats of water bottles. The other's cart was piled high with brown cardboard boxes. "MREs," the man said, by way of explanation or apology. "We got 'em from the National Guard armory. They ain't real exciting, but they beat the heck outa empty."

Meals, Ready to Eat. Three lies in four words, Vanessa discovered. Maybe not a world record, but in the running. After she choked hers down, she decided it made Del Taco a Wolfgang Puck special by comparison. Looking at the box, she discovered hers had an expiration date eight years in the future. On the one hand, that made it fairly fresh for an MRE. On the other, it said even germs wanted jack diddly to do with the goddamn thing.

Still and all, the Red Cross man had a point. A full belly was better than a hungry one.

Vanessa chucked her trash into one of the garbage bags the Red Cross people left behind. Then she went outside and down the hall to the john—which, of course, meant she gave up the chunk of floor to which she'd laid claim. The TP was just this side of wax paper: even worse than the cheap, scratchy stuff offices used. And the roll was almost empty. What would they do when they ran out? She didn't know, but she had the bad feeling she'd find out.

Mr. Class Clown came out of the boys' room at the same time as she came out of the girls'. "Boy, that was fun," he said, and held his nose.

"Yeah." Vanessa nodded. With one toilet backed up, the girls' room had been pretty rank, too.

"I wanna get outa here," he said. His name was Luke. She'd found that out.

"Who doesn't?" she said. "But how do you aim to do it?"

"I know how to hotwire a car," he answered. "If it'll take me out of the fuckin' dust before it goes belly-up, I'm golden."

Cop's kid or not, Vanessa considered that with less disgust and more interest than she would have imagined before the supervolcano went boom. How many thefts and robberies could you blame on the eruption? Hundreds? Thousands? Hundreds of thousands? That would have been her guess.

Luke went on, "Anybody thinks I'm gonna sit here scarfing down Meals Revolting to Eritreans, he damn well better think again."

Vanessa had heard *Meals Rejected by Ethiopians*, but not his take on the name. That might have been why she said, "Want a passenger? I've got some cash. I can pay for gas and stuff."

He looked her up and down. As he did, she realized she'd made a mistake. His wet gaze made her feel as if she had slugs crawling over her. "There's other ways to pay," he said, running his tongue over his lips as if he were running it into her ear. "Cheaper'n cash, and more fun, too."

"No, thanks. Forget I asked," she said, and hurried back to room K-1. He wouldn't try anything with people around.

"Hey!" He hurried after her.

She turned around. The .38 was in her hand, aimed a few inches north of his belly button. "I said no. I meant no. What part of that didn't you follow?"

"Okay. Okay!" He drew back a couple of steps. He was smart enough to see he'd get ventilated if he came forward instead, then. That was good—for him. "Don't get your bowels in an uproar. You ain't such hot shit, trust me."

He wasn't so very smart after all. He was trying to wound her, but he thought she'd give a rat's ass about anything that came out of his mouth. "Like you are. As if!" she said. "Just stay away from me, and we'll both pretend this never happened. Otherwise, I'll blow your fucking head off."

"You talked me into it." Luke eased around her, hands plainly visible, making no sudden moves. Vanessa got the idea he might have had a gun pointed at him before.

He went into the classroom first. She put the pistol back in her purse before she opened the door. He was already launched into a stupid joke by then. He didn't even look at her. That suited her fine. Not much in the way of brains, but at least some street smarts.

Night absent electricity was darkness absolute, darkness claustrophobic and scary. Vanessa would have loved it had someone lit a candle, but she, like everybody else in K-1, was left to curse that darkness. She hadn't tried sleeping in a crowd like this since summer camp when she was a kid. People muttering, people twisting and crunching as they tried to find half-comfortable positions on the hard floor, people snoring, people farting . . . People.

In spite of everything, she did fall asleep. Not too much later, someone tapped or kicked her in the ankle. She woke with a wildly pounding heart. For a few bad seconds there in the blackness, she had no idea where she was or what she was doing there. Memory came back piecemeal. Garden City . . . Red Cross shelter . . . Poor Pickles! . . . This stupid fucking classroom . . . Oh.

She tried to go to sleep again. It took longer this time. At least no one in here was having screaming hysterics. That was some-thing. A whole room full of people could forget about shut-eye if anybody did.

Asleep. Awake. Asleep. Awake. Asleep. *Awake*. It was still as black as the middle of an SS man's heart, but she knew damn well she wouldn't go back to sleep again. So she said to hell with it and waited till wan gray light started leaking through the windows. Then she discovered she wasn't the only one who'd given up and was sitting instead of lying.

The Red Cross people brought more MREs and water bottles. Mushrooms and beef tasted like mud with lumps, some squishy, others chewy. No way to boil water for the instant-coffee packet. She tore it open, poured the stuff onto her tongue, and washed it down with water. It was as bad as she'd thought it would be. Any caffeine, though, was better than none.

When she came back from the john, she pulled out a copy of *The Mill on the Floss* and started reading it. It was the only entertainment around. Unlike the vile instant coffee, it wasn't as bad as she'd thought it would be.

Luke disappeared two days later. Maybe he did know how to boost a car. Stuck in a room full of increasingly smelly strangers, Vanessa wondered if she should have gone with him. Wasn't escaping—this—worth some less than heartfelt fucking and sucking? She hadn't thought so then. As time dragged on in her crowded cage, she got less and less sure she'd been right.

XV

Every time Colin picked up the *Times* from his driveway, it got thinner and lighter. It might almost have been an African famine victim, slowly wasting away. It had started shrinking long before the Yellowstone supervolcano, of course; the Internet had been sucking the life out of newspapers for years. But less and less paper was making its way to the presses these days. The *Times* did wry stories about its own struggles for survival. And the *Breeze*, which remained Web-only, no doubt envied its bigger rival.

That wasn't the only struggle going on. When he drove to the cop shop in the morning, gas stations reminded customers ODD or EVEN: the governor had reimposed the every-other-day rationing scheme not seen since the Arab oil embargoes. Mother Nature could embargo Los Angeles, too. More and more stations flew red flags to show they had no gas at all. Thanks to Gabe's swoop right after the eruption, San Atanasio's police department still had a tolerable supply. How long that would last, and what the police would do when it ran low . . . Colin preferred not to dwell on yet.

A Burger King had a big sign in the window—SORRY, NO FRIES. TRY OUR ONION RINGS! When not enough spuds were making it into town to support the fast-food business, L.A. was in deep kimchi. Colin hadn't heard of a kimchi shortage, and San Atanasio abounded in Korean restaurants. Maybe they brought their Napa cabbage down from the nearby Central Valley.

It got cold—highs refused to climb into the sixties. A rainstorm came down from the Gulf of Alaska, and then another one, and then another one still. Anything could happen in the fall; everybody who'd lived here for a while knew that. People kept hoping things would warm up. Colin eyed the pale sun and the washed-out sky and the unbelievable sunsets. He hoped things would warm up, too, but he didn't expect it. That was what he got for falling in love with a geologist.

He doggedly kept on with his own job. If snow fell below 2,500 feet and didn't want to melt right away, if the mountains ringing the Los Angeles basin were white, white, white, he couldn't do anything about that. His own little corner of the world? There, he stood a chance.

Gabe Sanchez felt the same way, though he pissed and moaned more than Colin did. "Man, you figure the Honolulu PD's got any openings for an experienced cop?" he asked as he and Colin drove through chilly rain to a liquor store that had just been held up by a shotgun-toting robber.

"You can always hit Craigslist," Colin answered. "You want to get out of town, though, I bet there's less competition in Fairbanks."

"Fairbanks?" Gabe made a cross with his two forefingers, as if repelling a vampire. "Funny, man—funny like a colostomy bag. That fuckin' town was in the fuckin' deep freeze before this stupid superwaddayacallit blew its stack. What's it gonna be like year after fuckin' next? The July ice-cube harvest'll be terrific, that's what."

Maybe you didn't need to fall in love with a geologist to know how screwed up things were, and how screwed up they were liable to get. Maybe you only needed your normal complement of working brain cells. Colin flicked on his turn signal and pulled into the cramped liquor-store parking lot. A black-and-white was already there, red and blue and yellow lights flashing in the overhead bar.

He grabbed his umbrella and got out. "One thing," he said as he and Gabe squelched toward the entrance. "Rain's washed away most of the ash."

"Oh, boy," Gabe said. "Besides that, Mrs. Lincoln, how'd you like the goddamn play?" Colin shut up.

The clerk inside the liquor store was a short, plump Filipina. She looked pissed when Colin asked for her story. "I already tell it," she said, pointing to the two uniformed policemen in there with her.

"Well, tell it again, please," Colin said. "Maybe you'll remember something new."

"I don't think so," the woman said. Colin looked at her. It was the kind of look that got the message across. She changed her mind: "Okay, I tell. This motherfucker come into the store. He point big old gun at me. 'Give me your money or I blow your ass away!' motherfucker say. I open cash drawer. I put money on counter. Motherfucker grab it and run. I call police."

English as she is spoke, Colin thought. The Filipina used the twelve-letter endearment as if it meant *guy*. For all he knew, she thought it did. One of these years, maybe it would. He'd heard plenty of other people use it the same way.

"Do you have surveillance video?" he asked her.

"What you say?" she returned: English as it wasn't spoke.

Colin tried again. "A camera," he said patiently. "A TV camera." Was there anybody in the world who didn't savvy *TV*? Maybe a few luckless natives stuck in the bad reception of the

Papua New Guinea mountains. Everyone else bowed down before the great god of the modern age and his holy name.

"Oh. TV!" Yes, the Filipina got that. She pointed up and behind her, to a brushed-aluminum box with a lens at the business end. "Right there."

"We'll check that out, ma'am," Gabe said. "Was the robber wearing a mask?" He had to do a show-and-tell to get across what a mask was. When the clerk understood, she shook her head.

"Something, anyway," Colin remarked. "Have to find out what the footage looks like. If it shows the perp's face, and if he's nasty with that shotgun, maybe we can get one of the TV stations to run it. That'll help if somebody makes him." He might—he did—despise TV news, but he wasn't too proud to use it.

"There you go," Gabe said. "Maybe it's the same jerk who blasted that other clerk a while ago."

"Maybe it is," Colin agreed. "That'd be good. Well, we'll see."

"That motherfucker shoot somebody?" The clerk's voice rose in understandable horror.

"We're not sure if it's the same guy yet," Colin said.

"You catch him! You put him in jail! You keep him in jail!" she said shrilly. "This not first time we get robbed. Nobody never get caught. What kind stupid motherfuckers work for police, huh?"

Colin would have got pissed off if he hadn't already figured out she didn't mean much by the word. Sighing, he answered, "Ma'am, there are smart cops and dumb cops, same as there are at any other kind of work."

She eyed him. "You smart cop or dumb cop?"

"Probably," he said. Let her make whatever she wanted of that. Back to business: "Let's see what the camera picked up."

After some fiddling with the controls, they played it back and watched it on the monitor next to the now-gutted cash register. It was in color and highly detailed. Colin remembered the black-and-white blurs you got from early-model surveillance cameras. No more. This was plenty good enough to ID the perp—and his shotgun—in court.

He was about eighteen, African American, in a cheap knit watchcap, a hoodie, and jeans. He had earrings and a tattoo on the left side of his neck, just below his ear.

"Damned if I don't think that's the same guy," Gabe said.

"It's been a while," Colin answered, but he suspected the sergeant was right.

Whoever he was, the way the robber yelled and waved the shotgun around ought to be plenty to rouse a TV anchorman's righteous indignation. Colin knew the numbers to call.

Channel 7 sent a gal out to look at the video. "Oh, yes, we can use this," she said, beaming at Colin and showing off teeth undoubtedly capped. "Do you have a hotline number where people can call if they know something?"

"Sure do." He wrote it down on the back of one of his cards. Under it, he printed SAN ATANASIO PD HOTLINE. She might not think to turn the card over and remind herself where she'd got it. She didn't especially look like a dummy, but you never could tell.

"Thanks." She stuck it in her purse. "Now, what was the name of the liquor store? Where exactly is it? When did the robbery take place? The clerk was a woman?" She could see that on the video, but he didn't mind if she made sure. By the time she left, they were both pretty well pleased with themselves.

The only trouble was, the footage didn't run. The big headline on the evening news was that the governor had ordered mandatory statewide rolling blackouts. "We have to conserve energy because less is reaching us due to the impactful nature of the supervolcano eruption," he declared earnestly.

Just because he'd ordered blackouts and power cutoffs didn't mean he'd get them right away. Half a dozen different groups—right, left, and center—converged on his mansion, waving picket signs and demanding that he change his mind this instant, if not sooner. A judge way the hell up in Siskiyou County had already issued a preliminary injunction against the blackouts. Colin felt a certain amount of sympathy for him. Siskiyou County was cold and mountainous. Without electricity for several hours a day, it would be colder yet.

And there was a car chase on the Long Beach Freeway. The station had to cover that live—or thought it did, anyway. So the people out there in TVland never got a glimpse of the robber with that shotgun and the tat.

It turned out not to matter. One of the San Atanasio cops took a look at the video and said, "Fuck me if I don't know that asshole. That's JerWilliam Ellis. I busted his sorry butt for armed robbery year before last. I didn't know he was outa juvie."

"JerWilliam?" Colin said.

"That's his name. One word, capital *J*, capital *W*," the cop said. "Don't ask me why. I just work here. Ask his mama."

"O-kay." Colin shrugged. It wasn't his business. He'd seen plenty of names stranger than that. "Know where he lives?"

"Last I heard, in the projects on Imperial."

That was north and east of San Atanasio. The big housing projects there had gone up after the 1965 Watts riots, a monument to LBJ's Great Society. They'd been breeding gangbangers ever since. As projects went, there were plenty of grimmer examples back East. That didn't make the Imperial Gardens a garden spot.

"Have to talk with LAPD," Colin said unenthusiastically. The projects were in the Big City's jurisdiction. Sometimes LAPD cooperated well. Sometimes the Big City cops treated their small-town cousins like a bunch of scrounging hicks. You never could tell till you tried.

"Better call quick," the cop said. "Way things are going, they'll start canceling phones pretty soon, too."

"Heh," Colin said, for all the world as if it were a joke.

Louise Ferguson grabbed a shopping cart and headed into Vons. The supermarket on Reynoso Drive had been there for as long as she could remember, and for longer than that, too. Some of the regulars who'd come in when she was just getting started were still regulars now: regulars whose hair had gone white or light blue or pink, regulars with wrinkles and bent backs and polyester tops. *Microfiber, my ass*, Louise thought. *I say it's polyester, and I say the hell with it.*

Was that how it ended up? Was that how she'd look twenty-five years from now? Would that cheery newlywed going up the produce aisle see her a lot further through the century and shiver as if a goose had walked over her grave? Probably. You couldn't win. The only way you could get out of the game was by walking in front of a truck or something. Louise didn't want to do that.

But she didn't want to get old, either. She especially didn't want to get old with a lover so much younger than she was. Men turned distinguished as they aged. You respected their experience. Women went invisible or grew hideous, one. Who gave a flying fuck, or any other kind, about some old broad's experience?

Did you come to the store to piss and moan, or are you going to shop some, too? Louise asked herself. She chuckled wryly. She had the cart. She had her list—she was an organized shopper. Might as well drop some cash.

As usual, she headed for the produce first. The newlywed looking unhappy now, not cheery, had her reasons. Not much filled the bins. Most of what was there didn't look very good. The prices were through the roof. A sign above a bare bin that should have held potatoes said SORRY! WE'RE DOING THE BEST WE CAN!

The scary part was, Louise believed it. Nobody who could get his hands on higher-quality veggies would have put these sorry specimens on display.

"Sucks, doesn't it?" the newlywed said.

"I couldn't have put it better myself," Louise answered. They smiled at each other and rolled their eyes. At least for a moment, misery loved company.

Things got no better in the rest of the market. The shelves had lots of odd, spotty gaps. Louise had noticed a few of them the week before. Now they came right out and poked her in the eye. She didn't need long to see what the pattern was. You could still buy local stuff. Anything that came from back East was in short supply.

She got what she could. Some of what she couldn't get, she could work around. No tissues in sight, but they had plenty of TP for some reason. If you had to, you could use it on your nose as well as your rear end. And rice could substitute for potatoes: oh, not exactly, but close enough. *Where there's a will, there's a lawyer*, she thought. Then she tightened her lips so her mouth turned into a thin, bloodless line. That had been—and no doubt still was—one of Colin's jokes.

Well, what's-her-name—Kelly—was listening to them now. She hadn't heard all of them a million times yet. Only a few hundred, say. If she stuck with him as long as Louise had . . . He'd be pretty ancient by then, and Kelly would be no spring chicken herself.

People said you were crazy for two years after your marriage sank. Much of what people said was bullshit, nothing else but. That, though, seemed pretty much true. Louise felt a lot more stable, a lot more grounded, than she had when she walked out the old front door for the last time.

Grounded or not, she couldn't get away from what had been so familiar for so long. Would Colin and the things he'd done and said keep bubbling up inside her for the rest of her life? It sure looked that way. On the outside, the break was clean. On the inside . . . She could still hear him, dammit.

She steered the cart to a checkout stand. As she displayed her Vons Club card for the discounts, the Hispanic kid bagging groceries said, "Hope you don't mind plastic bags. They're the only ones we were able to get."

"That's okay," Louise said. They were supposed to be phasing out plastic. No, they were supposed to have phased it out. Maybe they'd won some kind of dispensation on account of the supervolcano.

The Pope gives dispensations. You mean an exemption. Damn straight she could still hear Colin in her head. Oh, Vanessa would have said the same thing, but not in the same tone of voice. And she hadn't heard one damn thing from Vanessa since Yellowstone fell in on itself.

Reminding herself of that made her miss whatever the bagger said next. "I'm sorry?" She tried to look interested and attentive.

"I said, if you've got some of those cloth totes with the handles, it might be a good idea to bring them the next time you come in. Who knows how much longer we'll be able to get any bags at all?"

"Okay. I'll do that." Louise had several of them in a drawer. Who didn't? Some people were bound not to. And they'd be the ones who raised a stink when the market didn't—couldn't—help them corral their groceries.

Louise stowed the Vons Club card and took out her trusty Visa. She was signing the store copy of the register printout when the checkout gal remarked, "Maybe you're lucky to get plastic bags today. It's coming down in buckets out there."

"It is?" Louise hadn't paid any attention to what the weather was doing. Now she looked out through the big plate-glass windows. "It is!" she agreed in dismay. It hadn't been when she got there. "Can I run back and buy an umbrella?" That would make the two women behind her in line love her to death.

The checker turned to the bagger. "Run get Mrs. Ferguson an umbrella, Orlando. Hustle!"

"*Sí*, Virginia," Orlando said, and he was off like a shot. He came back with an umbrella—an umbrella with a tacky floral pattern, but what could you do?—a lot faster than Louise could have got it for herself. She paid cash; it was quicker than plastic, and she did care what people thought, even if they weren't people she knew.

Buckets was barely the word for the way it was pouring. L.A. didn't usually get deluges like this. The umbrella kept her top half dry. From the waist down, she was soaked anyhow; it was blowing almost horizontally out of the northwest. The plastic grocery bags *were* a blessing. Brown paper would have disintegrated in rain like this. Louise threw the sacks into the trunk and waded around to the driver's door.

Getting in, wrestling the umbrella shut, tossing it down in front of the passenger seat, and slamming the car door took only a few seconds. All the same, Louise let in enough water to fill a hazard on the golf course down the street. Quite a bit came down on her in the process, too. "Yuck!" she said. That wasn't nearly good enough. She tried again: "Shit!"

Better. Definitely better. She'd given up trying to understand why people told you not to swear. It didn't help the human condition as much as getting drunk or screwing, but it made a pretty fair Band-Aid.

Then she said "Shit!" again. Getting in, letting in all that water and wet air, and having the gall to go on breathing had steamed up the inside of the car windows. For all the seeing out she could do, she might as well have been in the middle of her own private fog bank.

She turned on the motor and hit both front and rear defrost.

Blowing warm air across the inside of the windshield made things worse before it improved them. She'd known it would, so she didn't bother cursing. Weren't a couple of old paper towels hiding under the passenger seat?

They were, and they weren't too wet, either. She used them to wipe off the side windows, or as much of the side windows as she could reach. Once she finished, she started to wad them up so she could give them the old heave-ho once she got home. Thoughtfully, she caught herself. Kleenex was gone from the shelves. How long would paper towels last? These would dry out, and she could use them again. She shoved them back under the seat uncrumpled.

Start the windshield wipers. Turn them up to high. She couldn't remember the last time she'd done that, but she sure needed to now. Turn on the headlights. If the wipers were going, you had to do that. It was the law. As a cop's wife—yes, yes, dammit, a cop's ex-wife—she not only knew about stuff like that, she took it seriously. And in a downpour like this, you needed to give the other jerks out there all the chance to see you they could get.

A ginormous SUV was shoehorned into the space on her left. As it always did, that made backing out a special delight. She wondered why the damn things had got so popular and stayed so popular so long. She shrugged. Nothing she could do about it now but escape this one without getting rear-ended.

She managed that. She pulled out of the parking lot and onto the street. She started back toward the condo, trying to look every which way at once. She'd been driving for thirty years. She'd seen from experience that people in L.A. didn't know how to handle rain. They went too fast and they tailgated. If she hadn't seen it for herself, the stories Colin brought home from the cop shop would have rammed the lesson home.

So she wasn't astonished when things ground to a halt

halfway home. Disgusted? Yes. Ticked off? You betcha. Astonished? No way. It was about time for the news station to run its traffic report. On the off chance, she hit the third button on the radio.

"—fic on the fives," came out of the speakers. Freeway crashes—and there were a slew of them—came first. Then the announcer said, "And there's a bad surface-street accident in San Atanasio, near the corner of Sword Beach and 169th Street. At least four cars are involved, and a light pole is down across the road. *That'll* put a hitch in your git-along."

He sounded absurdly cheerful. Of course, he wasn't stuck in it. Louise was. She slid into the right lane, ignoring the horn from the asshole who didn't care for it. Then she got off Sword Beach with almost as much relief as soldiers must have felt escaping the genuine article in 1944.

Stores and restaurants and gas stations and banks and all the other impedimenta of Western civilization fronted the avenue. As soon as you got away from it, things changed. White clapboard houses from before the war sat side by side with faded stucco ones from not long after. The house where she'd raised her family with Colin was only a couple of miles away, but in a much better neighborhood.

A much whiter neighborhood, too. Louise might be living with a Hispanic man, but when she didn't watch herself she still eyed faces darker than her own with suspicion. That was one more inheritance from being married to a cop, even if it was one she wished she could have escaped.

Not many white faces here. Mexicans, Salvadorans, blacks, Koreans, Filipinos . . . You could find everybody, and every kind of hole-in-the-wall eatery, in San Atanasio. A lot of lawns hadn't been mown any time lately. Some of these men mowed other people's lawns for a living, and had no time or energy to worry about their own. Before the rains started, the grass would have been yellow or brown. It greened up in a hurry, though. A few lawns had cars on them.

An Asian woman with an umbrella pushed a stroller along the beat-up sidewalk. A black guy who'd got up onto his roof with an aluminum ladder secured a blue plastic tarp with broken bricks to bandage a leak till the roofers showed up. That wouldn't be till after it quit raining, of course, if it ever did.

Nobody paid any attention to her as she drove along. It wasn't a neighborhood like South Central, where people stared at any white face. San Atanasio's *everybody* included honkies, too. And when you were in a car, especially a car closed up against the rain, you were halfway towards invisibility anyhow.

She hit the brake as a boy on a bike zoomed out from no-where. Plenty of kids ran here and there, rain or no rain. Well, okay. It was Saturday. No doubt their older brothers had scrawled the graffiti that marked fences and garage doors the way cat pee marked toms' territories. San Atanasio had a graffiti-abatement program. You could call in and get them painted over for free. You could, but nobody here seemed to care.

And how long would a program like that last now that times were hard and getting harder? Probably not long. But then again, who could say where spray paint came from? If it wasn't made here, the gangbangers would have trouble getting any more.

Would they go back to buckets and brushes? Or would they . . . ? *Cut it out*, Louise told herself sternly. It wasn't her worry. Even if it had been, she couldn't do anything about it these days. Back when she was married to Colin, she'd fed him tips, and he'd used some of them. She was damned if she'd call him or e-mail him now. Unless it was about the kids, she wanted nothing to do with him. She didn't *want* that, either, but she knew she was stuck with it.

If she turned left here, she ought to be able to get back on to Sword Beach beyond the accident. She turned—carefully. The rain was really coming down in buckets. You never saw rain like this in the fall. You hardly ever saw rain like this in January or February, as wet a season as L.A. had.

There was the stop sign at Sword Beach. Louise didn't California it, the way she would have in good weather. It wasn't only that she'd lost the immunity to tickets cops and cops' spouses enjoyed in their hometown. Some jackass barreling along the street after going slow for so long was liable to cream her.

She made good time after she turned on to the thoroughfare. The accident receded in her rearview mirror. She saw a lot of smashed sheet metal, two black-and-whites, an ambulance, a fire engine, and a yellow truck with a cherrypicker from the Department of Public Works. A mess, all right. She supposed the Public Works guys were in charge of the downed light pole.

Back to the underground parking lot that had become as familiar as the old driveway used to be. She popped the trunk and grabbed as many sacks of groceries as she could carry. Rainwater dripped from the bumper. It rilled down to the center of the concrete expanse and vanished into a softball-sized drainage hole with a metal grate over it.

Louise got soaked all over again lugging the groceries up to the condo. "Oh, you poor thing!" Teo exclaimed when she came in. "Are there more? Let me fetch the rest."

"Don't bother. Why should you get wet, too?" Louise said. But he wasn't listening to her. He plucked the keys out of her handbag and vanished down the stairs. He came back with the rest of the sacks a couple of minutes later. Sure as hell, he was as wet as if he'd just come out of the shower. The keys clanked when he put them back in her purse.

"Forty days and forty nights," he said, more happily than the sentiment deserved.

Louise was already putting stuff in cupboards and the fridge. She missed her old kitchen; she didn't have room to swing a cat in here. "I wouldn't be surprised," she agreed. "There was a god-awful wreck on Sword Beach, too. I had to kinda go around it to get home." She told him about it.

"Did you?" Teo said. Louise nodded. So did he, as if that explained something he'd wondered about. And it did: "I thought you were taking a while getting back."

"Well, I was. Couldn't help it," Louise replied. "Hand me that chub of ground round, will you?" She stuck it in the freezer. "You can still get beef," she said. "I know it's fatty and everything"—Teo worried much more about nutrition than anybody she'd known before—"but you can still get it."

"The earth is angry at us," he said. "Who would have imagined a volcano could throw all our plans for a loss?"

He was a football fan. Louise . . . tolerated that. As for who would have imagined—well, Colin had been tiresome about it even before the supervolcano erupted. Of course, that was because his new squeeze worried about such things. People rubbed off on each other as they rubbed against each other. You couldn't help it.

She smiled. Teo smiled back, and ran a hand through her wet hair. As far as Louise was concerned, she'd got the best of the bargain.

There was a technical term for what riding a bike through heavy rain was like. It bit the big one, was what it did. Marshall Ferguson had a plastic poncho that kept him at least partially dry. It bit the big one anyhow.

But so did the UCSB parking policy. There weren't nearly enough spaces on campus. The ones that were there cost too bloody much. A bike was a lot more practical.

Most of the time. This past week, riding the bike to school tempted Marshall to take the bus instead. But he would have got drenched waiting for it, and it stopped three blocks from his place, so he would have got drenched walking to and from, too. You couldn't win.

A car zoomed by. It kept its distance; most Santa Barbara drivers, unlike their counterparts in a lot of Southern California, at least had some notion that they shared the road with people on two wheels. That didn't mean the tires didn't pick up water and plaster it against Marshall's side, then splash him in the face as the Toyota got ahead of him.

This happened at least half a dozen times before he finally got to campus. As he did every day when he arrived, he wondered if the bus wasn't a better idea after all. He wondered the same thing every time he pedaled home in the rain. *Maybe I should suspect a trend*, he thought. Somehow, though, he climbed aboard the bike every morning instead of walking to the bus stop. He always figured things would get better this next time. He might have been like that annoying song about tomorrow, tomorrow. Or he might have met one of the short definitions of insanity: doing the same thing over and over while expecting a different result.

"Hey, at least I have fun," he muttered as he escaped the nasty traffic at last. Whether getting cold, dirty water flung in his kisser from speeding Michelins honest to God counted as fun was something he'd worry about some other time.

Campus bike racks took up less room than parking lots did, but they filled up just as fast. He found a space, put his bicycle in it, and locked the machine to the rack. He used a lock and a chain his father approved of. He'd got el cheapos at first—and, one unhappy day his sophomore year, he'd had to take the bus back to his place after biking in that morning. His old man made him pay for the new bike, lock, and chain out of his own money, too. He hadn't appreciated that. He also hadn't had his bike stolen since.

Everybody else on campus looked as wet and miserable as he

did. Well, almost everybody. A tweedy prof strolled along under an umbrella big enough to keep the supervolcano crater dry. The guy was almost bald on top, but his gray hair came down to his shoulders all the same. He'd probably grown it out when he was a kid around 1973, decided it looked way cool, and never bothered to change his mind in spite of changing styles and changing hairline. Tenure could do that to you. You stopped needing to change, so you didn't. And if people snickered at you behind their hands, so what? You still had tenure.

Marshall wished students could get tenure. That was what he'd been trying to do all his years here. He liked imagining himself at fifty-five, paunchy, maybe balding, too, still living in an apartment with ratty furniture in Ellwood or Goleta, still soaking up units, still smoking dope, and still laying coeds whenever he got the chance. What more could anybody want?

He was mournfully aware it wouldn't happen. For one thing, his father wouldn't keep fronting him cash forever, and you couldn't make enough money odd-jobbing it to pay for your place and your food and your car and all the other shit you needed, to say nothing of university fees. One more thing that bit. Bigtime, in fact. For another, even if his old man had been willing to leave him on the gravy train for the next thirty years, UCSB wasn't. By rights, he should have graduated long since. He'd passed—way passed—the ordinary limits on time of attendance and total units. Adroit major-changing and a couple of petitions the administration had carelessly approved left him still working toward his sheepskin.

Pretty soon, though, he'd graduate no matter how much finagling, how much wiggling, or how much kicking and screaming he did. He hadn't had many expectations before the supervolcano knocked the economy flat and stomped on it. Now life with a bachelor's degree looked depressingly like going back to San Atanasio, back to his room at the old house, and sponging off his dad while he flailed around looking for work that wasn't there.

Rain or no rain, people were out on campus collecting donations for all the millions who'd had to evacuate on account of the eruption. Cash, canned goods, old clothes—they'd take anything. Marshall had given them money. He couldn't see how canned goods or beat-up jeans would make it from Santa Barbara to the Midwest.

He'd even asked about that. "They won't," an earnest guy with a Red Cross pin on his pocket replied. "But there are plenty of refugees at the western edge of the ashfall, too."

"Oh." Marshall hadn't thought about that. The next day, he'd donated a can of roast-beef hash and a can of mandarin oranges. So they didn't exactly go together. BFD.

Today, he walked past the wet volunteers. He was low on funds, and he hadn't stuck any cans in his backpack. The rain lowered everyone's spirits. The volunteers didn't try very hard to get people to stop. They stood or sat under polyethylene sheeting that didn't keep off enough of the rain, and looked as if they would have donated their souls to go somewhere warm and dry.

Marshall could actually do that. Campus buildings weren't *very* warm, because thermostats got pushed way down after the eruption. But it wasn't raining indoors. He could shed his poncho. He could even go into a men's room and use a paper towel to dry off a little. New stickers in there warned DON'T WASTE PAPER GOODS! What wasn't in short supply these days?

On to the room for the creative-writing class. Professor Bolger wasn't what Marshall had expected. He made the students write. Well, surprise! But he also made them submit what they wrote: submit it to markets where they were competing against people who'd been freelancing longer than they'd been alive.

When Bolger had announced that requirement, a girl bleated,

"We'll get rejected!" Marshall would have beaten her to it if he hadn't been exhaling at the moment instead of inhaling.

The prof answered a squawk with a question: "Suppose you do. How are you worse off?"

"Because!" the girl explained. Marshall nodded. That sure made sense to him.

"Listen to me," Bolger said grimly. "You are here to learn something about writing. And you are here—with luck—to see if you can make money writing. To make a living at it, even, if you're good enough and stubborn enough and lucky enough. You cannot possibly sell your work if you never submit it. And so . . . you will."

"How often do *you* get rejected?" Marshall asked. He assumed Bolger did; if the answer came back *never*, what the hell was the guy doing teaching here? Why wasn't he all over the best-seller list?

"I have a stack of slips this high." The prof held his hands six inches apart. "And that doesn't even count e-mails. Nobody's going to like your work all the time. You have to get hardened to that. It doesn't mean you're a bad person. It just means that editor didn't like that piece that day."

He made it sound simple and logical. Marshall still quailed at the idea of some hard-bitten, probably cigar-chewing, editor laughing at something he'd worked hard on. Logic would take you only so far.

XVI

When Vanessa heard loud diesel engines outside the Red Cross shelter in Garden City, the first thing she wondered was whether she'd slipped a cog. Hardly any motor noises had been around lately. The cars that could get out of town had got. Hardly any more vehicles were coming in out of the west.

So what the devil was going on? Curiosity felt odd. She knew more about the people cooped up in room K-1 with her than she'd ever wanted to find out. She knew how they smelled: worse by the day. So did she. She knew how *The Mill on the Floss* came out. Knowing didn't stop her from wondering why the Garden City school district inflicted it on defenseless high schoolers.

Some of the refugees passed the time by playing cards. That had already caused two fights. Money seemed like a joke when you couldn't buy anything with it—till you started losing. Then, to some people, it stopped being funny.

And if Vanessa never saw another MRE . . . it was liable to mean she'd starve to death. Which was worse seemed less and less obvious.

The MREs did give her and her fellow inmates at the refugee

center the strength to complain. They complained about the food, though nobody did the old Catskills shtick and added *and such small portions!* Not even the most dedicated complainer—and Vanessa was right up there—wanted more of the military rations. As far as she was concerned, they only proved GIs were heroes.

They complained about the accommodations. They complained about the stinking heads. They complained about having to go outside through the dust to use the stinking heads. (They complained even more about the idea of using a bucket behind a curtain in the room, not that there was enough space to set up that kind of niche anyhow.) Everybody complained about how smelly everybody else was.

They complained whenever somebody farted. Since they were eating MREs all the time, people farted a lot. Some were sound and fury, signifying nothing. Some could have cleared out Madison Square Garden. Clearing out K-1 wasn't so easy. You had to flee into the dust. Farts were only noxious. That stuff was whatever came after noxious.

Pickles was out in it. She wasn't the only one who complained about having to abandon a pet. Maybe somebody out there had taken in her poor, dumb kitty. She could hope so, but she couldn't make herself believe it. Guilt gnawed at her.

One of the Red Cross people came into the classroom in the middle of the morning. That alarmed Vanessa the way a change in routine alarmed a guy halfway through a twenty-year sentence. It was different! Something had to be wrong with it!

"Grab your stuff, put on masks if you've got 'em, and come outside in a neat line," the woman said, for all the world like a kindergarten teacher. But she added something a kindergarten teacher wouldn't have: "We are going to evacuate the people at this center to a site farther east."

"There *is* a God!" Vanessa exclaimed amidst the general hubbub the announcement set off.

A doughy, middle-aged woman gave her a disapproving look. "Of course there is," she said, her voice a harsh Kansas rasp that sounded straight off a Depression-era farm. "Have you accepted our Lord Jesus Christ as your personal Savior?"

"I don't think Jesus had shit to do with the supervolcano, and I figure I saved myself when I got the hell out of Denver," Vanessa answered. To make herself perfectly clear, she added, "You can do whatever you want with your own stupid religion, as long as you don't dump it on me."

When her father talked about religion, he described himself as a born-again pagan. *His* father had been a dour Baptist, but Dad got over it. Vanessa's mother had messed around with various New Agey things without letting much stick. Her brothers were as pious as she was. Rob enjoyed getting into debates when Mormon missionaries came around. One memorable summer afternoon, Marshall tried a more direct approach: he turned around and dropped his pants. No Mormons—or even Jehovah's Witnesses—rang the doorbell for a long time after that.

Ms. Doughface looked as if Vanessa had sprouted bright red horns and a long, barbed tail. "You'll burn forever!" she said.

"Yeah, well, suppose you let me worry about that, too, okay?" Vanessa said. She pushed past the woman. She would have hauled off and belted her with any more provocations. None of the squabbles in K-1 had left anyone badly hurt, but everyone's temper was frayed.

Vanessa wasn't close to the front of the line. She also wasn't close to the doughy woman, who'd ended up near the back. *Serves her right*, Vanessa thought.

Lines were also forming in front of the other overcrowded classrooms. A man's voice floated through the air (so did volcanic ash people were kicking up, but Vanessa tried to ignore that): "Wherever we're going, it's gotta be better than this!"

Now there was something to say *Amen!* to. One by one, each

classroom's worth of refugees headed up toward the front of the high school. At last, a Red Cross man shepherded K-1 forward. Vanessa hoped with all her heart she never saw—or smelled—this miserable place again.

Some of the buses growling out front were commandeered from schools: they were bright yellow, with the names of rural districts stenciled in black below the windows. More were as military as MREs, and painted olive drab. All of them had big, fat, super-duper filters sticking out from their engine compartments. If you were going to go anywhere with all this shit blowing around—and it was—that was how you had to go about it.

The bus into which Vanessa climbed was a military model. That didn't, and probably couldn't, make it less comfortable than a school bus. The driver was also military. He wore desert camouflage and a gas mask.

He touched a door when the bus was full. The doors rasped shut. Vanessa, who was sitting not far from the front, got the idea they were supposed to hiss instead of rasping. You couldn't put super-duper filters on everything. Even if grit didn't murder the engine, this bus had a strictly limited life expectancy.

As long as it got her away from Garden City, Kansas, before it dropped dead, she couldn't have cared less.

"Where are we going?" someone asked as the bus pulled away from the high school.

"It's called Camp Constitution, sir," the driver answered. Vanessa could hardly hear him over the roar of the bus in motion. Military specs plainly didn't worry about noise inside the cabin. "As for where it's located at, it's between Muskogee and Fayetteville."

Oklahoma? Arkansas? One of those states. The ass end of nowhere, either way. Why on earth would they dump—how many?—refugees there?

No sooner had the question occurred to Vanessa than the

woman right behind her asked it out loud. "Ma'am, they briefed us on account of that's where the dust from the volcano stopped falling," the driver said, which made a certain amount of sense. He continued, "So that's how come FEMA was tasked with setting up Camp Constitution there."

By the way he repeated the name, he seemed to like it. Vanessa didn't. To her, it sounded like some bureaucrat's effort to make squalor and misery sound patriotic. Hearing that FEMA was running the place did nothing to reassure her, either. Had FEMA ever run anything it hadn't screwed up? If it had, it wasn't within her memory.

How many people aboard the olive-drab bus were having that same reassuring thought? At least one besides Vanessa: a man yelped, "How come the Army isn't running this camp?"

"The Army can't do that!" The driver sounded as shocked as anyone could through a gas mask. "It isn't the military's responsibility to run a civilian facility inside the USA."

"But the Army might do it right. FEMA sure won't," the man said, which was exactly what Vanessa was thinking.

This time, he got no answer. The driver was concentrating on the Interstate in front of him. He needed to concentrate, because he was going through a pretty fair sandstorm. Less dust and ash floated in the air than right after the eruption, but more lay on the ground. The bus convoy stirred it up again.

The Army bus boasted air-conditioning. Soldiers traveled in more style than Vanessa would have guessed. What kind of fancy filters kept the A/C from overloading and crapping out? She didn't much care. Breathing air that wasn't close and moist and didn't smell like too many other people felt wonderful, or whatever one step up from wonderful was.

Then there was a *pop!* outside. One of the windows on the left side blew in. At the same instant, or close enough, one of the

windows on the right side blew out. So much for the air-conditioning.

Even as people were screaming and squealing and trying to
get bits of glass out of their hair, the driver grabbed an M-16
Vanessa hadn't noticed by his feet. He fired a burst out through
his window. The din was horrendous, and set the passengers making
even more noise than they were already.

Another shot from outside punched through sheet metal. By
what would do for a miracle, it didn't punch through any people.
The driver squeezed off a fresh answering burst. He hadn't a
prayer of hitting whatever maniac out there who was shooting at
them. Maybe he could make the asshole duck, anyway.

"What's he *doing*?" a woman howled. Vanessa thought it
was the gal who had a personal savior. That didn't make it a
dumb question, though.

"Some people are kinda unhappy we're evacuating from west
to east, and on account of we're taking folks out of Red Cross
shelters first," the driver answered with commendable calm.

Kinda unhappy, here, meant something like *pissed off enough
to try to commit murder*. Vanessa had no trouble working that
out. She wasn't so sure about her fellow refugees; she'd never
been one to underestimate the power of human stupidity.

Then she imagined herself on a lifeboat in the middle of the
Pacific instead of in a freshly ventilated olive-drab bus that all of a
sudden stank of cordite. She imagined some poor bastard treading
water as the boat went by. It wasn't going to stop for him and let
him climb aboard. If he had a gun, wouldn't he use it?

No wonder the guy out there in the dust started shooting.
Vanessa supposed they ought to count themselves lucky he only
had a varmint gun, not an RPG. For whatever reason—maybe
his car bought a plot right away—he was stuck in the middle of
the dust. How much longer could he, or anybody else, last here?

How many more like him were scattered from Nevada to

here? How many of them would be able to get out? How many would die of one lung disease or another, or else starve because the continent-wide food-distribution system suddenly had a hole you could throw a few states through? Bound to be hundreds of thousands. Millions, more likely.

How many acres of corn and wheat and soybeans were dying under the dust? How many cows and sheep and pigs and chickens? They weren't going to evacuate livestock, not when they didn't have a prayer of getting even a fraction of the people out.

Which meant . . . what, exactly? *It means I'm goddamn lucky to be on this bus*, Vanessa decided. That was obvious, and made obviouser by someone in the blood-warm water with the circling dorsal fins opening up on her.

Less obvious, maybe, was that, if things kept on the way they were going, pretty soon an MRE would be something to fight over, not something to swear at. That might have been the scariest thought Vanessa had had since the supervolcano blew up.

The man from the National Park Service and the man from the U.S. Geological Survey nodded in jerky unison. "Yes, if you want to do this you have to sign all the releases," the USGS guy said. "You have to acknowledge in writing that you are doing this at your own risk, that you know it is dangerous, and that the federal government is not liable if you are injured or killed. We have a little too much on our plates right now to worry about nuisance lawsuits."

"Yeah, just a little," the National Park Service guy agreed.

Kelly was ready to sign on the dotted line. Kelly was, in fact, eager. She wouldn't have come to this meeting if she weren't. A chance to fly over the supervolcano crater, look down, and take pictures? She thought she would have signed away her immortal soul for that, let alone a chance for her heirs and assigns to take a bite out of Uncle Sam if something went wrong.

And something was liable to. She hadn't told Colin about

this little jaunt, for fear he would call her ninety-seven different kinds of idiot. If the supervolcano so much as hiccupped while they were over it, they'd be toast—to say nothing of toasted. They'd fall out of the sky and go into the magma pit. Three-quarters of a million years down the road, they'd be part of the next big show. A tiny part, but part even so.

She signed on the dotted line. She signed, repeatedly, on the dotted line. The government's attitude seemed to be that anything worth doing was worth doing in quadruplicate. Several other grad students and a couple of profs also indited their John Hancocks in all the requisite places.

What did it say that more graduate students than faculty members were willing to risk their lives for science? That people who'd got tenure had more brains than those who merely dreamt of it? Or that profs lived a better life than grad students and didn't want to chance throwing it away? Was *all of the above* an acceptable choice?

One of the other intrepid grad students asked, "Do we know it's safe for the plane to take off?"

"Son, we don't *know* the sun'll come up tomorrow," the USGS man answered. "It may go nova between now and then, or the Earth may quit rotating, or whatever the hell. What I do know is, when the plane takes off I'm gonna be on it. I've already signed all this bullshit paperwork. If that's not good enough for you, I don't know what else to say."

No one seemed to have any more questions after that. The National Park Service man said, "Be at Oakland International by five a.m. day after tomorrow. Airport security will be in place for our little jaunt."

"Wait. Run that by me again," Kelly said. "We sign all this stuff saying we know we're risking our lives, but they've got to make sure nobody'll hijack the plane and crash it into the crater? Where's the sense in that?"

The USGS man grinned at her. "Hi! Welcome to Catch-22!" he said. "It doesn't have to make sense. It's government policy. Those people may pay me, but they don't pay me enough to lie for them."

And so, at a few minutes before five in the morning—well before dawn, in other words—Kelly sleepily put her cell phone and laptop in a tray and took off her shoes. She passed her little bag through the X-ray machine. "Can you open this, please?" a stern-looking black woman said when it came out the other side.

When TSA people said please, they didn't mean it. Kelly unzipped the bag. The woman pawed through her meager stuff, then grudgingly nodded. "What was wrong?" Kelly asked.

"Your bagels looked like something they weren't supposed to," the black woman answered.

She told the story of the bagels of mass destruction to the other geologists waiting to go out to their chartered Learjet. They gave back the mixture of laughs and groans she'd looked for. "What else do you expect from a system designed by very sharp people for very dull people to work?" one of them said. Kelly hadn't thought of it like that; when she did, the rituals of airport security made more sense.

She'd never been on a private jet. Having enough room to stretch out in her seat made her want to abandon Southwest, American, and United forever. "I could get used to this," she said as the plane taxied toward takeoff.

"In that case, what are you doing studying geology?" asked her chairman, who had the window seat beside hers. Geoff Rheinburg was gray-haired and pudgy, but more than plenty sharp. "You should have gone into programming and turned into an Internet billionaire. Then you'd have a jet for every day of the week—two for Saturday, if you wanted."

"I spend more time doing geology than flying," Kelly answered after a little thought. "And I can use computers, but I'm not much for making them sit up and beg. This is more fun."

"Then you may possibly be in the right place after all," Rheinburg allowed. Was he old enough to have started out on a slide rule, back in the days before pocket calculators? If he wasn't, he came close.

The plane shot down the runway and zoomed into the sky. Air traffic here and most places in the USA was still screwed up, with flights way, way off their usual level. Maybe that tough black gal had checked out the bagels for no better reason than that she was bored stiff.

"This is the pilot speaking." The Learjet's intercom had better sound quality than a commercial airliner's. The man's voice didn't sound as if it were coming through a tin-can telephone. He went on, "I am going to give you the usual advice—keep your seat belts fastened at all times. I mean it more than usual, though. We will be flying over the crater at forty thousand feet. Look for turbulence all the same. That sucker is enormous, and it is hot. Hot air rises—why do you think old politicians float away and never get seen again?"

That won him a few startled laughs. Kelly wondered if he'd ever flown for Southwest. She hated the seating stampede, but enjoyed the way the crew sometimes spoofed the usual instructions about seat belts and exit rows and oxygen masks.

"My brother-in-law told me I needed my head examined when he found out I was making this flight," the pilot went on. "I told him I needed some help with the down payment on a house I want to buy. . . . That doesn't necessarily make him wrong, you understand. What's *your* excuse, folks?"

"He ought to be doing stand-up," Kelly said.

"We can't throw things at him when he's behind that locked door," Professor Rheinburg said. "Too bad, isn't it?"

They flew on. The engines . . . sounded like engines. Kelly approved. There was still a lot of dust and ash in the air, and the supervolcano's afterbelches—major eruptions on any normal scale, but the scales weren't normal now, and wouldn't be for a long time—kept adding more. The planes that were flying needed much more frequent engine overhauls than anyone had dreamt they would.

From Oakland to Yellowstone was about an hour and a half. No, not to Yellowstone: to the supervolcano crater. Yellowstone was gone, dead, off the map in the most literal meaning of the words. Yellowstone had either fallen half a mile toward the center of the earth or was buried deep in lava or pyroclastic flows or volcanic ash. Yellowstone was screwed, blued, and tattooed, not to put too fine a point on it.

People worked on laptops or fiddled with the sensors and other instruments that were the real reason for the flight. The pilot didn't make the usual announcement about electronic devices. The geologists might have lynched him if he had. Without electronic devices, they fell all the way back to the start of the twentieth century, or maybe even to the nineteenth.

After a while, the pilot did come on to say, "Folks, we are getting close. I'm going to do what I'm supposed to do when turbulence is likely. I'm going to tell you to make sure you're in your seats with your belts securely fastened. Don't be dumb, now. If there isn't turbulence flying over this critter, then there's no such animal. We don't want to have to scrape you off the ceiling—or off your neighbor's lap."

Geoff Rheinburg gave Kelly a wry grin as he checked his belt. "No offense, but the only gal I want on my lap is my wife," he said.

"Okay by me," she answered, tightening her own a little. She knew he was happily married. Nice that somebody was. She figured Colin would get up the nerve to propose one of these days before too long. She also figured she would get up the nerve to say yes when he did. What happened after that was a crap-shoot—as far as she could see, just like every other marriage since the beginning of time.

"Three minutes till we reach the edge of the crater," the pilot said. "Welcome to the biggest goddamn roller coaster in the world."

Kelly peered out. Unlike a commercial airliner's, the Learjet's windows were big enough to give even somebody in an aisle seat a good view of the wider world. She'd looked down into active volcanoes before. She'd gone to the Big Island of Hawaii: yeah, work as a geologist could be rough. But the volcanoes there, which went off pretty much all the time, were as different as you could get from the Yellowstone supervolcano. The supervolcano was like the little girl saving up more spit. It saved and it saved and it saved till its igneous cheeks couldn't hold any more. Then—

Then it went and trashed half the continent. And that was only the first act. The follow-up, which did a number on the whole planet, was just getting started.

Even in the wide-windowed Learjet, she leaned toward happily married Professor Rheinburg to see better. He didn't wince, so she hadn't forgotten her deodorant even though she'd crawled out of bed at some heathen hour. Lots of gray and brown down below. Nothing green, not any more. Life would be trying to reboot down there. It had likely already succeeded in a few tiny spots, but not in a way you could see from eight miles high.

Or eight and a half . . . The edge of the world fell away, down below. As soon as it did, the plane started bouncing in the air. Yes, the crater was heating things up, wasn't it? Oh, just a little.

Here and there, the floor had already crusted over and looked like, well, bare rock. One of these days, one of these centuries, it would form the bottom of the new caldera that would take the place of the one at the heart of Yellowstone. They'd need to give it a new name. Kelly wondered whether they'd still speak English when they got around to it.

Lava still boiled and bubbled in between the congealed places. It wasn't as impressive as the stuff in *The Return of the King*. For one thing, that lava was CG. For another, you were looking at it up close and personal, not from forty-odd-thousand feet. Kelly, who'd first read *The Lord of the Rings* when she was nine, wondered what would happen if you dropped Sauron's dread creation right into the middle of this. She expected it'd be gone for good. Hell, if Mount Doom happened to sit on top of a supervolcano hot spot, one of these days *it* would have been gone for good. That was why there was a big stretch of the Rocky Mountains without any mountains.

"Some of those patches of molten rock are miles wide," Rheinburg murmured, most likely to himself.

Even if he wasn't talking to her, it was a useful reminder. The scale of this thing was . . . *ridiculous* was one of the words that occurred to her. Then the Learjet did some up-and-downs she devoutly hoped it was designed for. As urgently, she hoped the bagels of mass destruction would stay put.

"For anyone who needs the reminder, you have airsick bags in the pockets of the seats in front of you," the pilot said. "If you need them, I do hope you'll use them. We don't want the next batch of passengers to think we were playing Vomit Comet, now do we?"

"Oh, shut up," Professor Rheinburg said under his breath. He looked green around the gills. Kelly suspected she did, too. She'd never been airsick, or even feared she might be. Now she discovered there was a first time for everything. She grabbed her bag, just to stay on the safe side. Next to her, her chairman did the same thing.

Neither of them needed to use theirs. Horrible noises from behind them and an acid reek in the conditioned air warned that someone hadn't been so lucky. "Oh, dear," Rheinburg said sympathetically.

Kelly kept her mouth shut—kept it clamped shut, in fact. That sour stink sure didn't help her stomach. She tried her best not to think about it. Wasn't lava fascinating? Sure it was!

Then they were past the great pockmark in the earth's skin and over more devastation of the same kind they'd seen on the approach. The air smoothed out. Kelly's insides relaxed—until the pilot said, "We'll turn around now, and make our second pass over the crater while we're heading for home."

She'd been about to stuff the airsick bag back where it belonged. On second thought, that could wait till they got back to the Idaho side of things—although Idaho, or big parts of it, was an idea that had come and gone.

"What's that song about how much do you have to pay to keep from going through all these things twice?" Professor Rheinburg asked.

"Beats me," Kelly said. Whatever the song he was thinking about was, it came from his generation, not hers. She added, "What I keep thinking about is, we volunteered for this."

"Proves the Army guys know what they're talking about when they say that's a bad idea, doesn't it?" Rheinburg said.

A U-turn at upwards of 500 miles an hour took time and space to execute. They didn't fly back over the supervolcano crater right away, then. They had a little while to brace themselves. Then the plane started bouncing some again. Kelly didn't think it was quite so bad this time through; she might have been more ready for it. As she had before, she stared down at the broad expanse of what was as close as anyone was likely to see of hell on earth.

Beyond it lay the ash beds and stuff that would become tuff. "How many towns and farms and roads somewhere under there?" Professor Rheinburg said. "'Vanity of vanities—all is vanity.'"

"Hey, no fair," Kelly said. "You can't not build something because the supervolcano goes off every 700,000 years. Besides, they built a lot before they even knew it was there."

"They sure did—and it's gone now, along with everything they built after they knew." The gray-haired prof spoke with a grim relish that reminded Kelly of Colin. Then he switched gears and grinned at her. "Of course, looking at the bright side of things, you've got a straight shot at a tenure-track position. You're one of the top experts on the world's biggest problem for at least the rest of your life."

"Well, sure, assuming there are any universities left once everything shakes out." Kelly wouldn't let anybody outgloom her without a fight.

"Yes. Assuming," Rheinburg said, so he probably won that round.

Marshall Ferguson had long since stopped taking snailmail seriously. When you could e-mail or text or talk on the phone, mail with stamps on it that took days to get from hither to yon seemed downright medieval. And snailmail from the other side of the continent had got slower and more erratic since the supervolcano went off. To think they'd said it couldn't be done!

He opened the box on the ground floor of his apartment building only every other day or so. He did need to check every so often, because some bills still came by snailmail. Corporations lacked a sense of humor when you forgot to pay for cable or your utilities.

Most of the rest of what he got was junk—spam on paper, spam that cost the senders a little something to print and mail. That had dropped off dramatically after the eruption. Paper was scarce and expensive these days, which made junk mail a losing proposition. Even the local restaurants had quit mailing out discount coupons, and that was a goddamn shame.

He almost chucked the envelope with the bland corporate return address unopened. Somebody back in New York City was trying to get him to do something he likely didn't want to do. Whoever it was either had a stock of old envelopes or money coming out of his ears, because the paper was uncommonly fine.

The only reason he did open it was the off chance it might be a fancy bill. Otherwise, it would have gone straight into the recycling bin for paper. He unfolded the crisp sheet inside. It was stationery, with the same address as the one on the envelope. Below that . . .

Dear Mr. Ferguson, he read, *We are pleased to accept your story titled "Well, Why Not?" for a future issue of* New Fictions. *A contract and a check for $327.00—the appropriate payment at our standard rate of eight cents a word—are forthcoming. I look forward to working with you on the story. Cordially,*—and an editor's scribbled signature below.

He read it again, and then one more time. By the end of the third go-round, he began to believe it. "Holy shit," he said softly.

Then he started to giggle. He'd sent out the story because that was part of his assignment. Hell, he'd written it because that was his assignment. If he hadn't been in Professor Bolger's class, he never would have done it. And now somebody wanted to pay him money for it? How funny was that?

A moment later, he said "Holy shit" again, on a different note this time. If he'd sold once, chances were he could sell more than once. Having some cash coming in that wasn't straight out of his old man's wallet would be nice, which was putting it mildly. He didn't think you could get rich writing stories—eight cents a word wasn't bad, from everything he'd heard, but it would never make you a millionaire, either—but that might set the stage for bigger and better (which is to say, more profitable) things.

He went up to his place and sent Bolger an e-mail announcing the sale. If that didn't do good things for his grade in there, nothing ever would. Then he fished his phone out of his pocket and called his father.

"What is it, Marshall?" came the familiar growl. Of course Dad would know who it was—he could see the number on his screen, after all—and of course he'd be busy at the cop shop. He'd likely be surprised to get a call in the middle of the afternoon, too. Sure enough, the next thing he said was, "Are you all right?"

"I'm fine." Marshall was just starting to realize how fine he was. Once the amazement wore off, what replaced it was, well, more amazement. "Guess what?"

"Chicken butt," Dad answered, as Marshall had known he would. That had cracked Marshall up when he was little. Dad still did it, though. Did he do it with other cops, too? Marshall wouldn't have been surprised. After a couple of seconds, Dad did add, "Well, what?"

"I sold a story." Marshall couldn't remember the last time he'd sounded so proud of himself.

"Sold?" Dad pronounced the word with care, as if he wasn't sure he'd heard it right. "As in, for money?"

"As in. Three hundred and twenty-seven dollars of money." Marshall was sure he'd remember the size of his first check as long as he lived, even if he hadn't seen it yet.

"How about that?" his father said—one of the few phrases, as Dad himself noted, you could use almost anywhere. Then his voice warmed: "Congratulations, son. That's something, all right. What's the story called? What's it about?"

"It's called 'Well, Why Not?' I never know what to call things." Marshall hated titles. He had no idea how anybody ever came up with a good one. "It's about . . . a guy going to college while his folks get a divorce."

"Oh." Dad chewed on that for a little while. "They do say you're supposed to write about things you know, don't they?"

"Yeah, they say that. They say the opposite, too. The way it looks to me is, you can get away with anything when you're writing, as long as you do it well enough."

"Huh." That didn't sit well with Dad. Marshall had known it wouldn't. Dad believed in Rules with a capital R. He wasn't a cop by accident. As if to prove as much, he went on, "Just remember it doesn't work that way in real life."

"If I can get them to keep paying me, maybe writing will turn into real life," Marshall said.

"Maybe it will." His father sounded surprised at the idea. But getting paid resonated with him. "Here's hoping—and congratulations again. Sorry, but I've got to get back to it."

"I know you're working. I did want to call and tell you, though."

Marshall checked his e-mail. He had an answer from Bolger. *WTG!* the message said. *I hoped somebody in the class would make a sale. Now you've given the others something to shoot for.*

"Yeah," Marshall said. How jealous would the rest of the class be? Bigtime jealous, that was how. They'd have to compete against a real, live published (well, to be published) author. And the girls in there would think anyone who could sell was freaking awesome. He could hope they would, anyhow.

In the meantime . . . In the meantime, Marshall rolled himself a doobie about the size of Pittsburgh. Even triumph went better with weed. He was happily wasted when the sun went down towards another ridiculous, gaudy, over-the-top beautiful sunset. Did dope improve that, too? He smoked some more to find out.

XVII

Camp Constitution. Vanessa wondered what dumbshit adman or bureaucrat got himself a bonus for coming up with the name. Whoever the bastard was, she would have bet her life he not only didn't live here but had never got within a thousand miles of the place. Camp Hole in the Ground would have come a lot closer to the truth.

Truth? You can't handle the truth! What movie was that from? She couldn't remember. Back a long time ago—she couldn't think of exactly when, either—swarms of people trying to get away from the Dust Bowl packed up whatever they had and headed for California. Some places in the state, being of Okie blood still mattered.

Well, the supervolcano had made a bigger, more horrible Dust Bowl now. The only reason even more people hadn't washed up in these camps was that a hell of a lot of would-be refugees ended up corpses instead. As things were, tens of thousands, more likely hundreds of thousands, maybe millions of people from at least half a dozen states wound up in Camp Constitution and others like it on the eastern fringe of the supervolcano eruption, and more streamed in every day.

And there were more refugee centers in the West. The biggest—imaginatively tagged Camp Independence—was somewhere near Pasco, Washington. People who'd gone west, young man, instead of east to flee the ash and dust wound up in them. Again, those camps would have been larger if a lot of the folks who tried to get away from the supervolcano hadn't gone west for good. Fewer refugees squatted in the western camps, because the population in those parts hadn't been much to begin with.

Vanessa wondered if they could possibly be anywhere near as fucked up as Camp Constitution and the others around here. The FEMA functionaries and National Guard officers with the power to bind and loose in these parts swore they were doing their level best. The really scary thing was, Vanessa believed them.

A Welsh corgi that ran yapping at a rhinoceros was doing its level best, too. That wouldn't stop it from winding up smeary goop on the bottom of the rhino's big foot, though. The federal government and the sovereign states of Oklahoma and Arkansas and Texas and Missouri were fighting just as much out of their weight.

No one had looked for cities to spring up out of nowhere around here. There wasn't enough of, well, anything to take care of the swarms who'd got out of the ash clouds the supervolcano dropped all up and down the USA's midsection (and Canada's, too). FEMA had caught and deserved holy hell for the shitty job the organization did when Katrina drowned New Orleans. Next to this, New Orleans looked like a stroll through the park.

Most of the evacuees there had had homes to go back to. Those homes were wrecked, yes, and needed repair and re-building. But what were you supposed to do when whole states were wrecked? It wasn't a question of when people could start rebuilding in Wyoming. The question at the moment was, did anything bigger than a microbe or possibly a windblown bug or two survive in Wyoming? Vanessa had no idea how many people from the Denver metropolitan area had died (neither did anyone else, not to the nearest hundred thousand). She did know she was damn lucky not to be one of them.

FEMA had housed some of the people who'd lived through Katrina in trailers that stank of formaldehyde and had swarms of other things wrong with them, too. Some of those trailers—or some kind of trailers, anyway: trailers that looked old enough and ratty enough to have gone through the aftermath of Katrina—were here at Camp Constitution. Vanessa had seen them.

She didn't get to stay in one. They counted for luxury housing in these parts. There weren't enough to go around. (There wasn't enough of anything to go around.) To rate a trailer, you had to be a family with a bunch of little kids, and there weren't enough for all of them, either.

Instead, she was under canvas. Back in the day, she'd gone camping a few times. She'd done all the dumb things you do: looked for moss on the north side of a tree, toasted marshmallows over an open fire, slept in a sleeping bag in a day-glo nylon tent that would have horrified every claustrophobe ever hatched.

This wasn't like that. Vanessa hadn't dreamt even the circus had tents the size of the one she lived in. Hell, didn't the circus mostly play in the same arenas that hosted basketball teams and jowly metal bands these days? She thought so, but, since her interest in the circus was only slightly higher than her interest in suicide, she wasn't sure.

Somebody had run up four-decker bunks inside the tent. Probably somebody from the National Guard: her respect for the competence of the guys in the camo unis had gone up by leaps and bounds since she landed here. FEMA people seemed more interested in explaining why you couldn't have what you wanted. The Guard got it for you if they possibly could.

She had two inches of foam rubber over a sheet of plywood for a mattress. She bitched about that, but not for long. If she had no shoes, the refugees who came in after her had no feet. Try as the Guardsmen would, they didn't have enough tents for everyone. They couldn't build bunks fast enough. They ran out of the mattress pads even sooner than they ran low on tents.

Yes, the mantra of FEMA and the Guard was "We're doing the best we can." The Guard meant it. FEMA went through the motions.

Morton mined salt. Somewhere far underground ran endless tunnels and columns that glistened white when electric light shone on them and were altogether black when it didn't. (Wasn't that in Kansas? If it was, the salt biz had as much trouble as everybody else.)

Vanessa had started to suspect that they mined MREs the same way. People swapped them around, trying to get the varieties they found least obnoxious. Vanessa played the game, but more to make the time go by than because she really cared about the relative demerits of MREs.

Making time go by was as big a challenge here as it had been back at good old Garden City High, and for the same reason: no electricity. There were charging stations for cell phones, powered by chugging generators. The line for them was never shorter than two hours, 24/7. Vanessa braved it anyhow.

"I'm alive," she greeted her father when he answered her call.

"You would have had a harder time phoning if you weren't," he agreed.

"Dad!" She might have known he would come out with something like that, especially when she handed him such a juicy straight line. All the same . . .

"It's good to hear from you," he said. "I'm sure your mother will think so, too."

Call her next, that meant. Vanessa was less than thrilled. For one thing, Mom still treated her like a baby, and no doubt would till the end of time. For another, Vanessa blamed Mom for breaking up her folks' marriage. But, if blood was even slightly thicker than water, it needed doing. Otherwise, Dad would have to take care of it himself. He would, too, and then probably get plowed to wash it out of his system.

So she sighed and said, "Right." Then she added the essentials: "I'm in Camp Constitution. The refugee camps are all over the news, I bet."

"Yup," Dad said. "How bad is it?"

"Camp Concentration would be a better name," she dished. "It sucks."

He wasn't impressed. She might have known he wouldn't be. "They're swamped," he said. He wasn't here, either, or he wouldn't have added, "I'm sure they're trying as hard as they can."

"My ass!" Vanessa said, and then, quickly, "Listen, I'm gonna go, and save my battery. You wouldn't believe what a hassle recharging is, and that's almost the only electricity here." He might have said good-bye, but she didn't wait to hear.

Mom said, "Oh, thank God!" and burst into tears when Vanessa called. Vanessa kept the call even shorter than the one to her father. Again, hanging up was a relief.

After that, Rob. She got his voicemail. He'd updated it to include gigs in Maine, so she figured he was up there. Denver winter was bad enough. Maine was bound to be worse. She left a message and called Marshall.

"Yankee Stadium, second base." Yeah, that was him.

"Hey, kid bro. Believe it or else, I'm alive." Vanessa waited for him to do the same kind of number on her as Dad had a few minutes earlier.

"Good kind of way to be," was as far as Marshall went. He asked the next reasonable question: "Like where are you alive?"

"Camp Constitution."

"Where's that?"

"About five miles southeast of the middle of nowhere. Don't you ever watch the news?"

"Huh? No." By the way Marshall said it, that was one of your basic dumb questions. He was probably sitting there in Santa Barbara, totally wasted, without a clue about how lucky he was. Then he said, "Guess what I did."

"I don't know. Are you out on bail because of it?" Vanessa was thinking about getting busted for dope, although these days that wasn't easy in California. The acid bite of malice felt good any which way.

It would have felt even better if Marshall had noticed it. As if she hadn't spoken, he went on, "I sold a story. To *New Fictions*. They're gonna pay me real money for it."

"You did what? No way!" That was more sea-green envy than disbelief. Like any good editor, Vanessa was sure she would make a good writer as soon as she found the time. As with a lot of good editors, somehow she never did. That Marshall could have appalled her.

"Way," he said, and she couldn't doubt the smugness in his voice, however much she wanted to. "I bet I never would have done it if I wasn't taking that writing class that made me submit."

"Rrr." Vanessa wasn't grinding her teeth, just making a noise as if she were. How many times had she told herself that quitting school and making a real living instead was a good idea? "*Weren't* taking. It's contrary to fact," she said automatically.

"Whatever." He not only didn't know, he didn't care. And he was in Santa Barbara, with electricity and hot water and food that didn't come out of cardboard boxes and taste like cardboard, *and* he'd sold a fucking story? As a matter of fact, yes. Where was the justice in that?

"I'll talk with you more later. I'm going to save my battery." Vanessa trotted out her built-in excuse once more.

"Right. Take care, y'know?" How baked *was* Marshall? Short of calling the Santa Barbara PD and having them bust him, Vanessa had no way of doing thing one about that. And, since it was Santa Barbara, half the cops probably got lit when they were off duty.

"Shit!" she said loudly. People were walking by her through the mud. Nobody even looked up. You heard plenty worse than that in Camp Constitution. Vanessa heard plenty worse in her own tent from the trailer-trash single mom whose eleven-, eight-, and six-year-old girls were going out of their tree because they couldn't watch TV or play video games or get on Facebook—and from the little darlings, too.

She looked up to the uncaring heavens. The uncaring heavens started raining on her. Well, where else would the mud have come from? By the look and feel of things, it was liable to start snowing pretty damn soon. Wouldn't that be fun, when she was living under canvas?

And speaking of shit . . . The wind blew harder, from out of the west. It brought the stink of row upon row of outhouses. Running water? A sewage system? It was to laugh. How long since cholera last broke out in the land of the free and the home of the brave? How long till it did again? The only thing Vanessa could do about it was hope she didn't get sick.

"Wow!" Rob said, and then, "Oh, wow!"

Justin Nachman nodded. "This is white like white on rice." They'd both seen snow before, on Squirt Frog and the Evolving Tadpoles' earlier winter forays into the cold parts of the country. Only this wasn't winter, and Rob didn't think anyone this side of an Eskimo had ever seen snow like this.

Justin's thoughts ran along different, though related, lines. He was driving, and had his nose about six inches from the windshield—it looked that way to Rob, anyhow—to try to see out better. He said, "I keep expecting to spot a St. Bernard by the side of the road. I wouldn't mind, either. A slug of brandy right now would go down nice."

"Uh-huh." Rob nodded. The SUV's heater was doing its brave best, but how long would that stay good enough? He had no idea what the outside temperature was, but he would have bet dollars to dill pickles he'd never been anywhere colder. "You might want to be careful if you do see a St. Bernard," he added. "This is Maine, remember. Stephen King country. It could be Cujo."

"You know how to cheer a guy up, don't you?" Justin said.

The wipers on the SUV went back and forth, back and forth. So far, they were staying pretty much even with the swirling snow. Rob just hoped they could keep doing it. Justin had the lights on, but sensibly kept them on low beam. All the blowing white would have reflected brights straight back into his face, making it even harder for him to see where he was going.

"Hey, there are worse things than giant rabid dogs." Rob was determined to be helpful—or something like that. "Maybe some vampires from 'Salem's Lot still flitting around."

"It's daytime," Justin pointed out.

"Oh, yeah. That's really gonna bother 'em in weather like this," Rob said. "Besides, nowadays they probably wear shades and smear themselves with SPF 50 sunscreen. Using technology to solve problems. That's what engineering's all about."

"Thank you, Albert Speer." Justin gave a straight-armed salute truncated by the SUV's roof.

Rob had only a vague notion who Albert Speer was. A Nazi: what more did you need to know? "That wasn't him," he said. "That was Professor Dinwiddie, explaining why engineering majors should be proud of what they were doing."

"And are you proud?"

"I'm so fucking proud, I play bass in Squirt Frog and the Evolving Tadpoles so I never have to worry about another circuit board as long as I live."

"Sounds about right," Justin agreed. "Now where the hell are we?"

Rob grabbed the trusty road atlas. "We got off I-95 at Newport, right?"

"Right." Justin's head bobbed up and down. "Maine roads suck, you know?"

"Now that you mention it, yes," Rob said. Once you got off the Interstate, you fell back in time, probably back to the days before Beaver Cleaver was even a glint in Ward's eye. Two-lane winding blacktop roads, too many of which hadn't been resurfaced for a long, long time . . . California, it wasn't.

"And we're heading north up be-yoo-tiful Route 7," Justin went on.

"Roger," Rob said. "With a little luck, Biff and Charlie are, too."

"Or what would be beautiful Route 7 if I could see through this goddamn snow any farther than I can piss," Justin said. "And we passed through the grand metropolis of Corinna, otherwise known as a wide spot in the road."

"We sure did." Rob started singing "Corina, Corina." The way he sang showed why he played bass. Then he looked at the map again. "And we're coming up on lovely, romantic Dexter. Dexter is a bigger dot than Corinna. Not a big dot, mind you, but a bigger one. Might even be big enough for a traffic light or two."

"Wowww!" The way Justin brought it out, he might have been stoned. He might have been, but he wasn't, or Rob didn't think he was. Driving while loaded was more trouble than it was worth. Being a cop's kid, Rob had impressed that on the band. The amount of dope he smoked when he wasn't driving also impressed, if in a different way.

But the *Wowww!* wasn't undeserved. A Maine town big enough for stoplights was well on its way to cityhood . . . or, more likely, had been the same size for the past seventy-five years. This part of the country wasn't into cancerous growth like California.

They drove past a roadside traffic sign. It was a yellow diamond, there and gone again in the snow. You might have seen the like back home. But no traffic sign in California bore the silhouette of a big old deer with honking antlers. "Bullwinkle crossing," Rob said: it wasn't the first moose sign they'd spotted.

"There you go." Justin nodded. "Enough signs, though. I want to see some more real moose."

"Supposed to be bunches of 'em over by Greenville. They do tours," Rob said.

"The mooses do?" Now Justin sounded surprised—and with reason. He slowed down some more, and he hadn't been going real fast to begin with.

"Um, no." Rob pondered antecedents.

"Well, that's a relief, anyhow," Justin said. "I think the snow's getting worse."

"I didn't think it could," Rob said, not wanting to admit he was right.

"Yeah, well . . ." Justin took a hand off the wheel for a vague gesture. "Not like we'll have to worry about global warming for a while. We should've torched more dinosaurs while we had the chance."

At the moment, what they had to worry about was staying on the road and not drifting onto the shoulder—when there was a shoulder. Some of the yellow signs that didn't warn about moose did let you know when there wasn't. What happened when you went off the road there? Rob had no trouble finding an answer: you flipped over and burst into flames, that was what.

"Stick to the paving," he urged.

"Yes, Mommy. I'm working on it, believe me," Justin answered. Rob shut up.

They finally made it into Dexter. It was indeed a town of some stature: two or three traffic lights, two gas stations (a sure sign it was no dipshit village), a church with a tall white steeple, a graveyard now blanketed in snow, and, along with the Subway that seemed to be far and away the most common fast-food joint in this part of Maine, a mom-and-pop Chinese restaurant.

"I wonder what Chinese food tastes like in the middle of moose country," Rob remarked.

"I dunno, but an hour after you eat some you're curious again," Justin said.

"I've had some shit do that to me, but never the goddamn beef chow mein," Rob said.

Which, of course, made Justin break into "Werewolves of London." Warren Zevon wasn't exactly a spiritual father to Squirt Frog and the Evolving Tadpoles, but he was no further removed than spiritual uncle. And the kind of almost-fame he'd won was at the top end of what they could hope for.

Even if Dexter was a fair-sized place by the standards of Maine away from the Interstate, rolling through it took only a few minutes. Then they were out in the country again, with snow-covered meadows and fields going back from the increasingly snow-covered road to the snow-draped pines. Sometimes, for variety's sake, the snow-covered pines came right up to the edge of the road. No need for the NO SHOULDER signs on those stretches; it was pretty obvious.

They'd switched to Route 23 halfway through Dexter. It offered a more direct path to Greenville than 7 did. It was also even narrower, which hadn't shown on the map. Rob started wondering if the switch was smart. He wondered even more when Justin hit the brakes—carefully, to keep from skidding. And he didn't skid, either. For a guy from California, he was doing okay with the funky white stuff. "What's up?" Rob asked.

"Accident ahead," Justin said. "Flashing lights and stuff."

And damned if there weren't. Rob hadn't noticed them through God's blowing dandruff. Good thing Justin was keeping an eye peeled. *That's why we pay him the big bucks*, Rob thought vaguely.

An accident it was, with two cars and an SUV. One of the cars lay on its side next to the road, unpleasantly reminding Rob of his fretting before they got to Dexter. There was a big dent in the sheet metal above the rear wheel on its other side. The second car and the SUV were both upright, but pretty well crunched. A couple of the people milling around were bleeding. A cop was tending to one of them. Red and yellow and blue lights flashed on top of his cruiser.

Glass crunched under Justin's tires as he steered around the wreck. Only a couple of cars skirted it ahead of him. On any road in L.A., it would have tied things up for an hour. On the 405 at four in the afternoon, it would have screwed traffic for the rest of the night. Well, L.A. County all by itself had more people than forty-two states—or was it forty-three? Rob couldn't remember. Maine was definitely one of them.

"Charlie and Biff *are* still with us," Justin said as he picked up a little more speed. "I could get used to a heated side-view mirror. I wouldn't be able to see squat without it."

"Okay, great. But how often would you need it in California?" Rob asked.

"Depends on how cold it gets, right? If California turns into, like, Washington state, it'll freeze sometimes."

"Huh," Rob said thoughtfully. That hadn't occurred to him, and it should have. Then something else did: "If Los Angeles is the new Seattle—"

"Like fifty is the new thirty?" Justin interrupted helpfully.

"My ass," Rob said. They both laughed—easy enough, when neither of them had seen the old thirty yet. He went on, "Like I was saying, if L.A.'s the new Seattle, what does that make Maine? The new North Pole?"

"Nah. Won't be that bad," Justin said. "More like the new Labrador."

"Happy day!" Rob said in distinctly unhappy tones. "Ten months of winter and two months of bad skiing."

"You think you're kidding, don't you?"

"I wish!" Rob rolled his eyes. "The next interesting question is, how the hell do we ever get out of here? If the snowdrifts are as high as an elephant's eye and they stay that way, nobody goes in or out, near enough."

"You've got something, I'm afraid," Justin said. "And when they start running out of food and heating oil . . ." His voice trailed off. If you wanted to, you could imagine this whole state—hell, you could imagine everything north of Boston—fading away like that.

"Remind me again why we took that gig in Greenville," Rob said.

"It's called money," Justin explained. "Bringing some in every once in a while instead of spending it all the goddamn time is supposed to be good. I think I remember that, anyway."

"It's been a while, hasn't it?" Rob sighed. "I still wish like hell we'd been going down to Key West or something when the supervolcano blew. New England . . . It's over with here."

"Uh-huh. And you knew ahead of time that Yellowstone was going to go kablooie like Hamster Hughie." Justin was as big a Calvin and Hobbes fan as Rob was. That sensibility—if you wanted to call it a sensibility—also rubbed off on the band.

The bitch of it was, Rob *had* known, or known as much as anybody not a geologist could. It wasn't as if Dad hadn't gone on about the supervolcano whenever they talked. Rob had tuned out most of it. What were you going to do when your father went on and on about stuff he got from his new girlfriend, especially when she wasn't a whole lot older than you were?

"Too late to worry about it now," he said with another sigh.

"You got that right." Justin clicked the wipers from regular to high. It did less good than he must have hoped it would. He slowed down some more. The snow on the road was getting thicker. "I wonder if we're going to make it to Greenville."

"This thing is the size of an armored personnel carrier. It's got four-wheel drive and snow tires," Rob said. "You gonna let Mother Nature dick around with us?"

"I may not have a choice. You fight with Mother Nature, you're fighting one big mother," Justin answered. Rob looked out the window. Not much to see but blowing white and, through it, already-fallen white. He wondered if he ought to be looking for gigantic rabid St. Bernards, or maybe vampires, for real. No sunshine to slow 'em down, and none likely any time soon.

Dexter was a big enough deal that the next village up 23, instead of enjoying its own name, went by North Dexter. Up the road a ways from it was an Italian-Mexican restaurant. Rob saw the neon sign in spite of the snow; the restaurant itself, set back from the road, was barely visible.

"Mexican food in Maine," Justin mused. "You think the Chinese'd be weird, what about that?"

"You're not stopping, are you?" Rob said with mock—perhaps not so mock—anxiety.

"Nope. Greenville or bust," Justin said. They chugged on.

A streak of red shot across the road. It was there and then gone. Justin had time to take his foot off the gas, but not enough to bring it down on the brake. "The fuck was that?" Rob asked, wondering if he'd really seen it.

"Well, I'm pretty sure it wasn't a moose."

"Brilliant deduction! A lesser mind would be incapable of it."

"Yeah, I know," Justin said smugly. "My best guess is, it was a fox—and not the kind that walks on two legs."

"A fox! Cool!" There weren't so many of them in California. California had coyotes instead. Coyotes thought four-legged foxes were tasty.

The map insisted there was a village called Sangerville just before Route 23 ran into Route 6. Rob saw another snow-covered graveyard off to the right, which made him look out for vampires again. Other than that, damn all suggested human beings had ever lived anywhere near here. He flipped to the back of the road atlas. It insisted that Sangerville had 475 people. If the place did, most of them, in the classic phrase, came disguised as empty seats.

When 23 dead-ended at 6, Justin said, "I go left, right?"

"Right—left," Rob agreed. "If you go right, you head away from Greenville and toward Dover-Foxcroft."

"Dover-Foxcroft?" Justin echoed. "Bizarre, man. I mean, I know a lot of people with hyphenated names. These days, who doesn't? But a town?"

"I just work here," Rob said. "That's what the map says. However they got married, they're a bigger place than Dexter, or even Newport. They're in bigger type, and the town sign is a white circle with a little black dot in it, not just a black dot."

"Place'll be Boston before we know it." Justin dutifully swung the SUV to the left.

"Next town ahead is Guilford. It's a mile or two from here," Rob said, still eyeing the Rand McNally. "The road forks there. We stay on 6, heading northwest. Next place after Guilford is Abbott Village, and then North Abbott."

"No North Guilford?" Justin asked.

"As a matter of fact, there *is* a North Guilford. But it's not on 6. It's on some half-assed side road."

"This road we're on is half-assed," Justin said accurately.

"Well, then, the other one's quarter-assed." Rob corrected himself.

As things turned out, they were counting chickens they never got to see. They didn't even make it quite as far as Guilford. It wasn't that the blizzard got worse, though it did. The accident down below North Dexter hadn't closed down the whole damn road. This one did. A Hummer had slammed into an eighteen-wheeler head-on.

Rob didn't know how fast the guy in the Hummer had been going. *Fast* seemed a pretty good guess. A Hummer was half again as big and twice as heavy as any other SUV in captivity. A Hummer was a fucking bad joke, was what a Hummer was. No wonder the market for them tanked—*le môt juste*—when gas prices took off at the end of the Aughts.

This particular Hummer was scrap metal, with the whole front end stove in. The windshield glass was starred and bulged outward on the driver's side. What cop's kid couldn't read that sign? The jerk behind the wheel—hey, he was speeding in a Hummer, so of course he was a jerk—hadn't been wearing his seat belt. The only question now was whether he only needed a dentist and a plastic surgeon or a neurosurgeon. That assumed he had any brains left at all, which also wasn't obvious.

And he'd done a number on the eighteen-wheeler, too. He'd rammed it hard enough to flip it over onto its side and jackknife it. That would have shafted the Santa Ana Freeway. On a narrow two-lane road in Maine . . . The broken-nosed cab lay on the shoulder to one side, diesel fuel dribbling out into the snow from the punctured fuel tank like blood from a cut jugular. The trailer stretched all the way across the asphalt to the other shoulder.

"Fuck me up the asshole," Justin said, and that about covered that. He eased to a stop.

Several other cars had already had to stop in front of them. Some people had got out to do what they could for the injured, or else just to get a better look at the mess. Charlie and Biff stopped two cars behind Justin and Rob. More cars pulled up behind them. Nobody would be going anywhere around here any time soon.

Justin found a question: "Where are the cops?"

"Maybe they're on the Guilford side, and we can't see 'em," Rob answered. "Or maybe they're on their way from Dover-Foxcroft." He would have bet on the latter. Dover-Foxcroft was a good bit bigger than Guilford. "In the meantime, let's see if we can do anything useful."

He opened the door. Cold bit at him. L.L. Bean knew their business, though. As soon as he zipped up his anorak, he stopped freezing. He'd never owned long johns before this trip to Maine. He was damn glad now that he'd bought some. His nose stayed cold, but what the hell? He figured that made him a nice, healthy mutt.

An older guy who'd already got out nodded at him. "I ain't seen nothin' like this since I was in Eye-raq," he said, and pointed to a body lying behind the Hummer. Someone had draped a coat over its head. "You're lucky he's covered up. He ain't pretty, not even a little bit."

"I believe it." Like anyone from L.A., Rob had seen road carnage now and then. He'd also seen some of the grisly photos in his father's books. When he was a kid, he'd used them to gross Vanessa out. He wasn't supposed to look at those books himself, much less give his little sister nightmares with them. He'd got a spanking when Vanessa ratted on him; Dad wasn't the kind to figure corporal punishment warped you for life. *His* old man had licked him plenty, and he'd turned out all right, so. . . . Thinking about that was more pleasant than remembering what lay under the coat. Rob made himself ask, "Anybody else in the SUV?"

"Ayuh," the older man answered, which meant he came from these parts (and also meant yes). "There was a gal. She had her belt on, so she didn't go into the windshield. But her leg got tore up pretty good, and she maybe busted some ribs. They done took her back to the clinic in Guilford."

"How about the trucker?" Rob found the next logical question.

"He ain't bad. Cuts, bruises, somethin' sprained—maybe busted—in one foot. He was up high, like. Might not've got hurt at all, hardly, if the goddamn Hummer didn't flip his rig."

"You've got to be nuts to drive like that in this kind of weather," Rob said.

"Ayuh," the older man repeated. "Well, some folks are, and that's the long and short of it. They figure their shit don't stink, and nothin' can go wrong with 'em no matter what kind of ass-holery they pull. I'm here to tell you, things don't work that way." He jerked a thumb at the Hummer's late driver. "He ain't gonna tell you nothin', not no more."

"How long will it take to clear this mess off the road?" Rob wondered.

"Beats me." The local didn't sound worried about it. Of course, he didn't have a gig in Greenville tonight. Almost cheerily, he went on, "Christ only knows where from they'll have to bring in a tow truck big enough to shift these fuckers. Guilford ain't got one—I know that for a fact. I don't believe Dover-Foxcroft does, neither. Greenville, mebbe, or Newport where the Interstate goes through. All this snow, take forever to get here, too. Might as well relax and set a spell, know what I mean?"

"Yeah." Rob was damned if he'd make a noise like *ayuh*. He unhappily mooched back to the waiting Justin. Seeing him coming, Biff and Charlie got out of the trailing SUV to hear the news. Rob made it short and sweet: "We're fucked. They've got no idea when they're gonna be able to clear the road."

"That, like, sucks." Biff wasn't long on words, but he got the point.

"We can't even turn around," Charlie said. There were cars

behind them and westbound cars in the eastbound lane. Some jackasses always figured they could dodge trouble if they broke the rules. Once in a while, they did. More often, as now, they screwed things up for themselves and everybody else.

"I think I'd better call Greenville and let 'em know we ain't gonna make it." Rob reached into his pocket for his cell phone.

The promoter didn't sound brokenhearted. "We'll cancel, all right," he said. "We didn't get as much advance sale as we wanted, and people sure won't be coming into town in weather like this." Which was all true, but left Squirt Frog and the Evolving Tadpoles stranded in the middle of Maine with not a gig in sight.

XVIII

When flights to Los Angeles finally resumed, Marcus Wilson gave Bryce a ride from Lincoln to Omaha. "Thanks for everything," Bryce said when they pulled up in front of the terminal. "I don't know what I would have done without everybody from the department here."

"Hey, man, after what you went through, I don't know if I'd ever have the nerve to get on another plane again as long as I live," the other grad student answered.

"If I'm gonna get home, I've gotta fly," Bryce said. That wasn't exactly true. I-10 was open, and some ordinary travel was allowed on it—but not much. It was the lifeline between Socal and points east, and most of the traffic was trucks. Passenger rail service had been cut off altogether. It was all freight all the time as far as the railroads were concerned.

He got out and strapped on his backpack. All his meager stuff fit in it. No need to pay the thieving airlines for the great privilege of checking a bag. Since he had a boarding pass, he headed straight for security. Getting through was a breeze—all the more so when you were used to dealing with LAX and

O'Hare. Close to 400,000 people lived in Omaha, which made it a city of decent size, but you'd never mistake it for Chicago.

His gate had a big TV screen hanging down from the ceiling. Like most airport TVs, it was tuned to CNN Headline News. Bryce usually turned his back on the goddamn things—was there no place you could escape them? But the headline below the pretty girl who read the teleprompter made his eyes snap back, even if she didn't: NUCLEAR STRIKES ON TEL AVIV, TEHRAN.

"Oh, fuck," he said, and then looked around to see if anybody'd heard him. No one was giving him an offended look, anyhow. He would have bet he wasn't the only one here who'd come out with something like that. When you saw a headline with NUCLEAR STRIKES in it, what else could you say?

The screen cut away from the pretty announcer to show slagged ruins. "Loss of life in the Israeli coastal city is believed to be extremely heavy," said a correspondent with an English accent. "The Prime Minister has vowed an eye for an eye and a tooth for a tooth."

Bryce expected footage of devastated Tehran to follow hard on the heels of that biblical threat. Instead, the attractive newsreader came back on. "This just in," she said breathlessly. "A flash of quote sunlike light unquote has appeared over the Iranian holy city of Qom, and communications with Qom seem to have been lost. It is not known whether the Grand Ayatollah—the real powerholder in Iran—was in Qom when it was struck."

The woman who'd stopped next to Bryce to watch the news crossed herself. That was more elegant and restrained than cussing. Whether the sentiment it expressed was so very different might be another question.

"With us now is retired Marine Lieutenant Colonel Randolph Cullenbine, our military analyst," the pretty newswoman said. "Colonel Cullenbine, what is America's likely response to this double tragedy in the Middle East?"

Randolph Cullenbine wasn't pretty. He looked like, well, a retired Marine officer: short-haired, blunt-featured, wide-shouldered, tough. He talked like a TV guy, though: "It seems probable that Iran was trying to take advantage of the USA's perceived weakness. We've had the middle of the country badly degraded, and the launch sites of many of our land-based ICBMs are currently unusable due to ash and lava laid down by the supervolcano."

"Huh!" Bryce said, and he wasn't the only one in the boarding area to make some kind of surprised noise. He hadn't worried about where Uncle Sam parked his missiles. Uncle Sam hadn't, either. Maybe he should have.

"But we still have our missile-carrying submarines and our manned bombers, right?" the newswoman asked.

"Oh, absolutely." Cullenbine nodded. "We aren't defenseless, no matter what the ayatollahs may believe. And neither are the Israelis. These were their strikes, not ours. I have multiple sources confirming that."

"What's . . . likely to come next?" The newswoman asked the question as if she feared the answer—and well she might.

"I don't know, Kathleen. Right now, the only people who do know are whoever's in charge in Iran and the Israeli Prime Minister." The military analyst sounded thoroughly grim, which made more sense than most of what you saw on TV these days. "It depends on how many missiles the Iranians have left, and on whether they feel like using them. And it depends on how massive a retaliation the Israelis intend to take. They have enough bombs to destroy most if not all of Iran's major cities. That would put the death toll in the millions, if not the tens of millions."

"Thank you," the pretty newswoman said, in about the tone you'd use to thank a dentist after a root canal. "Do you think this would have happened if the supervolcano hadn't erupted?"

"Not a chance," Lieutenant Colonel Cullenbine replied at

once. "The perceived weakness"—he liked that phrase—"of the United States after the disaster had to be what galvanized the Iranians into motion." He bared his teeth in what wasn't quite a smile. "They forgot that Israel was plenty able to take care of itself. But we may have to look for other trouble spots coming to the boil, too, and we won't be able to do as much about them as we might have before we landed in so much trouble of our own."

They started boarding then. When his group got called, Bryce turned away from the TV and walked to the jetway. Along with the rest of the paying sheep, he filed aboard the airliner. He tried not to think about what had happened the last time he flew. Trying not to think of a green monkey after somebody talked about one would have been easier. He didn't expect to end up in a lake again. Ending up dead . . . That, he worried about.

Takeoff was smooth enough. The pilot came on the intercom to say, "We'll be using a southerly route to get to Los Angeles today. There's no report of any unusual activity from the super-volcano caldera, but we'll give it an extra-wide berth anyhow. We expect to arrive at LAX on time—maybe even fifteen minutes early if the headwinds cooperate. So relax and enjoy the flight."

Bryce wondered if he'd ever enjoy a flight again. Right this minute, he would have bet against it. He had a window seat. Before long, he started seeing signs of the eruption. Despite rain and snow, gray volcanic ash still dulled broad swaths of land-scape. Things wouldn't have been very green at this season in any year. Less so now, and that got truer as they flew farther west.

Even the Rockies looked like gray ghosts of their old selves: not nearly so rocky as they should have. Up right by the eruption, where lava and ash and sludge or whatever the hell they called it lay hundreds of feet thick, they would, given enough centuries, turn into more rock. Down here, they just made a godawful mess of hundreds of thousands of square miles.

A southerly route, the pilot had said. Presumably, that took the plane well south of whatever was left of Denver. Buildings—not a lot of people, not any more. Vanessa had made it out of town before things got as bad as they could get. Bryce had heard that from Susan, who'd heard it from Colin. For quite a while, Susan had been weirded out because Bryce stayed friends with his ex's dad. For all Bryce knew, she still was. But she'd decided it didn't threaten her, so she didn't worry about it out loud any more.

Bryce was glad he knew Vanessa was alive. That she'd dropped him like a live grenade wasn't enough to wish on her the kind of end those 12,000,000-year-old rhinos on display in Lincoln had got. Marie's disease . . . Bryce's mouth twisted. Before the supervolcano, not one person in a million had ever heard of it. He knew damn well he hadn't.

Since the eruption, though, everybody knew its name. It was on the news all the time, sometimes called HPO because no one but a medical specialist wanted to come out with hypertrophic pulmonary osteodystrophy if he could help it. It had sickened and killed thousands in Denver and Salt Lake City and Topeka and Pocatello and Saskatoon and all the places in between.

So far as anybody knew, it was incurable. There were cries for research, for treatment. In normal times, the Feds and private foundations would have thrown money at it till it yielded up its secrets. Bryce supposed some research on it was going on. But with untold millions of refugees, with the country's economy shot to hell, with hideous crop failures, with the prospect of years if not decades or centuries of frigid weather, even Marie's disease had to stand in line and wait.

Flight attendants came down the aisle flogging their overpriced boxes of what was allegedly good. Bryce hadn't bought anything in the airport, the way he usually did: he hated giving the airlines money for stuff that shouldn't have rated a fee.

He didn't pay them this time. Rubbery cheese on what the stewardess kept calling artisan bread (why did they grind artisans into flour?) was less than appealing. He'd be hungry when he got back to L.A., but he wouldn't starve.

Then he said, "Urk!" The guy in the aisle seat gave him a funny look. Bryce didn't care; *Urk!* was exactly what he meant. His car had been sitting in one of the satellite parking lots at LAX since he headed for Chicago before the supervolcano blew. The battery was bound to be dead by now. And, at twelve bucks a day, he'd have to come up with several hundred dollars to get it out of hock.

In a rational, reasonable world, he would have been able to talk to some parking honcho, explain how he was lucky to be alive and even luckier to be back in California, and let people know he hadn't meant to leave his car in the lot so long. The honcho would have nodded and forgiven his fee, except for the part he would have paid had he come home on time.

The words *rational* and *reasonable* did not go along with the acronym *LAX*. They never had. Odds were they never would. The airport was as dedicated to separating the people who used it from their cash as the airlines were themselves. That was saying something—something filthy. Bryce resigned himself to forking over the dough.

He wouldn't even try to take care of that today. All he wanted to do was get back to his apartment—oh, and jump on Susan once he did. The car would wait another day or two. The bill would get correspondingly bigger, but WTF.

Everything the airliner flew over now seemed to be the same shade of grayish brown—everything, for hundreds and hundreds of miles. No doubt the depth of the ash varied, but Jesus God there was a lot of it! And the sunlight that shone on it seemed weak, almost consumptive. Bryce had wondered if getting seven miles up in the air would make the light look more the way it had in pre-eruption days.

Nope. A nice thought, but no. And that made sense, when

you worked it through. If the supervolcano had blasted particulate matter twenty or twenty-five miles up into the stratosphere, a mere seven wouldn't make much difference.

When the engines' roar changed pitch, Bryce tensed. He feared he'd be a nervous flier the rest of his days. "We're beginning our descent into the Los Angeles metropolitan area," the pilot announced, and he relaxed . . . some. "We *will* be landing about ten minutes ahead of schedule."

Coming in to LAX from the east, you flew over built-up country for about fifteen minutes. At jetliner speeds, that translated into a lot of miles and a hell of a lot of metropolitan area. Bryce didn't know of any other flying approach even remotely like it.

Lawns here were green. That jolted him with its novelty. For one thing, the ashfall in Southern California hadn't been bad enough to kill off the grass before rain could wash the ash away. For another, they hadn't had any freezes. From what Susan told him, the weather was colder than usual, but not that much colder.

Not yet.

The last thing an airliner did before touching down on the runway was to fly low across the 405: almost low enough to look out the window and read the cars' license-plate numbers as they zoomed by. If they zoomed by. If the San Diego Freeway had coagulated, as it so often did, you could probably tell whether a driver's fingerprints were whorls or loops.

A bump—not a very big one—and they were down. Bryce let out a long, slow sigh. He'd spent a lot of time wondering if he'd ever make it back. A few minutes of that had been sheer terror, wondering whether he'd stay alive longer than those few minutes. The rest was on a rather lower key, but no less sincere even so.

"Please remain seated with your seat belts securely fastened," a flight attendant droned. "You may now use your cell phones and other approved electronic devices."

Passengers were already doing it. Did the airlines really believe people didn't know the ropes? Bryce didn't think it was about controlling the occasional moron. More on the order of dotting i's and crossing t's. This way, if anything did go wrong, some corporate lawyer could truthfully testify it hadn't gone wrong because the airline failed to make the proper offerings to the gods—uh, failed to deliver the appropriate warnings.

Since they were early, he made his own call to be sure Susan had got there. "Hi, sweetie!" she said. "Yeah, I'm down in baggage claim. Can't wait to see you!"

"Boy, does that work both ways," he answered. "We're coming to the gate now, so it'll only be a few more minutes."

It took longer than that. His seat was well back of the wing. Everybody in front of him seemed to need to wrestle a carry-on the size of a well-fed Nebraska porker out of the overstrained overhead luggage bins. Airlines hadn't intended that to happen when they started charging for checked baggage, but it did.

At last, he escaped the plane. A stewardess' insincere "Thank you" seemed a fitting sendoff for what got more unpleasant every time he did it. But the whole crew had worked wonders when his last flight had to go into Branch Oak Lake. Remembering how nasty air travel was these days, he also needed to remember that.

He trudged past shops and restaurants and other gates. They gave you every chance to part with your money, all right. Bryce bought a 3 Musketeers and inhaled chocolate and nougat. His steps got bouncier as soon as he did. Blood sugar was a good thing, yes indeed. Now he'd last till he could get outside of some real food.

Down the escalator. Past one baggage carousel after another, some still, others spinning, all of them made from articulated bits of armor plate as elaborate as Henry VIII's steel suit. There was his flight number, up in glowing red above a carousel that had just started to move. There was Susan. She saw him at the same time as he spotted her. Jesus, she looked good! He hurried toward her.

Then he saw his mother standing behind Susan. Barbara Miller was easy not to notice. She was short and plain, with mouse-brown hair going gray these past few years. She had on her usual outfit: trainers (she still called them tennis shoes), track-pants, and a polyester top. She'd taken off a cotton sweater and draped it over her arm.

Bryce hugged her, too. "Hi, Mom," he said. Then he said it again, when he saw her eyes on his mouth. Her hearing was starting to go, though she was too vain to admit it. He loved her without taking her seriously. He'd outgrown her by the time he turned sixteen. What could you do?

"Susan sent me an e-mail and asked if I wanted to come along to pick you up, so I said sure," she told him.

"That's great, Mom." He lied without worrying about it. "Good to see you."

"Good to see *you*," she said after he repeated himself again. "I was so worried! Such a terrible thing!" She was inventing emotions after the fact. She couldn't have known he was airborne while the supervolcano erupted till after it happened. Well, people did such things all the time. Then she added, "Your father would have been proud of you for being so brave."

His father had died when he was twelve. Maybe Colin Ferguson filled some of the hole that left in his life. Maybe that was why Bryce had stayed close to him after Vanessa said bye-bye. He could worry about such things later, though, if he bothered. For now . . . "Brave? There wasn't any time to be brave. We got out as fast as we could and we floated in the lake till the boats got us."

"You're too modest. You're always too modest. Listen, I made a chicken last night. The prices these days! It's robbery, I tell you! But I've got almost a whole bird left over. If you and

Susan want to stop in when you drop me off, you could have something to eat. There's potatoes, too, and a Black Forest cake from Ralphs."

Bryce raised an eyebrow at Susan. She threw the ball right back to him: "Whatever you want is fine with me."

Thanks a bunch, he thought. Should he make like a dutiful son? Or go back to his place, screw himself silly, and then sleep for about a week? He knew what he wanted to do. He also knew he'd hurt his mother's feelings if he did it. Mom wouldn't say anything, but she'd find plenty of other ways to rub his nose in what was going on. She always did.

With a sigh he couldn't quite swallow, he said, "Chicken sounds good. I haven't eaten much home cooking lately." That had the added virtue of being true. He appealed to Susan one more time: "If it's okay with you."

"It's fine. I already told you," she said quickly. She wasn't going to play the villain, whisking Bryce away from Barbara so she could work her carnal wiles on him. *Damn! I sure wish she would*, he thought as they started off toward the parking structure.

Squirt Frog and the Evolving Tadpoles still hadn't seen Greenville and the haunting, romantic shores of Moosehead Lake. By now, Rob was as near certain as made no difference that the band never would get there. He wasn't nearly so sure about whether they would ever get out of Guilford.

It wasn't where he'd expected to end up, which meant as close to nothing as didn't matter. By the time the locals finally cleared the smashed Hummer and the flipped and jackknifed eighteen-wheeler from Route 6, he and Justin and Biff and Charlie—and a lot of other people trapped by the wreck—were glad to get into Guilford. That was definitely preferable to freezing to death in the snow, the other main choice.

The longer he stayed, the odder and more interesting Guilford seemed. For a town of just over 1,500 people, it had a lot going on. The Piscataquis River ran through it. Once upon a time, every Maine town with a stream had had water-powered mills and factories. Guilford still did. No one seemed to have bothered to tell the locals water mills were hopelessly outdated. This nineteenth-century anachronism remained a going concern a lifetime after most of the others had closed down.

And there was the Trebor Mansion Inn, where the band currently resided. You took a diagonal right—not a straight right, or you'd end up somewhere else—by the Shell station near the eastern end of town, went past the slough and the high school on the other side of the street, climbed a hill, hung a left into a long driveway whose outlet you barely noticed from the street, and there you were. The Trebor, by God, Mansion Inn.

Charlie stared at it in something approaching awe when he and his bandmates got out of their SUVs. "Wow!" he said—not the usual stoner's slurred *Wow!*, but one that showed he really meant it. He proceeded to explain why: "If this place doesn't have an 'H. P. Lovecraft slept here' plaque, somebody dropped the ball somewhere. Of course, old H.P. spent most of his time down in Providence, but he should've made a side trip for this."

"No, dude." Biff shook his head. "H. P. Lovecraft started in Chicago, but they were working out of San Francisco when they made their records."

Confusion and argument followed. Charlie had never heard of H. P. Lovecraft the band. Biff didn't know about the writer from whom the band took its name. Rob vaguely knew about both. Justin, by all appearance, knew neither. "How come you know about this band?" he demanded of Biff. "They're way older than you are, and they never got big." That was an understatement, and a healthy one, too.

"My dad got me into them, believe it or else," Biff answered, suitably shamefaced at the admission. "He told me he lost his cherry with 'White Ship' on the stereo."

"You'd remember that, all right," Rob agreed. He didn't think of creepy horror writers or San Francisco psychedelia when he looked at the Trebor Mansion Inn. He remembered a couple of enormous pseudo-Victorian office buildings he'd seen in the San Fernando Valley the last time the band played there. Steep roofs, funky shingles, a tower or two . . . Yeah, this place had the look, all right.

But there was a difference. L.A. had buildings that looked like anything and everything that had ever been under the sun. And they were all phonies, run up by modern-day real-estate guys and construction crews to make some client happy, or at least willing to spend money. Roman, Spanish, Victorian, half-timbered Tudor, the odd hot dog or donut . . . You name it, Socal imitated it.

Whatever the Trebor Mansion Inn was, Rob was convinced it was no imitation. It had been sitting here since sometime in the 1800s. It was older than some—all?—of the snow-covered pines around it. That steeply pitched roof was no architect's whimsy. It helped keep snow from piling up there.

A cat gave the newcomers a once-over. It was very large and very furry: both assets in weather like this. There was a name for that breed, a name Rob was still groping for when Justin said, "That's a Maine Coon!"

Rob thumped his forehead with the heel of his hand. "D'oh!" he said, as if he'd escaped from a *Simpsons* episode and magically acquired a third dimension. If you were in Maine and met a big, fuzzy feline, what else would it be? Rob had a bad habit of answering his own rhetorical questions, even when he didn't ask them out loud. If you met a big, fuzzy feline around here, it was liable to be a lynx.

A man came out of the inn. He was a generation older than

the guys from Squirt Frog and the Evolving Tadpoles, with a full head of graying brown hair. He wore a thick wool sweater over a shirt whose collar protected his neck from the scratchy stuff and a pair of black jeans. The sweater looked warm, but not warm enough for this weather. But Rob knew he was a wuss about cold.

"Hello, gentlemen," the fellow said. "If one of you is about to give birth, I may be able to offer you a manger."

A pregnant pause followed. After a couple of beats, Justin said, "Somebody at the gas station told us you might be able to put us up for a while."

"Um, that's what he just said, Justin," Rob pointed out.

Justin worked it through. He looked comically astonished when he finished. "You're right!" he exclaimed. He made as if to tug his curly forelock to the . . . innkeeper? "Sorry about that. I try not to be stupid all the time."

"An admirable ambition," the older man said, fog gusting from his mouth at every word. "About as much as anyone can hope for, too, the world being what it is. I'm Dick Barber, at your service." He stuck out his hand.

One by one, the guys in the band shook it and gave their names. Rob, who was last, added, "Put us all together and we're Squirt Frog and the Evolving Tadpoles."

"Are you?" The name didn't faze Barber. "And here I thought that was a plastic band, even without an Ono."

"Not plastic. Us," Biff said proudly.

"When the Word was made flesh two thousand years ago, they started a religion about it. In our capitalist times, we incarnate the Sale Catalogue instead," Barber said.

"Wow!" Charlie repeated, in the same tone he'd used when he got his first good look at the Trebor Mansion Inn. "Who would've thought we'd run into a dude who was crazy the right way *here*?"

"*You* just washed up on these shores. I got here not too long after you were born," Barber said. Sure as hell, he didn't talk as if he'd lived in Maine his whole life. *Ayuh* might never have crossed his lips. He went on, "You will have to bear in mind that this isn't exactly our high season."

"No, huh?" Rob did his best to sound like a dry martini. That was the best way to deal with his father. He suspected it was the right approach with this guy, too.

Dick Barber smiled fractionally. "Not so you'd notice. But we will do our best to accommodate you—assuming the snow lets up sooner or later. If it doesn't, well, welcome to Guilford."

He *did* remind Rob of Dad, enough to make him ask, "Were you ever a cop before you got the, uh, Mansion Inn?"

"A cop? No." Barber shook his head. "But I did spend twelve years in the Navy. Maybe that's what you're noticing."

"I bet it is," Rob said. "My father was in the Navy."

"And he's a police officer now?"

"That's right."

Charlie broke in: "Did H. P. Lovecraft ever visit this place?"

"He's in the tower." Barber pointed up to it. Bob and his bandmates all goggled at him. That small smile came and went again. The older man condescended to explain: "In paperback. I've got a few shelves of books for guests who stay up there."

"Dibs!" Rob said before any of the other Californians could beat him to the punch.

"You do need to know the tower has no plumbing fixtures," Dick Barber said. "Those are off the room below. You should probably be on good terms with whoever's staying down there."

"Me." Did Justin sound pleased or just resigned? What he added didn't tell Rob much on that score: "We've been putting up with each other for a long time."

"So have Biff and I," Charlie said. "Is there another room on that floor?"

"There is, right across the hall from the one below the tower," Barber said. "If you need anything, holler and bribe the help. They're my grandchildren, and they can use the cash."

Rob started to laugh. Then he realized the older man meant it. This was an . . . interesting place all kinds of ways. He wondered if the tab would be similarly . . . interesting. How much more bad news could the band's plastic stand? Considering the rates places in Bar Harbor gouged out of customers, he couldn't begin to guess what Barber would charge. Figuring it was better to know what they were getting into before they got in too deep, he took a deep breath and asked the obvious question.

"You can stay on the house for a while," Barber answered. "We don't cook for you unless you bring in the food. Unless you pay off the laundry fairy, you won't get clean linen—but I already told you that, didn't I? You're not costing us much. Technically, we've been closed since Labor Day. That's when the season ends here, pretty much. But it's okay. You don't want to be sleeping in your cars in this delightful weather."

"For nothing?" Rob could hardly believe his ears. "Are you sure, man?"

Justin's look told him he was an idiot for checking a gift horse's teeth. Rob didn't need the look. He'd already realized that for himself. Now he'd given Barber another chance to shaft them.

"I said it. I meant it," Barber replied. "I usually mean what I say. These days, that means I'm hideously out of place in about ninety-eight percent of the country. In Guilford, I fit in fine. That's one of the reasons I like it here."

Dad would fit here, too, Rob thought. His father sure didn't fit in L.A., no matter how long he'd lived there. L.A. turned the lie into an art form.

But that was beside the point. "Thank you very much, Mr. Barber," Rob said. His bandmates chorused agreement.

"You're welcome—and I'm Dick. You may as well get used to it," the innkeeper said.

"You talked about bringing food in," Biff said. "Where do we get it to bring in?"

"We've got a little grocery and a meat market. Supermarket's in Dover-Foxcroft, ten, fifteen minutes east. Closest place to buy a meal is Calvin's Kitchen, down on Water Street. They make a decent breakfast and a halfway decent burger. They do dinner, too, but I wouldn't. A couple of blocks farther west, there's a Subway," Barber said. Rob found himself nodding. If there was going to be anything in a little place like this in Maine, odds were it'd be a Subway. Dick Barber added, "There's a Rite Aid close to the Subway, too. You can find almost anything there—maybe not the exact style or brand you want, but you can."

"Yup." Rob nodded. If you spent a lot of time on the road, that was one of the things you learned. Drugstores weren't always deep, but they were very wide.

"Anyway, if you're looking for something that isn't a breakfast joint or Subway, try Dover-Foxcroft," Barber said. "There you've got the Golden Arches. Not exactly an improvement on Subway, but not the same, anyhow. And there's a Chinese place. Cantonese, but it's sort of half Hong Kong and half Maine, if you know what I mean."

"Sounds like that Mexican place we ate at in . . . where the hell was it?" Justin looked to Rob.

Rob couldn't remember. He'd eaten in too many Mexican places in too many towns. But Charlie said, "I know the one you mean. Wasn't that Madison?"

"Madison!" Rob echoed. Once Charlie put a finger on it, it came back to him, too. "It wasn't bad, but it wasn't what you'd call Mexican, either. That cheese was *so* Wisconsin—oh my God!"

They brought their gear out of the SUVs and into the Trebor

Mansion Inn. There was a family area, which seemed overrun by cats, and a guest area not much warmer than the snowstorm outside. Barber hadn't been kidding when he said they weren't looking for business this time of year. "You've got radiators in your rooms," he told them. "They'll warm things up—eventually. And you've got plenty of blankets. Genuine wool, too. We haven't sheared any acrylics or skinned any naugas."

The tower room had a trapdoor and a ladder you could pull up after you. "This is awesome!" Rob exclaimed when he saw the arrangements. "When I was twelve years old, you never would have got me out of here."

"Well, maybe when you had to take a leak." Justin was more pragmatic.

If you weren't twelve years old, the tower wasn't perfect. You couldn't stand up straight in it, except right in the middle. The bed wasn't exactly a bed: it was a mattress and box spring on the floor. If you were six-one like Rob, your feet hung out over the trapdoor space when you lay down on it.

But there was plenty to read. The shelves set into the wall over the mattress held history books, mysteries, bestsellers from about the time Rob was born, and some science fiction. He always checked out the books when he walked into a furniture store or a restaurant that used them as part of the decor; he'd got the habit from his father. Now he had his own odd assortment.

Justin grabbed a fat book about tank battles on the Russian front in World War II. "This should either keep me awake all night or knock me out better than Valium," he said.

"Which would you rather?" Rob asked. He had a panoramic view up here. At the moment, he had a view of snow swirling this way, that way, and now and then the other way, too. Through it, he could dimly make out the back sides of some of the buildings on Water Street. That tall stack . . . Did it belong to the water mill?

Closer was snow-covered ground with pines of assorted sizes sticking up out of it at random. Something prowled across it: another Maine Coon. The critter peered up into one of the pines. A red squirrel stared down at it, bushy tail lashing as the squirrel chewed out the cat from a safe distance.

Justin answered him, but he was so busy watching the little drama outside that he had to ask the lead singer to repeat himself. With a snooty sniff, Justin did: "I *said* it probably doesn't matter much one way or the other. It sure looks like we aren't going anywhere for a while."

"Winter in lovely, charming Guilford, Maine? A new reality show, coming soon to a cable network near you! The other title is *Say Hello to the New Ice Age*."

"Hello, new Ice Age," Justin said obediently.

Rob laughed. Then he looked out at the blowing snow again. "I was just kidding," he said.

"Oh, sure," Justin agreed. "But was God?"

"Well, the blame's gotta stick to somebody. Why not to Him?" Rob answered. Justin said not a word. Outside, the snow kept falling.

XIX

The computer in Colin's study had a twenty-five-inch monitor—a good size, even these days. All the same, he had trouble taking in the scale of the photos from the flash drive Kelly stuck into one of his USB ports. "I see red and black. Could be just about anything. Maybe a volcano, or maybe a bunch of shots from somebody's colonoscopy."

Kelly gave him a severe look. "Back when we first met in Yellowstone, you said the country didn't get its enemas there. It got 'em in Providence."

He kissed her. "Migawd—you were listening to me! I'm not used to that any more. Nobody who's raised children is."

She laughed. He only wished he were joking. One of these days, she might find out for herself. That was part of the reason he'd asked her down to L.A. Not all of it, but part. She said, "You're looking down at Yellowstone—for all I know, the part of it where the West Thumb used to be—from about forty thousand feet. No telephoto, no zoom. This is pretty much what I saw when I looked out the Learjet's window."

"You were dumb to go."

"I knew you'd say that." Her look got more severe. She was an adult. She expected to be treated as one. Colin only sighed. He couldn't do anything about it, especially after the fact.

He studied the picture again. "So it's . . . miles from one side here to the other?" He thought about it for a little while and whistled softly. "That's—something, isn't it? Reminds me of the spaceprobe photos from . . . which moon of Jupiter is it that looks like a sausage-and-anchovy pizza?"

"Io." Kelly dropped severity and laughed again. "It *does* look like a pizza, doesn't it? You come out with the strangest stuff sometimes, but you're right about that."

"Wish I could take credit for it, but I read it somewhere," Colin replied. "And speaking of coming out with strange stuff—" He stopped, muttering to himself. This wasn't how he'd wanted to do things, dammit. Open mouth, jam in foot. *The story of my life*, he thought.

"Why? What other strange stuff was on your mind?" Kelly asked.

He sent her a sharp look, but couldn't read the one she gave back. That he couldn't read it threw gasoline on his ever-active suspicions. Did she already know, or at least have suspicions of her own? They'd been going together for two and a half years now. Probably something wrong with her if she didn't have suspicions by now. Or maybe something was wrong with him for not getting to this point a hell of a lot sooner.

Only one way to find out. He took a deep breath. Even so, it was a good thing they were sitting side by side, because when he asked, "D'you want to marry me, Kelly?" she couldn't have heard him if she'd been on the far side of the room.

"Sure," she said. He blinked. He'd been expecting and hoping for yes and braced against no. Anything but one of those or the other screwed up his mental IFF for a few seconds.

Then he processed the meaning in the unexpected response.

"Is that anything like yes?" he said, wanting to leave no possible doubt.

"Sure," she said again, this time with mischief in her voice.

"You!" He pulled a small velvet box out of the trouser pocket where his keys usually lived. "Well, since it is kind of like yes, you may want to have a look at this, too."

Kelly opened the box; the spring hinge clicked when she did. Even the compact fluorescent in the ceiling fixture was plenty to make the diamonds in the ring sparkle. Her eyes widened. "Ooh!" she said softly. "Pretty!"

"Try it on," Colin urged.

"Okay." She slipped it onto her finger. Then she smiled. "I like the way it looks. And it fits, too. I won't need to get it sized or anything. How did you do that?"

"I hired a guy who used to work for the KGB, back when there was a KGB and a USSR and a bunch of other initials running around loose. These days, he smuggles blintzes and borscht in from Brooklyn. He went through your credit-card records and your cell-phone bills till he found your ring size in there. And he only needed to start working on it a year and a half before I met you."

He spoke with such assurance, he might have been convincing a jury that no one else could possibly have pulled off this home-invasion robbery. "When you talk like that, I start believing you, no matter how much BS you come out with," Kelly said. "It's a good thing I love you, or you'd really be in trouble."

"It's a good thing you love me, or I'd really be in trouble," Colin echoed. By his tone, he meant something different with the same words. He went on, "Good thing I love you, too. Darn good thing—best thing that's happened to me since I don't know when."

"I like that." Kelly nodded. "And if we both say it the same way thirty years from now, we'll have done something right."

"Here's hoping," Colin said. He'd thought the same thing, or close enough, when he said *I do* with Louise. And they did, and then they didn't: not thirty years' worth, anyhow. "I would drink to that here, but I'd rather go out to dinner and do it there. How does Miyamoto sound?"

"Too funky for words," Kelly answered; he'd taken her there before. "Let's go," she added, pulling the flash drive out of the computer. Then she spread her fingers, the way women do when they flash a new ring. The diamonds did some more flashing of their own.

Miyamoto was a San Atanasio institution of sorts. Despite the Japanese name, it was a Polynesian place, one of the last survivors of what had been a common breed of restaurant in Southern California around the time Colin was born. It had Easter Island heads and tiki torches out front. The appetizers featured things like rumaki and foil-wrapped chicken, things you just didn't see in other places any more. The surf-and-turf was lobster and teriyaki steak. The waitresses wore leis. The bartender made rum drinks you normally wouldn't find anywhere this side of Honolulu.

"Two scorpions," Colin told the waitress as they sat down in their bamboo-framed booth.

"Hey! What am I gonna drink?" Kelly said. Colin probably gaped. The waitress cracked up—she hadn't heard that one before, and it caught her by surprise.

"One scorpion for each of us," Colin said carefully. Still chuckling, the gal in the lei went back to pass along the order.

Colin wondered how many times he'd come here with Louise over the years. A lot, but he liked the place too much to cede it to her after they broke up. He'd never seen her here since. That might have been coincidence. Or maybe Teo was too organic to want to pollute his system with the high-cholesterol goodies Miyamoto dished out. *More for me if he is,* Coin thought. Less happily, he'd also come back once since the split to investigate a robbery.

The waitress brought back a couple of scorpions, each almost big enough to swim in. They spelled *drink* with a *u* here. Even they wouldn't serve you more than two zombies. That made sense, because you weren't just drunk after two of those. You were fucking embalmed.

"Are you ready to order yet?" she asked. She scribbled what they wanted and went away again.

Before the food came, the owner wandered over to say hello. Stan Miyamoto was short and stocky. He was about Colin's age; his son had graduated from San Atanasio High in Vanessa's class. "I want to say one more time what a good cop you are." He was talking more to Kelly than to Colin. "The way you caught those guys who held us up, the way you sent them to prison—"

"Part of the job." Colin didn't want to tell Miyamoto the only way the crooks could have been dumber was to wear BUST ME! signs. To change the subject, he went on, "Stan, this is my fiancée, Kelly Birnbaum."

The owner, of course, had come over to say hello when Colin visited with Louise, too. You never would have guessed by his smile. "Congratulations! You are a lucky lady, Ms. Birnbaum."

"I think so. I hope so," Kelly said.

Miyamoto turned back to Colin. "So you celebrate tonight, do you?"

"We sure do," he agreed.

"And you choose to do it here? Dinner on the house!"

It was kindly meant. Colin knew that. Back when he was starting out, he would have thanked Stan and enjoyed it. But the world had changed. For better? For worse? For different, anyhow.

"Stan, I can't," he said. "I'd like to, but I just can't. Too darn many regulations about police officers and gratuities. You're gonna have to take my money whether you like it or not." Now there was a sentence you didn't get to trot out every day.

"I am not doing this for Lieutenant Ferguson," the owner said stiffly. "I am doing this for Colin Ferguson, who is my friend. I hope he is my friend."

"I hope so, too. But if you want to put your friend's behind in a sling, you'll feed him a free dinner. The city council and the accountants would land on me like a ton of bricks."

"They should get in an uproar about things that need uproar. Heaven knows there are enough of them in this town." By the way Stan Miyamoto said it, he could think of three or four himself. But he didn't try to insist any more. Shaking his head, he went back to the kitchens.

Quietly, Kelly said, "I bet a lot of cops would have taken him up on that. I bet they would have got away with it, too."

"I bet you're right." Colin shrugged. "If it doesn't bother them, it doesn't, that's all. It bothers me. If I keep my nose clean all the time, I never need to worry about remembering which lies I told to which people. And if I don't give an inch, I don't have to worry about giving a mile, either."

"Makes sense to me." She quirked an eyebrow at him, though. "If I get a ticket, I guess you won't fix it for me."

"Good guess." Colin had never fixed any for Louise or the kids. Nobody in his family was a bad driver, so he hadn't had to worry about it much. Once or twice, a cop might have decided not to write them up when he realized who they were, but that was something he didn't officially have to know about. He found a more interesting topic: "Here comes dinner."

There was enough food for at least half a dozen people. Leftovers in styrofoam boxes would make lunches and dinners for days. Stan Miyamoto had his own kind of stubbornness. He was going to be generous, by God, whether Colin liked it or not. Sensibly, Colin decided he might as well like it.

Louise Ferguson yawned. She'd been doing that all morning, and she couldn't figure out why. She'd had a good night's sleep the night before, but she kept wanting to nod off anyhow.

Mr. Nobashi started to yawn, too. It wasn't the first time he'd done it today, either. Yawns were as contagious as the common cold. This time, he caught himself in the middle, and almost dislocated his jaw trying to stop. He frowned at Louise as if that were her fault.

"You okay, Mrs. Ferguson?" he asked in his heavily accented English. What he did to her last name was a caution, but she'd been deciphering Japanese accents for as long as she'd lived in San Atanasio—the town had always had a sizable Asian population. The ramen company hadn't put its American headquarters here by accident.

"I'm fine, Mr. Nobashi, thanks. I really am," Louise answered, and then made a liar of herself by yawning again.

"You need more coffee," he declared. He ran on the stuff the way a car ran on gasoline. If Louise guzzled it the way he did, she didn't think she'd ever go to bed. He poured himself a fresh cup now. He also poured one for her, and set it on her desk.

"Thank you very much, Mr. Nobashi," she said in amazement. Subordinates took care of small things for superiors here. It rarely worked the other way around.

With him watching her, she took a sip. She smiled and nodded and thanked him again. She didn't yawn, even if she wanted to. He nodded back and took his own refill into his sanctum. He got on the phone there and started barking at someone in Japanese laced with English profanity.

Louise . . . yawned yet again. She started to drink some more coffee, but set the cup down. It didn't taste right somehow; it seemed harsh and metallic. The trouble wasn't in the brew. She was sure of that. She'd made it herself. Neither Mr. Nobashi nor anyone else noticed anything out of the ordinary.

If it wasn't the coffee, it was her. She wondered if she needed to go to the doctor. She hoped like hell she didn't. She had medical coverage because she worked here, but it wasn't nearly as good as what she'd got through Colin. You didn't think about such things when you'd just fallen in love. Unfortunately, they didn't go away just because you weren't thinking about them. Deductibles, copays . . . Seeing Dr. DiVicenzo would cost her more than it had in the old days, dammit.

What could make her sleepy all the time—and tired, too, because she had been the past few days—and make coffee taste lousy, too? Whatever it was, it seemed unfair. Coffee was the best legal weapon when you got worn out.

She couldn't remember the last time she'd felt like this. And then, all of a sudden, she could. She let out a startled squawk of laughter. She hadn't even thought about *that* in twenty-odd years. Yes, her period was a few days late, but so what? Her cycle was getting erratic anyway. Pretty soon, it would stop. She wouldn't miss tampons and pads and cramps, not even a little bit.

"It's nutso," she said out loud. Had she worn her diaphragm every single time she'd gone to bed with Teo? She knew damn well she hadn't. When you started making love, pausing to go into the john and smear the contraption (Colin had called it a manhole cover—the kind of thing he thought was funny) with contraceptive goop was a great way to break the mood. She hadn't thought she was taking a chance, or much of one.

She still couldn't believe it. *The rabbit died—laughing.* That was what the gal on the '70s TV show said when she found out she was going to have a change-of-life baby. She hadn't wanted her life to change that way, so she got an abortion instead.

"Ridiculous," Louise said. This had to be something, anything, else. Dr. DiVicenzo would tell her she'd come down with a virus. Or he'd tell her it was all her imagination. His fee would be real, though.

Not long before the lunch break, Louise did nod off. It was only for a couple of minutes, and she was sure she woke up again before anybody saw her, but even so. . . . Sometimes you felt refreshed after a little nap. Louise felt she needed another little nap. A big one would be even better.

In lieu of coffee, she went into the ladies' room and splashed cold water on her face. That did help, some. She had to repair her makeup afterwards. No one walked in on her. Sometimes lucky was better than good: one more notion she'd heard from her ex. You could wash a man right out of your hair, but washing him out of your brain was a hell of a lot harder.

She gulped her brown-bag sandwich (Swiss and turkey ham on rye) and apple at her desk. Then she drove to the Walgreens a few blocks from the ramen works. Half a dozen brands to choose from. The supervolcano hadn't kept them from getting here, or maybe they were made locally. When she went to the register, she started to pull out her Visa, then thought better of it and paid cash instead.

You didn't have to kill a rabbit nowadays, or mess around with frogs, or anything icky like that. Louise went back into the ladies' room. In the privacy of a stall, she peed on the Clearblue test strip. She supposed she'd bought that one because this whole thing came out of the Clearblue sky.

She didn't wear a watch any more. She used the clock in her cell phone to count off the minutes till the result that showed was reliable. She didn't, she wouldn't, she flat-out refused to, look at the strip till then.

Time. "Ready or not, here I come," she muttered, as if at hide-and-seek. She looked.

PREGNANT. The letters were bright red. It didn't feel like a red-letter day. It felt like . . . She didn't know what it felt like. The end of the world as we know it. She heard the bouncy song in her head. She didn't feel fine, though. She felt—sleepy, dammit.

No one else had come in while she sat on the pot waiting out the test. No one was in there when she chucked the Clearblue box and the test strip. She covered them with paper towels even so. Afterwards, she scrubbed her hands like Lady Macbeth. Germs wouldn't trouble her. Like exes, other things were harder to wash away.

"You better now?" Mr. Nobashi asked her in his telegraphic English as she tried to settle herself at her desk.

"I think so," she lied. The rabbit might have died laughing. What would Teo say? She didn't suppose he'd be so amused. She didn't think things were very funny herself, for that matter. *What am I going to do?* she wondered. *Have it? Get rid of it?* Both prospects seemed equally appalling.

She checked some inventories for Mr. Nobashi. He wanted to figure out why shrimp ramen was selling better in Seattle than anywhere else in the USA. They hated beef ramen there, but it outsold shrimp two-to-one in Chattanooga. Again, he wanted to know why. Louise couldn't have cared less, but she could scare up numbers for him to plug into his spreadsheets.

Her cell rang. She fished it out of her purse. "Hello?"

Colin growled in her ear: "Hi, Louise."

"*What* is it?" she snapped. Of all the people in the world she wanted to hear from right this minute, he couldn't have rated higher than next to last.

He paused for a moment, then said, "Thought for a second there I called Vanessa by mistake."

"Sorry." Again, Louise lied. "Look, whatever it is, make it snappy, will you? I'm pretty busy here." One more fib.

"Well"—he breathed out hard, a sure sign she'd pissed him off—"all I wanted to tell you was that I asked Kelly to marry me, and she said yes. If you don't care about that, I'll go off and eat worms, I guess."

"Sorry." This time, Louise sounded more like someone who

meant it. "Congratulations! Or do I say good luck to the groom? I never remember."

"You congratulate me and wish her luck. Sounds about right." Colin still sounded very much like Colin. He went on, "How are things with you?"

Not bad. I'm going to have a baby. Louise didn't say it. The only thing she was sure of was that Colin hadn't had thing one to do with it. Sooner or later, if she decided to keep it, she'd have to let him know. Later. Not sooner. "I'm tired," she answered: a tiny fragment of the truth, with none of the reason behind it.

"You sound like it," he said. Was that a dig, something on the order of *You sound like an old lady*? Louise wouldn't have been surprised. You always had to look twice—sometimes three times—at things that came out of Colin's mouth. You'd be sorry if you didn't.

Well, he could dig and jab as much as he pleased. She wasn't an old lady by the most fundamental way to judge that. Her biological clock wasn't just ticking. The alarm on the damn thing had gone off. She was alarmed, all right.

"You there, Louise?" Colin asked when she didn't say anything right away.

"I'm here," she replied.

"Are you okay? Is Teo treating you the way he ought to? Anything like that, you let me know, you hear? I'll take care of it."

"Teo is treating me fine. Don't do anything dumb because you've got a case of the imaginaries—do you hear me?" she said sharply. *He treats me better than you ever did.* Louise didn't come out with it. Vanessa would have. She knew that. But living most of her adult life with Colin left her convinced he'd done his best, at least when he thought of it. Trouble was, his best didn't come close to being good enough.

"Okay," he said. "So long, Louise. Take care." He hung up.

Teo was treating her so fine, he'd gone and knocked her up. And what would he say when she told him that? Whatever it was, she expected she could take it at face value. Unlike Colin, he didn't think sarcasm was a spectator sport.

At about half past three, Mr. Nobashi came over to her and said, "You want to go home early? Not much going on, and you maybe could use some rest, *neh?*" He was, she supposed, doing his best to be tactful in a language not his own. What could that mean but *You look like something the cat dragged in?*

"It's okay, Mr. Nobashi. I'll make it till quitting time. Thank you, though." Louise got paid by the hour. She didn't want her check docked—and it wasn't as if she were actually sick. She managed a smile, adding *"Arigato"* so he'd know she was picking things up on the job.

He grinned in surprise and bobbed his head in what was almost a bow. "You go," he said. "We not worry about clock, okay?"

The thanks in Japanese must have done it. That wasn't a corporate thing for him to say, but maybe a nice guy lurked under the salaryman after all. Louise wouldn't look a gift horse in the mouth. "Thank you very much, Mr. Nobashi!" she said, and then *"Arigato!"* one more time.

She was out of there before he had the chance to change his mind. When she got back to the condo, she lay down on the couch for a little while and closed her eyes. *Just to rest them*, she told herself. Next thing she knew, Teo was unlocking the door.

He laughed when he saw her confusion. "Hello, sleepyhead!" he said, hurrying over to kiss her. "You must have had a tough day if you sacked out as soon as you came in."

"Mr. Nobashi let me off a couple of hours early," she said. "On the company's dime, if you can believe it."

The way he blinked said it wasn't easy. "Why'd he do that?" he asked. Louise explained about *arigato*. Teo was still puzzled when she finished, wondering, "Okay, but why did he want to let you off early to begin with?"

"I was all tired, and I guess I looked kind of green around the gills, too," Louise said. She hoped the morning sickness wouldn't be too awful this time around. Colin had dubbed her the Duchess of York for the way she kept tossing her cookies when she was pregnant with Rob. She'd hardly been sick at all with Vanessa, and kind of in-between carrying Marshall.

"You look fine now," Teo said. "You always look good to me, love."

That made her smile. Teo had a knack for making her smile. She wasn't surprised to hear she looked all right now. She'd been asleep for—what?—close to two and a half hours. She wondered if she'd be able to sleep later on tonight. From what she remembered, she wouldn't have any trouble at all.

Teo went on, "But what made you so out of it at work? It must've been bad, or he wouldn't've turned you loose like that. You need to go to the doc or something?"

She would need to see her gynecologist soon. Frank Russell, who'd delivered her babies, had long since retired. Last she'd heard, he was living in Palm Springs, painting watercolors of the desert, and selling some of them for pretty good money. She didn't like Dr. Suzuki so much, but she thought he knew his business.

"I think I know what's cooking with me," she said.

"Yeah? Tell, love, tell."

You couldn't be a little bit pregnant. You couldn't break the news by easy stages, either. Louise wished you could. Her life was about to get more complicated. No. Her life had already got more complicated. Now she had to announce the fact. She wanted a drink—but that wouldn't be good for her passenger. She took a deep breath instead: as inadequate a substitute as you could find. "I'm going to have a baby, Teo."

He giggled. "That's the funniest thing I've heard in I don't know when! I didn't know you could do a straight face like that, either. Oh, my God!" He was practically holding his sides.

"I'm not kidding," Louise said. "I'm pregnant. I'm sleepy like you wouldn't believe, my coffee tastes weird—tastes lousy—"

"That stuff doesn't mean squat," Teo broke in. He didn't want to believe it. Well, how could she blame him when she didn't want to believe it herself?

"I wasn't done," she said. "My period's late. I know it's getting erratic"—*I know I'm getting old* lay behind that—"but still. And today at lunch I got a pregnancy test at the drugstore, and I peed on it in the head at work. I'm pregnant, all right."

He stared at her. For the very first time since they'd been together, his dark eyes seemed opaque. She couldn't tell what was going on behind them. "You mean it," he said slowly, and his voice was as guarded as his expression.

"I sure do." Louise nodded. "You're going to be a daddy, Teo."

"Well . . ." If he was pleased, he did a mighty good job of not showing it. He licked his lips. He'd never been a father before, and he hadn't looked to be a father now. She'd already been through pregnancy three times. *Not out of wedlock, though*, she thought. Maybe this would make him do something about that. Louise hadn't worried about a piece of paper, but it mattered when a child was involved. He pulled in a deep breath of his own, then expelled it in a sigh. "It's still real early, right? You could, um, dispose of it, like?"

"Yes. I could." Louise didn't know why she was so disappointed. It wasn't as if she hadn't had the same thought. But she hadn't looked for it to be the first thing she heard from him. "I don't know that I want to, though. It's something we made together, after all, something wonderful."

"It's an oops. We didn't intend to do it," Teo said.

"No, we didn't," she agreed. And if that didn't win next year's Oscar for Best Understatement, whoever did take the statuette home was bound to have cheated. "But it happened, and we've got to deal with it."

"Getting rid of it is dealing with it," Teo said. "Then we don't have to worry about it any more."

"I'm not sure I want to do that," Louise repeated. "You shouldn't make up your mind right away, either. We don't have to decide anything tonight. We've got some time to think about it."

"What's to think about? It just messes everything up. You ought to know that better than I do," Teo said.

Kids did mess up your life. Louise sometimes thought that was their sole function in life. They didn't stop when they got to be self-winding, either, the way you thought they would. Even so . . . "They give back more than they take away," Louise said. "Ask your folks."

"What do they know?" Teo said. His father was a carpenter, his mother a housewife. They weren't educated people, but they were plenty nice enough. "They went crazy trying to keep us all fed and in shoes and like that. Who needs the hassle if you don't have to put up with it?"

"Let's talk about it later." Louise had never seen Teo like this. Plainly, he needed some time to get used to the idea. He didn't want to look at it yet, much less to like it. She could see him outside jogging with a little boy who looked just like him. She could see the little boy staring up proudly at the great big man who was his daddy. How sad Teo couldn't picture it, too.

Later didn't happen the rest of the evening. They slept together, the way they always did, but it didn't feel as warm and loving as usual to Louise. Teo might have been on the far side of the country, or on the far side of the moon. Louise tried to tell herself she was having the vapors, but she had trouble convincing herself. She also didn't have long to do the telling; she fell asleep as if someone had slipped a Mickey Finn into the water she drank after she brushed her teeth.

Next morning was no better. She staggered around like a zombie, awake but not alive. She made coffee, but she couldn't get more than a third of the cup down. It tasted nasty, so nasty she wondered if she'd give it back.

And Teo was out the door in nothing flat. He did remember to kiss her good-bye. She didn't think he'd missed a day since they got together. But if ever anyone was going through the motions, he was then. Again, Louise tried to think she was seeing things that weren't there, or it was nothing but her hormones running wild (which they were, and would be), or—anything. Again, she had trouble believing it.

Mr. Nobashi greeted her at Ramen Central with, "You better today?"

"I sure hope so," Louise answered. "Thanks again for giving me some time off yesterday. It helped a lot."

"Good," he said gruffly, and went back into his inner office. Which was a good thing, because not thirty seconds later Louise yawned almost wide enough to make the top of her head fall off.

Wondering how she'd ever make it till half past five, she sat down and started messing around with the inventory spreadsheets. She wondered what would happen if she just entered numbers at random. Would ramen-scarfers all over the country start pining for their favorite flavors, or else find themselves swamped with them? Would she get fired and find herself unemployed as well as knocked up? Or would nobody notice or care?

Mr. Nobashi bawled for coffee. Then he bawled for sweet rolls. Then he hollered for sweet rolls *and* coffee. Hopping up to bring him goodies every so often kept Louise from sacking out at her desk. Nice to think Mr. Nobashi was good for something.

When she carried in the sweet rolls and coffee, he was just getting off the phone after a conversation with headquarters in

Hiroshima. "Weather very bad in Japan," he said. "Very cold. Hiroshima is warm. Like Los Angeles warm, only sticky. They have snow there, thirty centimeters snow." He paused. "A foot, you say."

"Wow! That's a lot of snow," she said. It hadn't snowed here, but it was the rainiest winter she remembered.

"Only get worse, too. Supervolcano number-one bad," Mr. Nobashi said. She couldn't very well argue with that.

Patty came by her desk to yak for a bit. After a little while, she asked, "You feelin' okay, sweetie?"

"I'll live," Louise said, as dryly as if she were Colin.

"Well, okay. You seem a little peaked, that's all." Patty was gossip-hungry. She'd have something to gab about when Louise's belly started swelling. For now, though, Louise didn't feel like sharing the news. Patty eventually went away.

Somehow, Louise staggered through the day. She was fixing dinner when Teo came in. He was bright and cheerful—in a superficial way. He talked about how his day at the exercise studio had gone. He told a dumb joke he'd heard. He didn't say word one about the elephant in the room.

After dinner, Louise tried to bring it up. Teo changed the subject. He hardly even seemed to have heard her. If he kept on doing that, Louise knew she would get mad at him. If she'd had a little more energy, she might have got mad then and there. Or she might not have. He'd built up a lot of capital with her. A couple of days of acting like a jerk—even if it was about something important—didn't come close to burning through it.

She wondered if making love would help. But, even though she did everything except send up a flare, he didn't take the hint. He just went to sleep, earlier than usual. Disappointed, so did she. Disappointed or not, she zoned out as if knocked over the head. She'd always thought you slept a lot while you were pregnant because you sure as hell wouldn't afterwards.

He was gone the next morning before she got up. That was funny; they usually woke up together. Maybe he'd told her why the night before, but she was too sleepy to recall. The condo felt strange with her fixing breakfast alone.

Another day at the ramen mill. She survived it. She didn't doze off or do anything to give Patty more ideas than she had already. It was raining again when she went out at half past five. On the way home, somebody rear-ended the VW in the lane next to hers. No one got hurt, but neither car would be going anywhere without making a body shop happy.

When she walked into the condo, her first thought was that a burglar had hit it. Then she realized the only stuff missing was Teo's. Favorite chair. Clothes. DVDs. CDs. Computer. TV. Gone.

A note lay on the bed. *I am sorry,* Louise read, *but I am not made to be a father. If you can make the payments, keep the place. I won't give you no trouble about it. It was fun while it lasted, wasn't it? But nothing lasts forever.*

He'd scribbled a signature under the last four words. No forwarding address. She could try his cell, but what were the odds he'd answer? She tore the note into little pieces before she started to cry.

XX

"Been a while since the Strangler did anybody," Gabe Sanchez remarked. "Not since the supervolcano went. Maybe he was at Yellowstone when it blew."

"Too much to hope for," Colin said. All the same, he imagined the son of a bitch watching Old Faithful when everything for miles around fell down onto the magma. Yes, he knew that was ridiculous. The area around Old Faithful had been off-limits for months before the big eruption. All the same . . . "Less than he deserves, too, you know."

"Oh, yeah. Lethal injection!" Gabe snorted contempt. "If we ever do drop on him, here's hoping some of the big, muscle-bound studs at San Quentin get some action with him. Let him find out about some of what he gave the old ladies."

"That'd be nice," Colin agreed. Before he could go on, his phone rang. He picked it up. "Lieutenant Ferguson."

"Hello, Colin." His former wife had been calling this number since before either of them had a cell phone. No doubt she did it now from force of habit.

"What's up, Louise?" he asked. Whatever if was, it wasn't

good. She sounded as if she'd just watched a cement mixer run over her puppy.

"I don't want to talk about it on the phone," she said. "Could you pick me up here at the ramen office for lunch?"

"Okay." He tried to hide his astonishment. Since she left him, she'd made a point of *not* wanting to see him. "What time? . . . Twelve straight up? All right, I'll be there. . . . Yes, of course I know where it is. 'Bye."

"Your ex?" Gabe knew the variations on this theme, too— probably better than Colin did. His kids were young enough to live with their mother most of the time, so he had to keep dealing with her. However painful it was, Colin's break was clean. Or it had been, till now.

"Yeah, that was her. Something's wrong. I don't know what yet, but I'll find out at lunch," Colin said.

"Lucky you." Sanchez rolled his eyes. "What'll you do to help?"

"Damfino." Colin shook his head. "Have to see what it is first. I don't aim to buy a pig in a poke. Things aren't the way they were right after she trotted out the door."

"Nope. You found somebody else." Gabe didn't sound— very—jealous. He'd dated a double handful of women since his breakup. Nothing lasted long.

"Uh-huh. If she thinks she can walk back in the same way she walked out . . ." Colin shook his head again. If Louise had wanted to do that a few months after she left, chances were he would have dumped Kelly to get his old life back. Now? The train had rolled on.

He thought it had, anyhow.

"Luck," Gabe told him.

"Thanks a lot." For the rest of the morning, Colin went through the motions at his desk. He went through the emotions inside his head. When the time came, he drove north up Hesperus

Avenue to Braxton Bragg, then hung a right to the ramen place. He shook his head when he turned in to the lot. He hadn't remembered how heavily fortified the perimeter was. One more sign of San Atanasio's changes—not for the better.

Louise came out at twelve on the dot, a couple of minutes after he got there. She looked the way she always looked—which is to say, she looked good to him. But no, not quite the way she always looked: she was pale and she'd been crying.

"Thanks," she said as she got into the Taurus.

"It's okay. Where do you want to go?"

"How about that Carrows on Reynoso Drive?"

"You got it." Colin nodded. "Want to tell me about it now or after we get there?" Colin pulled back onto the street. He noted the way the armed guard kept an eye on him till he did. If that guy wasn't a vet, and likely a combat vet, he'd eat his shoes.

"Teo left me yesterday," Louise said. "He skipped. He's gone. He took his things and he bailed. I have no idea where he is."

"Okay." Colin didn't say anything more until he got into the left-turn lane that would put him back on Hesperus. Then he asked, "Did he . . . hurt you before he left? Am I looking at a domestic-violence case? Last time I talked to you, you said everything was fine with you guys."

"The last time we talked, everything *was* fine." Louise laughed bitterly. A moment later, she yawned and covered her mouth with her hand. "I keep doing that," she said, as if annoyed at herself. "No, he didn't hurt me, not the way you mean. Not so you could bust him for it."

"Then what do you want from me?" He tried to sound patient, not pissed off. "If you need a shoulder to cry on, I'm not your number-one candidate any more. I'm sorry, but I'm not. When I called you, you know, it was to tell you I'm gonna marry Kelly." Louise was the kind of person who could forget things like that when forgetting them looked convenient.

"Colin, I'm going to have a baby. That's why he ran out on me."

It was a good thing traffic on Hesperus was light, with no cars anywhere close to his. The Taurus jerked out of its lane for a split second. He had to haul it back over the yellow stripes. He hadn't been so surprised since—since the day she walked out on him.

He started to ask if she was kidding, but he swallowed that question. She wasn't. She'd never hurt him for the sake of hurting him—if anybody in the family enjoyed pulling wings off flies, it was Vanessa. He asked something else instead: "Are you sure?"

"Oh, you betcha," Louise said. "The home pregnancy tests they have nowadays are just about as good as the ones doctors use. It says I am. And I feel like I am. I know what it's like, even if it's been a while. You don't forget."

"If you say so." Colin hung a right on Reynoso Drive. "Do you, ah, know what you're going to do about it?"

"No. Teo wanted me to get rid of it right away. I may, but I'm not going to do it like that—" She snapped her fingers. "I didn't mean to get pregnant, but I may have it anyway."

The Carrows was on the south side of the street. He waited in the center lane till he could turn left against the eastbound traffic without getting creamed. Most of the shops and eateries in the little center catered to Japanese. The lot was crowded. He finally found a space and slid in. He and Louise walked to the restaurant a few inches farther apart than they would have before they broke up.

He didn't say anything till they were seated at a table that gave them a fine view of the cars going back and forth on Reynoso Beach. "What exactly do you want me to do about all this?" he asked then, picking his words with great care.

"Are you ready to order?" The waitress couldn't have been more than twenty, and sounded as if she had not a care in the world. That was what twenty was for. Too goddamn bad it didn't last.

"I'll have the BLT," Louise said.

Colin ordered a cheeseburger. The waitress went away. He repeated the question.

"I heard you the first time," Louise said sharply. "Can you find out where he's gone? Phone records or his plastic or whatever? His parents don't know or they won't say—I've already tried them."

"Maybe," Colin said. "If he's left the county, I don't have so many contacts. If he's out of state, it gets a good bit harder. I can try, I guess. Where does he have relatives?"

"Some down in San Diego. Some in Mexico, too." Louise looked rueful. "If he's south of the border, it's impossible, isn't it?"

"Pretty close," Colin agreed. "Nobody down there would get excited about that kind of case." Not many people up here would, either, although he might be able to call in some favors. On the other hand, he might not. The supervolcano and its disruptions made small stuff too small to worry about. And if Teo felt like disappearing into a refugee camp, he might not surface for years, if he ever did.

The food came then, interrupting his gloomy thoughts. The cheeseburger was . . . a cheeseburger. Better than fast food or Denny's, nothing to jump up and down about even so. The way Louise demolished her sandwich said morning sickness hadn't kicked in yet.

"Why did he just split like that?" Colin asked. "You two have—uh, had—been together a while now. Wasn't it something you could have worked out between you?"

"I thought so, but he freaked. He didn't want to be a daddy—no way, nohow." Louise's mouth twisted. "Sometimes you don't find out what somebody's really like till it's crunch time. I got crunched, all right."

"Yeah, you did. Sorry about that."

"What am I going to do?" Her eyes filled with tears.

"Either you'll have the baby or you'll decide you don't want to have it and you'll take care of that." Colin was no enormous fan of abortion. He could see, though, that a woman might not want to bear the child of a man who'd abandoned her—especially if she was a woman with some gray in her hair unless she touched it up. Raising a kid on your own was never easy. It got harder as you got older and tireder.

Through the tears, his ex looked indignant. She eyed him as if this were somehow his fault—or, at any rate, anyone's but hers. "I can figure that much out for myself, thank you very much," she said tartly. "What I wanted to know was how much help from you I could count on."

"Huh? What kind of help? I'm not made of money, especially when I'm putting Marshall through school and he never seems to graduate."

"But he sold that story! To a magazine! For money! Isn't that wonderful?"

"Well, it's pretty good. But what he got is not quite a week's rent on his place, and that's before you chop taxes out of it. Besides, you pretty much cleaned out my bank account when you left." He'd kept the house. She'd taken just about everything else they'd built up over all the years they were married. The lawyers called it a fair split. Colin hadn't loved lawyers before the divorce. He was even less fond of them now.

"You're being mean!" Louise exclaimed.

He exhaled through his nose to try to hide how angry he was. "Louise, you walked out on me. You were in love with Teo, and he was in love with you, and the two of you were going to live happily ever after. You got your half of the community property. Except for that, you didn't want thing one to do with me any more. Months could go by without us talking. But now Mr.

Happily Ever After finds out you've got a bun in the oven, so he takes off. And all of a sudden I look a lot better by comparison, huh? Is that where we're at, or did I miss something?"

"You're not going to help me?" If the Mask of Tragedy had a voice, it would have been hers then.

"You were the one who didn't want me darkening your towels any more. You called me every name in the book. We *are* divorced, remember? Why should I care about the bastard of the guy you left me for?"

"Never mind the baby," she said impatiently. "Didn't you love me?"

"Yeah. I did. Past tense. I loved you longer than you loved me, as a matter of fact. I was a mess after you dumped me." Colin bit back several other things he might have said. This was more than bad enough without looking for ways to make it worse. The waitress chose that moment to bring the check, too. After she hurried away, he went on, "Now I've found somebody else, too. I'll do the best I can with Kelly. I think we've got a decent chance. That's about as much as anybody can hope for these days."

"And so you'll throw me under the bus." Louise would have been a star in Victorian melodrama.

You did that to yourself. One more thing Colin swallowed. "Look," he said, "if I have a little extra, maybe I can chip in something. But if you think I'm going to go one inch further than that, I'm here to tell you it ain't gonna happen. It's over, Louise. I'm sorry—Christ knows I'm sorry—but it is."

She glared at him. "You are a cruel, hard man. Your Kelly doesn't have the faintest idea what she's getting into, poor thing."

"For all I know, you're right," he answered. "But I'll tell you one other thing."

"What is it?" Louise spat the words at him.

"If I'd knocked you up, I wouldn't've run out on you. And you know darn well that's so."

She did. He could see it in her face. He could also see that she would sooner have been dropped into the supervolcano than admit it. "Maybe you'd better take me back to work," she said glacially.

"Okay." He tossed a five on the table, then paid the bill at the register. Rain started spattering down as they walked across the lot to his car. He held the passenger-side door open for her. She got in with the air of Marie Antoinette heading for the guillotine.

Neither one of them said much as he drove north to Braxton Bragg Boulevard. Just before he turned in to the fortified lot, Louise murmured, "I wish . . . I wish things could have been different."

"A lot of people do," Colin agreed. Cops saw that every hour of every day. "But by the time they make the wish, it's already too late. Take care of yourself, Louise, whatever you decide to do."

"Like it matters to you!" she flared.

"It does," he said. "We can't go back to square one, though. You've got your life to live, and I've got mine, and they aren't on the same track any more."

She slid out and slammed the car door. Then she hurried inside; the rain was coming down harder now, and she didn't have an umbrella with her. The guard nodded to Colin as he left the lot. He gave back a wave that was half a salute.

When he sat down at his desk again, Gabe asked, "Do I want to know how that went?"

Colin thought for a moment. "Even worse than I expected," he said judiciously.

"Aii!" Gabe winced. "They said it couldn't be done!"

"Oh, it could, all right." In a few bleak words, as if he were summarizing a case on the witness stand, Colin explained how.

"Oh, man. Oh, wow, man." Sanchez shook his head. "That happened to me, I wouldn't've come back here. I'd've found somewhere quiet and got loaded."

"I'm on city time now, not on mine," Colin said. "And I did too much drinking right after we broke up. It's a bitch, all right, but she's just not my problem any more." He packed the words with more emphasis than he usually used. Was he trying to convince himself as well as his friend? He wouldn't have been surprised.

"You're a better man than I am, Gunga Din," Gabe told him. "Now, are you gonna give your new squeeze the good news?"

That was a more interesting question than Colin really liked. Reluctantly, he nodded. "Don't you think I've got to? If we're going to make some kind of life together, she needs to know what's going on with me."

"I guess." Gabe sounded anything but sure. "I don't know who it'll be rougher on, though, you or her."

"Oh, my God, Colin! How totally awful for you!" Kelly exclaimed when her fiancé reached the end of his story. Here and there getting through it, he'd sounded more like a machine running on clockwork than a flesh-and-blood human being. She had the feeling he couldn't have made it through without shutting down most of what he was feeling.

"I've had lunches I enjoyed more," he allowed. "Hey, I've had teeth pulled I enjoyed more."

"I believe you. I wish I could be down there to give you a hug," Kelly said.

"That'd be good," Colin said. "So now I've got to set up a skip trace on this clown. Just what I want to do." He couldn't get it out of his mind.

"You could just tell her to forget it. She's got a lot of nerve, dropping that on you after she sashayed out the door." Kelly thought she needed to remind Colin of that. If Louise wanted to sashay back into his life, how interested would he be? They'd had a lot of years together. If she could work it so the ones that had passed since she left him somehow didn't count . . .

Carrying her lover's baby made that harder. But if she decided to visit a doctor, she wouldn't have to carry it long. Then again, Colin had never struck Kelly as being good at forgetting.

His electronically transmitted sigh in her ear did everything a real one would have except ruffle her hair. "Hon, if some guy ran out on a woman I'd never heard of before and left her pregnant, I'd put out a skip trace on the so-and-so." He sighed again. "I wish this were some gal I never heard of. I wouldn't get all messed up inside dealing with her then."

"I bet you wouldn't!" Kelly exuded righteous indignation. "She gave you one in the eye, and now she wants your help? Some nerve!"

"Yeah, well, I pretty much told her the same thing." Colin hesitated, then went on, "In case you're wondering, like, I wouldn't take her back on a silver platter. That's all over now. I'm better off, and I've got the sense to see it. Just so you know."

The supervolcano had shot global warming right behind the ear. The ice pack in the Arctic Ocean and the one around Antarctica were both spreading and thickening. Kelly had some satellite data on her kitchen table somewhere. She could dig it out. . . .

Thickening ice packs or no, a glacier in the middle of her chest suddenly melted all at once. Glorious warmth spread from the spot where it had been. "I did know," she said, which was true and false at the same time in a way scientific data couldn't be. She'd been pretty sure of the one thing, while still worried about the other.

"Happens I love you," Colin added, as if he'd been an innocent bystander when that somehow happened to him.

"It works both ways," Kelly assured him. She didn't like to get mawkish. She had no intention of going Bridezilla when they made things official. She still marveled that he'd got up the nerve to propose, and that she'd had the nerve to say *yes*, or even *sure*.

The percentage of women who passed thirty single and stayed that way permanently was large, and getting larger by the year. She was bucking the odds.

"Okay. Good." He sounded like someone who needed assurance, or at least reminding. Then he said, "Keeping that in mind makes it easier to cope with Louise." He chuckled harshly. "Teo was always everything I wasn't. He was sweet. He was caring. He listened to Louise—"

"You listen!" Kelly interrupted. "Whenever we talk, I always think how I've never known anybody who listens like you."

"Louise didn't think so. She wanted out, and Teo was her way out." Another chuckle. "Then he wanted out, too."

"He *was* everything you weren't," Kelly said. "You never would have done anything like that. Even if you had got somebody pregnant, you would have stuck around afterwards."

"One more thing I told Louise. I do like to think so," Colin said. "But who knows? Sometimes you just can't cope, so you run."

Kelly snorted. It was much easier to imagine Colin sticking like glue even when that made him a goddamn nuisance than to picture him breaking and running. She wouldn't have minded had he run from Louise—just the opposite, in fact. But that wasn't his style, and never would be.

"Anyway, now you know," he continued. "You needed to, because I'll have to give Louise whatever cop-style help I can." No, he wouldn't run. He said, "If she ends up having this kid, though, you've got to remember it ain't mine."

That made her laugh in surprise. "I promise," she said.

"Okay." Another pause from Colin. Then he said, "Son of a—" and broke off very abruptly indeed.

Kelly had long since seen that he didn't like to cuss in front of her. He must have bitten off something juicy. And he must have had reason to bite it off. "What?" she asked.

He sounded thoroughly grim as he answered, "Somebody's gonna have to tell the kids about this. Two guesses who draws the short straw. Won't they be thrilled to find out they're gonna have a new half brother or half sister?"

Quite a few words for grown children's reactions to news like that went through Kelly's mind. *Thrilled* didn't make the list. "Don't say anything right away," she urged. "Maybe your ex will take care of it for you—"

"Ha!" Colin delivered a one-word editorial.

"—or maybe she'll decide to get rid of the baby, and in that case there won't be anything to tell." Kelly resolutely pretended he hadn't broken in.

"No, huh?" he said. "She'll have to explain—or I'll have to explain—how come dear, sweet, wonderful, loving Teo isn't in the picture any more. He just disappeared for no reason at all, right?"

"If there's no baby, you don't officially have to have any idea why he flew the coop."

"Maybe." Colin sounded dubious, and proceeded to explain why: "Way it looks to me is, there'll be a baby. Teo wanted her to get rid of it. Teo got rid of himself when she didn't go okey-doke fast enough to suit him. She'd have the kid now just to spite him, even if she wasn't looking for any other reasons."

That made a crazy kind of sense to Kelly: just enough to worry her. It wasn't something she would do herself, but it was something she could see somebody else doing. "If Louise thinks that way, let her tell your children," she said again.

"I won't spill the beans right away," Colin said. "If I did, that might look like I was gloating about it. But if she decides— chooses: that's the word they always use these days, isn't it?—if she *chooses* to have the baby, the kids will need to know."

"I guess so," Kelly said unwillingly.

"And what have *you* been up to?" he asked. "I hope like any- thing you had a better day than I did."

"I'm working on a paper about increased geyser activity as a warning sign of a supervolcano eruption," she said. "Whoever's in charge of Yellowstone three-quarters of a million years from now can dig it out of the archives if their geyser basins start getting frisky."

"For a second there, I thought you meant that," Colin remarked.

"You never can tell, but I won't hold my breath," Kelly said. "This lets me use some of the photos I took at the end of my first hike to Coffee Pot Springs after things started heating up." Her eyes welled with tears. "All that stuff is gone forever. No one will see Yellowstone again."

"I'm glad I got the chance. I'd be glad even if I hadn't met you there, but I'm especially glad now," Colin said.

"Good," Kelly answered. "Me, too."

By the time Squirt Frog and the Evolving Tadpoles could have got to Greenville, going there had lost its point. The local promoter wasn't wrong to say that nobody in that part of Maine could have got to their show. People in Maine understood snow, and they understood how to keep roads passable. But even they weren't used to dealing with weather like this.

If they weren't up for it, the guys from California who were stranded in Guilford were, not to put too fine a point on it, freaking out. "Doesn't the Iditarod start somewhere around here?" Rob asked Dick Barber.

Before the proprietor of the Trebor Mansion Inn could answer, Justin started doing background vocals: "Rod, rod, ditarod, I ditarod! Ditarodrodrod, I ditarod!" It was as if the Beach Boys had met a denizen of the State Home for the Terminally Loopy.

"Would you please stick that in the deep freeze?" Rob asked him, in lieu of suggesting that he stick it up his ass. He amplified the request: "Go outside, in other words."

"Cold out there," Justin observed accurately.

"Cold in here, too," Rob said, which was also accurate, if to a lesser degree. He quickly turned back to Barber. "We're not looking a gift horse in the mouth, believe me."

"I know it's cold. That's why God made long underwear," Barber answered. "I've been running the furnace as little as I thought I could get away with, trying to stretch the fuel oil as far as I could. It'll run dry in the next few days no matter what I do, though."

"When does more fuel oil get to Guilford?" Rob asked. He was used to gas or electric heat. As far as he knew, nobody in California used fuel oil.

"Good question!" Barber said. "The way things are, I have no idea. I have no idea if any fuel oil is getting into the state. It doesn't grow on trees, you know. Quite a few people in town are already out."

Rob believed that. Barber was one of the more stringently efficient people he'd met. His military background might have had something to do with it. Dad was the same way, only not quite so much.

He tried a different question: "What if no more fuel oil gets here?"

Dick Barber clicked his tongue between his teeth. "In that case, things do get more . . . interesting, don't they? The way it looks to me is, we have two choices in that case. Either we freeze to death or we start cutting down trees."

"That doesn't sound like two choices to me. More like one," Justin said.

"Oh, I agree with you," Barber replied. "But I promise, there will be folks who don't. Some people in this state—influential people, too—feel it's not just wrong but evil to harm a tree for any reason. They feel that way very strongly, and they're not shy about saying so."

"There are people like that in California, too," Rob said.

The proprietor of the Trebor Mansion Inn let one eyebrow climb toward his shock of graying hair. "Why am I not surprised?"

"I don't know. Why aren't you?" Rob had a crooked grin of his own. "I'm kind of a tree-hugger myself, but—"

"That *but* suggests you're young enough to get over it," Barber said.

Rob shrugged. "Whenever you can take care of trees without hurting people, that's a good thing to do, I think. But if people are going to freeze to death unless they've got logs in the fireplace, that's the time to break out the axes and the chainsaws."

"Sounds reasonable. Are you sure you're from California?" Barber said. "The other thing is, all the questions about fuel oil apply to gasoline, too. The Shell station's closed, in case you hadn't noticed. So the chainsaws won't keep working forever, or even through the winter . . . assuming the winter does eventually end."

"I've checked out the Year without a Summer online," Rob said. "Snow in June! That doesn't sound like a whole lot of fun."

"No. And the Yellowstone supervolcano is a bigger, nastier beast than the one in the nineteenth century," Barber agreed. "So it may come down to men working up a sweat even in our lovely winter weather chopping down pines the old-fashioned way. But chances are they won't be leveling old-growth forest. There's still quite a bit of that farther north, but not around here. A lot of the woods in these parts have grown up since the war. People stopped trying to farm. They gave up the land and moved to the cities—or else they pulled up stakes and headed for the Sun Belt. There are more people in Maine now than there were in 1950, but there aren't three times as many or six times as many, the way there are some places."

"I believe that," Justin said. "You're more settled here than we are on the other coast."

"And nobody moves here on account of the weather," Rob added. "Nobody moved here on account of the weather even before the supervolcano."

"You forget the summer people," Barber reminded him. "I can't afford to do that, no matter how tempting it is. I make my living off them. They come to Maine to get away from Boston and New York City and Philadelphia. If there's no summer next year, there won't be any summer people. I don't know what I'll do then."

Rob wondered how many times he'd heard that since the supervolcano erupted. More often than in all the years before then, he suspected. It was too big to plan around. You just had to wait and see what happened next and try to roll with it as best you could.

"Suppose there isn't just a year without a summer," Justin said. "Suppose there are five or six or ten years like that all in a row. What does Maine look like by the end of that time?"

"Hell," Barber answered promptly. "Dante's hell, I mean. The book is called *The Inferno*, but Satan's buried in ice. At the end of ten years like that, we'd probably have enough ice to keep Old Scratch from getting loose for quite a while."

A cat wandered in, a cat almost big enough to be a bobcat. The Barber family semiprofessionally bred Maine Coons. They handled the weather in these parts as well as a critter was likely to. And they were also uncommonly good-natured. Vanessa would go gaga over them, at least at first. Rob suspected she'd get bored with them, though; they weren't contrary enough to suit her.

This beast rubbed his leg. It made motorboat noises when he bent down and stroked it. "I ought to keep one or two in the bedding, the way the Australian Aborigines did with their dogs," he said. "They're like hot-water bottles with ears, you know?"

Justin nodded. "A three-dog night was really cold. That's how that turkey of a band got its name."

"Once upon a time, I liked them," Barber said. "I got over it."

Thinking about warmth made Rob think about electricity. He rather wished he hadn't. "How long will the power stay on?" he wondered out loud. "Won't storms start knocking the lines down? And if even the utility companies can't get gas to send out repair crews . . ."

"In that case, we welcome back the nineteenth century in all its glory." Barber made his tongue-clicking noise again. "Whether that level of technology can support this level of population . . . Well, we'll all find out, won't we?"

"Won't be as much fun playing acoustic sets all the time," Justin said.

Rob stabbed a forefinger at him. "I was just thinking the same thing! You came out with it before I could."

"You two might as well be married. I was married once upon a time," Barber said. "I got over that, too, but it was expensive."

That only reminded Rob of his own parents' divorce. And he didn't know what was up with Teo suddenly running out on Mom after such a long stretch of not-quite-wedded bliss. He had the feeling more was going on than Mom was telling. If Dad knew what, and chances were he did, he wasn't talking. All he said about it was *Ask your mother.* He wanted to know what the chances were for Rob's coming back to California when he tied the knot with Kelly.

Rob feared those chances were anything but good. Getting from Guilford to Dover-Foxcroft was a major undertaking these days. Getting from Guilford to Bangor or Portland might not be impossible, but it sure wouldn't be easy. Rob would have liked to go to his father's second wedding. If he did, though, how would he make it back here? He didn't want to run out on the band. Justin and Charlie and Biff and the polymorphously perverse thing that was Squirt Frog and the Evolving Tadpoles seemed more like family these days than did the people connected by arbitrary ties of flesh and blood.

Justin said, "I'm getting hungry. You want to go down to Calvin's Kitchen for breakfast?"

"Do I want to?" Rob echoed. "Not so you'd notice. But we've got to eat, don't we? Are Biff and Charlie up yet?"

As if to prove they were, they chose that moment to thunder down the stairs. Off to the diner they all went. It was only about a five-minute walk. The place just didn't cut it for dinner. Despite Dick Barber's opinion, Rob didn't think it was all that wonderful for breakfast, either.

Still, you couldn't mess up eggs and sausages and bacon and hash browns too badly. What got to Rob more than the food was the isolation. The waitress and the cook behind the counter were polite enough, but they were serving strangers. They knew the locals—and vice versa—the way Rob and Charlie and Biff and Justin knew one another. A black Baptist family moving onto a street full of Chasidim could have felt no more cut off from the neighborhood.

He was almost done with his breakfast when it occurred to him that isolation could have more than one meaning. If fuel oil and gasoline had trouble reaching rural Maine north and west of the Interstate, how about food? You could cut down trees and burn them, and maybe you wouldn't freeze, yeah. But could you feed half a state's worth of people on moose and ducks and whatever else you could shoot?

It didn't seem likely. What were people going to do if the food ran low, though? All the L.L.Bean gear in the world didn't help against hunger. Only eatables could. But where would they come from?

XXI

Bryce Miller dropped three copies of his dissertation—thump!—on his chairperson's desk. The physical copies were a formality, left over from the days when theses were actually typed. Professor Harvey Harriman had had his finger in every chapter of the Word file from which the diss was printed. There seemed to be two kinds of chairpersons: the ones who didn't do enough and the ones who did too much. Harvey Harriman was of the second school.

He stuck out his hand now. "Congratulations, Bryce," he said in his soft, precise voice. He was heading towards emeritus status, but looked twenty years younger than he was. Maybe, like Dorian Gray, he had a portrait somewhere that was taking a beating.

He'd been at UCLA since dissertations were typed on Selectrics, and since the University of California system had money. He'd probably had his plaid jacket about that long, too. His father's translations of Aeschylus and Sophocles were classics among classicists. He'd never done anything so illustrious himself, but he was more than capable.

"Thanks," Bryce said. "I'm only sorry it took so much longer than I thought it would."

"They have a way of doing that," Professor Harriman said. "And it may be *agathe tykhe* in disguise, you know. Suppose you'd finished when you expected to. Suppose you'd taken a job at the University of Wyoming or Idaho State or some such place." By the way he spoke, all the colleges and universities in the mountain West were interchangeable.

Even if that was naive, he had a point. It *was* good luck not to have wound up somewhere like that. Bryce might not have got out if he had. "I had my brush with the supervolcano any which way," he said.

"Yes, so you did," Harriman agreed. "I'm glad you made it back in one piece. And I'm glad to have one copy of the thesis for myself, one for the department library, and one for the University Research Library."

How often had Bryce wrestled with Doric verb forms in the classics library? Lots. One whole bookcase was full of bound dissertations going back half a century and more. Did anybody ever look at them? He knew he never had. Some eventually got turned into proper books. The rest . . . must have seemed important at the time, at least to the shlubs cranking them out.

And was the world ready for a fat new study of Theocritus and the other leading Hellenistic poets? Would Oxford and Cambridge and Harvard get into a ferocious bidding war over the publication rights? If they did, they might run the advance they paid him all the way up into three figures. But they wouldn't. Or it sure wasn't likely.

As if to underscore that, Professor Harriman asked, "What will you do now that you've finished?"

"Look for work. What else can I do now?" Bryce said.

"Mm, yes." Harriman didn't need to worry about it. He might not have been tenured since the Hellenistic Age, but he seemed as if he had. He coughed delicately now. "The job situation is . . . difficult at the moment. In the present emergency, classics departments find themselves under unprecedented pressure. Surely you are aware of this."

"Surely," Bryce said, deadpan. Slots opened up only when the current holder dropped dead. Even then, a university was at least as likely to cut a position as to fill it. It wasn't just positions, either. Whole classics departments were facing the axe. So were French and Italian departments and anything else that didn't immediately help people dig out from the supervolcano. What kind of world they'd have once they dug out—if they could dig out—they'd worry about later.

"Well, then . . ." Harvey Harriman spread his well-manicured hands.

"Oh, I'll take any kind of job I can get," Bryce said. "If somebody wants me to teach Western Civ at a community college, I'll do that. If a Catholic high school needs a Latin teacher, I can do that. Or if all I can come up with is a job job, if you know what I mean, I'll do that, too."

"I do understand. The wolf at the door is a harsh taskmaster," Harriman said, as if he knew anything about the wolf at the door. Yeah, as if! His father might have grounded him if he'd messed up too many declensions, but that was about it. Sighing, he went on, "It seems a shame to have to turn your back on what took so long and required so much work and study to accomplish."

Bryce thought it seemed a shame, too. But starving seemed an even bigger shame. "You don't always get to do what you want to do," he said. "Sometimes you do what you have to do, and pick up the pieces from there."

"Will you come back to UCLA in June for the year's commencement?" Professor Harriman asked.

"I hope so." Bryce had blown off the ceremony after his A.B. and M.A. His mother would probably disown him if he did it again. So would Susan, whose opinion mattered more to him—and who was waiting for him right this minute.

He said his good-byes to Professor Harriman. He wondered when he would ever see the inside of the UCLA Classics Department again. Once upon a time, business weenies had infested the Public Policy building. Now they had a bigger, newer, spiffier one all their own: the Anderson School of Management. Classics got some of their leftovers—or their sloppy seconds, if you were feeling uncommonly cynical.

Susan called the North Campus Center Maxim's. Maybe that was a History Department in-joke; Bryce had never heard it before he started hanging out with her. She sat at one of the big tables outside. Unusually in this winter of the earth's discontent, it wasn't raining. She got up as he drew near. "Are you official?"

"I'm done, all right—like a roast," he answered.

"Hey, you did something special," she said. "How do you want to celebrate?"

"People would talk if we did that right here," Bryce said.

Susan made a face at him. "How about coffee and a danish instead?"

"Talk about second prizes!" he said mournfully. She poked him in the ribs. That didn't do much—she was far more ticklish than he was. They walked into Maxim's together.

Susan did get coffee and a danish. Bryce got a danish and a Coke instead. Susan bought. "You just turned in your diss," she said. "How awesome is that?"

"I don't have a job. I don't have much chance for a job. I was just talking with my chairperson about what I was gonna do. He didn't have any terrific ideas, either. How awesome is *that*?" One more reason for Bryce to let Susan buy.

"Something will turn up for you," she said. "Something will turn up for me when I finish, too. Would you have put all that time and effort into it if you really thought you'd never get the chance to use it?"

They sat down at a couple of chairs facing the brickwork around a circular gas fire. The warmth was welcome. No doubt Susan had meant the question rhetorically. Bryce gave it serious consideration all the same. At last, he said, "You know, I think I would. What else would I have been doing instead? Retail? Real estate? I might have made more money in real estate—"

"The way the roller coaster goes, you might not have, too," Susan broke in.

"You've got that right," Bryce said. "Whatever I did, I wouldn't have had much fun doing it. Here I am, close to thirty, and I've got away with not working for a living yet. Can't go on forever, not unless you inherit or something, but I've had a pretty good run."

One of the reasons he'd got away with not working for a living was that Vanessa had dropped out and did work. Add her real salary to the dribs and drabs he brought in, and they'd done tolerably well. He'd had more trouble staying afloat since the breakup. But he didn't want to remember Vanessa now.

"You're—not practical," Susan said. Vanessa had told him the same thing. He seemed to have to remember her, like it or not. She'd said it with intent to wound, though, if not with intent to condemn. With Susan, it was just a statement of fact.

"Guilty," he said. It wasn't as if he didn't know it himself. "I'm afraid nobody who writes poems modeled after ancient pastorals will get a lot of ink in the *Wall Street Journal*."

"That's not what I meant. You've published them. I think that's wonderful," Susan said.

Bryce thought it was wonderful, too. Of course, he'd made exactly no money from any of them. And here, out of the blue, Vanessa's brother sold—really sold—a story. If that made Bryce jealous (and it did), he was sure it drove Vanessa nuts. He said,

"But no one should hang out with me because she expects to get rich doing it. Or even eat, necessarily."

"I'm hanging out with you because I want to, silly," Susan said. "One way or another, we'll make ends meet. Who needs more than that?"

Plenty of people did, or thought they did. Vanessa had always had filet mignon tastes, even when the budget yelled for ground chuck. She was never happy with what she had. He sometimes thought, especially toward the end, that she couldn't be happy without something to be unhappy about.

Susan wasn't like that. For a while, Bryce had wondered if something was missing in his relationship with her. Before long, he'd figured out what it was: tension. Once he realized that, he quit missing it.

"I wonder what's out there in the big, wide world," he said. *The big, wide, ugly world*, he thought, but he didn't come out with that. "I don't have any excuses left now. I've got to find out."

Selling his story gave Marshall fifteen McLuhan minutes of fame at UCSB. Because of paper shortages, the campus rag was down to a weekly, but it ran a story about him. The photographer who snapped him holding up a printout of "Well, Why Not?" was seriously cute. She seemed impressed with him, too: impressed enough to let him have her cell number, with the air of an aid worker handing out sacks of wheat to pipe-cleaner-legged famine victims in Zimbabwe or somewhere like that. But when he tried it, it turned out to be bogus. Well, you couldn't win 'em all.

Professor Bolger gave him an A in the course, which he was glad to have, and advice, which he found as welcome as the phony phone number. "Congratulations. You've sold to a market I'd—mm, maybe not kill, but commit armed robbery, anyway—to break into," Bolger said. "Now you have to figure out where you go from here."

Where Marshall wanted to go was away from the prof's journal-crowded office. Unfortunately, that didn't seem practical for the next few minutes. "Uh-huh," he said, and tried to keep looking interested while he tuned out.

"If you've got anything else you like, you should send it to the editor there right away," Bolger went on. "Anybody—well, lots of people, anyhow—can get lucky once. Being able to do it over and over is what marks the difference between a writer and somebody who just writes, if you know what I mean." He waited expectantly.

Thus prompted, Marshall nodded and went "Uh-huh" again, for all the world as if he'd been listening.

"The other side of the coin is, you don't want to get a swelled head because somebody sent you a check," Bolger said. "Twenty-five years ago, when I was a senior in high school, a friend of mine sold two stories to a magazine that's long since gone under. He decided he knew everything there was to know, the way you can when you're that age. He dropped out of the University of Washington halfway through his freshman year to become a writer, and he sold a couple of novels, too. But he's made his living moving stuff from here to there at Sears ever since." Another pregnant pause.

"I'm not gonna drop out now," Marshall said, "not with my degree right around the corner." He'd avoided it as long as he could, but they were going to pitch him out into the real world no matter how little he liked it.

"I should hope not," Professor Bolger said, politely horrified at the mere idea. "If you work hard at it, and if you don't expect too much, writing is a good trade in difficult times. There's not much overhead—hardly any. And you can do it part-time, to add to your income from a more ordinary job. I've been doing that for a long time now."

"Right. Makes sense," Marshall said. Of course, the prof was bound to have some fancy degree piled on top of his bachelor's. You didn't get to teach at a university without one; Marshall was sure of that. One sold story, or even several sold stories, wouldn't win him possession of the office next door here.

"Students in my classes don't often place pieces. It happens, but not every quarter. Nowhere near," Bolger said. "You have a right to be proud of yourself." He glanced at the clock on the wall across from his desk. "And do keep writing. I always hate it when people who have the ability don't use it."

That had to be *Okay, I've used up as much office time on you as I'm going to.* Marshall said his good-byes and got out. It was late afternoon. The sun was sinking in one of those ridiculously over-the-top sunsets people had started taking for granted since the supervolcano erupted. Oranges, reds, purples, sometimes greens . . . The light show usually started a good hour and a half before actual sundown. You didn't even have to be loaded to enjoy it, though that sure didn't hurt.

As Marshall walked to the bike rack, somebody behind him said, "Hey, isn't that the guy who—?"

He walked a little taller, a little straighter, for a few steps. After all, he was *the guy who.* He was right this minute, anyhow. Before long, somebody else would do something worth noticing. Then, for a little while, *he'd* be *the guy who.*

Marshall unlocked his bike and climbed aboard. How did you keep it going once you weren't *the guy who* any more? How did you keep it going when you never got to be *the guy who*? His brother's band had always had to deal with that. More hype stuck to the third runner-up from *American Idol,* who was only *almost the guy who,* than Squirt Frog and the Evolving Tadpoles had seen in their whole career.

One good way to keep it going was not to let the jerk in the Lexus flip you over his—no, her—fender. "You dumb asshole!"

Marshall said. The Lexus' driver went on her way with the lordly indifference of those who didn't need to use their own muscle power to get from hither to yon.

A moment later, though, Marshall had his *Come the revolution* moment as he pedaled past two gas stations on opposite sides of the street. Prices had been zooming up and up since the eruption. One of the stations had topped six bucks a gallon the other day—and it wasn't a tourist trap by the 101, either. A sign in front of the other said SORRY—NO GAS TODAY.

Lots of the petroleum that got made into gasoline came from the Middle East and other distant places. Israeli nukes on the Iranian oil fields hadn't done that supply any good. But some of it was homegrown. The supervolcano hadn't done domestic production any good, which was putting it mildly. And some of the big refineries in Texas and Oklahoma were still out of action, while transportation between the West Coast and anything east of Yellowstone remained totally screwed.

Which meant high prices and shortages. Here were both of them. Pretty soon, gas prices would get to the point where they pinched a bitch in a Lexus. Or else even her Majesty wouldn't be able to fill up at all. Then she'd have to stick her rich ass on a bicycle like the peasants or damn well stay home.

Come the revolution . . . When Marshall got back to his place, he drank a Coke (they were plugging them as *Better than ever with real sugar!* because you couldn't get high-fructose corn syrup when the corn crop lay under volcanic ash) and fired up his computer. He did his e-mail first.

After that, though, he started working on a new story, one about somebody who was rich enough to drive a Lexus and live in Santa Barbara, but who found that her money was buying her less and less, and that it couldn't buy some things at all. He knew a bit about failed relationships; all he had to do was think of the one that had blown up on his folks.

He stopped after a couple of hours and a thousand words and went back to reread what he'd written. He cleaned up some clumsy phrasing and put in foreshadowing to show that Ms. Lexus didn't have it as together as she thought she did. Then he nodded to himself. It . . . felt good. He didn't know how to put it any better than that. If he stayed at it and finished it, he thought he had a chance to sell it somewhere.

So much he still didn't know, not just about writing but about finding markets and everything else that had to do with the business. He was at least as surprised as anyone else that somebody'd bought one piece. Could lightning really strike twice? Could he be, or become, a creative-writing major who'd got lucky?

How could you know something like that? The only answer that occurred to him was, by writing and seeing if anything else stuck. He was no more diligent than he'd ever had to be. You needed that stuff if you were going to go anywhere in this racket. That seemed obvious.

Did he have it in him? That seemed much less so. All he could do was give it his best shot, whatever that turned out to be. If he didn't decide to do something else in the meantime, maybe he'd find out.

The nurse took Louise Ferguson's temperature with a gadget she stuck into her ear. The old under-the-tongue thermometer was as antique as a Victorian thundermug. Measuring blood pressure still involved a cuff around the upper arm and a stethoscope, though. After writing the data on Louise's chart, the nurse said, "This all seems fine. How are you feeling today?"

The only way she could have made that more patronizing would have been to ask *How are we feeling today?* But *we* was, or were, involved, or Louise wouldn't have been sitting impatiently in this patient room. "Pregnant," she answered, her voice nothing but grim.

"Well, yes." Nothing dented the nurse's good cheer. "Dr. Suzuki will see you in a few minutes." She bustled out and almost closed the door behind her.

"Happy day," Louise said, but not very loud.

Travis Suzuki was several years younger than she was. He always seemed bright and self-assured; she'd rarely met a doctor short on self-confidence. By the way he swept into the examination room, he expected her to genuflect. "How are you doing?" he asked.

"I'm doing all right," Louise said.

He glanced at her chart. "Your numbers look good. None of the tests we've run show anything abnormal about the fetus. If you proceed with the pregnancy, chances are you'll have a healthy baby. If you don't . . . Well, you're approaching the end of your first trimester. If you wait longer than that to decide to terminate, things get more complicated, as I'm sure you know."

"Yes. I do know that," Louise said. "I'm not thrilled about any of this. I'm talking to lawyers again. Like I told you, my boyfriend lit out for the tall timber when he found out he'd knocked me up."

"That's . . . unfortunate," Dr. Suzuki said.

"Tell me about it!" Louise exclaimed. "Things might've been okay if I'd said right away that I'd get rid of it. When I didn't, Teo—split. If I dispose of it now, I'm still doing what he'd want. I'll be damned, if you know what I mean."

Dr. Suzuki nodded. "I think I do," he said, and she was inclined to believe him—hers wouldn't be anything close to the first tale of woe he'd heard. As if to prove as much, he went on, "If you have the baby, will you be able to keep from taking out your resentment about its father on it?"

That was a shrewd question. It was one she'd asked herself more than once. "I hope so," she said slowly. "It's not the baby's fault, after all. I understand that."

"Okay," he said, though that was more likely acknowledgment than agreement. *Snap! Snap!* He donned a pair of thin rubber gloves. "Let me call Terri back into the room, then, and I'll examine you."

Terri! That was the nurse's name. No matter how often Louise had come in here, she never remembered it. She pulled down her panties and put her feet in the stirrups at the end of the table. The underwear was cotton, severely functional but comfortable. For the first time since her early twenties, she'd worn little skimpy transparent nylon things while she was with Teo. He liked them. Well, now she didn't have to worry about what Teo liked—or about wedgies, either.

Terri came in to preserve propriety. Couldn't have a male doctor prodding a woman's private parts with no one around to make sure hanky-panky didn't ensue, no sir. As Dr. Suzuki started doing what he did, Louise asked him, "Do you get sick and tired of staring at pussy all day?"

He straightened up with a startled laugh. "Nobody ever asked me that before," he said. "You bet I do. You do it for a while, it's a job like any other job."

And maybe that was true, and maybe it wasn't. More likely, it was true and false at the same time. He wouldn't care about a little old lady's twat any more than he cared about her elbow. But if a cute young thing with a cute young thing came in, Louise guessed his interest might be more than strictly professional. She'd heard somewhere that gynecologists had one of the highest divorce rates of any kind of doctor. She couldn't remember where, and she didn't know for sure it was so, but she wouldn't have been surprised.

His fingering of her was nothing but businesslike. Dr. Russell had been the same way, even though she was younger then. Once, when she was pregnant with Rob, Colin had come in with her for an examination. He hadn't liked watching another man's fingers probing her. He understood it was in the line of duty. He hadn't liked it anyway.

Dr. Suzuki finished what he was doing. "You can put your pants on again," he said as he peeled off the gloves and dropped them into the trash can.

Louise got out of the stirrups and smoothed down her skirt before she redonned her underwear. "Is everything okay?" she asked.

"It certainly seems to be. You've taken good care of yourself," Dr. Suzuki answered, by which he could only mean *You're no spring chicken, sweetheart*. Well, that was nothing Louise didn't already know. Suzuki went on, "If you decide to bring the baby to term, I don't see any medical reason why you shouldn't have a successful delivery. I don't see any reason now, I should say. If your blood pressure rises, if you start showing protein in your urine . . . That's a different story."

"I understand," Louise said. "If I was going to end the pregnancy, my reasons wouldn't be medical."

"Well, yes." The OB-GYN frowned a little. "I'm not so well equipped to advise you on, uh, personal choices."

"I understand that, too." Louise's mouth twisted, as if she'd just tasted something bitter. "I loved that man, you know. I loved him like I hadn't loved anybody since I was a kid. And he loved me back. He did—till I got pregnant. He couldn't handle that, so he split. And so here I am."

"Here you are," Dr. Suzuki agreed. "Which brings us back to the question I asked you before."

"I have been wondering about whether I'd take it out on the baby," Louise said slowly, "but I really don't think so. I'd try to remember the good times with Teo, not the bad ones. There were some. There were quite a few, till he bailed on me."

"That seems like a commonsense attitude." Suzuki sounded cautious. Of course he did. What else were doctors for? He had his reasons, too: "Will you be able to keep it up at three in the morning, when the baby's got you up for the fourth time that night and you still have to go to work in the morning?"

"I don't know," Louise said. "But any mom alive is gonna want to punt her kid when something like that happens."

He smiled. "True. She may want to, but she won't do it."

"I don't think I will, either. I know it's not the baby's fault— that's what babies do. And by then coffee'll taste good to me again, so that'll help me keep going."

"Okay. I can't tell you what to do, and I won't try. But I do want to make sure you understand your options." Plainly, Dr. Suzuki believed she was off her rocker for even thinking about keeping the kid.

"I'd better, by now. I haven't done much but think about them since I found out I was pregnant." Louise didn't tell him she was one of those people who were more likely to do something because all their friends and relations thought they were crazy if they did. Leaving Colin for Teo, for instance.

Yeah, and look how well that turned out, her mind gibed. But she remained convinced she was happier now, in spite of everything, than she would have been had she stayed. Staying would have meant slow death. She'd never felt more vital, more alive, than she had since she walked out of the house.

And now somebody else was alive inside her. She hadn't expected that when she walked out the door. Did she really have the energy to raise another one? More and more, she leaned toward finding out.

Colin Ferguson sat in an uncomfortable chair in a windowless conference room at Torrance PD headquarters. Torrance was the biggest South Bay city, and had the biggest police department. Said department boasted the biggest building, and said building boasted the biggest conference room, in the region. Torrance was also centrally located. It was the logical place for cops going after the South Bay Strangler to meet. But Colin had seen interrogation rooms with a warmer human touch.

Beside him, Gabe Sanchez fidgeted in his seat. Colin didn't figure that was on account of the chair. No—chances were Gabe needed his nicotine fix. Hardly any town in California let you light up in a place like this any more. Colin had never got that particular vice. He didn't miss the smoke-filled meetings of his earlier days as a cop. Gabe had the jones, though.

Nels Jensen sat at the head of the long table. The Torrance captain had a lacquered mat of silver hair and features that would have seemed distinguished if his eyes weren't a little too close together. He wore an expensive suit that looked expensive. How he afforded it . . . was none of Colin's business.

Jensen glanced around the room. Everybody who should have been here was. Cops were mostly a punctual bunch. As soon as the wall clock showed two straight up, Jensen got to his feet, which naturally made everybody look his way.

He nodded heavily and pawed at some papers on the table in front of him. "Well, gentlemen, I got the DNA reports this morning," he said. "It's official, I'm afraid. We can chalk this latest one up to the South Bay Sonofabitch."

"No big surprise," Lou Ayers muttered. The Palos Verdes lieutenant sat a few seats up from Colin. And he was right. The murder of Margot Keller matched the Stangler's MO too well to leave much doubt. The bastard was back in business. Mrs. Keller—she was a widow—was seventy-three, she lived alone, she was throttled and raped, and there wasn't a fingerprint in her neat little tract home that didn't belong to her.

That little tract home was in Torrance, not far from the big shopping center at the corner of Redondo Beach Boulevard and Hawthorne Boulevard. One more reason for Captain Jensen to hold the meeting here. He went on, "We have got to catch this guy. We've got to. Every time he does another one, the media take out their knives and start raking us over the coals."

Block that metaphor! Colin thought. He had no use for the *New Yorker*'s politics, but appreciated the magazine's wit.

"The Strangler's made all of us look bad for way too long now," Jensen said. "I don't know about the rest of you, but I don't like it when the papers and the TV news calls—uh, call—me a no-good stupid stumblebum."

I won't make chief if they keep calling me names like that, at least not in any town around here. Those were the words behind the words. Colin heard them loud and clear. He suspected the other officers in the conference room did, too. Roy Schurz was happy as a clam being the boss cop in Orofino, Idaho. Colin was mighty glad that made Roy happy; otherwise, Kelly might still be stuck in Missoula. Even before the supervolcano went off, though, he wouldn't have wanted to live in Orofino himself—not for all the plastic junk in China, he wouldn't. There, if nowhere else, he sympathized with Nels Jensen.

"One of these days, the asshole's got to slip up," Jensen continued plaintively, a sad song Colin—and everybody else here—had also sung. "Someone will see something, or hear something, or he'll pick a cop's widow to go after and she'll blow his head off with her husband's service revolver. Something."

That was what you called whistling in the dark. None of the cops seemed to want to meet his colleagues' eyes. But it sparked a thought in Colin. He stuck up his hand, the way he would have in school. Jensen nodded at him.

"Have we got any idea at all how the guy picks his victims?" Colin said. "He doesn't cruise the streets till he sees a little old lady walking along. No way—he scopes things out before he breaks in and kills 'em. So how does he find 'em? Churches? Senior centers? Facebook, for cryin' out loud? If we can get a handle on that, we're a step closer to psyching out what makes him tick. It's something we haven't tried up till now, far as I know."

He waited to see what the other cops would think. Slow nods went up and down the table. "Gives us something to do besides cussing at the bastard, anyhow," Lieutenant Ayers said. More nods followed.

"We can follow it up." Captain Jensen sounded like the Pope approving something a cardinal had said in an ecumenical council. *If he thinks I'm gonna kiss his ring, he can kiss my ass*, Colin thought. "No way to know if we'll get any leads from it, but I can't see how it'd hurt."

The first thing Gabe did when they got outside after the meeting finally broke up was light a cigarette. The next thing he did was say, "You had a good idea there. Mr. High and Mighty shoulda got more turned on about it."

"Nah." Colin shook his head. "The only ideas that turn him on are the ones he gets himself." Then a reporter bore down on him—the press knew the South Bay Strangler had struck again. Since the Strangler had struck in Torrance this time, Colin could convincingly plead ignorance. He not only could, he did. He and Gabe got to their car more or less unscathed.

He turned on the news while he was eating dinner after he got home. There was Nels Jensen, telling a TV reporter, "It seems like a good idea to me to see if we can determine how the perpetrator targets his victims. Does he search for them in houses of worship, or at gatherings of senior citizens, or perhaps even by utilizing social-networking technology? We are actively pursuing several of these possibilities at this point in time."

Colin didn't Frisbee his dinner plate through the TV screen. The damn set was expensive. But he almost gagged at hearing Jensen not only lift his notion but turn it into mind-numbing bureaucratese. Was it really true that no good idea went unpunished? It sure seemed to be.

SUPERVOLCANO: ERUPTION | 395

He was glad when Kelly called half an hour later. She let him vent about all the different kinds of chickenshit chicken thief Captain Jensen was. She sympathized: "He's a lousy plagiarist, is what he is."

"Lousy is right," Colin agreed. "It sounded a lot better when I said it."

"I believe you," she said. "You aren't into bureaucratic BS."

That was true. It was one more thing that went some way towards explaining why Colin had probably come as far as he could in policework. Every once in a while, he wished he could quit calling a spade a spade, or even a goddamn shovel. Like kidney stones, those moments soon passed.

Kelly went on, "I've got news, too."

"Oh, yeah? What is it? Better'n mine, I hope, whatever it is," Colin said.

"Well, I think so. I picked out my dress today," she told him.

"All right!" he said. "What's it look like?"

Her reply got more technical than he was ready for. He gathered the dress was long and white and had a veil. He could have guessed that much without fancy explanations. He didn't worry about it. This was Kelly's first marriage, after all. She was more excited about tying the knot than he was. He'd put on a tux, march down the aisle, and say *Yes* or *I do* when that was called for. Then he'd hope for the best. With her, he thought—yes, he hoped—he had a fighting chance of getting it. If he didn't, he wouldn't march down the aisle.

"Hey," he said when she slowed down. "One thing I'm sure of. Whatever you're wearing, you'll look great. And when you aren't wearing anything, you'll look even better."

"You're impossible," Kelly said. "Or else you're just male. I'm not sure which." She didn't say *I'm not sure which is worse*, but Colin didn't need to be a practiced interrogator to hear it anyhow.

"Guilty on both counts," he said. "I throw myself on the mercy of the court—splat!"

"Splat is right. Not even married yet, and you're already hen-pecked." Kelly sounded proud of it.

"Worse things to worry about." For Colin, that was nothing but the truth. He could worry about Margot Keller, her body used, crumpled, and discarded like a paper towel. He could think about all the other old women killed before her, and about the guy out there living what looked like a normal life till he got the urge to add one more to his list. Next to that, imperfect married bliss was no big deal. "Somehow or other, we'll make it work. What do the Brits say? We'll muddle through—that's it."

"There's what I like: confidence," Kelly said. "Won't be long now, Mister."

"Good," Colin answered, and she purred at him over the phone.

XXII

The Piscataquis chuckled through Guilford. In the western part of the little town, it powered the mill. Farther east, its northern bank turned into a park that would no doubt be pretty when the grass was green and the trees had leaves on them. Eyeing the bare branches of those trees and the snow that was burying the river-view benches, Rob Ferguson wondered whether Guilford would ever see days like that again.

A monument, also splotched with snow, listed Guilford's war dead from a history longer than towns on the other coast knew. The letters on one of those names were still bright and shiny and new. Sooner or later, they would mellow to match the others. By then, though, chances were newer names would have gone up on the monument.

Rob was getting used to wearing too many clothes all the time, and to being cold anyway. What heat there was in the Trebor Mansion Inn rose to his little tower room—where it leaked out through the walls and windows. The glass in the windows was double, with an insulating air space between the panes. They routinely did such things here. Heat leaked out all the same.

Kids in the park slid down slopes toward the river on sleds. They flung snowballs at one another. They thought a winter with all this snow in it was fun. Rob might have felt the same way if he hadn't wondered when—or whether—the weather would let up.

One of the books in his tower room was a sort of informal history of Maine. It told him more about the Year without a Summer after Mt. Tambora erupted than he'd found out online. Quebec City had got a foot of snow in June 1816. Ice stayed on the lakes and rivers that long as far south as Pennsylvania. Crops were ruined in North America and Europe: ruined to the point of widespread hunger. The haze was so thick, you could look at the sun with your naked eye and see sunspots. And Mt. Tambora was just one of these kids banging on a toy drum next to Charlie's fancy amplified kit when you compared it to the Yellowstone supervolcano.

Shaking his head at such gloomy reflections, Rob trudged up Library Street toward the Trebor Mansion Inn. The library was another historic building. Books in there would no doubt have even more to say about that summer that wasn't. He didn't stop in to go look for those books. Why bother reading about it when he'd be living through it—and then some—before long?

Both SUVs from the band remained in front of the inn, along with the Barber family's cars. Nobody was going anywhere. The Shell station still hadn't got more gas. All the stations in Dover-Foxcroft were dry, too. Tankers weren't even trying to come up here any more. North and west of the Interstate, Maine was on its own: the big part of the state, if not the populous part.

But something new had been added. Out there next to the nearly useless motor vehicles stood a one-horse open sleigh straight out of "Jingle Bells." In lieu of a hitching post or rail, the horse—a well-curried bay—was tied to a doorknob. It munched contentedly from a feed bag.

When Rob went inside, he took off his hat and his overshoes, and that was about it. With even firewood in short supply, the place stayed cold. Dick Barber greeted him with, "Come into the parlor, why don't you? Someone here I'd like you to meet."

"Whoever's in charge of the sleigh there?" Rob asked.

"That's right. Your cohorts have already made his acquaintance." Barber sometimes had an old-fashioned turn of phrase. He could use it or not, as he chose, which made Rob classify it as a special effect.

He wasn't inclined to be fussy. A fire burned in the parlor hearth, perhaps in honor of the newcomer. The man stood with his back to Rob, savoring the warmth. He was talking to Justin and Charlie, who listened in what was plainly fascination.

Hearing Rob and Barber come up behind him, the fellow broke off and turned toward them. He was in his late sixties, and looked like . . . Rob needed a moment to realize who he looked like. If you took John Madden down to about five feet eight, that would do for a first approximation. He was ruddy and fleshy and had a sharp nose, bushy eyebrows, and silver hair.

He didn't dress like John Madden, though. John Madden looked like an unmade bed, even in a suit. This guy could have been a 1930s dandy. A lot of his hair was hidden under a broad-brimmed black fedora. His overcoat boasted fur trim. When he shrugged it off, he was wearing a double-breasted, pinstriped wool suit underneath, with lapels sharp and upthrusting enough to cut yourself on.

"Jim, this is Rob Ferguson, also of Squirt Frog and the Evolving Tadpoles," Barber said. "Rob, here before you stands Jim Farrell, recent unsuccessful Republican candidate for Congress in the Second District—most of Maine, even if it's not the part with most of the people in it. The ones who do live their chose, in their wisdom, the usual blow-dried airhead over someone who actually had some idea of what he was talking about."

"Glad to meet you, Rob," Farrell said in a resonant baritone.

"Dick helped run my campaign, such as it was. He tends to forget that it's over, and that we got trounced. Ancient history now, like any failed campaign."

"Speaking of ancient history, Jim taught it for years at SUNY Albany," Barber said. "Then he retired and came home—claimed the good weather in Albany was wearing him down."

Albany and good weather didn't strike Rob as a likely mix. Farrell raised those extravagant eyebrows. "I've got over that," he rumbled. "The way things are these days, so has Albany."

Barber went on as if the older man hadn't spoken: "He picked up a fair amount of fame—"

"Notoriety," Farrell broke in, not without pride. "It was definitely notoriety."

"—for his newsletters called *To the Small-Endians*. They skewered PC academics the way they deserve. Skewered 'em, hell—screwed 'em to the wall."

Charlie jerked on the couch where he was sitting. He startled a cat sleeping beside him. "Oh, my God! Those things!" he said. "My older brother picked up a couple of them at an sf convention. I think he's still got 'em. I've read 'em. They're wicked!" He eyed Farrell with newfound regard.

Farrell doffed the fedora, showing off a hairline that hadn't surrendered even half an inch. "I finally quit doing them. I gave up, in short. The real academic world proved madder and sadder than anything I could invent."

"And he's known for his comparative study of the campaigns of Alexander and Julius Caesar," Barber added. "I can't speak as a professor—I never even played one on TV. But as a career military man, it impressed the bejesus out of me."

Rob, Justin, and Charlie eyed one another. Sometimes you got a song cue when you least expected one. Charlie started beating out a rhythm on his thighs and on the coffee table in front of the couch. That was a long way from his usual industrial-strength noisemakers, but it would do. It was plenty to make the cat, which had tentatively settled down again, head for the hills with a tail bristling in indignation.

And Justin and Rob launched into "Came Along Too Late." Not every band had a song about Alexander the Great—one that even mentioned Julius Caesar, too—but Squirt Frog and the Evolving Tadpoles wasn't every band. Not even close. The words were mostly Charlie's, with some tweaks from Marshall back when he'd got into ancient history. They'd done it before larger audiences, but never before a more knowing one:

> "Dozing before the idiot box
> When hoofbeats awakened me—
> History Channel, three a.m.:
> So-called documentary.
> Swords and sandals
> Maps and blood
> Watching the conquests spread and spread
> Darius' name was mud.

> "Came along too late to see Alex the Great
> Mopping up the Persian cavalry.
> Came along too late to see Alex the Great
> Found his Hellenistic monarchy!

> "Now some will stand out from the mass
> In good times or in rage
> For King Philip's son by Olympias
> Greece was too small a stage.
> Had to spread out 'cross the world—
> Couldn't help himself, I think.
> Everywhere his flags unfurled;
> He won fantastic ink.

"*Came along too late to see Alex the Great*
Mopping up the Persian cavalry.
Came along too late to see Alex the Great
Found his Hellenistic monarchy!

"*I know I live in the here-and-now.*
It can't be helped—that's true.
But thinking of long-vanished days ... Oh, wow!
All the things he got to do!
Lift a bottle with Aristotle,
Start Alexandrias all over the place.
One got a library
Founded by his longtime friend,
Good old Ptolemy!

"*Came along too late to see Alex the Great*
Mopping up the Persian cavalry.
Came along too late to see Alex the Great
Outdoing Julius Caesar's infantry.
Came along too late to see Alex the Great
Found his Hellenistic monarchy!"

"Came Along Too Late" was supposed to end on a wild flourish of cymbals. You couldn't do those on your person or a tabletop. Justin solved the problem by using a doo-wop shout—"Woo-hoo!"—instead.

Jim Farrell looked from one member of the band to the next. (Biff was probably down at Calvin's Kitchen. He'd fallen for a brunette who waitressed there. Whether she'd fallen for him was a different question, but he was in there pitching, anyhow.) "These are men of parts," Farrell said at last, to Dick Barber. "I suspect some of the parts stand in desperate need of repair, but he that is without sin, let him first cast an aspersion at them."

"Ouch!" Rob said, a noise with more admiration in it than pain. Farrell gave him a tip of the fedora if not a doff. But Rob quickly turned serious again. Here was a real, if unorthodox, politico in front of him. He hadn't expected to have a chance like that. Since he did, he asked, "What do we do—what can anybody do—about everything the supervolcano's doing to us?"

"Well, I can't say I'm completely sorry the government seems to have forgotten about this part of the country. Sometimes being forgotten by the government is the best thing that can happen to you," Farrell answered.

Rob wasn't so sure he bought that. He was a liberal more often than not and in most ways. But he turned libertarian, if not reactionary, four times a year: when his estimated-tax payments came due. The band made raw money, with not a dime withheld. Rendering what Uncle Sam and the state demanded hurt more than it would have were he working a nine-to-five like most people.

Farrell hadn't finished: "But it also seems as though *everybody* on the far side of the Interstate has forgotten about us. I think—I hope—we can get through one winter like that. When things warm up, if they ever do, we'll have to see about stocking up for another long, hard, cold stretch next winter. If we can stock up. If there's anything left to stock up on. It's not just a Guilford, Maine, problem, you know. It's worldwide."

"It's not so bad in a lot of other places," Rob said.

"True enough. But it's worse in some," Farrell said. "How would you like to be in Salt Lake City or Denver right now?"

"My sister was in Denver. She's one of the lucky ones—she got out quick. I guess she was lucky. Now she's stuck in one of those camps in the middle of nowhere," Rob said. "She can't stand it, but she's alive, anyway."

Vanessa Ferguson commonly acted on the principle that the squeaky wheel got the grease. She didn't believe in depriving herself of the pleasure of complaining. The only trouble was, there were a hell of a lot of squeaky wheels in Camp Constitution. The miserable place had to have a couple of hundred thousand people in it by now, and it was awful. A saint would have hated it. Ordinary people? Vanessa had heard the suicide rate at the camp was ridiculously high, and she believed it. It was much too easy to decide that staying here was a fate worse than death.

The people who ran Camp Constitution were from the government, and they were there to help you . . . provided you did exactly what they told you to do. If you didn't, or if you were otherwise unhappy, well, they had Procedures for that.

To get your problem settled, or even noticed, you lined up at the Camp Constitution Administration Building. That only roused further resentment. As far as Vanessa knew, it was the *only* building in the whole enormous goddamn camp. It was flimsy and rickety and had been run up in a tearing hurry, but still. . . . Federal bureaucrats deserved no less. That was what they and their paymasters in Washington thought, anyhow. Tents and FEMA trailers were for the rabble stuck in the camp 24/7.

You lined up regardless of what it was doing outside. Raining? You lined up. Snowing? Same deal. They did, in their mercy and wisdom, put up an awning that gave some modest protection from the elements. But that was all it gave: some modest protection. The ground under your feet still got gloppy. The weather still got beastly cold. People said it was the worst winter in these parts in they couldn't remember how long. Everybody blamed it on the supervolcano. Everybody was likely to be right, not that that did anybody any good.

If you didn't feel like shivering in the muck for however long you needed to see the people with the power to do something about your complaint (if they happened to feel like it), you could turn around and trudge back to your tent through even more of that same muck. The bureaucrats inside the administration building wouldn't mind. Not one bit, they wouldn't.

There weren't nearly enough of them to handle all the people in the camp with problems. That made the line start well before the awning did. It inched forward with glacial slowness. Considering the weather, the comparison struck Vanessa as much too apt. She had a hooded, quilted anorak with a pink-and-purple nylon shell that was at least three sizes too big for her: charity, of a sort. She had long johns, too. More charity. She was cold anyhow.

She was also itchy. There were bedbugs in her tent. There were bedbugs all over Camp Constitution. Somebody'd brought them in, and they'd thrived like mad bastards. Several eradicating campaigns had failed to eradicate. The same was true for head lice, though she didn't have those—yet. There was talk in Washington of making DDT to fight the vermin at the refugee camps. So far, it was nothing but talk. Vanessa had always thought of herself as a pretty green person, but she would cheerfully have shot a spotted owl to rid herself of her six-legged companions.

A heavyset, bearded man wearing a coat even uglier than hers—and they said the age of miracles had passed!—gave up and stumped away. He muttered a stream of obscenities as he went. Maybe they were what made his breath smoke. More likely, it was just the cold.

The queue moved up to fill the space he'd occupied. "One more we don't got to wait for," said the black woman behind Vanessa.

"One more the yahoos up ahead won't have to deal with," Vanessa said, pointing to the still far too distant building ahead. "I *hate* lines, you know?"

"Jeez, honey, who don't?" the black woman answered. "But what you gonna do?"

Vanessa still carried the .38 in her purse. A few people at the camp had gone postal. One guy gunned down seven of his tent-mates before somebody brained him from behind with a baseball bat. For a nasty instant, Vanessa savored the brief, scarlet joy of flipping out like that. If the alternative was worming forward an inch at a time till you got to talk to some dumb fuck who couldn't have cared less . . . Sighing, she wormed forward another inch. Maturity and sanity sucked sometimes. They really did.

Half an hour later, she scraped the mud off the bottom of her Nikes on the sharp edges of the aluminum steps leading up to the administration building. Those edges already had a lot of mud on them, from others who'd done the same thing before her. The instinct not to track dirt inside remained strong, even when there was next to no inside and what seemed like all the dirt in the world.

A sign on the glass doors said PLEASE KEEP CLOSED. The administration building had a real heating system, not a half-assed propane heater in the middle of a tent. Nothing too good for the folks helping our refugees. The building had power, too, and computers and phones and broadband Internet and everything else Vanessa was missing except when she got in the line even longer than this one to go to the charging station to give her cell more juice.

In due course, she reached a counter behind which sat a thir-tyish dweeb with glasses and a broken front tooth. Before she could get down to brass tacks, he asked for her name, her Social Security number (only he called it her "Social," which she wouldn't have understood if she hadn't already heard it from other pen-pushers), and her tent number. "And the nature of your difficulty is . . . ?"

"It's not just mine," Vanessa said. "It's everybody's except for this one woman named Loretta. She has three horrible brats. They're going stir-crazy, they've got no video games to play or TV to watch, and they drive everybody nuts. You can't even sleep at night, 'cause they scream and fight for the fun of it. If you don't do something about it, somebody's going to pinch their little heads off."

He fiddled with a computer. "That would be Loretta Baker, it seems. What do you want me to do?"

"Move her and the monsters out of there," Vanessa said at once. "If you can't do that, get *me* the hell out."

"You realize conditions may be no better in the tent to which you are reassigned?" he said. Her heart sank. He wouldn't move Loretta and the snotnoses, which was what she really wanted.

Sighing, she said, "I'll take my chances."

"It might not be so easy to make the adjustment." He eyed her over the tops of his specs. "An attitude of cooperation would be expected."

"What does that mean?" Vanessa figured she knew what it meant. Make nice for Mr. Federal Functionary and he'll help you out, too. Don't make nice and stay stuck where you are.

"Why, what it says, of course," he answered primly. The son of a bitch had practice at this. He wouldn't come out and tell her *Fuck me or get lost.* That might land him in trouble. But if you were that kind of bastard, you had to have opportunities galore in a place like this. Chances were he got laid a lot.

Vanessa got up from her uncomfortable folding chair. "Forget about it," she snarled, thinking again of the revolver in her handbag.

The guy with the broken tooth only shrugged. "The choice is always yours, Ms. Ferguson. If you change your mind, consult with me again. I promise you excellent service if you do."

And how did he mean *that*? Just the way it sounded, no doubt. Vanessa stormed out of the administration building. What really worried her was, those little assholes of Loretta's were so very appalling, she feared she might come back and come across if somebody didn't murder them first. She'd worried about this kind of thing before. Now, if push came to shove . . . She swore louder than the bearded guy had when he gave up on the line.

"It's so wonderful!" Miriam Birnbaum gushed, and reached out to straighten a lock of Kelly's hair that didn't need straightening.

"Mom!" Kelly pulled away. She wished more and more she'd just gone through a simple civil ceremony with Colin. Her folks had almost given up on the idea that she'd ever get married. Now that they had the chance, they were trying to turn the wedding into a production number.

Well, they were footing the bill. That gave them a certain right to have things their way. Only to a point, though. It wasn't their wedding, even if they were paying. It was hers and Colin's.

"I'm happier than I know how to tell you," her mother said, and either proved that or gave it the lie by crying.

"Don't do that!" Kelly exclaimed. "You'll mess up your makeup!" She dabbed at Mom's cheek with a Kleenex. It repaired most of the damage, anyhow. Her father—one of the best dentists in the South Bay, if he said so himself (and he did)—put an arm around her mother.

"It's okay, Miriam," Leonard Birnbaum said. "Colin's a good guy."

"I wouldn't be crying if he wasn't," Mom said, which might have made sense to her but left Kelly mystified.

She was also gobsmacked that the lecturer's slot at Cal State Dominguez Hills fell into her lap right after her parents hired the hall here. Whether she was obsolete or not, they wanted her. She would have had second thoughts about taking the job most of the time. If the University of California system was hurting, the California State University system was on the critical list. But CSUDH wasn't more than fifteen minutes away from San Atanasio. As long as any gas at all got into the L.A. area—and as long as any money at all got into the Cal State system—she could go teach.

She wondered if Geoff Rheinburg knew the gal who ran the Dominguez Hills Geology Department. That would explain a lot. It would also be odds-on the best wedding present she got.

One side of the hall was packed with her relatives and friends. The other side was mostly cops: square, solid men in suits that had been stylish a while ago or maybe never. How many of them had shoulder holsters under their jackets? Marshall was there, of course. *I'm a stepmother*, Kelly thought in bemusement as she went up the aisle on her father's arm. She hoped Colin's other two kids were doing all right.

Next to Marshall in the front row sat Colin's sister, Norma. Kelly'd never set eyes on her before. She and her husband, Earl, both worked nights, though, and didn't show themselves when most people did. Kelly didn't think there were any hard feelings between her and Colin, but they weren't exactly close, either.

Colin waited under the *chuppah* with a Reform rabbi, Wes Jones, and Kelly's first cousin, Loreen Samuels. Damned if Wes didn't wink at her as she came near. There'd be never a dull moment living across the street from him. He wore a yarmulke with as much ease as the rabbi did. Colin's kind of stuck up on his head. He'd agreed to a Jewish ceremony with good grace, but nothing would ever make him look Jewish.

Some chanted Hebrew prayers, some marriage advice that was sensible but perfectly ordinary, Colin's shoe coming down on a cloth-wrapped glass to remember the fall of the Temple, a ring, a kiss . . . It was official. She'd have to start getting used to her new last name. Well, she wouldn't *have* to, not these days, but she intended to. Kelly Ferguson? For once, it sounded as if her first and last names went together.

After champagne toasts at the reception, Colin said, "I saw a study that showed guys who marry younger wives live longer and are happier."

"Oh, yeah? Wonder how come that is," Gabe Sanchez said. Everybody laughed. Gabe struck Kelly as a slightly rougher, Hispanic version of the guy she'd just married. He went on, "Congratulations, man. Looks like you got a real good one. Gives us all hope, y'know?" His heavy-featured face clouded. Kelly remembered Colin saying Gabe had gone through a divorce even uglier than his own. Evidently he hadn't found anyone new since.

They ate. They drank some more. They danced. Colin moved as gracefully as anyone with two left feet. "Man, I know white folks got no sense of rhythm, but can't you at least try?" a black cop said, softening the dart with a grin.

"This ain't the 'hood, Rodney. You got to do the dozens on me at my wedding?" Colin said.

"Any time at all," Rodney answered. He was strutting his stuff with a Latino woman—his wife, Kelly decided after checking for rings. She still hadn't got used to rings on her own finger. She expected she would.

At last, they changed back into street clothes. A limo laid on by Kelly's folks waited under an awning outside the hall. A good thing the awning was there. A nasty, chilly rain came down; it couldn't have been far above freezing. "It wouldn't be this cold if it wasn't for your dumb old supervolcano," Kelly's mother said. She was right, but she made it sound as if the supervolcano wouldn't have erupted if Kelly hadn't studied it.

The driver—a Samoan big enough to have played pro football— whisked them up the Harbor Freeway to the Bonaventure Hotel downtown. Colin slipped him fifty bucks. "Thanks a lot, man," the guy said, touching a blunt forefinger to the brim of his cap. "Happy wedding, y'know?"

Their room was high up in one of the hotel's round, glassy towers. Colin lifted a squeaking Kelly over the threshold. A bottle of champagne with a card waited in an ice bucket in the room. Colin opened the card. He grinned. "From Gabe," he said.

"He's sweet." Kelly was looking at the city lights and at cars streaming by on the freeway just to the west. In spite of gas shortages, there were still lots of them. She wondered if things would pick up or just keep going downhill.

"Yeah. He is," Colin agreed from behind her. "And he'd clout us one if we said so to his face." A muffled pop announced he'd opened the bottle: carefully and neatly, so as not to waste any. On the nightstand stood two glass flutes, not plastic like those at the reception. He poured for them both and handed her one. Then he raised the other. "Here's to us, babe. I love you."

"I love you, too." She clinked flutes. "To us." After they drank, she said, "If I do too much more of this, I'll fall asleep on you. Some wedding night that'd be."

He mimed a leer. "I'd just have my way with your unconscious body—mwahaha!"

Kelly snorted. "It's better when both people in the game want to play."

"I won't argue." Colin shut the drapes. "So—do you want to play?"

"Right this minute, there's nothing I want more in the whole wide world." Kelly stepped into his arms. Things went on from there. Some considerable and very happy time later, she said, "Don't you ever let that Rodney sass you about your sense of rhythm again, you hear?"

"Yes, ma'am," he answered from a distance of about three inches. Then he patted at his hair. Kelly made a questioning noise. "I was wondering if you took the top of my head off there," he explained.

"You!" she said fondly.

"Me," he agreed. "Is there anything left in that champagne bottle?"

"If there isn't, we can always call room service," she answered.

There wasn't, and she did. "Spending my money already," Colin said.

"No way," Kelly told him. "Dominguez will pay me . . . a little something, anyway."

They eventually went to sleep. When Kelly woke, wan gray light was leaking past the drapes. She put on sweats and a T-shirt and went to look outside. She must have made a noise—probably a startled grunt—because from behind her her new husband asked, "What is it, babe?"

"Come see," was all she said.

He needed a moment to get decent, too. Then he joined her at the window. He let out a low whistle of astonishment. Snowflakes danced in the air. It was white down below, white in the middle of downtown L.A. The Harbor Freeway was white, too, white and empty: ghostly, even. Any snow at all would screw traffic here from A to whatever came after Z.

No sooner had that crossed her mind than a car on the surface street down below skidded sideways into a pickup truck. Neither, luckily, was going very fast. Both drivers got out and glumly eyed the damage.

Colin turned on the TV. A chipper local weatherman said, "Be careful out there, folks. The last time we had snow all over the L.A. basin was in January of 1949. I have to say, we aren't really equipped for it. If you can possibly stay home, you'd sure be smart to do it."

Kelly and Colin exchanged stricken looks. Marshall had been planning to pick them up and take them back to the house. From there, they would have gone to the Hotel Coronado in San Diego: a honeymoon on a tank of gas. Now . . . Kelly had no idea what they'd do now.

Colin did: "Call room service again. Tell 'em to send up coffee and some breakfast. And after that—hey, we'll just go on from there." By the way his gaze roamed her, she didn't need to have bothered dressing.

"Sounds good to me," she said, and padded over to the phone. Outside, the snow kept coming down.

Along with Gabe Sanchez, Colin spooned up ramen—fancy ramen, not the packaged stuff college kids ate and Louise dealt with—in a little place on Reynoso Drive. It was in the mostly Japanese shopping center that also held the Carrows where he'd had that lacerating lunch with his ex. If he looked out the window, he could see the other place. As long as he kept slurping up soup and noodles and chopped pork, he didn't have to look out the window.

"So you and Kelly were stuck there, huh?" Gabe said. "That's funny, man!"

"Worse places to be than snowed in with your brand-new wife," Colin answered. In the two and a half days before enough snow melted to let traffic start moving again, he'd done more than he'd figured a man his age could do. And he'd managed all right once they finally got to San Diego, too.

"Yeah, I guess." Gabe didn't sound completely convinced. No, he hadn't had much luck with his love life since his marriage hit a mine and exploded. "It's good to have you back in the saddle, though."

"Good to be back," Colin allowed. No matter what kind of carnal excesses he'd managed at the Bonaventure and the Coronado, a man his age couldn't do that all the time, not unless he wanted to roll up like a window shade, thwup, thwup, thwup!

"You figure we'll ever drop on the goddamn Strangler?" Gabe asked. It wasn't out of the blue. There'd been a fresh killing over in Manhattan Beach while Colin and Kelly were on their abbreviated visit to San Diego. Colin hadn't heard about it till he came home. Watching the news hadn't been his biggest worry while he was there. As long as no more snow came down, he hadn't cared what happened in the outside world.

Now he did. Now he had to. And now he said what cops all over the South Bay had been saying all along: "He's bound to goof sooner or later. Trip over something in the dark and break his ankle, maybe. Something." Some bad guys got away with things for a long time, either through fool luck or because they were the uncommon smart people who turned to crime. Very few went to their graves uncaught. Colin was sure of it. He had to be, if he wanted to keep thinking he was doing something that mattered.

"This one's not in our jurisdiction, same as the last one wasn't," Gabe said. "Let the guys in Manhattan Beach take the heat. See how they like news vans lined up outside the department all the time and the clowns with the expensive haircuts asking dumbass questions."

"I'm sure they enjoy it as much as we do," Colin said. Gabe laughed harshly. Colin went on, "What I want to be is, I want to be the one who busts the son of a bitch. I don't know if I can be that lucky twice, but I sure want to."

"Twice?" Now Gabe sounded puzzled. Colin had been a solid, steady, capable cop for a hell of a long time now. He'd caught a lot of perps, some smart ones and even more of the jerks and losers who went wrong. But he'd never pulled a coup that even came close to what arresting the South Bay Strangler would mean.

He wasn't thinking of policework, though. "Lucky. Uh-huh," he said. "Only reason I ever went to Yellowstone was to get away from everything after Louise walked out on me."

"Me, I went to Vegas when things hit the fan," Sanchez said. "I bet you got away cheaper—I'll tell you that."

"I bet you're right," Colin agreed. "So there I was, walking around in this cold, miserable drizzle, still kind of hungover, looking at the hot pools in the West Thumb Basin, and I reamed out this gal for going off the boardwalk."

Gabe chuckled. "Once a cop, always a cop."

"Tell me about it. So Kelly showed me she had every right to be where she was 'cause she was doing her research, and I felt two inches tall and covered in dogshit. But then I got lucky one more time. This earthquake hit, and it gave us something to talk about besides what a moron I was. I ended up getting her e-mail, and I gave her mine, and we just went on from there. Fool luck all the way, nothing else but."

Instead of answering right away, Gabe concentrated on getting to the bottom of his bowl. Then he said, "If you tell me the same thing ten, fifteen years from now, I'll be more impressed."

"Mm, I know what you mean," Colin admitted. People went into first marriages sure theirs was a passion for the ages, and just as sure love would last forever. They went into second marriages hoping things worked out. Even that might have been the triumph of hope over experience. But it also might have been a more realistic attitude.

"Sometimes even ten, fifteen years aren't enough. Look at us. Our first ones both lasted longer'n that, but when they died, they fuckin' *died*, man," Gabe said.

"I know. Sometimes you grow together, sometimes you grow apart," Colin said. He worked at his own ramen. The broth was salty and porky and delicious. His doctor would probably scream that it was a sodium bomb—and a fat bomb to boot—but sometimes he just didn't care.

"You know what I'm really jealous about?" Gabe asked.

"What?" Colin worked to keep his voice neutral. How could his buddy help being jealous of his happiness? Gabe didn't have a hell of a lot of his own these days.

But the sergeant's answer blindsided him: "I'm jealous you

got to see Yellowstone. See it while it was still there *to* see, I mean. Nobody's ever gonna be able to do that again, but you did."

"You're right," Colin said in surprise. "Kelly goes on about so much stuff being gone, but I hadn't thought about it that way. Hell of a lot of stuff nobody'll see again."

"You were there." Gabe paused. "Wasn't that the name of a TV show a million years ago?"

"I think it was. Something like that, anyway." Colin finished his lunch. Before the eruption, this place had served its ramen in big old styrofoam cups. You could wash bowls and use them over and over. The only time you needed a new one was when you dropped an old one. Once these people ran out of styrofoam, they fell back on Plan B.

Plan B . . . Plan C . . . A lot of the time these days, it seemed as if the country was on about Plan Q. Nobody had any good ideas to pull it out of its mess. Or, more likely, the mess was simply too goddamn big for anything so trivial as some human's good idea to make much difference.

And, as Kelly kept pointing out, this was only the beginning. The eruption was over, but the aftereffects lingered on. How long would it be before the Midwest was the world's breadbasket again, not buried under ash and dust? How many people would go hungry on account of that? Would the Midwest be the world's breadbasket again, with the weather getting so much colder? How long would the chill last? Years? Decades? Centuries? Nobody knew for sure, but everybody was going to find out.

Things probably wouldn't be anywhere close to the same for the rest of his life. What were you supposed to do?

Gabe put money on the table. "Here, Mister Just Back from His Honeymoon, this one's on me."

"Thanks." Colin stood up.

So did Gabe. As they walked out to their car, he asked, "So . . . You got your ducks in a row to testify at the Ellis trial?"

The kid from the projects was up for three counts of armed robbery and one of first-degree murder. The case looked open-and-shut to Colin, but nothing was open-and-shut if you messed it up. "I'm getting there," he answered. "Still reviewing the video-tapes and the reports and all. How about you?"

"Pretty much the same," Gabe said. "If they don't stick a needle in his arm, they need to make damn sure he doesn't get out again."

"Yup." Colin nodded. Maybe *this* was what you were sup-posed to do: what you'd always done, as well as you could for as long as you could. What else could any one person do?

He unlocked the car and slid into the driver's seat. Gabe got in on the other side. They drove back to the cop shop under a sundogged sun in an ague-cheeked sky.

Author's Note

Whenever you happen to read *Supervolcano: Eruption*, it opens the following Memorial Day weekend. I sure hope it does, anyhow!

The supervolcano under Yellowstone National Park is quite real. When it will next erupt—next year, fifty thousand years from now, or maybe even never—is anybody's guess, and a subject for learned argument among geologists. The Sour Creek magma dome, and the Mallard Lake dome farther southwest (not mentioned in the text), are real, and are bulging. The Coffee Pot Springs dome is fictitious. Again, I hope it stays that way.

Also fictitious is the town of San Atanasio, California, though the surrounding South Bay cities are real. So is the Trebor Mansion Inn. I couldn't possibly make it up.

Special thanks for hospitality and help go to Robert Shaffer, John Frary, CthulhuBob Lovely, Justin Barba, and Joanne Girvin. I also need to thank my father and mother, though sadly they aren't here to read this. More than fifty years ago, they first gave me a subscription to the *National Geographic*. They kept it up even when times got tough, and I've done so ever since. I found out about the supervolcano in its pages.

If you're so inclined, you can sing "Came Along Too Late" to the tune of "Josephine Baker," from Al Stewart's excellent album, *Last Days of the Century*. When my youngest daughter, Rebecca, was taking Western Civ in college, she asked my wife—Broadway maven Laura Frankos—and me for songs on historical themes. Laura gave her ersatz Sondheim. My contribution was an earlier version of "Came Along Too Late." It also seemed to fit what was going on here. Thanks again, Rebecca.